TAMING SERAPHINE

GIGI STYX

For all the girls who like to clutch at pearls...
this ain't for you

TRIGGER WARNING

This is a dark romance that includes dub-con, graphic depictions of torture and violence, and sexually explicit scenes. If any of this content is triggering for you, please do not read this book.

Triggers:

    Abduction
    Abuse
    Attempted somnophilia
    BDSM
    Body modification
    Bondage
    Blood and gore
    Cannibalism
    Car crash
    Castration
    Child abandonment
    Child sexual abuse
    Degradation
    Dismemberment

Drugging
Dubious consent
Electrocution
Exhibitionism
Grief and loss
Humiliation
Knife play
Male genital mutilation
Mental illness
Murder
Organized crime
Organ trafficking
Orgasm denial
Primal play
Psychological abuse
PTSD
Revenge
Rape
Serial killing
Sexual Assault
Step brother
Torture
Trafficking
Trauma
Violence
Voyeurism

Reader discretion is advised. If you find any of these topics distressing, please proceed with caution or consider choosing a different book. Your mental health matters.

To all the pretty little psychos who crave a blade to the throat

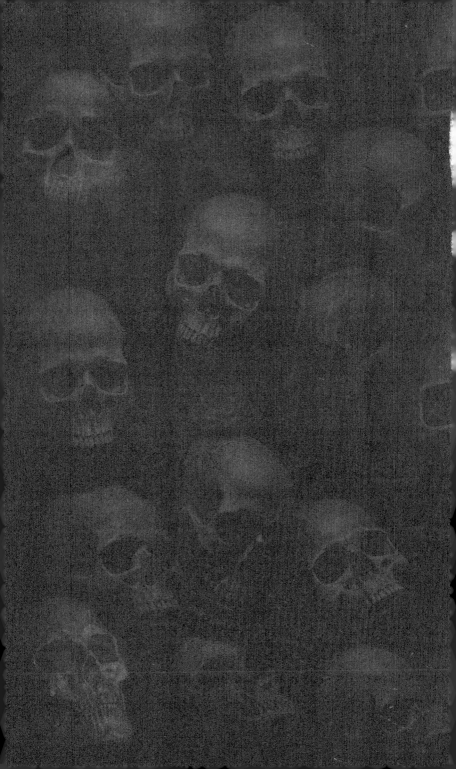

PROLOGUE

SERAPHINE

To save my grandmother, I must murder a stranger.

Loud techno music pounds through my ears as I walk toward the Phoenix, a nightclub on the edge of Beaumont, New Alderney. Partygoers pass on my left in various states of drunkenness and traffic rumbles by on my right, everyone blissfully living their lives, unaware that I have been a captive for months.

I wonder if anyone even noticed I didn't turn up at school.

Flashing blue lights catch my eye from across the road. A police car pulls into the Tropicana Bar, and a tall officer and his partner steps out.

My heart skips. I should shout, raise a hand, let them know that I'm being held hostage and being forced to commit a murder. As I turn toward the cops, the chip embedded behind my ear emits a snap of electricity.

Shit. This is worse than the old collar.

I glance over my shoulder, only to lock eyes with the

handler, who raises his remote. My captors have left nothing to chance.

With one last deep breath, I focus on my instructions. I am to skip the line, tell the doorman that I'm joining Mario at his VIP table, enter the club, and not talk to anyone but my target. When my target has isolated me, I am to inject him with the syringe, and then escape through the fire exit.

Once my mission is complete, they'll set Nanna free.

My throat tightens.

I must do this.

Moments later, I'm blinking away bright strobe lights and navigating through the club using the map they made me memorize. Before I even reach the VIP room, a pair of large hands grab my shoulders, and I'm crushed against a broad chest.

Nausea grips my throat, even though nothing he's doing causes me any pain. I can't stand to be touched—especially by men. This new captor's eyes are already bloodshot and glassy. At about six-two, he eclipses me by a foot and looks even more imposing with his lanky frame. He stares down at me with a lazy grin.

"Wanna dance, blondie?" he slurs, the scent of stale alcohol heavy on his breath.

My jaw tightens. If he knew about the proverbial noose around my neck, he'd choose someone else to harass. I pull my arms out of his grip, but his fingers tighten around my arms.

"Let go," I hiss at him through clenched teeth.

His grin widens. Of course, it does. This man sees me as nothing but sport. Even if he knew I'd been captured, tortured, violated, and corrupted, he wouldn't give a shit. All he sees is a toy.

I reach for a hairpin at the back of my head, but his grip

around my shoulders slackens. When I glance up at the man, he's stumbling backward, his eyes now half-lidded. He falls, only to reveal a familiar and unwelcome set of eyes.

The handler shoves the man into a group of women hovering by the dance floor. His sharp nod is the only sign he gives for me to proceed.

With a gulp, I continue toward the VIP room and my target.

The guard at the door sweeps his gaze down my form, his eyes lingering on my bare legs. I'm wearing a pastel pink summer dress, a variation of something I would have worn when I was twelve, when I was still Daddy's little princess.

To my shock, the guard lets me into the VIP room. I can't tell if it's because nightclubs don't give a shit about underage girls, or because he's working with the handler.

The temperature immediately drops as I step inside, and goosebumps break out across my arms. I tell myself it's from the cold, but a weight settles in my gut when the door slams behind me and the sound of the club on the other side disappears; the muffled thump of the bass matching the manic beating of my heart.

It's really happening.

I'm really going to murder a man in cold blood.

After tonight, Nanna will be free.

Each table in the VIP room glows with a dim blue light that casts scant illumination over the men and women gathered around on sofas. Remembering my instructions, I force myself not to glance around for my target and make my way to the bar.

Like the tables in this exclusive space, the bar casts a gentle hue. I perch on a stool and make eye contact with the bartender, order a glass of water, and wait.

Over the next several minutes, different men approach

me. Some offering drinks, others dances, one asks if my parents know I'm at a club but I ignore them all. The handler made me memorize both my target and his guards in case he sends a lackey to do his dirty work.

My hands should be trembling. I should be sweating with nerves, but nothing that happens tonight could ever be worse than my so-called training. I've been beaten, broken, and torn down. Everyone I love who isn't already dead is now their hostage. The only way to set them free is with these murders.

As I take another tiny sip of water, one side of my vision fills with a large figure. I ignore him until he grabs my arm and ignites my veins with an explosion of fury.

"Come with me," the man says.

My lips tighten. I glance from the hand encircling my bicep and lock gazes with one of the faces I was ordered to remember. He's an employee of my target, although I don't know his name. The handler said it wasn't necessary.

"Alright." I slip off the bar stool and let the man march me through the VIP room to an empty table at the far end.

My target likes his girls innocent and sweet. The younger the better, according to the handler, which is why he forbade me to wear makeup, save for a coat of clear mascara to make my eyes look larger. Based on the number of men who tried to buy me drinks, my target isn't the only one here with a taste for underage girls.

The man who brought me to the table orders me champagne. There's no chance to refuse. He looms over me and watches me sip. Wine tasting wasn't part of my training, but this drink is more bitter than anything my parents ever let me try.

Pain surges across my chest the way it does every time I

think of Mom, but I tuck that memory into the back of my mind. I can't think about her. The memory of how they killed her is seared into my soul. The only thing I can do for her now is save everyone they've left alive. Sucking in a sharp breath, I continue drinking, wishing the alcohol would numb the agony. It doesn't. The handler made me drink a concoction of chalky liquid earlier to dampen any effects of alcohol, drugs, or whatever else might have put in my drink.

I'm already tipsy by the end of the first glass since I made the mistake of inhaling the bubbles. The buzz isn't enough to affect my reflexes, but it takes the edge off my hurt.

My head lowers, and I rest my chin on my chest, pretending to be drugged. Any more of that champagne and no amount of antidote will keep me alert.

"Hey." The guard nudges my arm.

Rocking to the side, I let a curtain of blonde hair fall across my face. The citrus scent of the lemon the handler made me use to make my tresses youthful and bright washes over me and clogs in my sinuses.

I try not to shudder as the man hauls me to my feet and walks me through a different door guarded by two other faces I memorized from the intel. My heart is beating so hard and fast that every inch of my skin throbs with both anticipation and terror.

This will be my first kill—the price for Nanna's freedom. After that, I have a second target to murder so I can rescue Gabriel, and then a third to free myself.

Since my head is bowed and I'm pretending to be semi-conscious, I don't see the faces of the armed men who pass us as we walk down the hallway. I stumble into the wall, so I can compare the layout with the map I learned, but the man scoops me off my feet and carries me through another doorway.

Strangely, I don't feel the usual surge of disgust. Maybe that's because someone's about to die.

"Is she prepared?" asks a deep voice from within the second room.

"I watched her drink the whole glass," the man carrying me replies.

The room is dark, decorated in shades of black and crimson with low lighting and rich, opulent fabrics. I peer through my lashes, catching a glimpse of a gray-haired man standing beside a bed adorned with oversized cushions.

My breath catches.

It's him.

The man I'm going to kill.

I glance at a set of small curtains on the far-left wall in the room that will become my escape route. If the handler is correct, there should be a serving hatch that leads straight to the kitchen.

"Put her on the bed," says the target.

A heartbeat later, I sink into the softest surface I've lain upon since the night Dad turned on us. Closing my eyes, I hold my breath and pray to Mom's spirit that they don't use any restraints.

The handler warned me that this was a possibility, since the target likes his girls docile. If that happens, I have to hold still until he frees my arms. Dread swirls in my gut, followed by the bitterness of disdain. They're all sick, including the handler. They all deserve to die.

"Leave us," the target says.

I exhale, but it's too early for relief. Even without the bodyguard, the target is still more than I can handle alone. I didn't learn his name or what he does. He'll be dead soon, anyway. He's a looming presence with eyes so dark they meld into the shadows. In the dim light, he barely looks human. My heart pounds so hard and fast that I'm sure he's feeding on my helplessness and terror. He's just like Dad, a man who surrounds himself with armed guards. If I'm right, then he's dangerous.

Which is why I need to wait until he's distracted.

My breathing shallows when a huge, warm hand begins a slow path up my inner thigh. Revulsion roils across my skin and gathers in my shrinking stomach. I can't let another man touch me like this. Not again. Not while I'm awake and able to fight.

But I will.

I clench my jaw, resolving to endure this for Nanna.

"Sweet girl," he croons. "Are you a virgin?"

Not anymore. I'm tainted because of men like him. Men like him I want to punish. Men like him I want to erase from this earth.

My teeth grind as he pushes my panties to the side and explores me with his fingers. I have to swallow back a scream when he invades me with two digits.

Every instinct in my body tells me to rear up and finish him before he goes any further, but I'm cautious. Even with my eyes closed, I feel his gaze sweeping my face.

I lie back, endure, and wait. I'll only have one chance. The moment must be perfect. When the target pulls out his fingers, my stomach lurches because I know what will happen next. When he enters me with one thrust, a silent scream lodges in the back of my throat.

"So tight," he grunts into the side of my face.

Blood roars through my ears, drowned out by his breaths that punctuate each thrust. As he picks up speed, I peek through my lashes to find his eyes squeezed shut, his craggy features contorted with a sick combination of pleasure and malice.

My hand curls into a fist.

Not yet.

When I'm absolutely certain he's lost in his pleasure, I slide a hand up the mattress and extract the hairpin infused with poison. The handler made me practice using it from every possible angle and assured me it would work in seconds.

Just as I'm about to ram it into his jugular, the target's hand clamps around my neck.

My eyes fly open, and I stare into his twisted grin.

Cold shock hits me in the gut. I gasp, but he grabs the hand holding my weapon and quickens his pace.

"Come for me," he growls.

I twist the hairpin around in my fingers, stab its pointed end into his hand, and push down on the plunger.

The target rears back with a roar, raises his fist, and slams it into my face. "Bitch. I'll—"

Pain explodes through my sinuses, but it's nothing compared to what I had to endure during my training. The target collapses on top of me before he finishes his sentence. With my free hand, I check his pulse. It's still beating. Freeing my wrist from the hand I injected, I find it's wet with the poison.

Shit.

What if I failed to give him a lethal dose?

I thrash my arms and legs, trying to dislodge his dead weight. When I finally slide out from under him, he's gasping for air. Sweat beads across his forehead and his lips part. He tries to speak, but the words that come out are garbled.

He's still alive.

"No."

I scramble off the mattress, my gaze darting to an armchair where I spot a gun holster. If I shoot him, his death will be quick, but the noise will alert the guards. Instead, I pick up a crimson cushion from the bed and press it over his face.

The target gasps and struggles, trying to buck me off, but I push down with all my weight. Minutes pass, and he stops moving. I continue holding the cushion until I'm certain he's dead.

My heart thrashes within its cage, reminding me I have to leave before someone knocks. I check his pulse again. Finding no heartbeat, I throw down the cushion and rush to the serving hatch.

The escape goes as planned. At this time of night, the kitchen is closed, so I navigate the maze of stainless steel tables on trembling legs until I slip into a darkened hallway that leads to a fire exit.

Outside, cool air fills my lungs, and I step into the alleyway, where a black sedan awaits with dimmed headlights. I exhale a noisy breath of relief and rush into the car, only to find a computer tablet on the back seat.

"Where's the handler?" I ask the driver, confused.

Without a reply, he activates the central locking, then pulls out of the alleyway and speeds down the road.

I pick up the tablet, press the power button, and find a message already waiting:

Congratulations on completing your first mission. The man you killed was Enzo Montesano, the leader of the syndicate that rules New Alderney.

From today, the Capello family will assign you further missions in exchange for protection from Montesano's associates.

I regret to inform you that your grandmother died in captivity; however, your brother is still safe.

Good luck and stay alive.

A sob bursts from my throat. There's no mention of our bargain. No mention of setting Gabriel free.

At the bottom of the handler's note is a thumbnail, I tap it and a video of Gabriel appears. He's sitting up in a hospital bed with electrodes taped to his chest and a tube in his nose. Every bone on his torso protrudes through skin as pale as death. It looks as though he's lost a quarter of his body weight.

My heart shatters. "What have they done to him?"

The car speeds through the streets of Beaumont, back to where Dad's legitimate sons are holding me hostage in their basement. They're twin demons with hearts as black as souls. I play the clip of Gabriel over, transfixed by the rise and fall of his chest, taking small comfort in knowing he is still breathing.

How many more murders will I need to commit to earn our freedom? From what's in the letter, it looks like they've changed the terms of our agreement.

My hands curl into a fist.

The only way I'll ever get free is to kill my dad and his psycho sons.

ONE

LEROI

FIVE YEARS LATER

A job as big as this needs a full team of operatives—a hacker to kill the alarms and block outbound communications; snipers to take out the guards at the mansion's perimeter; inside men to give me the all-clear; and an armored truck to get me the hell out of this stronghold.

It's a pity that all I have is a getaway driver and a stack of explosives that will light up the estate like the Fourth of July.

Anton would be the best person to ask for advice. My mentor is a veteran hitman, from back in the days when you had to identify targets with Polaroids. But I already know what he would say. Killing the entire Capello family isn't just risky—it's suicide.

"Leroi," Miko's voice whispers in my earpiece. "Morning guard just arrived."

It's taken weeks of analyzing the family's routine and security system to work out the easiest way to take down Frederic Capello, which is why I infiltrated it as part of the hired help for the sixtieth birthday party he threw for himself. Instead of leaving the Capello mansion after the festivities, I stayed behind to enact the final stages of my plan.

Having arranged a series of altercations in the Capello Casino, I know the bulk of his security staff will be across town dealing with the shitstorm, leaving me free to execute this family.

Three hours later, with my face mask secured, I crawl out of the laundry room's ventilation duct and make my way through the halls. By now, anyone that came into contact with the toothpaste, water bottles or painkillers I doctored should be passed out until at least noon.

I take the back staircase and make my way into the guest bedrooms. The silencer on my 9mm Glock keeps the noise at a minimum while I take out the distant Capello relatives who were unfortunate enough to have stayed the night.

I push open the bathroom door, and a long-haired figure jumps out from behind the shower curtain, thrusting a knife to my throat.

On instinct, I jump back and fire a shot into the person's chest. He falls into the bathtub with a loud splash.

Shit.

The person I just shot is Capello's first-born, Gregor, but noise wasn't part of the plan. I fire another bullet between his eyes to make sure he's dead and back out of the bathroom. Next time, I'll have to be more careful.

One down, three to go.

The next bedroom belongs to the second son, Samson. He's sprawled face-down on the bed, passed out from the revelry. I squeeze the trigger and lodge a bullet in the back of his skull.

In the master suite, Frederic Capello snores in an

armchair, still dressed in his tuxedo. According to my research, he has liver problems, but he looks like the picture of health for a man of sixty. Placing the barrel of my gun against his forehead, I shoot.

Marisol Capello is in the bedroom, dressed in a black lace camisole. Her features are obscured by her long blonde hair, but there's no mistaking her from the massive diamond on her ring finger. She's the old man's much younger, fourth wife. With the twins dead, she stands to inherit the syndicate's assets if she survives the night.

My jaw clenches. No women or children. That's my code, but it's something I must break if I'm going to eliminate the Capellos and free my cousin from death row.

Damn it.

I take aim and shoot her in the heart.

So far, killing the Capellos is easy. Finding the recordings that will prove my cousin innocent will be tricky.

I return to the suite's lounge area and extract a saw from my backpack. On a less perilous job, I would leave the target alive to open the biometric safe, but my time here is limited.

With a deep breath, I grab a cord, loop it into a tourniquet just above Capello's wrist and pull it tight. After positioning his hand on the armrest, I get to work.

Blood splatters on the cream carpet. I step out of its path and continue sawing until I've secured the hand adorned with the Capello signet ring.

It's still warm when I reach the safe. His thumbprint activates the lock, and I open the safe, finding stacks of folders, hard drives, and a bunch of shit I don't have time to catalog.

Most syndicates gain strength through hard work, determination and the skillful application of violence, but Capello's currency was information. He had dirt on every judge, every politician, every high-ranking police officer ,and official in the state of New Alderney and beyond. That, and a copious amount of backstabbing.

Everything goes into my bag, except the hand, which I still need. According to my intel, Capello's secret weapon is in the basement.

The first rays of morning light filter in through the windows as I head down the stairs. A flash of movement at the far end of the manicured gardens tells me that my time is running low. I press the old man's index finger up to the reader and the door to the basement unlocks with a deafening click.

It's dark inside, save for a flickering TV at the far end of the vast space. I don't bother turning on the light in case that triggers an alarm, but I raise the pistol and make my way toward the screen.

"Leroi," Miko hisses through the earpiece. "A delivery van's approaching the gates."

"Good," I whisper. "Keep me informed."

The driver of that van is a poker buddy who will attempt to deliver an incorrectly addressed package. His job is to distract the guards with his incompetence, in case what's in the basement is time consuming.

I flip on my headlamp to illuminate my way, passing exercise equipment and a tiny kitchenette. So far, there's no sign of another safe. There is, however, a small figure lying on a bed.

It's a girl with pale blond hair and a bruised eye. It's hard to tell her age in the dark, but she's frail. Her breaths are shallow, and the tightness of her jaw tells me she might be awake.

She lies in the fetal position wearing nothing but an

oversized t-shirt and a metal collar. It's a four inch wide band of steel with a thick compartment at the front that glows with red light. Everything about it reminds me of the device Anton uses on his farm to train his sheep dogs.

My nostrils flare when it dawns on me.

It's a shock collar.

Fuck. I knew Capello was dirty, but sex slaves in the basement? That bullet through the skull was too merciful.

A D-ring at the front of her collar connects to a chain that disappears beneath the bed. Based on the level of security in this house, it's probably linked to an alarm system.

The weight of my backpack settles on my shoulders, a reminder that my cousin, Roman, is in prison for a crime he didn't commit. I have enough information to free him, but it will only help if I leave now, before the guards realize the family is dead. Now, before they come after me in a rain of gunfire.

My breath hitches. Can I really leave this girl in the basement?

If the only people who can access this place are dead, then it's only a matter of weeks before she starves. If she's found, then someone might hand her over to another monster for the same treatment, or worse.

I can't leave her to either fate.

Maybe I should shoot her in the head and send her straight to heaven. I dismiss that thought in an instant. I don't kill kids.

Crouching beside her, I pull up my mask and whisper, "Can you hear me?"

The girl doesn't move, but her breathing stills for a moment before resuming. She's probably terrified. Who knows how long she's been down here and what she's suffered?

"The people who did this to you are dead," I say, my voice soft. "I'm going to get you out of here, but you'll need to stay quiet, understood?"

She cracks open her swollen eye and inhales a sharp breath.

"Is your collar alarmed?"

She nods.

Fuck. I could cut the mansion's power, but there's no time. Any sudden lack of lighting might also alert the guards. I clench my jaw so tightly that my molars grind. Anton has always said there's a loophole to every alarm. I just need to ask the right question.

"Does it sound in the house?" I ask.

She shakes her head.

My jaw unclenches. "Does the alarm alert a device?"

She nods.

"Whose?"

She lowers her lashes.

"Leroi," Miko whispers. "The guards are making the delivery guy unload his van."

My pulse quickens. Time is running out. By now, I should have found the alleged second safe and retrieved the secret weapon. There's only so much time the guy I paid to pretend to have the package can keep the guards occupied before they point a gun to his head and tell him to get lost.

Fuck the secret weapon. This innocent girl needs saving. I need more information on the workings of this collar. And fast. Without thinking, I raise a hand, and she flinches.

"Hey..." I lift my palms. "I won't hurt you, but I need you to answer some more questions. If I disable your collar, will any of the guards know?"

She shakes her head.

My adrenaline surges. I could ask if anyone other than the Capellos would know if I tampered with the collar, but this going back and forth is already taking too long.

I reach into my backpack, extract a set of bolt cutters, and snap the D-ring. The chain attached to it falls, but I catch it before it hits the floor.

The girl shuffles to the corner of the bed, wraps her arms around her chest, and gazes up at me through terrified, blue eyes.

I slide off my jacket and toss it in her direction. "Put this on."

Even with my head turned away and the light shining in another direction, I'm aware of her scrambling into the jacket. Her desperate little breaths awaken long-forgotten stirrings of conscience. Did I really consider putting a bullet through her head?

In the twenty years I've spent on this job, I've never felt an ounce of emotion for any of my targets—not even contempt. That spreads to the rest of my life. The only exception is the small family I've formed with Anton and Miko. Seeing this girl chained up like a dog reminds me too much of the reason why I became an assassin.

As soon as I'm sure she's ready, I offer her my hand. "We need to go."

The girl stands on trembling legs, her arms wrapped around her middle. She's vulnerable and small and still hasn't uttered a word. What did those sick bastards do to her?

"Come." My fingers twitch.

She motions with her head at something over my shoulder. I turn to find what's on the monitor. It's a shirtless and emaciated man sitting up on a bed with his head bowed.

The rise and fall of his chest is the only thing indicating that he's alive.

With his surroundings so dark, there's no telling his location. But one thing's for damn sure is that we need to leave. Now.

"The driver's backing out," Miko says into my earpiece.

"Don't activate anything until you see us approaching the car," I mutter.

"Us?" he asks.

"Later."

Pulling my mask over my face, I turn to the girl, who shrinks away and points at the screen. Frustration wells in my chest, but I keep the impatience out of my voice. "You can tell me who that man is on the road."

Her trembling fingers meet mine for an instant before her knees buckle. I scoop her into my arms, snatch the backpack containing the information needed to free my cousin, Roman, and sprint across the basement.

In a few minutes, Miko will detonate a bomb at the other side of the property, and all hell will break loose.

TWO

SERAPHINE

My arm shifts, setting off an explosion of pain that forces my eyes open. The man races through the house, clutching me like the spoils of war, passing tall windows I've never seen in all the years this place has been my prison.

Each of his rapid movements aggravates my bruises from whatever havoc the twins wracked on my body after they shot me with the tranquilizer gun. The man told me they were dead, but the enemy of my enemy has always been a fickle friend. My limbs are still too sluggish, too heavy from the effects of the drugs to break free, so I'll let him take me... For now.

Outside, a blast of fresh air hits my nostrils, lingering with the coppery tang of blood that always coats my sinuses. The morning sun bathes the mansion's exterior in pale light, but even that makes my eyes sting. I squeeze my eyes shut, my mind too foggy to remember the last time they let me out to kill. Or at all.

My head pounds with each footfall that hits the gravel, making me shudder.

I'm finally getting to leave the basement, but what about Gabriel?

If what the man said about killing Dad and the twins was true, then who's going to take care of my brother? Without my missions to pay for his upkeep, the people holding him will either put a bullet through his head or leave him to rot.

"Now, Miko," the man says, his sharp voice cutting through my thoughts.

A heartbeat later, the air fills with an ear-shattering boom. I flinch, and the man picks up speed.

Gunshots ring through the air, accelerating my frantic pulse. My eyes snap open to find him racing us through a row of trees with a canopy so overgrown and thick that they block out the morning light.

Even though gunfire echoes from far away, it's only a matter of time before Dad's guards realize what's happening and track us to this side of the grounds.

I turn my head in the direction the man is headed, finding an armored truck with its side door open. It's the kind of vehicle used for collecting cash from banks. Inside is a red-haired boy about my age who stares at us through wide eyes.

His gaze locks on mine. "Who's that—"

"Get in front and drive," the man growls.

Another explosion sounds from the direction of the mansion. The man shoves me into the truck and I land on its cold metal floor. Before I can take in my surroundings, the door slams shut, and the vehicle lurches forward. I roll across the floor and bash my head against something hard.

"Shit," the man says as I'm dragged into unconsciousness.

———

The drone of male voices pulls me back to awareness. I lie on my side atop a smooth surface, my nostrils filled with the mingled scents of metal and polished wood.

Warm hands pull my hair off the back of my neck, making me stiffen. The touch is pleasant, seeming to chase away my darkest thoughts, even though the drugs have left me with a blistering migraine, made worse by hitting my head.

I crack open an eye and take in the sight of a wooden bench surrounded by guns hanging on pegboards. Strangely, there's a sack of cat litter on the floor.

Playing dead, I tune into their conversation. The man who pulled me out of the basement is called Leroi. Next to him is Miko, the red-haired boy from the van. From the way he talks, he knows a hell of a lot about computers and remote devices. Their gazes are so fixed on my collar that they haven't even noticed I'm awake.

"So, where did you find her?" Miko asks.

"Can you disable the collar or not?" Leroi snaps.

"Maybe, but it's not that easy." He rubs his chin. "Some of these devices are set up to release their full charge of electricity as a penalty for tampering."

"Is it lethal?"

Miko chuckles. "An electric chair needs to discharge at least two-thousand volts to kill. The most a DC battery of that size can hold is twelve."

"Alright then." Leroi nods at my collar. "Remove it."

"No," I rasp.

Both gazes snap to my face. I push myself up, my limbs screaming in protest.

"There's a chip." I raise a trembling finger to a spot

behind my ear. "They told me it would overload if I ever messed with the collar."

The two men exchange glances, but it's Leroi who speaks first. "Who are you?" he asks, his voice soft. "What's your name?"

My eyes dart to the redhead, who backs away under the other man's command. It's only when he's completely out of reach that I turn to this stranger. My savior. He's in his early thirties, about the same age as the twins, with eyes so dark they appear black and bottomless.

They're as expressionless as the rest of his face. It's the first time in years someone has looked at me—really looked at me with anything other than fury or lust. My breath catches, and alarm tugs at the pit of my stomach. I shrink away, not wanting to fall into those depths.

"Maybe she's shell shocked?" the red-haired man asks from the other side of the room.

"She isn't," the man says, his gaze breaking away from mine.

The pressure around my lungs loosens, and I exhale, finally able to look the man full in the face. His features are angular—sharp eyes, sharp cheekbones, straight nose, cruel mouth. It's softened by olive skin and a dusting of stubble, but there's still a hardness to him. He has the look of a man whose hands are soaked with blood.

Like mine.

"Seraphine," I mumble. "Seraphine Capello." I cringe at the sound of my full name on my lips. It's been so long since anyone's asked, and my head is so messed up that I forget to lie. What if he kills me next?

His gaze snaps back to meet mine. "Any relation to Frederic?"

"He's my..." I clear my throat. It's not like I can make up anything clever now. "He's my dad."

"Frederic Capello didn't have a daughter." He leans into me, his dark eyes boring so deeply into mine that I swear he's trying to yank the answers out of my soul.

The fear in my gut twists into the same fury that's kept me going for years. It's venomous and cold, a fierce determination to prove them all wrong.

"Dad had two families," I say from between clenched teeth. "I didn't know that until he brought me to his second house and handed me to his sons."

"Shit." The man glances away.

"Leroi?" asks the younger man.

He shakes his head in a motion to shelve that line of conversation, pinches the bridge of his nose, and clenches his jaw. "Who was the person on the monitor?"

"My brother," I say, my pulse quickening. "They're keeping him in another building. I need to find—"

The man raises a palm. "Another Capello son?"

"Yes," I rasp.

Leroi exhales, his gaze dropping to my neck. "Let's work on removing your chip and collar, then we'll find your brother, alright?"

My ears ring with alarm. Who sent Leroi, when everyone who ever cared for us is dead? There's the handler, but after five years, he wouldn't help me now. Not when he was such an eager participant in my training.

Mom is dead. Dad's guards strangled her until she stopped moving while he and the others looked on and jeered. Nana died months later in captivity. Gabriel is still a hostage, and he's too emaciated and weak to arrange a mass murder. This man killed Dad and the twins. No one else with any power knows I was kept in that basement.

Asking questions might lead to him discovering why I'd been held captive, then he'll find a way to hack into my collar and bring me under his control. I need to play along, treat this interaction like any other job, and act like an innocent, harmless victim.

"Seraphine," Leroi says, "Will you keep still while another colleague takes out your chip?"

My breath catches. Another man? I shrink away, not wanting to be trapped in a room with a trio of strangers.

"He won't hurt you," Leroi says. "I'll stay at your side and keep you safe."

Nodding, I raise my finger to the skin behind my ear and trace over its hard edges. "Alright."

"I'll call Dr. Sal and tell him it's urgent." Miko walks out of the room, leaving me alone with Leroi.

My head bows under the weight of his gaze. He hasn't asked about what they made me do, both in and out of the basement. Maybe he doesn't know. Either way, I'll stay quiet until it's time to escape and find Gabriel.

And if they try anything, I'll slit their throats.

THREE

LEROI

Thank fuck I have a qualified doctor on staff. Admittedly, Dr. Sal had his license revoked by the state medical board for malpractice. Now he works in our clean-up crew —there isn't much call for healers in this line of work.

Removing the chip is more complicated than cutting out a square of plastic. Sal sedates the girl to extricate tendrils of metal from her flesh. Over time, her body must have healed around the foreign object, making it impossible to extract without expert help.

After Sal cleanses the wound and pieces her back together with medical glue, I lift her off the table and move her out of the armory and into my spare bedroom. I lay her atop the mattress and watch her sleep. Her thin chest rises and falls beneath an oversized sweatshirt, making her appear even smaller and younger. More vulnerable.

She can't be much more than eighteen. It's hard to tell when she's so frail.

Shit. Only the sickest of bastards could keep their own daughter in a basement. If I could, I would bring him back to life again just to give him the slow, tortuous death he deserves. Him and everyone else involved in her imprisonment.

I back away from her and press down on the bridge of my nose. My mission was to wipe out everyone connected to Capello, whether through birth or marriage. Not just so that Roman could get out of jail, but to wrestle back control of an empire the sick bastard stole after the death of my cousins' father.

That mission should include killing Seraphine and her brother, but something in her innocence tugs at the frayed remnants of my conscience.

She's suffered enough.

Besides, no one but her knows she's Capello's daughter, and it's going to stay that way.

With one shake of my head, I step out of the room.

Miko waits for me in the hallway with his hands clasped. "Are you going to tell me what the deal is with her?"

"You don't want to know," I mutter.

Miko is the side-kick and little brother I didn't know I needed. I stumbled across Miko on a job to kill his asshole stepfather. He was fourteen, bruised and neglected, and had walked in on me while I was strangling the bastard with a garrote.

He'd looked me straight in the eye and nodded, urging me to continue snuffing out the bastard's life. Afterward, he'd begged me not to leave him alone with his drug addict mother. Anton had retired and left me to run the firm, so I took him with me. From then on, he became my shadow.

He's a hacker, researcher, and a getaway driver, wrapped up in a nineteen-year-old package.

"What are you going to do with her?" Miko nods toward the girl.

"Keep her safe," I reply. "At least until Roman's hold on the Capello empire is secure. After that, he and his brothers won't give a shit if she exists."

Miko gives me a slow nod, his gaze assessing. I'm certain he's thinking about how I took him under my wing all those years ago, but I haven't even thought as far as what will happen when Seraphine awakes.

I doubt that Seraphine could become my next protégé. She's too fragile and has seen more darkness than a girl her age should ever have to endure. After she recovers, she can work with Miko to track down her surviving relatives. If they were the ones who sold her into sexual slavery, then I'll follow her lead on how she wants retribution.

"You did well tonight," I mutter. "Take tomorrow off."

Miko gives me a tired smile. "Good night, boss."

———

I spent the rest of the night lying awake in bed, wondering how the hell any man could keep his daughter chained up in a basement. The thoughts twist and turn into the recesses of my mind until they fade to blackness.

It's past noon by the time I wake up, and I bring Seraphine a selection of items lying about in the kitchen. It's mostly potato chips, fruit, crackers, oatmeal, bottled water, and juice. Sal will order any supplements she might need, but until the next food delivery arrives, she has to manage with what's available.

She lies on her side, still sleeping. Sunlight streams in through the window, brightening the ends of her blonde hair into strands of gold. The unbruised side of her face looks so peaceful, it's almost angelic, and I'm transfixed.

Could she really be a Capello? Everyone related to the old man was brown-eyed and dark-haired. She could be a stepdaughter. It wouldn't surprise me if she wasn't trafficked to fulfill some sick daddy-daughter role play. I clench my jaw at the thought and tear my eyes away from the sight of her frail form. As long as I'm still breathing, no one will hurt this innocent girl.

The phone rings in the kitchen. I set down the tray and walk back to the device. Anton's number appears on the display, and my jaw ticks.

He's my mentor, a distant cousin of my mother's who brought me into the business. The man who taught me that mixing emotions with murder was the fastest way to get a hitman killed.

"Anton," I say, my voice tense.

"Did you hear about the disaster that took place early this morning at the Capello mansion?" he asks.

My mind races. Anton is strangely well-informed for a man who's been retired for over five years.

"What happened?" I ask.

"A lone gunman entered the building and killed the entire family, along with several cousins."

"A tragedy," I mutter. "The Capellos were excellent customers."

Anton falls silent, waiting for me to give further commentary, or maybe a confession. I trust this man with my life. He's the one who taught me everything I know about surviving this business and has saved my ass more times than I can count.

Admitting I was the lone gunman might lead to

explaining what I found in the basement. I can't bring myself to tell him about Seraphine. Not yet.

"Are there any leads?" I ask.

"Nothing," Anton says. "Whoever did this was careful not to leave any traces. Their security cameras fed old footage to the cloud, and the gunman reduced one wing of the mansion to a pile of flaming rubble."

The corner of my lips lifts into a smirk. Thank fuck Miko is also a genius with explosives.

"I'll ask around," I say. "See if anyone heard anything."

He grunts. "Don't you usually have the boys around on Thursday nights for poker?"

Shit. By the boys, Anton means a selection of men with loose tongues and extensive connections. With enough booze and weed, they'll give you the information you need or tell you where to start looking.

Every instinct says I should cancel this game, but doing so might arouse suspicion. Capello wasn't the most respected leader, but I don't want to risk anyone thinking I might be linked to the massacre.

"I'll see what they say," I mutter.

"The lone gunman also stole something that belonged to Capello."

I hesitate. "What?"

"A Lolita assassin."

A... I don't even want to think of the implications. That has to be some bullshit rumor. My eyes squeeze shut, and my mind speeds from fifty miles an hour to a hundred. Anton carried out a few jobs for Capello before he retired, but I didn't think they'd been well acquainted enough to share such sensitive intel.

"There's no such thing as a Lolita assassin," I say.

"Trained her myself," he replies with a touch of pride. "Face like an angel with the instincts of a killer."

Fuck.

Disgust coils in my gut, and a sour taste spreads across my tongue. I draw back and exhale a shocked breath. He can't be talking about Seraphine, but she's the only person I found in the mansion that even vaguely fits the description.

"What did he use her for?" I ask.

"I didn't ask questions. The less I know, the better." He clears his throat. "Sniff about. I don't want her falling into the wrong hands."

A dozen more questions rise to the surface, such as why the hell Anton trained someone so innocent and young to be a killer, but I bite them back. No one is supposed to know I have Seraphine. That would lead to questions about who killed the Capellos.

"I'll drop a few hints at poker," I say, my voice even. "Maybe one of the boys knows something."

"Doubtful. Are you still in contact with your cousins?"

My eyes narrow. Anton is getting too close to the truth. "I sometimes see Benito and Cesare at the Phoenix. Why?"

"Last night's slaughter could be revenge for Enzo Montesano."

"Didn't he die of a heart attack?" I ask, my brows pulling into a frown.

Anton hesitates. "Capello moved in on Montesano's empire after he died. Around the same time, his eldest was taken out of the picture with a well-timed death sentence. Then Capello shut out the other two of his sons. It doesn't take a genius to work out that Montesano didn't die of natural causes."

"True." I nod. That much is obvious, but my cousins never voiced their theories on how Capello could have caused Montesano's heart to fail. "But I doubt Benito and Cesare would admit to anything so incendiary, even to a distant cousin."

"Keep your eyes open. Upheaval in the underworld is good for business. The fall of such a huge family leads to a power vacuum, and everyone's going to be scrambling for control."

He hangs up, leaving me rubbing the spot between my brows. Anton is correct about the Montesano brothers being behind the Capello massacre. The information in those hard drives I took will be enough to get Roman out of jail, but Anton would have said something more if he suspected I was the hired killer.

I set down the phone and walk over to the coffee machine, my mind racing. Seraphine needs to stay somewhere else tonight. It's the only way to host poker night and keep her safe.

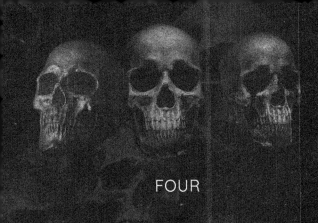

FOUR

SERAPHINE

My head pounds when I wake up in the strange room, but what's stranger is the freedom of movement around my naked neck. I'm free of the collar, but the situation I've landed in might be even worse.

My body still feels weighed down from the sedative, and it takes every effort to drag myself off the bed. I need to get out now and find Gabriel. He's out there somewhere, clinging to life now that the people who were holding him hostage are dead.

I creep through a bedroom of parquet floors and pale gray walls—a vast upgrade from the basement I was kept in for five years. It's lit by filtered sunlight, telling me that only hours must have passed since we left Dad's house.

Leroi, the man who took me, is an assassin. A professional one. Not someone coerced to kill targets with a knife or a poisoned hairpin. He has weapons, explosives, a getaway driver, and a physician who can extract chips.

With as much stealth as I can muster through my wooziness, I step out into an open-plan living room of whitewashed brick walls with enough leather sofas to seat a small army. A long dining table takes up the left side of the space, but there's no sign of a kitchen. Something tells me that's not the only place he keeps his knives, but I'm not about to return to the room with all those guns.

Ignoring the floor-to-ceiling windows that provide a hair-raising view of Beaumont city, I ease open the nearest door. At the first sight of the man sleeping in a four-poster bed, my heart jumps to the back of my throat.

After seeing all those guns on the wall, I thought this was some kind of facility, but this is his home.

White bedsheets pool around his waist, exposing sculpted pectoral muscles and defined abs. His chest rises and falls with each light snore, and the effect is hypnotic.

Leroi would make the perfect prey. There's no thick growth of hair obscuring his anatomy, no greasy layers of fat. He's textbook perfection, a killer's dream.

I force myself to look away. The twins aren't holding me hostage anymore and I don't even know if Leroi wants to put me to work, or if he has other motives.

Easing the door shut, I move to the next room, until I find the kitchen.

Bright light bounces off pristine white cabinets, creating a glare so intense that I have to squint. I rush past the breakfast bar and move to where a knife block sits beside a stainless steel stove. I pull on each handle and examine the implements until I find a boning knife.

Its blade is long and thin and flexible, with a tip sharp enough to slice through ligaments and glide through the ribs to reach the heart. After checking through the other blades, I open the drawers and extract a steak knife, which is small enough to conceal in my pocket.

I should search through the apartment for cards, cash, a

phone—anything that could help me find Gabriel, but I don't want to risk waking Leroi. Waking up with only a pounding in my head tells me he isn't the type of predator who thinks with his dick. Though I don't doubt he's the type who would hunt me down in a second if I stole anything valuable.

When I reach the front door, it's locked, with no sign of keys—not even for the balcony.

Clenching my teeth, I sneak back into the gray bedroom, slip the knives under my pillow, and curl up into a ball.

Leroi can't keep me here forever. Eventually, he'll let me out, and I'll use that opening to find my brother. If he doesn't, I'll kill him in his sleep and pick through his handsome corpse.

The next time I wake up, sunlight sears through my eyelids. I can't block out the glare, even when I squint.

On the bedside table is a tray filled with bottled water and nearly a week's worth of rations. I reach for a cracker and slip it into my mouth. The cheesy flavor is a welcome distraction from the bitterness that coats my tongue.

A soft knock on the door has my hand reaching for the steak knife. Heartbeats later, Leroi strolls in, holding two steaming mugs.

My throat tightens under his appraising glare. His eyes are so dark, and his mouth so sharp that he makes me feel like prey.

"Do you drink coffee?" he asks.

I stare up into his eyes, searching for clues behind his expressionless features. He seemed okay yesterday. Maybe a little impatient, but decent. It's hard to tell with men. One minute, they're nice and the next, they're feral hounds barking to be euthanized.

When the corners of his eyes narrow, I realize he asked a question. Mom never let me drink coffee, saying I was too young. I was too young for a lot of things when she was alive, but that was a lifetime ago.

Leroi steps toward the bed with the mug, and my muscles tense, ready to lunge with the blade if he throws the hot liquid. Instead, he places the coffee on the bedside table before backing away.

"It's there if you want it."

I nod.

"Are you hurt?" he asks, his voice deceptively soft.

My jaw tightens, and I don't answer. I'm not about to reveal any vulnerability. This might be a trick.

"Do you have a family I can contact?"

Nanna is dead. So is Mom. Leroi killed Dad. Not that I'm mourning the bastard; he handed me over to the twins and never once looked back.

"My brother," I rasp. "His name is Gabriel."

He exhales a long breath. "The man on the screen?"

I nod.

"Do you know who's holding him?"

"Gregor and Samson Capello."

His lips tighten. "They're dead. Did they have any associates who knew about your brother?"

I gulp. "Maybe their driver?"

"His name?"

"They called him Pietro," I whisper.

"That's a start." Leroi rolls up his sleeves. "Leave it with me. I'll put out some feelers and see if we can track him down."

My breath catches.

He runs a hand through his hair. "I need you to stay somewhere else tonight. A few associates are coming over to play poker. You don't want to be in the same space as them. They're dangerous."

My breath catches. My heart skips several beats. Is this where he hands me over to another man and I become his prisoner?

"No." I shake my head.

His brow furrows. "It won't be safe here."

"I'm not leaving," I say, my voice rising several octaves. "I can take care of myself."

He studies me for what feels like an eternity. Weighing his options, as if I'm an injured bird trying to fly on broken wings—does he offer aid or does he put me down? I'm not helpless, but I can't reveal my skills without putting myself in danger. Straightening, I hold his gaze until he nods.

"Lock the door tonight and don't open it until tomorrow. Is that understood?"

I nod, my lungs deflating with relief.

As Leroi walks to the door, the words slip out before I can stop them.

"Wait."

He pauses, staring at me from the corner of his eye.

"Why are you helping me?" I ask, my voice hoarse. "What do you want in return?"

His expression softens. "No one should have to suffer what you've been through. Especially not a kid."

My shoulders droop as he leaves the room, taking with him some of my peace of mind. Five years ago, I was sixteen and my biggest problem was failing my driving test. I had friends, a mother and father, and an older brother who was about to go to college. Now, all traces of that life are gone. The last vestiges of my childhood were corrupted by blood.

I don't believe Leroi wants to help me out of the goodness of his heart because I'm young. Every sick bastard I killed thought my baby face and small stature made me easy prey. He might even want to use me as an assassin. If he plans to use Gabriel as leverage, I'll just have to strike out at him first.

———

Leroi wasn't joking about the men being dangerous. At some point in the evening, I woke to the smell of cannabis fumes and raucous laughter. When I peeked out through the door, there were over eight men sitting around the dining table playing cards.

I'd gone back to sleep with a stomachache from overeating, but now I'm wide awake. My head no longer hurts, and the pounding between my ears has dulled to a roar. A large hand roams beneath my sweatshirt, and calloused fingers close around my nipple.

Disgust clogs my gorge. My jaw clenches, but my training commands me to remain perfectly still. I must have forgotten to lock the door when I spied on them earlier. The groper's hand travels down my jogging pants to my crotch.

"You like that?" he murmurs, his breath hot against my ear. It stinks of tobacco and stale alcohol.

Images surface from the dredges of my memory. I'm crouched at a door, helpless and cowering, while a crowd of men—

No.

Fury surges, filling my mind's eye with a haze of blood. I can't be disappointed in Leroi because I've been in these situations more times than I can count. He's just the same as the rest of them, and he'll suffer the same fate.

"You're a pretty little thing," he whispers.

My fingers close in around the steak knife.

The blunt tip of his penis presses against my lips, making my eyes snap open.

It's not Leroi. The man grinning down at me and holding his shaft is shorter, paler, fatter, with bloodshot eyes. Years ago, a situation like this would have thrown me into a flurry of panic.

But not now.

Anticipation wraps around my throat like a garrote, choking off my air. Now, I'm holding my breath, waiting for the right moment to spill blood.

Fuck the steak knife. I'm about to need something sharper.

"Mmmmm," I make a pleased sound in the back of my throat.

"You want it, baby?" he rasps.

I gaze up at him, bat my eyelashes and mod.

His eyes shine with lust. "Then take it."

Not taking my gaze off his, I wrap my fingers around his shaft. The man hisses through his teeth, his barrel chest rising and falling.

"That's it, baby. Now, take it all."

He doesn't need to ask twice.

I bring the boning knife up from beneath the pillow and slice through his dick. He screams, blood spurting on my face like a geyser.

He staggers back, his hands cupping his crotch. "You fucking bitch!"

That bastard doesn't know half of it. Slipping his penis in my pocket, I rush at him with the knife. He skids on his blood and lands on his ass.

"Get away from me." He raises a palm, trying to fend me off, but I dart around to his side and slice his throat.

The man gasps, his eyes wide, his hand clutching at the

gash in his neck. Blood spills through his fingers and onto his shirt, forming pretty blooms of crimson.

I stand over him, my chest heaving, and watch the life fade from his eyes. The dull roar between my ears settles into a steady beat, and I can finally exhale.

"What..." he croaks as though confused about how he's ended up dickless.

"You told me to take it all," I say, absorbing every flicker of pain, every anguished breath. "And I liked it very much."

"Psycho... Bitch."

My lips curl into a smile.

An agonizing death is the only thing I enjoy about being in the company of a man. However, as with most of his kind, he's left me unsatisfied. I step through the puddle of his blood and out of the room, needing to see more blood. Craving it.

That's when I spot Leroi sleeping on an armchair with his throat exposed.

FIVE

LEROI

I only get a crick in my back when I've slept in the armchair, but I'm too mellowed out to open my eyes or bother to move.

A dry cough chokes through my parched throat. The air is still thick with the scent of weed, but someone must have been smoking something much stronger because I never fall asleep during poker nights.

I didn't mean to drink so much whiskey, but fuck it, I deserved to let loose. After weeks of preparation, the Capello job went off with only one small hitch, and she hasn't once left her bedroom. I managed to get some leads on the location of her brother over the course of the evening too.

My mind drifts to that conversation with Anton. He didn't just know about Seraphine. He's one of the bastards responsible for keeping her in that basement. Did he know about the collar? There's no way he wouldn't.

Anton trained me before I was about Seraphine's age, but he sure as hell didn't keep me like one of his dogs. The man was the only father figure I had at a time when I needed guidance. My head throbs at the thought of him corrupting a child.

It's excruciating.

I can't even ask him about Seraphine without anyone knowing I killed the Capellos. My mind is so twisted in a loop that I can't even imagine him mistreating Seraphine.

Rhythmic ticking from somewhere high on the wall interrupts my relaxed state. I try to meditate so it can fade into the background, but the sound becomes insistent.

Shit. I envy the fuckers who can sleep through alarms and all kinds of shit, yet the sound of a clock is grating on my nerves.

If only I cared enough to reach for my gun...

Tick, tick, tick.

TICK, TICK, TICK.

The clock won't shut the fuck up, and I'm starting to take this personally. My fingers twitch toward the pistol digging into my waistband, the real source of my back pain.

I crack open an eye, only for the sun to sear my retinas with bright light.

Damn it.

Hours have passed, judging by the painful glare, and I'm still half drunk. When I open my eyes again, it's to peek through my lashes. I can't sleep all morning. I have responsibilities. Someone needs to check on the girl, give her breakfast, coax her out of the room. She's spent so much time locked up in a basement that she doesn't know how to be free. I also need Miko to follow those leads I gathered from the poker crew.

I crack my eyes open a few extra millimeters. The light stings, but I'm ready for the burn. *Wake up, you lazy fucker.*

You have responsibilities. You can't pick up a stray and leave her to her own devices.

My eyes snap open, and all I see is blood.

Blood coats the floors, the walls, the sofas. Blood runs down the fronts of the poker crew's shirts. It's everywhere.

Alarm explodes through my chest, propelling me out of the armchair.

Fuck.

I pull out my pistol.

Someone just killed six men in my living room while I was too drunk and stoned to notice. Adrenaline surges, sharpening my senses. My heart pounds hard and fast, sending sensation to every nerve ending. I glance around, searching for signs of movement.

Everyone is dead, from Larry the delivery driver to Nathan, who mowed the Capellos' lawn.

Shit.

Why did the killer leave me alive? I need to investigate. Need to find out who the hell infiltrated my apartment. Need to know if this was an act of revenge for killing Capello or something else.

My heart skips a beat. Did they take the girl?

Cold sweat breaks out across my brow and trickles down my back. I don't give a shit about the poker crew. They were temporary allies I'd gathered to complete the Capello job, but I do give a shit about Seraphine. I charge through the living room, my feet sticking in the congealed blood, and burst through her bedroom door.

The bed is empty, but the room is coated in blood. Billy Blue from Capello Casino sits dead on the floor, his eyes wide open, his mouth slack.

What the hell happened?

There's no time to ask why he was in her room. Not

when whoever else might have tortured her in that basement could have taken her back to another hellhole. Not when Anton might have put two and two together and worked out the location of his missing Lolita assassin.

I'm out of the door in an instant, my mind racing for clues.

"Seraphine," I roar.

There's no answer.

She's either dead or suffering a punishment that will make her beg for oblivion. It was supposed to be different with Seraphine. What was the point of all that training if I couldn't protect one girl?

My feet skid to a halt. What about the cameras? I could watch the footage, see who snuck in to take the girl, track their registrations, and—

I need Miko to pull up the footage.

Glancing from side to side, I skim the blood-covered remnants of poker night. Beer bottles, open pizza boxes, plastic chips, eight dead men with their throats slit, but no sign of my fucking phone.

Did I leave it in the kitchen?

My footsteps are loud and sticky across the tacky floor. I fling the door open to find a small blonde figure standing at the counter between the sink and the stove.

"S-Seraphine?" I rasp.

She glances over her shoulder and gazes up at me through huge, blue eyes. Her face would be the picture of innocence if it wasn't smattered with blood.

The relief that sweeps through my system is so intense that my knees almost buckle.

She's alive.

I couldn't bear the thought of someone stealing this innocent girl away to yet another basement, especially after promising her she would be safe. Despite being happy to see her, something about this picture doesn't look right.

Seraphine turns back to the counter, her right arm making slashing motions with a knife. I glance around, finding a plate with two slices of buttered bread and frown.

"What are you doing?" I ask.

When she doesn't answer, I cross the kitchen, following the path of her delicate, red footprints. My pulse continues to pound. Did she see what happened to the poker crew? I imagine her curled up in a tiny ball beneath the bed, hiding from the killers until it was safe.

Fucking hell.

The poor kid.

She continues slicing something on the chopping board, using the precision of a sushi chef. I glance over her shoulder to see what she's cutting, and my heart stops.

It's a severed penis.

"What the fuck are you doing?" I rasp.

She looks up at me with those huge blue eyes. Blue eyes that radiate something more sinister than having simply borne witness to the murders of my poker buddies. I grab the wrist of the hand holding the knife and squeeze.

"Seraphine," I hiss. "Where did you get that cock?"

Her face hardens, but she doesn't speak. The only time she seems to answer my questions is when I ask about her brother... or her collar and chip.

"If you want me to help you find Gabriel, you will answer my question," I snarl. "What the fuck happened?"

"That man touched me, so I cut off his dick," she says, her voice flat.

"Billy Blue?"

"The one in my room."

Guilt squeezes my chest, tightening my throat. I should

have carried her out of the apartment and dumped her with Miko when she refused to leave. Now, I've gotten her traumatized by someone else.

"What happened next?" I ask.

"I cut him." She raises a boning knife into the space between our bodies. "With this."

Shit.

I step back.

"And the others?" I rasp.

"I had to make sure they wouldn't do the same."

Seraphine has a way of distorting reality, so all you see when looking at her is a sweet little angel. It doesn't matter that Anton trained her as a Lolita assassin—my brain won't allow myself to believe she's capable of mass murder. Still, when she drops her gaze to my hand encasing her wrist, I release my grip.

"You killed them all?" I wheeze.

She turns back to the chopping board and continues slicing through Billy Blue's cock. My gaze darts to the two slices of bread, and realization hits me in the gut.

"You're making a sandwich?" I ask, incredulous.

She nods.

My stomach churns. "Why?"

"They need to know I'm not afraid."

"The voices in your head?" I whisper, my pulse quickening.

What the fuck did I bring to my home? Why the hell did I think the situation with Seraphine would be anything like with Miko? When I met the boy, he was bruised but fully clothed and unshackled.

Sure, there was a gleam in his eye when I strangled his stepfather, but that was satisfaction wrought from years of being powerless against a bully. I brought him into my spare room, but the worst thing he did was leave trash on the floor.

Did I bring home a serial killer or did she go too far with her self-defense?

As Seraphine continues to slice Billy Blue's penis into wafer-thin pieces, my patience cracks. I can handle a room full of dead poker players, or even a castrated creep, but I can't stand by and watch a girl make a sandwich out of a cock.

"Stop that." I snatch the knife out of her hands and toss it across the counter.

Without skipping a beat, she reaches for the sliced meat.

I yank the chopping board off the counter and throw it and the severed penis across the room.

Seraphine whirls around, her nostrils flaring.

"You will not eat that sandwich," I snarl.

"There's nothing worthwhile in the fridge," she spits back.

I clench my fists. "There's wings and pizza left over. Oh wait, you drenched that in blood."

Her lips tighten into a thin, and she glares up at me like a feral kitten, looking ready to make me her new target. I bare my teeth, daring her to pounce.

We stand so close that I can feel the rapid thrum of her heart. She wants to fight, I can tell, and I'm ready for her next move. Before I can think of what to say next, her shoulders sag.

"I'm sorry for ruining your leftovers," she says, sounding genuinely contrite.

My face drops.

What?

"Anything *else* you'd like to apologize for?" I ask, my

arm sweeping toward the trail of blood leading out toward the murdered men.

"If this is about the mess, I can clean it up," she says.

I pinch the bridge of my nose. "Really."

It's not even a question. There's no way a five-foot nothing girl with a face like an angel can move eight male bodies out of the building and dispose of them without breaking her back or getting caught.

She gives me a sharp nod, her features hard with determination. "Really."

Deluded as well as dangerous.

I should put a bullet through her pretty head before she causes any more mayhem, but I won't.

"Alright then, Little Miss Murderer, get to work."

With my eyes still fixed on Seraphine's, I step backward to where I left my phone by the sink. I'll be damned if I leave the cleaning up to this pretty little psycho.

It's time to call my own men and teach her a lesson about not biting off more than she can chew.

SIX

LEROI

The firm I inherited from Anton has a number of valuable assets. Firearms, explosives, and facilities across New Alderney. None are more vital than the clean-up crew. They're quiet, discreet, and can handle any size of job efficiently and without complaint.

I draw the living room curtains, encasing the space in gloom and survey the mess of spilled blood, slumped bodies, and slit throats. This is worse than the chaos I created at the Capello mansion.

Seraphine must have worked her way through the poker crew one by one when we were too high to realize she was picking us off with her stolen knife. I run a hand over my face and pinch the bridge of my nose.

Shit.

I can't even blame the girl.

Billy Blue's groping must have unlocked her pent-up rage from being powerless under the Capellos' control. They didn't just keep her prisoner, they put a shock collar around her neck and a chip under her skin.

What those sick fucks must have done to her. In her position, I wouldn't have stopped at castrating one man. I raise a hand to my neck, wondering if she spared me for a reason, was saving me for last, or had simply forgotten?

I don't dare to ask.

Her trauma, combined with Anton's training, makes Seraphine a walking disaster.

The kitchen door opens, and Seraphine walks out, holding a half-eaten sandwich. Blood soaks the front of her sweatshirt, rolled up jogging pants, and coats her dainty little feet.

There's no telling if she's just pressed two slices together or has gathered up the dubious meat, but she stares straight into my eyes, brings the bread to her mouth, and takes a bite as though issuing a challenge.

"Stop that." My jaw clenches.

Without stopping to chew her mouthful, she takes another bite. Her gaze fixes on mine with open defiance. She's like a cat that's eaten the proverbial canary and gives no fucks that it has feathers sticking out of its jaw.

At the third bite, something inside me snaps. I close the distance between us and pry the shit out of her hand. "You are not eating a cock sandwich," I snarl. "Not in this house."

Seraphine raises her chin and glares up at me, pretty eyes burning with insolence.

"You're supposed to be cleaning up," I snarl.

"I am," she replies in a monotone.

My nostrils flare. What is it with this girl? One minute, I'm sympathizing with her, the next, I want to wrap my hands around her scrawny little throat.

"Pick one man," I say, forcing my voice to stay even. "Drag him to the front door and put his shit in a bag."

Still glaring up at me, she parts her lips, but I'm no longer interested in what she has to say.

"Trash bags are in the cupboard under the sink. Go."

Seraphine slopes into the kitchen, letting the door swing shut, and reappears a moment later with a roll of bags. Trudging across the room like she's on a death march, she cuts me a glower before disappearing behind her door.

My jaw drops.

She wants to clean up her attacker? Of the eight men she killed, she chooses him.

I run a hand through my hair and pull on the ends. What the hell have I gotten myself into?

The doorbell rings, snapping my attention away from Seraphine's room. On the other side are six familiar faces, including Don. Standing at six-six, only two inches taller than me, but built like a barn, Don's crew consists of relatives who share family genetics.

He offers me a broad smile and a raised brow. "You said it was a big job?"

"In here." I step aside and sweep an arm toward the corpses.

Don steps through the threshold and lets out a low whistle. "Messy."

"Good thing I don't pay you for commentary," I say. "Are you up for the task?"

His grin widens. "Sure, but we'll have to wait until nightfall for the disposals. Anything more than two bodies attracts attention."

"Fine."

I leave them to it and walk across the living room to check on Seraphine, fully expecting to find her crouched in front of Billy Blue and carving out his balls.

When I open the door, she's bent over his corpse and

removing his shoes. The bed has been stripped and two full trash bags lean against the wall, presumably filled with blood-soaked sheets. She glances up at me before pulling off his socks and adding it to the pile.

"There's a crew in the living room cleaning up dead poker players." I want to make a barb about her having killed them, but I'm already feeling bad about putting someone so delicate to hard labor. "Don't attack their dicks."

Her pretty features twist into a scowl.

A chuckle rises from my gut. This situation is beyond fucked up. If I don't laugh, I might turn a gun on everyone and keep shooting until someone puts me down like a rabid dog.

———

Hours later, long after the clean-up crew has bagged up every corpse, broken the down blood-sodden armchairs into transportable pieces, and scrubbed the walls and parquet floors clean, I'm standing in the spare room over Seraphine with my arms folded over my chest.

Billy Blue's naked and castrated corpse sits in a corner of the room, his eyes staring unseeingly into the void.

This is cruel, and what I'm doing to her makes me an asshole.

I should be a gentleman and help the girl, but this is part of her education. Anton always said not to kill more men than you can clean up after unless you have a crew on standby or you're working behind a long-range rifle. This is a lesson best learned through blood and sweat.

After scrubbing her room clean and changing into another set of Miko's old clothes, she sits in the passenger seat of my Jeep with her arms folded over her chest.

We're parked by the woodland at the edge of Anton's land, waiting for the sun to set before she completes the final stage of her clean up. Resentment rolls off her narrow shoulders in shockwaves, although she hasn't asked why I didn't allow the crew to take care of Billy Blue.

"It's time." I reach beneath the dashboard to pull the lever to open the trunk.

She shoots me a scowl.

"Find a spot to bury the body." I flick my head toward the woodland. "Avoid the roots and stones, or you'll be here all night."

Her features turn sour.

"Go."

She opens the door, hurls herself out, and flounces out into the woods. As she passes the treeline, she casts me one last plaintive glower.

My lips twitch, and I shake my head.

"What a brat," I mutter.

I sit back and watch Seraphine traipse around, trying to find the right patch of ground. The more time I spend with her, the more I'm convinced that she really could be Capello's daughter. Or at least the child of someone wealthy enough to spoil her. I can tell that much by her inability to operate a mop.

The burner phone I set up for the Capello job rings. I pick up, already expecting to hear from one of my two cousins not trapped behind bars.

"It's Benito."

"Did you get the files we sent?" I ask.

"Yeah," he sighs. "Capello gathered a shit-ton of information. It's a lot to sift through, and Roman is getting impatient."

"Not surprising," I mutter. "How is he holding up?"

"He wants to speak to you."

"You're sure?"

Benito grunts. "You know what he's like."

I do, but few other people know I grew up around the Montesano brothers until I was nine. We even share the same last name. Our fathers were like brothers, though they were only first cousins. When Dad died, Enzo Montesano was like a second father.

A shitstorm of circumstances tore us apart, and by the time Anton found me, my situation wasn't much better than Miko's had been. I trained under Anton, and the Montesano brothers worked in their father's empire until his unexpected death and Roman's false imprisonment for murder.

Eliminating the Capellos was my way of repaying the Montesanos. I enjoyed the company of my blood relatives.

Seraphine's sullen face appears at my window.

"Got to go," I mutter. "Text if you need help finding the right info. My tech guy can tear through those drives in hours."

Benito thanks me and hangs up, and I roll down the window to speak to Seraphine. "Found a spot?"

She points toward the trees.

I open the door, making her jump back several paces, and step out. A cool breeze wafts through the wooded area, bringing with it the scent of leaves and damp wood. I inhale deeply to cleanse the stench of death.

We walk around to the trunk, where Billy Blue lies wrapped in blankets secured with duct tape. After hauling him out and depositing him on the floor, I extract a shovel and a pickax, and lay them beside the corpse.

Seraphine remains motionless, making no attempt to reach for any of the items, until I extract a cooler and a fold-up chair.

"What are those for?" she asks.

"I'll need somewhere to sit and have a cool drink while you're digging the grave."

Her jaw drops.

She actually thinks I plan on cleaning the rest of her kill. The only reason I carried that corpse through the hallway and parking lot was to avoid leaving a mess that would lead back to my apartment.

I flick my head toward the dead body. "Get going. Billy Blue isn't going to bury himself."

The rage burning through her eyes tells me she wished she had slit my throat along with the poker crew. I carry my cooler and chair through the trees, waiting for her to drag the corpse and her equipment.

My lips twitch.

I'm going to enjoy watching her learn that her actions have consequences.

SEVEN

SERAPHINE

Leroi is an asshole.

I should have killed him, along with those men. Opened his shirt, slit his throat, and watched the blood spill down those perfect pecs and tight abs. Then I would wait, transfixed, as his chest fell still, and the red liquid darkened to brown.

The only reason I spared his life was because he'd proven he wasn't like any of the others. He'd killed Dad and the twins, freed me from the basement, had my collar and chip removed, and hadn't laid a finger on me the way others might.

I also need someone with resources to help me find Gabriel.

My biceps burn as I drag the heavy corpse backward through the trees. Every few steps, the pickaxe or shovel falls off its chest and I have to stop and pick them up. Leroi pauses, holding his chair and cooler and staring down at me like I'm delaying his nighttime picnic.

Annoying and an asshole.

By the time I reach the spot where the ground looks smooth enough, sweat pours down my face, my chest, and my back. I raise an aching arm, groaning from the effort, and wipe my forehead on a sleeve that's already drenched with exertion.

Leroi takes his seat with a triumphant smirk and opens the insulated box. My throat tightens as he extracts a bottle of water that glistens with condensation, and I moan as he twists open its lid with a crack.

"Drink." He points it at my mouth.

I hesitate.

This has to be a trick, or at least a trap. The twins used to make me earn my food and drink, despite risking my life and eliminating the targets they sent me out to kill.

Leroi's brows pull together. "Don't just stand there." He tosses the bottle at my feet. "Drink. Grave digging is thirsty work."

I snatch the bottle and gulp down half of its contents before setting it aside and picking up the shovel. The first shove into the ground doesn't even break through the soil.

"Put a foot on the spade and use your body weight," Leroi says, his voice lifting with amusement.

My jaw clenches, and the lining of my stomach burns with resentment. I don't need his condescension. I need him to dig this grave. Leroi is twice my size. Three times, if you add all those muscles. He could get this job done in ten minutes. Instead, he's cracking open a can of beer.

"Why don't you help me?" I drive the shovel into the ground and lean on it with all my weight.

The earth gives way under the pressure, and I scoop aside the first pile of dirt.

"Did you say something, Seraphine?" he asks with a long swig.

I ignore his question and my screaming muscles, refusing to give him the satisfaction of hearing me struggle, and continue digging. Leroi watches in silence as more sweat runs down my face and gets into my eyes. Every few minutes, I shoot him a glare while he sips his beer like a man of leisure.

It feels like I've been at this for hours and the grave is showing no signs of getting any deeper. Each shovelful of dirt feels heavier than the last, and my arms won't stop shaking. I plunge it into the ground and hit what feels like a wall, the shock of it reverberating up my arms.

"Tired already, Seraphine?" he asks.

My jaw tightens. I was tired before we entered the car. Tired before I dragged that bastard's dead body across the pristine apartment. Tired before he made me scrub the floors, wash down the bedroom's gray walls, and unclothe the corpse.

"Nope," I answer through gritted teeth. "Just hit something."

Leroi sets down his can, saunters over, and stops by the wrapped-up corpse. He points a flashlight into the hole and then shines it on the pick ax resting at his feet.

"Looks like you hit a rock. Use the other tool."

The indignation simmering in my gut erupts into a rage that burns through my exhaustion. I snatch the pickax and start to chip away at the stone, wishing it was his skull. Each strike at the hard surface wipes away his smirk until that handsome face is a mess of blood and broken bones.

Leroi backs away. I want to think it's because he can read my mind, but he's probably going back to his beer. What a dick.

I'm half dead by the time the ax finally hits something soft. My palms sting, my arms burn like molten lead, and

I'm cross-eyed from fatigue. Tossing the ax aside, I reach for the shovel, but the trees surrounding the clearing spin. Dizziness overwhelms my senses, and my legs wobble. I collapse into strong arms, which catch me before I hit the dirt.

Leroi shoves a sandwich under my nose. "Eat."

"Is it cock?" I snarl, wanting to get under his skin.

He flinches. "No, it's turkey and cheese. Sorry to disappoint, but no human men were maimed in the production of this meal."

I sink my teeth into it, relishing the taste of something that isn't soil. Leroi watches me eat like I'm some kind of spectacle, but I'm too exhausted to care. Hell, I'm too exhausted to even chew. He wants me to break, or at least apologize for killing his friends, when he should be the one groveling for keeping such shitty company.

"Thanks," I croak before swallowing.

"Take another bite," he says.

My eyes droop, and my jaw goes slack. All thoughts of proving my point drain to nothingness as the edges of my vision turn black.

Leroi scoops me into his arms and chuckles. "Have you learned your lesson, Seraphine?"

No.

I'd murder a room full of men again in a heartbeat.

But next time, I'd save him for last. Maybe even turn one of his body parts into a trophy. Or a snack.

Whatever he says next is lost on me as I drift into unconsciousness.

———

I wake to find myself wrapped in a soft, fuzzy blanket in the backseat. There's a rolled-up jacket beneath my head that smells of him. Of Leroi. He must have picked me up and finished digging the grave. Warmth seeps into my heart. Maybe he isn't so bad.

Leroi drives in silence, save for the rumbling of tires on the road. Sunlight peeps out from behind the tall buildings, coloring the sky a delicious shade of orange and the ends of his hair mahogany.

"Where are we going?" I mumble.

"Awake now, princess?" he asks with a tiny smirk.

My lips tighten. Does he actually think I fainted on purpose just to avoid digging the rest of that pervert's grave? My mind conjures up a hundred rebuttals, but I can't even muster up the courage to utter a single one.

I don't know this man. Leroi is a mass of contradictions. He's kind, annoying, and not a creep, but he's also a killer more dangerous than either of the twins. They only had the balls to come at me while I was drugged or incapacitated by the collar. Leroi looks like the kind of man who doesn't need tools to inflict pain or get me under his control.

"You try digging a grave after five years in a basement," I mutter.

The car slows. "Did you say five years?"

"Yes." I sit up and clutch the blanket.

"Shit." He exhales. "God, Seraphine, I'm sorry—"

"I don't want your pity," I whisper.

With a nod, he pulls into a gas station. My heart flips and I draw in a sharp breath. Is he going to leave me at the side of the road, now that he knows the extent of my damage?

"Where are you going?"

"Filling the tank," he says without looking into my eyes. "Want me to get you anything?"

"No," I rasp. "Thank you."

"Be back in a minute."

Leroi steps out and closes the door without giving me a backward glance. All traces of the man who delivered snide remarks are gone, replaced by someone carrying a burden they want to offload.

I gulp, my throat knotting, every ounce of me wishing I hadn't blurted the truth. I can only imagine he's thinking I'm a liability with a compulsion to kill men. That's not entirely true. I didn't harm any of the clean-up crew, even if they spoke loudly and their voices grated on my nerves. I haven't been tempted to harm Leroi or his red-haired sidekick. Much.

In the side mirror, I watch him fill the tank before walking into the gas station and disappearing through the door. I open the door, slip into the front passenger seat, and buckle up. Then I close my eyes and try to calm my racing thoughts.

Maybe I'm overthinking the situation. Leroi could just be overwhelmed with what I said and feeling guilty for making me clean up and dig that grave. After all, he had a crew of men handle the other corpses. The only reason he wanted me to do the clean-up was to be petty.

Two sharp knocks sound on the window, shaking me from thoughts, and my gaze snaps to the side. A man in a baseball cap motions at me to wind it down. When I don't respond, he points at the other side of the car, like he wants to come in.

I press the button, and the window whirs down, letting in the scent of stale cigarette smoke and gasoline.

The man sticks his head through the gap, his eyes flickering to my meager chest. "Hey baby," he says, his breath reeking of booze. "Want a ride? You look like you could use a good time."

He reminds me of another old man who used to leer at me, but then I was tied up or threatened with a shock from the chip embedded in my neck. My nostrils flare. Nobody gets to look at me like I'm a piece of meat.

Before I can stop myself, I've pushed the button to raise the window and trapped his head in the car. Using one of the stolen steak knives, I stab him up to the hilt in one of his beady eyes.

I pull back the knife at his loud roar, cutting through his skin and releasing a spray of blood. It soaks the front of my shirt and face. His screams and the blood coating me breaks me from my stupor, and I open the window and set him free.

The man falls backward, trips over his feet, and knocks his head on the pump. As he lies unmoving on the ground, I glance toward the gas station's door, hoping Leroi didn't witness my outburst.

Thankfully, he's not in sight.

I hunch forward in my seat and hope to god we can get out of here without him noticing anything wrong.

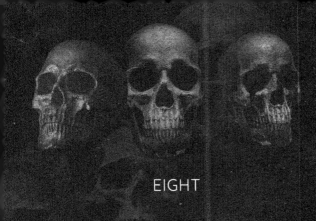

EIGHT

LEROI

Five years.

FIVE YEARS?

I'm so preoccupied with the thought of Seraphine spending half a decade in a basement that I don't hear the gas store attendant until he shouts out my total. With a jolt, I toss my card through the barrier and let him process the payment.

When I found her, I thought she might have been there for weeks, a few months at most. I was more concerned with getting us out of the Capello mansion unharmed and then removing her collar and chip that I hadn't dug deeper.

I can't begin to imagine how Anton thought up a concept as twisted as a Lolita assassin. Maybe it was one of the Capellos. No wonder he kept that quiet.

Fuck.

It's no surprise that Seraphine went on that killing spree. A psychologist I know once said that fifteen days of solitary confinement is enough to change a person's brain function irreparably, but five years? That kind of damage would be catastrophic.

The clerk hands back my card, and I collect my purchases in a plastic bag. Seraphine complained earlier about being hungry, so I grabbed a selection of snacks in case she still wants to eat.

As I walk back to the Jeep, my mind rings with a warning Anton gave me when I took Miko under my wing. He said that sometimes the only way to save those damaged by abuse is to put them out of their misery.

With a bullet.

I didn't like that idea then and proved Anton wrong by allowing Miko to find his own path and explore any interest he desired. Now, he's the best damned friend a hitman could have.

Seraphine's situation is different. I don't know if she's damaged beyond repair because there were extenuating circumstances. Would she have become so stab-happy if Billy Blue hadn't snuck into her room, trying to reenact what the Capellos did to her in that basement?

Even the sanest of women would make use of a knife in self defense. Some might even describe what she did to the poker crew afterwards as a preemptive strike, but the sandwich? I can't even tackle that kind of exercise in psychology.

I open the car door, slide into my seat to find her sitting in front, hunched over with her head bowed. A curtain of blonde hair obscures her face, even though I'm certain she'd tied it into a messy bun to dig that grave.

"Hungry?" I ask.

When she doesn't reply, my jaw ticks. I thought she'd overcome her silent phase.

"Seraphine?"

"Drive," she growls.

"What's wrong?" I reach out to touch her face, but she flinches.

At her movement, I catch the sight of blood. It's on her face, down the front of her shirt, and on her hands. It's even streaked on the window.

I was gone for less than five minutes.

"Who did this to you?" I snarl.

She shakes her head.

"What happened?" I ask. "Are you hurt?"

"It's not my blood."

"Then whose?" I glance around the empty gas station.

"A man came to the window," she says, her voice distant and flat. "He was rude."

"He touched you?"

"I stabbed him in the eye."

The words hit like a gut punch. "Where is he?"

"Over there." She tilts her head toward the window.

"Where?" I snarl.

"On the ground."

I open the door and walk around the front of the car to find a man lying wedged in the space between the passenger side and the foot of the pump.

Seraphine watches me with wide eyes, her features a blank mask. Ignoring her, I crouch by the fallen man and check his pulse. It's weak and thready, but he's alive. I stare down at the bleeding man, bristling at his continued presence and at the prospect of having to clean up another crime scene.

My fingers twitch toward my gun, but I'm not about to discharge it without a silencer or in a place so flammable. Instead, I reach into my pocket, extract a box cutter and slice his jugular. While he bleeds out, I call Miko.

He answers in two rings. "Hey," Miko says with a yawn. "Is everything alright?"

"There's a gas station at the intersection of Beaumont and Tourgis. Can you hack into its security system and wipe all evidence that I was there?"

"Did you pay for anything?" he asks.

"With a disposable card. Don't worry about that."

"Consider it done."

I rise from the soon-to-be corpse, my nostrils flaring, and return to the driver's seat. Anton's old warning returns two-fold, confirming that Seraphine is about to become a liability I can't afford.

"Sorry," she mumbles.

"For what?" I start the engine and ignore the pang of guilt that rises from her flinch.

"I made another mess."

That's an understatement. When I cast her a sidelong glance, she's staring up at me like a helpless little kitten. I tear my eyes off her and concentrate on the road.

Seraphine sighs, the sound so soft and forlorn that the fibers in my long-dead heart twitch back to life. She's trouble and her reckless killing is a nuisance, but there's a part of me that wants to wrap her in protective bandages and erase the past five years of her life.

But I can't allow her to continue a violent spree that will lead the cops, or worse, to my door. I'm also not about to sacrifice my life to save hers.

"You can't go around stabbing every man who shows you disrespect," I say.

"Why not?"

My molars clench and it takes every effort not to swerve. "Because it will get you killed," I grind out. "If the State of

New Alderney doesn't hand you a death sentence, someone else will."

"But you killed my dad and the twins, and that man who was lying on the ground."

"I know what I'm doing."

"So do I."

Frustration bubbles up to the surface, building up like a pressure cooker. I'm starting to suspect that Anton's training either failed or only went as far as how to commit murder. Maybe the Capellos originally kept her chained up in a basement because she's a danger to herself and others. Who the hell kills eight men without a plan and stays at the scene of the crime to make a sandwich out of one of their cocks? My pent-up frustration reaches a fever pitch and explodes.

"You have no vehicle, no means of hiding your tracks. No support staff and no understanding of the consequences of your actions. It's only a matter of time before you get caught."

She gasps as though insulted and turns her head to stare out of the passenger-side window.

I doubt that I've talked any sense into her pretty little head, but I already have a plan to turn her into someone else's problem. Like her brother's.

We pull into my building's parking lot and make our way back to the apartment. Instead of entering through door 101, I take her to 102.

She follows me into the empty space, her gaze wandering from left to right.

"This is the apartment next door to mine," I tell her. "I own both units on either side of mine, plus the three below. That way, I can live in the center of town and not worry about the neighbors overhearing or seeing anything that could get us arrested."

Her lips part, but I cut her off.

"You can stay here for as long as you like." I gesture to the open space. "Decorate it however you want. I'll give you a card with an allowance, you can go back to school—"

"I'm twenty-one," she says.

"Or college," I say, hiding my surprise. "You can start a new life here with your brother."

She bows her head, her hands clenched into fists.

"That's what you want, isn't it?" I close the distance between us. "To be reunited with Gabriel?"

Seraphine's chest rises and falls with rapid breaths. "You're sending me away?"

"I'll be right next door," I say, not knowing why I'm appeasing this little killer. "You're going to need space for when Gabriel returns."

Her eyes search mine, and I can see the wheels in her mind skidding on ice toward a precipice.

Finally, she asks, "Are you making me sleep on the floor tonight?"

"You can stay in your room," I say.

With a nod, Seraphine heads to the exit. I follow, already planning on sleeping with one eye open and a loaded gun under my pillow.

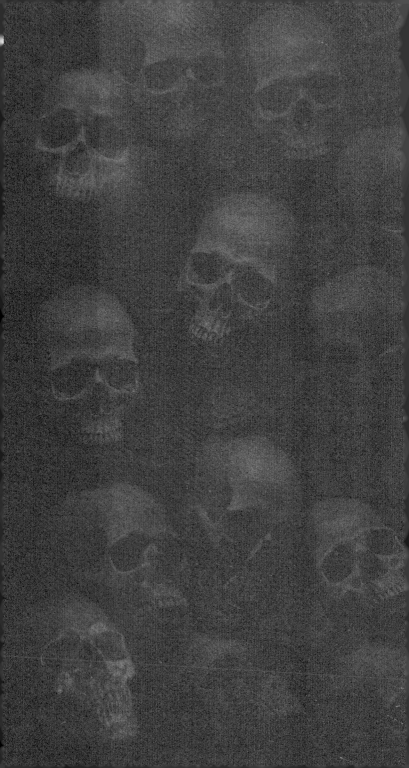

NINE

SERAPHINE

I lie in bed, my gaze fixed on the patterns of sunlight on the ceiling.

It's just as expected.

Leroi is ditching me along with his promise to help me find Gabriel.

Maybe I wanted to leave him at first, but he's already the best thing that happened to me in five years. Now, he's slipping through my fingers and I can't convince him to let me stay.

I only stabbed that man in the eye to make him stop leering. Leroi slit his throat while he was unconscious. Yet he claims I'm the one who doesn't know what they're doing?

Leroi is a hypocrite.

I curl my hands into fists, letting my fingernails dig into my palms. His rejection hurts worse than the collar. Maybe I should have killed him when I had the chance. I thought he was different. Perhaps even a little like me. Pressure builds up behind the backs of my eyes, and I squeeze them shut. He's just the same as Dad—kind one minute and casting me out the next.

Shit. I should have known better than to let down my guard, but I have no other options. I'll keep Leroi alive until I find Gabriel, and then I'll carve pretty patterns into his flesh and watch him bleed.

Until then, I can't move into that empty apartment. Leroi's presence is the only thing keeping away the intrusive memories. My mind is calm when I know he's near. Without him, every moment would descend into that twisting turmoil of screams.

My eyes snap open.

I need to prove to Leroi that I'm not a liability that's going to get him killed. I have to make him listen.

Sliding off the bed, I reach beneath my pillow for the stiletto daggers that I divested from the dead bastard I undressed. Payment for him forcing himself on me and Leroi making me clean it up. Leroi confiscated the knives I took from his kitchen and locked them up in the room with the guns.

Adjusting my oversized wife beater, I creep across the room and slide out of the door. A pang of guilt hits my chest at the sight of Leroi's living room. It's mostly empty now, all the blood-stained sofas were removed along with the corpses.

I cross the space on my tiptoes and ease open his bedroom door. Leroi lies on his back with his torso exposed, the sunlight caressing his olive skin. His sculpted chest rises and falls in a steady rhythm, and I pause for a moment to admire how his muscles flex and relax with each breath. He's a work of art, a perfect specimen of masculine strength.

With the pulse between my legs pounding hard enough

to fill my ears, I drift forward. My mouth waters at the sight of all that exposed flesh and how beautiful it would look smeared in red.

But I'm not here to kill him. Not today.

His rhythmic snores fill the air, the sound infusing my chest with bursts of warmth. Leroi might be an asshole, but he has a heart. Would it look as elegant as him if I removed it from his chest? Its pulse would slow in the palm of my hand and its arteries would ooze delicious red blood.

Clutching both knives, I mount the bed. My knees sink into the mattress, and I crawl the length of the bed toward my prey, and sit on his hips. Leroi loosens a deep groan that hits me low in the belly.

My breath shallows the way it usually does before a kill, only this time it's accompanied by an excited flutter. I never feel this way when I'm with a man. Ever. All I ever care about is the kill. Leroi is so handsome that it's distracting.

As I position the pointed tip of the blade to his carotid artery, I hold the second behind my back.

Leroi's eyes snap open. "Seraphine, what are you—"

"You're not sending me away," I hiss.

His gaze drops to the blade. "Put. That. Down."

I press its point into his skin, and he stiffens. "Not unless you let me stay with you."

Leroi's breath quickens, and the flesh beneath me shifts and hardens until his shaft nestles between my ass cheeks. Heat rises to my cheeks. I didn't mean to make him erect, but it's too late to think about that part of his anatomy.

"Seraphine," he says, the same placating tone someone might use to call a rabid rottweiler a nice doggy. "I won't ask you again. Put down the knife and we'll talk."

"Let me stay, and I'll put down the knife."

When I press the tip of my blade into a point of his flesh

adjacent to the artery, his hips jerk. The movement makes me shift a few inches down his erection, and its crown presses into my slit.

Heat floods between my legs in a rush of pleasure so sudden I'm forced to swallow back a gasp. Sensation rushes to my clit, which pulses and swells. My gaze drops to his heaving chest for an instant to find his nipples puckering.

In a flash of movement, Leroi produces a gun and points it at my head.

My jaw drops. I jerk backward, only for my clit to rub against his hardness. Tingles shoot up my core, making my breath catch. What the hell is Leroi doing to me, and why do I want him to do it again?

"Put that down," I whisper, my voice trembling.

"You first," he replies with a smirk.

I swallow, but my mouth is dry. Every drop of moisture in my body rushes south, accompanied by a rush of sensation. When my hips roll, it takes every effort to force my attention back to Leroi and his bullshit. "This is all your fault. We could have avoided a stalemate if you hadn't tried to throw me out."

"Seraphine," he says with an exasperated exhale. "You'll be right next door, where I can keep an eye on you—"

"Liar!" He's just saying whatever he needs to get out of trouble. I push the dagger deeper, making its tip glisten with a bead of blood. "You want me to leave."

Leroi's expression darkens, and he pushes the gun's safety off with a click. "This is your last warning."

My nostrils flare and the backs of my eyes burn. He thinks he can threaten me with a pistol when I know his weakness. The only time he ever lost his cool was when he found me slicing that penis.

I lower the knife behind my back to his erection. "Are you sure about that?"

He hisses through his teeth, his pupils darkening, his chest rising and falling with rapid breaths. My own breaths quicken in tandem with his and every nerve ending in my body thrums. Is this what it feels like to find someone attractive?

"Fuck," he groans. "A-alright. You can stay, but only if you take that knife off my cock."

"You first." I nod toward the gun.

He enables the safety and sets it down on the bed.

"Throw it."

With a growl, he tosses it off the mattress, letting it fall to the floor with a clatter. "Your turn."

When I put aside the second knife, he closes his eyes and sighs his relief. "You really need to do something about your castration kink."

"Are you making fun of me?" I growl.

"Believe me, angel, nothing about you holding a blade to my cock is funny. Now, please, take that knife off my throat before you puncture something."

I pull back the blade so it's no longer touching his skin. Blood trickles down his neck, and it takes every instinct not to lean down and lick it clean.

"Can I really stay?" I ask.

He nods. "But there will be no more knives. Understood?"

My heart thuds so loudly that its vibrations fill my ears. Is he really giving in or is he playing along until it's time to make his move?

"I asked you a question, Seraphine," he says, his voice stern. "And I expect an answer."

"Yes," I whisper, trying to keep my voice from trembling.

He flicks his head toward the dagger. "Put it down."

I pull it away, not releasing my grip.

Leroi smiles, but it's more like a grimace. "Good girl."

"You're still going to help me after what I did?"

"Seraphine," he says with a sigh. "When I pulled you out of that basement, you became my responsibility. I'll do everything I can to help you, but you need to trust me. Can you do that?"

Leroi looks me full in the face, his gaze steady. Everything from his body language to his words are consistent. He means exactly what he says... for now. My throat tightens. He could have shot me, but he threw away his gun to prove himself trustworthy.

"Can you trust me?" he asks again.

I nod.

"Alright," he says, his voice so gentle I could cry. "Now, get off the bed and get dressed. After getting you seen by a doctor, we'll go to breakfast, and I'll talk you through the leads I gathered last night."

I scramble off the mattress, my feet hitting the floor. Leroi smiles and nods, but I can't take my eyes off the thick erection pushing up the sheets. My fingers twitch with an urge to pull off the sheet so I can get a better look, but he follows my gaze and glances away.

"Go."

His voice is so commanding that I bolt out of the room, my heart thundering just as rapidly as the pulse between my legs.

This reaction to nearly killing him is unexpectedly arousing.

I want to do it again.

TEN

LEROI

Fuck.

I never thought I could get turned on by a girl holding a knife to my throat, but here I am, aching so hard it hurts. Seraphine is wild, untamed, reckless, but there's something about the way she handled that blade that has me in a chokehold.

It wasn't just the blade. The way she ground on my cock like a wicked little angel, her blonde hair a halo of gold cascading down her shoulders, forming a frame around her pert breasts. It took every effort not to fixate on her erect nipples and every ounce of self control not to stare at those lithe legs.

My gaze slips for long enough to catch Seraphine disappearing through the door, the fabric of her t-shirt clinging to her slender curves. I throw an arm over my eyes and groan.

She's off-limits, even if she's twenty-one years old and capable of slaughtering eight men in a fit of outrage. Seraphine is vulnerable. She needs help, and not the kind that involves her riding me until my vision explodes and I see stars.

I can't let myself get caught up with someone so out of control—not when my work is so dangerous. Losing focus right now would be foolish, especially when Capello's death will launch the underworld into chaos.

Ten minutes later, I'm still trying to pull my thoughts from the press of her sweet little pussy. I'm still painfully hard and desperate to bust, but I refuse to jerk off to my close encounter with the Lolita assassin. Instead, I haul my horny carcass off the bed and into the shower. The only thing that cools me off is the thought that my mentor helped turn a girl into a killer. Anton is of the sick bastards that taught her to lure in sick fucks with her innocence.

Seraphine waits for me by the dining table, dressed in a pair of jeans and a white t-shirt that arrived by mail earlier, with her hair pulled back in a high ponytail. She's breathtakingly angelic and sweet, but with a touch of darkness I can no longer unsee.

I take her in the Lamborghini to the complex of high-end stores and offices on Lower Saye Street. She agreed to see a mafia-friendly therapist to work through her issues while we search for her brother.

"This is the first time I've been here during the day," she says, her voice breathy.

"You were here during the night?"

Her features shutter, the way they always do when I get close to asking about the time she spent in captivity.

I open the car door for her and she steps out onto the sunny sidewalk, then we cross the street in silence. If she's not ready to tell me what happened, I won't press. That's why she's seeing a professional who won't balk at discovering she's an assassin.

"Remember," I say as we approach the glass-fronted clinic. "Monica is bound by her professional ethics, but she's still connected, so no mention of your last name, understood?"

Seraphine nods, and I let her into the office.

Monica Saint is a tall brunette I met through an associate who was going through a gambling addiction and was gracious enough to give Seraphine an appointment on short notice.

She steps out of her office with a bright smile. "Leroi, it's been a long time. How can I help?"

"I brought the new client I told your receptionist about," I say. "Angela Smith."

Monica ushers Seraphine into her office. I hover by the exit for a few minutes in case there's a commotion, but I shake off the thought. A female professional shouldn't be a threat to Seraphine, and Monica has dealt with a wide array of criminal clients. They'll be fine.

I step out of the door, lean against the window, pull out a burner phone, and speed dial my cousin, Roman.

He answers in one ring. "Leroi."

"How's prison treating you?"

"It's a dump. Benito told me your tech guy can find the dirt I need to get the fuck out."

"You want him to extract it?"

"Yeah, and congratulations on pulling off that job. Any loose ends?"

"No." The lie rolls off my tongue.

"I've got another one for you," he mutters. "Turns out that Capello was playing happy families with another woman. He has a daughter."

The words hit me in the gut. Two of the guys at poker night mentioned Capello kept something in his basement that was so top secret nobody could enter it but his sons. Now, here's another hint about Seraphine's existence.

"More offspring?" I drawl, feigning boredom.

Roman chuckles. "Don't worry, you didn't screw up. This daughter lived with her mother overseas until the woman died. Word on the street is that Capello's lawyer is trying to reach her about her inheritance."

"Shit."

"She doesn't even know about her billionaire father, and I want it to stay that way."

My pulse quickens. In other words, he wants me to kill Seraphine. If I refuse, he'll just employ one of the other contract killers in New Alderney. Maybe even the Moirai Group, who always gets their target, regardless of the collateral damage.

"Have you located her?" I ask, my voice even.

"She's a visual artist, whatever the fuck that means, and living uptown with a bunch of girlfriends."

"Her name?" I ask, my brows pulling together.

"Emberly Kay." The phone buzzes. "I just sent you a photo."

I glance down at the screen into the smiling features of a dark-haired woman who looks nothing like Seraphine but easily resembles the Capello twin I shot in the bathroom. I let out an exhale, my lungs deflating with relief.

"The family resemblance is unmistakable," I say.

Roman snorts. "You can take care of it, right?"

"No women or children," I say. "I broke my code to get you off death row, but no more."

My cousin falls silent for a few heartbeats before saying, "You're right. Don't think I won't forget how you saved my life."

I'm about to wax lyrical about how he and his family

were my rocks after Dad died, but a scream from behind the glass cuts through the tender moment. I barrel through the entrance, push past the receptionist, and barge into Monica's office.

Seraphine stands with a letter opener dripping with blood with Monica cowering behind her desk, holding a bleeding hand to her chest.

"Call 911," Monica says to the receptionist at the door.

"No." I advance toward Seraphine and squeeze the hand holding the letter opener until her fingers straighten and it drops to the floor. "Let me handle this."

"I'm professionally bound to make sure my client gets the right help," Monica says, her voice trembling.

My jaw tenses. Once again, I'm doubting my decision about not putting Seraphine out of her misery. She stares up at me with those huge, blue eyes, her bottom lip trembling, looking so vulnerable that the sight of her pulls at my frayed heartstrings.

I pull out my card. "How much can I pay you to make this problem go away?"

Monica's gaze drops to my hand. She might be a therapist with professional training and degrees, but she's also a realist.

"F-fifty," she says.

The corner of my lip lifts into a smile. If my life was a Shakespearian tragedy, my fatal flaw would be overestimating women. "The cost of a contract on a man's life?"

She flinches. "Twenty-five."

"Ten."

Her breath quickens. "F-fifteen."

"Done." I draw Seraphine into my side and hand the receptionist my card to process the payment.

Seraphine clings to me as the other woman's fingers

tremble over the credit card machine. I gaze down at her blonde head and sigh. She is going to be a handful.

———

Several minutes later, after I've ordered her out of Monica's establishment, she sits in the front seat of the car, breathing hard, her fingers tightening into fists. I give her a few moments to compose herself and explain, but she's too wrapped up in her own emotions to know where to begin.

"Why did you stab Monica?" I ask.

"I... I don't know." She glances away.

"Look at me, Seraphine," I say. "Are these outbursts out of your control? Do you black out?"

She shakes her head, her bottom lip quivering. "No, just..." Her head bows, and she exhales a ragged breath. "I can't stand being prodded. Or touched."

My brow pulls together. "What happened?"

"She wouldn't stop asking questions. Then she slid a box of tissues to me, and I snapped." Seraphine sniffs. "I didn't even think about it. My hand just moved."

I wince. This is more than just an aversion to physical touch. "We can find another therapist—"

"No. No more," she says in a rush. "The only person I can trust is you."

My breathing shallows. This reminds me of a TV show where the kidnapped girl fell in love with the cop who pulled her out of a basement. The woman from Internal Affairs called it white knight syndrome. Unease twists through my insides at the thought of an emotional attachment. I'm no hero. I get paid to kill strangers in cold blood.

She clings to my jacket, her eyes shining with unshed tears. "Leroi, could you be my therapist?"

ELEVEN

LEROI

I'd suspected she was building up to this request, but hearing it still takes me aback. My heart rate picks up several notches. Seraphine deserves someone better. Someone with ethics, training, experience. Someone who doesn't get hard at the thought of her with a knife pressed to my neck.

"That's not a good idea," I reply, keeping my voice even. "You need a professional. There's another woman in town—"

"Then I'll stab her too," she snaps. "I want you."

My eyes narrow. I take another look at Seraphine's face. There are no signs of the tears that were threatening to fall, and she looks just like the defiant girl who taunted me with a cock sandwich. Scratch that. She's more like the little vixen who sat and slid on my shaft.

She's cornering me. Trying to take away all options until I'm forced to agree to her demands.

"You're being a brat," I say.

Her expression softens, and she bites her lip. "I don't

trust anyone else. And I know I can trust you not to freak out."

So, she's not denying being manipulative.

"I know nothing about psychology."

"But you know how to control your urges."

I pinch the bridge of my nose. She thinks we're similar? The difference between us is that I've never killed in a fit of emotion. At least not after becoming an adult.

"My situation is different. I only kill for money or out of necessity."

"You didn't have to slit the gas station man's throat last night," she murmurs. "But you did it because that's what you wanted."

"I did it to protect you. And myself. He would have reported you to the authorities and led the cops to my door."

She hums as though dismissing my explanation as bull-shit. "Then it's in your best interest to teach me how to be more like you."

Any notion that Seraphine is innocent flies out the window when I remember that this is the same young woman who got me all hot and bothered this morning before conquering me with a knife at my cock.

She's trying to wrap me around her twisted little finger.

"I'm a monster, not a mentor," I mutter.

"Then teach me to be a better monster," she says with a practiced pout.

"Answer my questions truthfully."

She nods, knowing I'm not asking.

"Did you stab Monica because you wanted me to be your therapist?"

She hesitates. "No."

My eyes narrow. "Did you really lose control yesterday on your killing spree?"

"Yes," she murmurs. "And I know I need help."

It's on the tip of my tongue to ask about her end game. If the answer is her, Gabriel, and me playing happy families in my apartment, then my answer to her request is no.

I don't get attached to women. Certainly not a woman who has the face of an angel and the heart of a killer. Definitely not a woman whose darkness rivals my own, and especially not a woman trained to throw a man's common sense off kilter.

Before I can say anything, she slides a hand over mine. Electricity zips up and down my spine as she clutches my finger.

"You're the only one I can touch. You're the only person I trust."

I meet her pleading eyes. Eyes so clear and blue, I swear I can see the flames of her soul. Eyes that draw me in and won't let go. What's left of my resolve crumbles.

"I'm not a good man." I mumble.

"I don't need a good man," she replies. "I need someone who understands me."

"The training will be difficult."

She gives me an eager nod.

"There will be punishment for failure."

"Are there rewards for being a good girl?" she whispers, her voice husky.

Her words race straight to my cock, which pushes painfully against my fly. My mind is going in the wrong direction. She doesn't mean the type of good girl that gets on her knees and gets down and dirty to earn my approval. Seraphine probably wants chocolates or clothes or gadgets. Not my kind of reward.

I clear my throat, but it's already too late to clear my

thoughts. My filthy mind is already picturing her beneath me, naked and writhing and flushed.

"What kind of rewards?" I ask.

Pink blooms across her cheeks, and the fingers around mine intensify their grip. My brain won't stop picturing how tight she would be around my shaft.

"Well..." She licks her lips, and it takes every effort not to lean across the driver's seat for a taste. "I've never had an orgasm."

My eyes squeeze shut, along with the muscles of my throat. I rasp, "This conversation calls for a drink."

———

One of the few legit businesses my cousins retained after Uncle Enzo died is Phoenix nightclub. It owns the bar next door that serves food and hard liquor. It's also one of the few places where the tables aren't jammed so close together that you can hear the people next to you chewing.

Seraphine and I sit in a booth close to the fire exit. I knock back two shots of whiskey and she drinks from a strawberry milkshake.

"This isn't the kind of training I had in mind," I say.

"I can't think of any reward I want more than an orgasm," she says.

I shift in my seat. "What about perfume, clothes, makeup?"

"No."

My jaw clenches. "Tell me why."

She peers up at me through her lashes and slides her fingers up and down her straw. Her coy act is screwing with my judgment. "I liked sitting on top of you, and I think you could help me feel good."

My cock stirs, and I gulp. "Do you even know what you're asking for?"

"Yes."

The waiter brings me another shot. I turn the glass in my hand and swirl the amber liquid, still not sure she really knows what she's asking. When I screwed up with Anton, he made me run laps, perform press ups and burpees.

"If your reward is an orgasm, what kind of punishments can you tolerate?" I lean back in my seat to observe her reaction.

Her cheeks flush.

"Um... spanking. Maybe leather bondage. I've never tried that."

"How do you even know about BDSM?"

She raises a shoulder. "I'm not as innocent as I look. I learned a lot in the past five years."

My heart skips a beat. I try not to imagine the kinds of places she had to infiltrate as a Lolita assassin. She at least has some idea of what to expect, but her request still doesn't make sense. "How is that going to help you control your urges?"

She leans closer, her knee pressing against mine and sending a thrum of sensation where I need it the least. "It's like you said. You're going to teach me to be more controlled and every time I succeed in something, I'll get an orgasm."

"And you accept the consequences of disobedience and being a brat?"

She nods, her lips lifting into a smile.

My cock fills, and I let out a ragged breath. She's serious. If this arrangement between us is going to succeed, I'll have to keep a tight rein on my urges. She is, after all, another assassin. Seraphine doesn't know that I'm aware of her background, and I don't want to think about how she got close enough to her targets to murder them.

"I have two conditions," I say.

Her brows rise.

"No kissing and no orgasms for me."

Her face falls. "Why?"

"Because this is your training, not my opportunity to take advantage of you and get off."

She frowns. "But—"

"Take it or leave it."

Her shoulders droop, but the flush on her cheeks darkens. "Fine." She holds out her hand to seal the deal. "Let's get started."

Something about this agreement is off. Abused young women don't approach strange men for orgasms. Perhaps there are more layers to her than I thought, but then I remember a TV show where a woman's psyche was splintered by trauma.

"You're still Seraphine?" I ask, making sure she's not another personality because I still can't believe she's serious. "The girl I carried out of the basement?"

"Of course." Her fingers twitch, eager for my touch.

I take it, the corners of my lips lifting into a half smile.

This is going to be interesting.

TWELVE

SERAPHINE

Leroi's hand is warm and large. Touching his bare skin muffles out the music and chatter and turmoil. I first noticed it when I first arrived in his apartment and he drew my hair off my brow. It's like being encased in a cocoon during a storm, knowing nothing can break through and cause me harm.

Even when he's cracking stupid jokes and hinting that I have multiple personalities, he makes me feel safe. It's not just because he's steady and strong, but because he fills a part of me that I thought I'd lost forever.

I didn't realize how much calmer I felt with Leroi until he left me alone with that therapist. She kept asking me questions about my life, and I didn't know how to react. Everything she asked triggered horrible memories. She wouldn't shut up until my ears filled with excited male voices mingling with Mom's screams. When she tried to touch me with that box of tissues, I needed her scream to drown out the ones in my head.

It also didn't help that I noticed the way she smiled at Leroi, like she was angling to take him for herself.

He releases my hand, pulling back his warmth and letting in a rush of chaos.

I take a breath, my heart thudding so hard and fast that its vibrations reach my fingertips. I shouldn't trust this stranger, yet there's a part of me that wants to cling to him and never let go. I know to the marrow of my bones that he's the only person who can pull every inch of me out of the basement.

Even if my instincts want to give him my trust, experience has taught me to stay alert. If Leroi betrays me, he'll join all the other bastards in hell.

"Tell me why," he says.

"Why what?"

"Why do you want orgasms?"

Heat rushes to my cheeks, and I lower my lashes. "I felt something earlier." My tongue darts out to lick my lips. "When we were in your room."

He leans so close that it takes every effort not to fidget. "Explain."

"I really liked how you made me feel. That's never happened before," I say in a small voice.

He draws back. I don't dare to meet his gaze for fear that I might see pity. From the way he talks, he thinks I might be afraid of men. I'm not. I just want to hurt them. If I can get pleasure from the only one I can stand, then that's my business.

"Let's start with something simple," he says, his voice gentle.

My attention snaps to his face. "What are you thinking about?"

"I need to know your limits."

"Limits?" I cock my head to the side.

"Your boundaries. What can you handle? What things are a hard no?"

Up close, his eyes aren't so dark. They're a rich cinnamon, ringed with the deepest umber and flecked with varying shades of walnut. Toasty and warm and edible. I'm torn between tasting him and losing myself in his gaze.

"Seraphine?"

I blink, my eyes shifting to his furrowed brows. "Yes?"

"Are you listening?" He repeats his question about boundaries.

"I don't like shock collars. Or chips."

His lips tighten. They're back to looking cruel again, but I think his anger is directed at Dad and the twins. I raise my fingers to the band-aid behind my ear to check on my wound, which is now much less tender.

Leroi's eyes track the movement, and he swallows.

"Are you sure you want to do this?" he asks, his words halting. "We can research different—"

"If you're about to say professionals, the answer is no." I return my fingers to the straw. "You're the only person I can trust."

He knocks back his liquor and raises his glass to ask the waitress for another.

"Are you nervous?" I shift closer and lean into his side.

"Cautious," he replies. "I need to know your boundaries before we begin. What things make you uncomfortable apart from shock collars?"

"Rude men," I say.

"That much is obvious," he says, his eyes twinkling. "Anything else?"

"Don't tamper with my food or anything I drink, and don't shoot me with tranquilizer darts."

His face drops. "I wouldn't do that."

"Good, then can we begin?" I ask.

Leroi rubs the spot between his brows. I've observed him do this enough now to know it's because he's frustrated. I lean forward and take a sip of a milkshake that has the texture of melted ice cream infused with strawberry pulp.

I'm deadly serious about learning some self-control. Gabriel is going to be frail and weak when we find him. He's going to need a lot of care. I can't nurse him back to health if I keep lashing out at the first flash of temper.

Leroi is the only person who might be able to help us. He's cool and efficient, like the handler, only that man was creepy and cruel. He knew I was in that basement against my will, but all he cared about was getting me ready to execute the most powerful man in New Alderney.

"Let me take you somewhere that will help you understand my question," Leroi says, already sounding like he doesn't believe me.

———

Fifteen minutes later, we're standing in Wonderland, a huge store that smells of rosemary and sage. It's dimly lit with black furniture and racks upon racks of sex toys hung on its cherry-red walls. It looks nothing like Alice in Wonderland. Leroi strolls to the back as though he's been here a hundred times, and I stay close to his side.

It's empty, save for the woman standing behind the counter wearing a burgundy corset with chains looping out of its pockets. Blood-red hair spills down her tattooed shoulders, and the miniature top hat perched on her head tells me she's cosplaying the Mad Hatter.

She's only looking in our direction and not approaching, so I turn my attention back to Leroi. It might seem strange that I'm allowing him to take control of my pleasure when I don't understand his ulterior motives, but I trust Leroi not to take advantage since he's already been such a gentleman.

I've never heard of an aroused man with a gun not using his bargaining power to get off. For the first time, I've wanted to do more with an erection than slice it at the root. Leroi might just be the one who helps me feel good.

"When I asked about limits, this is what I was talking about." He gestures at a rack of leather belts and cuffs. "These are used for bondage."

Ropes of varying colors hang beside a display of small black shackles with silver studs, and realization dawns on me with the speed of a hurricane. Leroi wants to tie me up.

Memories surface, reminding me of the early days before I learned how to defend myself from the twins. I snatch my hand away. "No ropes."

"I'm not asking you to try any of these," he says, his voice low. "We need to know your limits."

"I'm not sure about the leather stuff," I say. "But definitely no ropes."

"Good." He places a hand on the small of my back, his warmth seeping through my shirt and infusing me with a sense of calm. "Let's move onto the other toys."

The next rack contains blindfolds. Leroi extracts a black leather one and holds it out to me. The fabric behind it is a soft suede that feels like velvet.

"These are for sensory deprivation."

I nod. "That's okay, but I want pink."

Leroi chuckles. "Good choice."

My gaze wanders to a delicate-looking blindfold with winged tips. Instead of choosing that, he picks up a padded one that's large enough to cover the ears. Since it's the color I want, I don't object, and we move onto the next rack.

"These items are for impact play." He gestures at some leather paddles.

They come in all shapes and sizes. One looks like a ping-pong paddle, another a hairbrush, and another resembles a spatula you'd find in a kitchen. Next to them is a rack of canes. Seeing them leaves me feeling indifferent.

"Spanking would be better," I reply with a shrug.

"Let's move onto the next."

It's a rack of what I can only describe as crocodile clips from science experiments attached to chains. I stiffen, wondering if they carry an electric current.

"What are those?" I whisper.

"Nipple clamps." He picks up a pair that's dipped in black rubber. "Give me your little finger."

I offer him my pinky, letting Leroi attach the clamp to its tip. There's pressure, but little else. "What's so special about this?"

His gaze drops to my nipple, which tightens under his attention. "The clamp isn't for fingers," he says, his voice husky.

Warmth surges low in my belly. I'm sure it has nothing to do with a silly clamp and more with the way Leroi is breathing so close to me. His face is expressionless and still, but the rapid rise and fall of his chest tells me he really likes this toy.

It reminds me of how excited he was when I held the knife to his throat. My clit throbs with the remembered sensation of rubbing against his thick, hard shaft, and my own breath quickens with anticipation.

"Would you like to try it over your clothes?" he asks and

I nod, unable to find the words. It's been so long since anyone's asked my permission to touch me.

He brings it to my nipple in a motion that's agonizingly slow. Its jaws open, and he hesitates.

"Do it," I say.

The clamp closes in around my nipple, sending a surge of sensation between my legs. It's so intense that I grip the edge of a shelf for balance and squeeze my eyes shut.

"Do you like it?" Leroi asks.

The pressure borders on pain, and my throat tightens, as do the muscles of my core. Samson and Gregor used pain to control me until I learned to dismiss the sensations. I don't understand why it's making me so aroused.

"Seraphine?" Leroi's voice breaks through my thoughts.

"It's nice," I say through shallow breaths.

"Look at me."

My eyes flutter open.

Leroi's irises are a ring of dark brown around dilated pupils, and his jaw is tight. The intensity of his gaze sends heat rushing through my veins, and the pulse between my legs quickens.

"It's more than nice, isn't it?" he asks, his voice a low growl.

"Yes," I whisper, my throat dry.

He removes the clamp, leaving my nipple sensitive and throbbing and wanting more. His gaze lingers on mine as he tosses it into the basket and pulls me toward the next rack.

Following him on trembling legs, I lean into his side, feeling more alive than I have in half a decade. When I was in that basement, I used to imagine someone would burst through the doors and set me free. The fairytale was better than facing my reality, but I knew better than to believe in a knight in shining armor. It was nothing more than a dumb fantasy.

My mysterious rescuer would slay my enemies, heal my wounds, and reunite me with Gabriel. We'd all live happily ever after in a castle with its own chocolate fountain. I never imagined this savior making me enjoy sex or giving me an orgasm.

I'm glad I spared Leroi's life.

At least for now.

THIRTEEN

LEROI

Seraphine is not the same woman I pulled out of that basement. Her eyes are alight with excitement at the prospect of the toys, and she even welcomes the red-haired store clerk's help. I stand back, observing the two women giggle and chat about toys, not believing that she just stabbed Monica with a letter opener for getting too close.

The taller woman places a hand on Seraphine's shoulder, and Seraphine doesn't even flinch. Instead, her smile is brighter than the sun. She seems mesmerized by the clerk's knowledge of kink.

Seraphine is mercurial–unlike anyone I've ever known.

For the next half hour, I lean against a blank patch of wall, volleying texts between Miko and my cousins, Benito and Cesare. Miko is tearing through the hard drives, trying to find the information needed to pull Roman from death row. Cesare is certain that Capello held something over the district attorney who presided over Roman's murder trial, but I want Miko to cast his net wider. Capello would have had dirt on politicians, judges, and the chief of police. We just need to find it.

Giggles erupt from the other side of the store, and I look up from my phone. Seraphine is holding out her forearm, while the store clerk runs the tips of a small flogger over her skin.

The sight of two beautiful women together should be arousing, but my gut twists with a surge of possessiveness. If anyone's going to tease Seraphine, even in jest, then that person is going to be me.

I push off the wall, slip the phone in my pocket, and walk over to the rack of whips and floggers.

Seraphine turns to me, her eyes bright. "Can we get this one?"

I grab her arm and pull her close, my gaze holding hers. "Anything you want, angel."

Her cheeks bloom a delicate shade of pink. She dips her head and gazes up at me through her lashes, making my heart skip. The look is so coy and innocent that I almost forget she's an untamed killer until I notice the tiny flecks of Monica's blood on her fingers.

I have to remind myself that she's off-limits. Seraphine has suffered enough and doesn't need to get involved with another killer, especially one also trained by Anton. Anton twisted and corrupted an inexperienced young girl until her knee-jerk reaction to stress became murder.

Taming Seraphine won't be as easy as giving Miko a place to stay. There's a darkness in her that calls to mine, not to mention this unwanted attraction. I like tall, kinky brunettes who don't form attachments, not tiny, angelic blondes.

Once she's learned to control her killer instincts and is

reunited with her brother, I don't plan on letting her stick around.

"Anything else?" I gesture at the overflowing basket.

She rushes to a bookshelf, extracts a coloring book along with a notepad covered in pink fur along with a pack of felt-tip pens. "Let's go home."

Home.

She's been in my presence for less than two days, and she's already claiming ownership of my apartment. My cock stirs at the reminder of her deadly wake up call. Seraphine is the first woman who wouldn't recoil at what I do for a living. Not that it matters because I'm not seeking romantic attachments.

After purchasing two baskets of items, I take Seraphine to a department store to pick out some clothes in her size. I'm not surprised to find that everything she chooses is a shade of baby blue or pink, but I'm taken aback that all she selects is loungewear. Perhaps she's sick of wearing the pretty dresses associated with her former job.

The apartment is pristine, with only a hint of bleach in the air when we return later. A testament to the proficiency of Don and his clean-up crew. At the dining table, we unload the bags from our shopping spree, and Seraphine doesn't wait even a heartbeat to bring up her training.

"Are we going to use the toys?" Seraphine asks, her eyes sparkling.

"You haven't done anything to warrant a reward or punishment," I say.

Her brows pull together. "What do you mean?"

"You asked for help with taming your compulsions," I reply. "I need to understand what went through your mind when you killed Billy Blue."

Her features darken, and all traces of the excited girl fade away, leaving her sullen and cold. "Nothing."

I wait for her to elaborate, but she falls silent.

"Did you black out?" I ask.

"No."

"Then how do you explain what happened?"

"I was protecting myself."

Familiar pressure builds up behind my eyes, and I rub the spot between my brows. She's determined to make me work for answers.

"Stabbing a man who's attacking you is self-defense. Why did you keep going? Why go so far as to cut off his dick?"

"Actually, that was the first place I attacked." She looks away and points her pert nose in the air.

"A blow like that would incapacitate any man. Why didn't you wake me?"

Her head whips around, and she glares at me, her eyes blazing with blue fire. "Are you on his side?"

"I want to understand why you took it so far," I say.

Her breath quickens, and she growls, her lips tightening into a grimace. "Because he deserved it."

"He did." I keep my tone measured. "But you still haven't explained your thought processes."

Her hands curl into fists on the tabletop, and her tiny frame trembles with a banked fury that can only come from years of pain.

What the hell did those people do to this girl?

My protective instincts rear to the forefront, urging me to give Seraphine a break. She doesn't need a refresher of what she suffered—it has to be unimaginable. Still, I can't work in the dark, and she can't continue to lash out and get herself in trouble. I won't allow it.

Silence continues until I remind her I need answers with a sharp, "Seraphine."

"I wasn't thinking anything," she says from between clenched teeth. "All I saw were their faces."

"Whose?" I ask, imagining her captors.

"The men Dad used to punish Mom."

"By Dad you mean Frederic Capello?"

Her face contorts. "He's not my father. He's a monster."

"But you call him Dad."

Deflating, she bows her head, hiding her face with a curtain of hair. "That's what I called him all my life. He used to be a normal dad, living with us in a house on the hills with Gabriel and Mom."

"What changed?"

"One night, I heard noises. My dad was supposed to be away on business. When I went to wake Mom, the bed was empty, so I took a bat and crept down the stairs."

Her breath quickens, and the fists on the table pull into her chest. I want to reach out across to place a hand on her shoulder, to offer some strength, but I don't want to risk interrupting her.

"The noises were coming from Dad's office," she rasps. "I peeked inside. Dad was there with his bodyguards, and they had Mom bent over his desk."

Silence stretches out for several seconds, punctuated only by Seraphine's rapid breaths. "They were taking turns with her. She was screaming, begging them to stop, but Dad said she was getting what she deserved."

My breath stills.

"How old were you?" I ask.

"I'd just turned sixteen," she whispers. "I didn't know what to do or how to help, and I froze. I was so scared that the men would turn on me."

"What did you do?"

"I ran upstairs." Her voice breaks. "I picked up the phone, called the police, and begged them to send help."

"You couldn't fight them," I tell her.

"The woman on the other line said she would send a squad car. She told me not to approach the men and to find somewhere to hide, but nobody came."

"The noises... they just got worse and worse, so I went back upstairs to fetch a gun." She pauses for several seconds, catching her breath. "I meant to go in and shoot the men hurting her, but I found one of them on the floor with his throat slit. There was blood everywhere, and I panicked."

Did Seraphine's mother have an affair with the dead man?

"What did you do next?" I ask.

"I left the house and ran across the grounds to where Felix lived."

"Who is Felix?"

"Our driver."

"Did he help you?"

She shakes her head. "Felix said the cops wouldn't come because Dad was too powerful. He said if I wanted to leave, he would take me anywhere."

In frustration, she fists handfuls of her hair, trying to tear it out by the roots. "I should have stayed. I should have shot the men and gotten my throat slit."

"Seraphine." I grab her hands and squeeze them until her fingers straighten and she releases her grip on her hair. Her skin is clammy and hot, as though she's reliving the moment. "You were a child. Nothing you could have done would have saved her."

The second she lets go of her hair, she slams her head into the table with a force that makes me flinch.

Shit.

I rush to my feet and pull her into my arms. "Don't hurt yourself."

Seraphine lashes out with her fists, trying to fight me off, but I hold tighter, letting her fight and rage until her punches slow and her body collapses.

My lungs deflate with a sigh. I understand these feelings all too well. Powerlessness, guilt, and rage. Three poisonous emotions that she's held in her soul for half a decade. She's probably just replayed that night over and over, cursing herself for not acting differently. It's no surprise that she killed Billy Blue and moved onto all the others. Her anger wasn't toward a lone assailant or even a trio. It was toward an entire group of men.

"Don't blame yourself. You did what you had to do to survive," I murmur into her hair.

"No, you don't understand. I asked Felix to take me to Nanna, and then Dad..." She exhales an anguished cry that makes the fine hairs on the back of my neck stand on end. "Dad came the next morning with those men and took us both. Now, Nanna and Mom are dead because of me."

My breath hitches.

Seraphine pulls back, her eyes bloodshot. "Let go of me. I want to go to bed."

FOURTEEN

LEROI

I thought I knew what I was getting into when I rescued the frail blonde girl from the Capello basement, but the extent of Seraphine's trauma goes deeper than her imprisonment and the abuse suffered at the hands of her own family.

Now I understand why she lashed out at Monica. Two women she loved were murdered. The rage and hopelessness that must have built up over the years had to be unbearable. Dredging up a memory like that would drive anyone to violence.

My arms slip free from around her shoulders, and she rises from the chair to walk around the table.

"Wait," I say.

Her steps falter, but she doesn't turn to meet my gaze.

"Did Capello ever explain his actions?"

She casts me a sidelong glance over her shoulder. "The dead man was our bodyguard, Raphael."

I nod, my brows furrowing, already suspecting where this is going. "So Capello found out he was having an affair with your mother. How?"

"Dad needed a liver transplant, and he had us both tested. When my DNA didn't match his, he tested Raphael's against mine, and found out that Mom had been unfaithful."

Shit

Without another word, Seraphine crosses the living room and disappears behind her door.

She feels responsible for involving her grandmother into this mess, so much so that she's prepared to slam her own head into the table.

I round the table, wishing once again that I had taken my time killing Capello and his sons. The man's sickness extends far deeper than that of the usual mafia boss. It's the first time I've heard of a man willing to use his own children as a source of organ transplant.

"Seraphine?" I knock on the door.

She doesn't answer.

"I'm coming in." I pull down the handle and slip inside.

She lies face-down on her bed with her blonde locks spread across the pillow like a halo. The sight of her delicate figure trembling with sobs pulls at the withered fibers of my heart.

"What happened to your nanna wasn't your fault," I say.

As expected, she doesn't respond.

"Promise me something," I say.

Her head twitches.

"Promise me you won't hurt yourself," I say, my voice tight. "That you'll save all your hurt and anger for the men who did this."

She doesn't move, not even to nod, so I lower myself onto the edge of her bed. "Look at me."

She flinches at the command.

"Now."

She turns onto her side and gazes up at me through blood-shot eyes. They're the only sign on her features that she's upset. I expect Seraphine has learned to hide her emotions as a form of self-preservation.

"I forbid you to inflict any pain, whether direct or indirect on yourself, is that understood?" I snarl.

Seraphine gives me a soft nod.

"Do you have any weapons hidden in your room?"

Her eyes narrow.

"Tell me."

She reaches underneath her pillow and extracts a long, thin blade.

"Where did you get that?" I ask.

"From one of the men I killed," she mumbles.

"Is there anything else?" I ask.

She hesitates.

I know why. It's because she doesn't feel safe. After what happened here with Billy Blue, I'm not surprised she's always on alert. I could turn the room upside-down, but that would resolve nothing. If she's ever going to break out of her compulsion to kill, she's going to need to trust me to keep her safe.

"If I promised not to allow anyone to enter this apartment, would you hand over the rest of your weapons?"

She nods.

I rise off the bed and crouch beside it to look her in the eye. "Nobody but you and me will ever step through the front door without your express permission."

"Alright," she says, her soft voice a balm on my heart.

"Gather the rest of the weapons you've hidden." I step back, letting her rise off the bed.

Seraphine slips a hand beneath the mattress and pulls

out an ice pick. My jaw clenches, but I remain silent as she extracts an array of items she duct taped beneath the bed.

"Is that all of them?" I ask.

She nods.

"There will be consequences if you're hiding anything else."

I glare down at her for several heartbeats, drilling the message into her skull. If she were any other woman, I would treat her with a little more tenderness, but Seraphine is a potential trip to the electric chair wrapped up in an innocent little package. She bows her head and lowers her lashes, which I take as a sign of her submission.

"Promise me you won't hurt yourself again." I lift her chin, making her look me in the eyes.

"Promise me you'll help me find Gabriel," she says.

"Do you remember the man who removed your collar?" At her nod, I add, "He's pulling together information on Capello's drivers and bodyguards. At least one of them will lead us to your brother."

Hope shines in her blue eyes, but the rest of her features remain stoic.

"I won't be able to rest until I kill each of those men," she says, her voice tightening with determination.

"Of course," I say with a nod.

Her eyes widen. "You'd let me hurt them?"

"Do you think putting those demons to rest will stop you from lashing out?" I ask.

"Yes."

"Then I'll help you kill every one of those bastards who assaulted your mother."

Her jaw clenches. "I don't need your help."

I chuckle, because I know she doesn't. She killed eight men in my apartment right under my nose. "Not with the stabbing part, but you'll need me to help track them down, break and enter their homes, and to leave no traces at the crime scene."

She swallows, looking like she's about to argue, but I add, "You only got away with that little massacre because one of the assholes in our poker crew was smoking something stronger than weed. We'd drunk several bottles of whiskey and were fucked out of our minds. If more than one of us had been awake—"

"Fine," she spits. "We'll do it your way."

I nod. "And you will learn how to kill without making a mess."

Her nostrils flare as though she finds my commentary on her methods an affront.

"Clean kills are what keep us away from getting caught and sentenced to death."

"But I don't want them to die slowly."

"Then we'll take precautions."

Her lips part as though to ask a question, but the doorbell rings. My eyes narrow. Miko lives in the apartment next door, and he always knocks.

"Wait here," I say and guide her toward the bed.

After gathering up her stash of stolen weapons, I place them on the dining table, pick up my phone, and fire up the security app. Whoever is outside has placed a hand over the doorbell camera, hoping to make me think it's malfunctioning.

Clumsy.

I walk to the door and uncock my pistol. Nobody but Miko visits without arranging it first and even if they did, they would call up via the concierge.

Positioning myself by the wall three feet away from the door, I ask, "Who is it?"

There's no answer from the other side of the door.

My jaw clenches. There were always going to be reper-cussions from the poker night massacre, but I didn't expect it this soon. Don and his team were careful to dispose of all the crew's cars at various locations around New Alderney, so there wouldn't be a fleet of abandoned vehicles outside my building.

Miko tampered with as much security footage as he could access, but even his hacking skills have their limits. No amount of technical know-how can erase a man telling a friend or loved one where they're going.

It's only a matter of time before someone comes looking.

When the doorbell rings again, my nostrils flare.

Another hitman would judge the distance of my voice, and know I'm not directly behind the door. They would wait until I'm tempted to use the peephole before shooting a round of bullets through the wood.

Raising my voice, I say, "If you don't tell me who you are, you'll stand in the hallway all day."

A feminine giggle sounds behind the door, and my eyes roll. There is such a thing as a female assassin—I might have one in my own home right now. I have two of them working in the firm, a blonde and a brunette, both with a one-hundred percent success rate. They're beautiful, cunning, and able to get close to even the most reclusive targets because no one ever suspects that the demure, attractive woman is a killer.

"Open the door, Leroi. It's me," says a voice that grates on my nerves and not because it belongs to an assassin.

Quite the opposite. This is a woman who likes to be choked. And spanked. And degraded. I didn't realize she was bad news until after we'd fucked for the sixth time, and I found her snooping through the apartment.

It turned out that she worked for the New Alderney Times, but she refused to confirm whether or not she was writing an article on me or my infamous cousins.

Fuck. "What are you doing here, Rosalind?"

"We haven't played together for a month." I don't even need to look through the peephole to know that she's pouting. "I've missed you."

I'm not stupid enough to think she's alone. It's a classic move in the hitman handbook—using the man's wife or lover to lure him into opening his door. Except she's neither, just an irregular hook-up.

"You know better than to come here," I say.

"Let me in," she whines. "There's something I need to tell you."

The sound of creaking has me turning around. Seraphine stands in the doorway of her room, her features a hard mask.

In her hand is a pistol. "Who the hell is Rosalind?"

FIFTEEN

SERAPHINE

Leroi glowers at my gun, his face a mask of fury. I walk toward the door, hoping there are enough bullets to get rid of the threat.

"Seraphine," he hisses. "Stay away from the door."

"Who is she?" I ask.

"Nobody," he growls.

"Leroi, let me in," the woman whines. "We have to talk."

"Stay." He holds out his palm, like I'm his dog.

I stop in the middle of the living room, my breaths shallowing. When he motions for me to stand out of the way, my jaw tenses. The only reason I'm obeying him is because he's going to help me find Gabriel. Stepping aside, I make a promise to myself to stay calm, at least until he's helped me get what I want.

"Take your finger off the camera lens," Leroi says, already sounding tired of her.

A moment later, he glances down at his phone, and some of the tension in his shoulders eases. His features are less murderous when he turns to me and asks, "She's alone. Can I bring her inside?"

My lips part with a protest, so he adds, "I could warn her against returning in the hallway, but she could have someone hiding in the stairwell. Let me drag her in."

I nod.

"Go into your room. I don't want anyone knowing about you until it's safe."

"You still haven't answered my question," I say. "Who is she?"

"Seraphine," he growls. "Go to your room."

A muscle in my jaw ticks. He talks to me as though I'm not capable of slitting his throat and watching him soak the sheets with his blood. It takes every effort to remind myself that I need him... for now. After he's helped me find Gabriel and track down Mom's rapists, I won't let him be so commanding.

Leroi continues glaring until my fingers itch with the desire to carve out both his eyes with a rusty blade. Since he's so stubborn, I'll have to obey his orders. I walk back to my room, open the door, and step inside, but I don't close it. Instead, I hold the pistol and peer through the crack.

He moves with surprising speed. Within a few short breaths, he's opening the door, yanking her inside, slamming her against the wall, and snarling, "I told you never to come here."

Rosalind and I are completely different. She's a gorgeous, tall brunette with loose waves. She reminds me a little of Monica, the elegant therapist. The only difference is their makeup. That therapist wears hers light and natural, but Rosalind has deep red lipstick and smokey eyes. Compared to them, I look like a pasty little kid.

From the way she's holding his shoulders instead of

clawing at his face, I can tell they're lovers. That, and the short red dress that displays miles of slender legs.

I swallow hard, my throat tightening. Is this his type? Tall, slender brunettes who show all their skin? I shrink against the door, my fingers tightening around the gun.

"Yes," Rosalind says, her voice husky. "Just like that."

She arches her back, pushing her ample breasts toward Leroi. One of her legs rises to hook around his hamstrings. My breath catches, and the pulse between my thighs pounds so hard that its vibrations reach my toenails.

Is this how Leroi likes to have sex?

His hand tightens around her neck. "What the fuck was so important that you would risk a getting shot?"

Her features drop. "Wait—what?"

Leroi raises his gun to her temple. "First, I told you never to come here uninvited." She whimpers as the gun slides down her cheek. "Then I told you never to return." He runs the gun over her bottom lip, pulling it down, marking the barrel with her red lipstick. "And now I'm thinking the only way to make you listen is with a bullet."

Her eyes widen, and her inflated chest rises and falls with panicked breaths. "Don't shoot. I just came to say..."

"What?" he snarls.

Adrenaline courses through my veins, and all sensation rushes low in my belly. This side of Leroi is thrilling. He's far more exciting like this than when he's nagging me about cleaning my room. I grip the edge of the door and grind my clit into its wooden surface. Seeing Leroi in this light excites me in a way I never imagined.

Rosalind's lips tremble, and my breaths quicken. I want him to make her open her mouth for the gun. I want to see her take its barrel down her throat before he pulls the trigger and paints the wall red with her blood.

"P-please," she rasps. "You can't hurt me. I'm pregnant."

My jaw drops.

Leroi's laugh is harsh. "Bullshit."

"It's true." Mascara-streaked tears spill down her cheeks, making her look like a clown. "I took the test yesterday and another one this morning to make sure."

Rosalind is an ugly crier, but I'm more concerned about this baby. If Leroi is about to become a father, he'll drop everything to take care of the mother of his child. He isn't like Dad or the other men I killed during my five years of captivity. If Leroi could show compassion for a stranger he found in a basement, then he would burn down the world to protect the woman carrying his baby.

My heart sinks into my stomach like an anchor, bringing up a throat full of bile. He won't have time to help me.

"If what you say is true, then go back to one of the other men you've been screwing because the child you're expecting isn't mine."

"It's yours. There hasn't been anyone else."

"In that case, you should consult a priest."

She hiccups. "What?"

"I had a vasectomy," he snarls. "We used a condom and you have an implant under your skin."

My chest fills with triumph, and I suck in a sharp breath. Leroi needs to end this stalker before she escalates.

Rosalind's mouth opens and closes like a fish. "But—"

"Get the hell out of my apartment," he snarls. "Don't come back unless you want the next time to be your last."

Her gaze shifts over his shoulder, and we lock eyes. When she holds my gaze for a second too long, I bare my teeth. She sees Leroi as her property, the same way Dad acted like I owed him something for doting on me under false pretenses.

Leroi turns around to see what Rosalind is looking at, and I shut the door before he can notice that I've disobeyed another of his orders.

Pressing my ear to the gap in the wood, I eavesdrop on the rest of the conversation.

Rosalind's voice is thick with tears when she says, "I'm sorry. I didn't know how else you'd listen when you blocked me—"

"Next time I see you anywhere near this building, your head will take a bullet," Leroi says, his voice cold.

Rosalind fills the apartment with desperate sobs. I crack open the door half an inch to witness him throwing her out into the hallway. He slams the door and turns the lock, then picks up the phone.

"Carl," he says into the receiver. "A dark-haired woman in a red dress is leaving the building. Make sure she never returns."

The other person says something before Leroi hangs up.

I step out of my room, hoping he was talking to one of the clean-up crew. "Who's Carl?"

His features sharpen. "I told you to stay in your room."

"But she's gone."

His gaze drops to my hand. "I also told you there would be consequences if you lied to me about having more weapons."

I glance down at the gun. "You said knives."

Leroi bares his teeth. "Do you remember accepting the consequences of disobedience and being a brat?"

Blood drains from my face and gathers between my thighs, making my core tingle. Even my pulse dials up several notches. I sway on my feet, dizzy with excitement.

I didn't think we'd get to use the toys so soon.

SIXTEEN

SERAPHINE

Leroi advances on me, his eyes hard. Raising my chin, I meet his gaze, trying to contain the surge of anticipation and desire. This is madness. I should be terrified after seeing how he slammed Rosalind against the wall and ran the tip of his gun over her face, but heat slams into me as he grips my chin.

"You disobeyed a direct order." His voice is so cold that a shiver runs down my spine. "And you lied to me about having a gun."

"I didn't—"

"I asked if you had handed over all the hidden weapons, and you nodded, knowing there would be consequences for not telling the truth." He strokes my chin with his thumb, infusing me with a delicious tingle.

My stomach flutters, and my heart rate ratchets to its maximum capacity. I take a deep breath, trying to remain composed, but the intensity of his stare makes my skin flush.

His gaze drops to my lips, and my brow breaks out into a

sweat. My arms twitch, but I hold them at my side, resisting the urge to kiss him.

"I-I'm sorry. I didn't mean to lie."

"It's too late for apologies," he says, his pupils dilating. "But I will give you a choice of punishment."

My breath catches, and every butterfly in my stomach takes flight. Will he finish what he started when he attached those nipple clamps in the fetish store, or will he bring out one of the other toys?

I run my tongue along my bottom lip, and his eyes track the movement, even though his face remains an impenetrable mask.

"What." I gulp, my throat suddenly dry. "What are you going to do?"

"That's entirely up to you," he says. "Are you ready for your punishment, or would you like to have it tomorrow?"

My chest deflates, as does my anticipation. Leroi was so ruthless with Rosalind, yet he's being soft with me. "Why are you giving me a choice?"

"Opening up about your past had to stir up old traumas. You might not be in the right state of mind to face being chastised."

"But we're still going to kill those men?"

"Of course."

I nod. "Then I'll take my punishment now."

He releases his grip on my chin, robbing me of his warmth. I whimper, my body trembling with the suspense.

Leroi stands back and says, "I'm leaving to fetch some of our purchases. By the time I return, I want you in your room, kneeling. Is that understood?"

My heart skips a beat. "Alright."

"You will address me as sir," he says, his voice stern.

Arousal hits me straight in my core, making my knees

tremble. It takes every effort to keep my voice even when I reply with "Yes, sir."

Leroi turns on his heel and stalks toward the dining table, where we left the bags of toys and equipment from Wonderland. I stand transfixed, my gaze glued to the muscles bunching and releasing beneath his shirt as he moves. It's no wonder Rosalind went to such desperate lengths to see him again. Leroi has an amazing body.

He reaches the table, turns, and arches an eyebrow. "Go."

I bolt into the room and pull off my shirt, thankful that everything I'm wearing is easy to remove with shaking fingers. After folding each item and arranging them into a neat pile at the foot of my bed, I kneel on the wooden floor and face the doorway.

Every second that passes feels like an eternity of torment. I'm so eager for Leroi to return that it's hard to be afraid, but as he turns the handle, my spine stiffens with dread.

Leroi steps in, bringing in a cool draft that makes my skin prickle into goosebumps, both with excitement and with the change in temperature. He pauses at the doorway for several frantic heartbeats, his breath catching, his eyes fathomless pools of black.

Replaying his instructions, I remember he only wanted me kneeling, not naked. Heat floods my cheeks, spreads down my chest, and tightens my nipples. Maybe he'll punish me with the clamps?

My gaze drops to what he's holding—I don't recognize the pink leather. Without looking in my direction, he walks around my kneeling form and places it on the bed. The gentle clink of metal tells me it's some kind of restraint.

Arousal surges, and I squeeze my thighs. All the leather

items we bought were buttery, soft, and lined with a velvety suede. They don't even compare with the twins' rope.

Leroi walks to the table on the side of the room and lowers himself into a chair. "Turn, so you're facing me."

"Yes, sir." I shuffle around on my knees and fix my gaze on the parquet floor.

"Eyes on me," he says.

I raise my gaze, running my eyes from his black leather shoes, to his black pants, and up to the black shirt that clings to his prominent pecs. His chest rises and falls with even breaths, as though he's used to dealing with a woman kneeling in front of him naked. I'm torn between looking into his face and glancing over to see what he deposited on the bed.

Disobedience might worsen my punishment, so I decide to look him in the eye.

He picks up a glass of whiskey and takes a sip before setting it back down. The movement stretches my anticipation until it's agonizing.

"Do you know why you're here?" he asks.

"Yes, sir," I rasp.

"Explain."

"I disobeyed an order and lied about not having any more weapons."

He leans back in the chair, his dark eyes studying me with a level of concentration that's as intimidating as it is thrilling. I'm not tall and curvaceous like Rosalind, and I'm not a brunette. My eyes are too large for my face, making me look like I'm constantly surprised. The only men who find me attractive are predators, who tend not to live long enough to regret it.

There's no lust in Leroi's gaze, only determination.

Determination to mold me into the kind of disciplined killer that doesn't get caught.

"Do you understand why lying to me was wrong?"

I nod. "Yes, sir."

"Tell me why."

Shivers skitter down my spine. Every man I've encountered in the past five years would have made some kind of lewd comment by now, yet Leroi remains completely in control. It's both terrifying and exhilarating. He's playing a game I don't understand, and I'm desperate to learn the rules.

"We had an agreement," I rasp. "You were going to help me control my urges, and I was going to follow your orders."

"Crawl to me."

The muscles of my core clench, but I get down on my hands and knees. The floor is cool against my palms as I make my way toward him, and I keep my gaze fixed on Leroi's face.

There's no trace of the furious man who slammed that woman against a wall, just a blank mask. I want to ignite that kind of passion in Leroi, to make him lose control, but I know better than to push a killer too far.

When I reach him, he trails a finger down my cheek and watches me with that same detached curiosity.

"If you can't be truthful or obey my orders, then being here with me is a waste of time. You may as well move into the apartment next door."

My stomach drops, and the excitement I felt moments ago vanishes, replaced by cold fingers squeezing my heart. Darkness creeps to the edge of my vision, reminding me of the endless stretches of time I spent alone in that basement.

"I'll do better," I say, meaning every word. "Don't cast me out."

Leroi studies my face for several painful moments before nodding. "You will submit to a spanking."

"Yes, sir," I rasp.

"Get up."

I stand on shaky legs, my heart galloping around my chest like a wild horse. The thought of Leroi's hand coming down hard against my bare ass makes the pulse between my legs quicken.

When I reach his side, he pulls me down so I'm lying on his lap, my head dangling toward the floor and my ass cheeks positioned between his spread thighs.

"Your punishment should be harsher, but I will be merciful since you've had a hard day and these are your first offenses."

My skin tingles and my nipples tighten to the point of pain. "Thank you, sir."

"You will count them. Fail to do so, and I will reset the count."

I squeeze my eyes shut and try not to moan.

This is either going to end in tears or my very first orgasm.

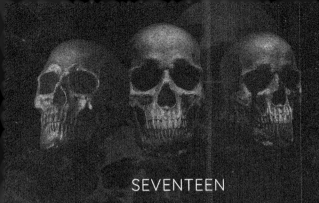

SEVENTEEN

LEROI

This is a mistake.

When I walked in to find her kneeling and naked, I should have told her to put on some clothes. Until this moment, she's been covered up. I hadn't imagined those baggy clothes were hiding such beautiful curves. Now, I can't look away.

I haven't yet touched Seraphine's skin, and my cock is already pushing painfully against my zipper. Her ass is perfect. Round globes of unmarked, porcelain flesh that beg to be spanked raw.

If Seraphine's tastes are anywhere close to complimenting mine, I'm in trouble. I can't resist a woman who likes to be pushed to the edge and brought back until she's begging and crying for me to pound into her until it hurts.

The stakes are high. If I screw up, she's more likely to show her displeasure in the form of my sliced throat, or worse. Regardless, the prospect of her is tempting.

I hover my hand over her pretty cheeks in preparation for the first strike. Warmth radiates from her skin. Skin that looks as smooth and soft as silk, skin that's too supple and untouched for the likes of me. I inhale a shuddering breath to remind myself why I'm here with her bent over my lap, but it still takes every effort not to stroke her tender flesh.

Seraphine is here to be disciplined. Not to be pleasured. She has to understand the seriousness of our agreement. If I'm going to train her to stop killing, she needs to give up her disobedience and lies.

I raise my hand and deliver the first strike. The sound of my palm connecting with her skin sends a wave of pleasure straight to my balls. She gasps, her back arching, the sight and sound of her surprise driving me deeper into a state of lust.

"One," she says, her voice breathy.

A handprint blooms on her creamy skin. I clench my teeth to keep from groaning. Without thinking about it, I stroke my palm over her warm flesh that's even more luxurious than I imagined.

My breath deepens, and my heart thuds painfully in its cage, pumping all blood and sensation south. I wrench my hand off her ass cheeks and remind myself that this is punishment, not play.

The next spank is harder and makes her flesh ripple.

Seraphine moans, sounding like she's interpreting the pain as pleasure. "Two!"

I swallow hard, trying to stay focused, trying to ignore the building urgency. When she proposed this to help control her murderous urges, I hadn't expected her to suggest a reward and punishment schedule that included orgasms. Now, my own discipline is being tested, and it's all I can do to stay detached.

The second handprint is darker than the first. While

waiting for the sting to subside, I smooth over it, letting her know the spanks are delivered with care.

Shivering prettily, Seraphine raises a leg, her dainty foot pointing toward the ceiling. I stifle a groan. Everything about this woman is ridiculously alluring, from her pretty little toes to her reddening cheeks.

"Get back into position." I give her calf a gentle push, only for her to shift on my lap.

Her legs part, and I'm treated to the view of her sweet pussy. The hairs are so pale and fine that they're barely visible, with her folds glistening and wet.

I'm certain she repositioned herself on purpose, just to drive me crazy.

It's working.

The third spank goes to her right cheek, which is paler than the left. Seraphine cries out and writhes against my thigh, like she's trying to create a little friction.

I smooth over the reddened skin. "Count the spanks or your punishment resets."

Her thighs part a little wider, displaying more of that beautiful little cunt. My cock jerks in response, and I grind my molars, trying to contain my arousal.

"Seraphine," I growl.

As she moves her ass from side to side, I'm painfully aware that she's torturing me or she's treating this punishment as a game. It's a game she won't win.

Pressing a hand on her hamstrings, I lean down to where her head dangles toward the floor. "This is your final warning," I growl. "Count the spanks, or we won't just start over. The next ones won't be so pleasant."

She shakes her head.

"You asked for it," I say.

In response, her spine stiffens.

I raise a hand and let it fly down to her ass in a spank more forceful than the last. Seraphine yelps and squirms, her body twisting and nearly slipping off my lap. I hold her down with a palm between her shoulder blades and deliver one and then another in quick succession.

After the sixth spank, she finally cries, "One!"

"Good girl."

I stroke her ass cheeks, soothing her reddened skin. Heat radiates from her flesh, and her pussy is even wetter. My index finger slides close to her folds, and she trembles. It would be so easy to slip into her slick heat, to circle her swollen clit until her cries reached a delicious crescendo. I remind myself that this is a punishment.

By the end of this spanking, Seraphine will regret her transgressions.

The next spank is equally harsh, and her legs move further apart. The corner of my lips lift.

She wants me to play with her pussy.

"Two," she says with a breathy moan.

As I soothe the sting with my palm, her hips lift, confirming my suspicions. Ignoring the sweet temptation, I deliver another swat that makes her gasp.

"Three."

The fourth spank lands lower down on her buttocks, where they meet her pussy. I make sure the sting reaches her where she needs my touch the most.

"Oh," she says through a gasp. "Four."

I stroke her ass, finding pleasure in her trembling frame. For a woman who claims to have never had an orgasm, she's dangerously close to the edge. It would only take a few quick touches to bring her to a shuddering climax.

As my fingers graze the few inches of flesh closest to her wetness, she moves into my touch.

"Please," she whispers.

"Please, what?" I ask, enjoying the sound of her pleas. "Tell me what you want."

"Touch me," she says, her sweet voice sounding like molten sin. "I need you."

I slide my knuckles down her spine, eliciting a delicious moan. Seraphine's back arches, and the sight is beyond tempting.

As much as I want to tease her to orgasm, she needs to learn the consequences of her misbehavior, but that doesn't stop me from sliding my fingers through her slick folds. When I reach her swollen bud, I caress it with the gentlest of strokes.

"This is your clit." I lean into her, my voice deepening. "Feel how I'm circling it with my finger?"

Her hips buck, and she releases a moan.

"You like that, little Seraphine?"

"Yes," she whispers.

"I'm going to shackle your wrists in one of the leather items we bought, alright?"

"A-alright," she replies with a groan.

I reach over to the bed and grab the arm restraints. Seraphine probably thinks I'll cuff her and continue teasing that sweet little bud until she orgasms, but she would be wrong.

Grabbing her wrist, I guide her hand through a soft leather cuff that's attached to another with a thick piece of the same material. The device is a separation arm binder, which will keep her in place for longer periods of time with minimal strain.

Seraphine moans, her hips wiggling from side to side. I shake my head. She's a deadly delight.

As I slip her second arm through the binder, she offers

little resistance, so bent on achieving her first climax. I tighten each strap, checking in with her that she's comfortable, and lift her off my lap.

She stands at my side, her cheeks flushed, her pretty lips parted and red. I keep my eyes on her face, though I suspect her nipples are erect.

"Lie face-down on the bed and spread your legs," I say.

Without another word, she scrambles onto the mattress.

I run my fingers down her back, loving how my touches elicit a shudder.

"Please, Leroi," she whispers. "I need you."

Leaning down, I place my lips to her ear. "Obedient girls get orgasms. Girls who conceal weapons from their Doms and disobey their orders get to lie on their beds with aching pussies and no release."

Her lips part. "But—"

"No, buts."

Tears glisten in her eyes. "But what if I want to pee?"

"Then you'll shuffle off the bed and make your way to the bathroom."

Her features harden, and her eyes glint with murder. I reach down and run my fingers over her cheek. "Now, take your punishment. I'll return later to free your arms."

"Wait—"

"This is what you agreed to, Seraphine. Don't be a brat." I turn on my heel and walk out of the door, leaving her gasping.

Now that she knows I'm more than capable of giving her an orgasm, I expect her behavior to improve.

EIGHTEEN

LEROI

I leave Seraphine writhing on the bed, trembling with frustration. She glares at me, her face reddening with each passing moment. I can't help but feel a sadistic thrill from working her to the brink of orgasm and then denying her release.

"Please," she whispers, sounding as helpless as she did when I found her in the basement.

My steps falter, only for a second, before I remind myself that beneath that sweet and delicate exterior is a young woman who could slit a man's throat for having the wrong friends or gouge his eye for leering.

Seraphine must be tamed.

I step out of her room, confident she won't be able to release herself from the binder. Nor will she be able to get off with her hands secured behind her back.

My phone rings, and I stride to where I left it on the dining table. It's a call from Rita, the firm's coordinator, who informs me that an assassin we employ has completed a job out of state.

Rita has been in the firm since before Anton retired. She's a sweet woman in her sixties who crochets while accepting phone calls on contract kills. She also handles customer satisfaction.

"Someone wants to open a contract to avenge Frederic Capello," she adds.

My nostrils flare. No one I left alive should be able to afford our rates. Keeping my voice even, I reply, "Oh?"

"Did you hear that a gunman wiped out the entire family this week?"

"He wants revenge?"

"Seems that way," she says. "He wants us to track down the killer and bring him to a specific place alive."

I pause, my jaw hardening. "We're not bounty hunters."

"That's what I told him." She chuckles. "But he's willing to pay a million to find the killer. That's why I'm passing on the inquiry to you."

Shit.

This is why I thought long and hard about striking at the Capellos. Whoever's after their killer won't give up if we refuse. He'll just give the job to one of our competitors, and I'll have another reason to watch my back.

"Did he leave a name?"

"Of course, not."

"Send me all the details," I say. "I'll take care of it."

"Will do." Rita hangs up.

I open the surveillance app and scroll to the cameras in Seraphine's room. She's still wiggling from side to side, trying to create some friction, but it's no use.

A frustrated scream sounds from behind her door, making me smile. I call Miko, who answers in one ring.

"Leroi?"

"Did you find anything useful in those files?"

He blows out a long breath. "Actually, there's a lot."

"I'm coming over."

Less than half a minute later, I'm in the apartment next door. It has only one bedroom compared to the three I have in mine, and a smaller living area with an open-plan kitchen. Miko has covered every wall in bookcases laden with volumes of manga and action hero figurines.

"What did you find?" I cast my gaze over his twin desks, one with an oversized monitor for playing video games and the other laden with the stolen drives where he sits, surrounded by more monitors.

"Enzo Montesano was a predator." He shudders. "I found video footage of him with underage girls."

"Shit." I rub the space between my brows, wondering how the hell Uncle Enzo could have kept something like that a secret. "How young?"

He shrugs. "Fifteen, sixteen. I didn't look too closely."

Enzo was my father's first cousin, and I grew up seeing him almost every day. He wasn't known for keeping secrets, which was why his wife yelled at him every day about his blonde mistress. Perhaps the woman was a cover-up for his true depravity.

"That explains how Capello took control of his empire. He blackmailed him."

"True." Miko spins around in his office chair. "I know you're friends with his sons. Do you think they might also—"

"Roman, Cesare and Benito aren't anything like their father," I say. "Did you find anything on the DA or the judge?"

"Take a look."

The monitor fills with clip after clip of the same man snorting coke, screwing hookers, and accepting a stack of bills from Capello.

"This is damning," I say, my voice low. "What about the judge?"

"Here." Miko opens a thumbnail, bringing up footage of an overweight man with gray hair. He's naked, on his hands and knees, being spit roasted by two clothed men.

I jerk my head away from the sight. "Is he married?"

"Yes, but it gets worse."

"How?"

"These guys." Miko points at the two men, bringing my attention back to the clip. "They're bank robbers who won their appeal in his court. Looks like they're paying him off."

"Fuck." I shake my head. "Forward those clips of the judge and DA to Benito Montesano."

With some dragging and dropping and a few clicks of a mouse, Miko sends the email. He turns to me and frowns. "What about the information Capello had on their father?"

"They don't need to know that," I say.

Miko's frown deepens.

"Enzo is dead, and Capello framed one of his sons for murder and made the other two suffer enough. Telling them their father was a pervert helps no one. If you identify any of those girls, send me their names and addresses. I will use my share of what we earned from the Capello job to pay for their therapy."

He bows his head.

"Any problems?" I ask.

"We always go fishing after a big job."

I suppress a sigh. "This one has come with an unexpected complication."

He hesitates for several heartbeats, looking like he's trying to muster up the courage to speak. "That girl you saved..."

"What about Seraphine?"

"Are you going to move her into an apartment like you did with me?"

"Eventually," I say with a smile. "But she's going to need a little extra help."

He nods.

"Is there anything else?"

"I want to learn how to use a gun."

"Why?"

"I'm tired of being behind the scenes. I want to help you out in the field."

Pressure builds up behind my eyes, feeling like the beginnings of a headache. Letting him sift through those files was probably a mistake. Miko doesn't have what it takes to look into a man's eyes and pull the trigger.

"I brought you here because I wanted you to have a better life. Not to train you to become a killer."

His gaze drops to the floor. "But I want to help."

"You do. You're the best hacker in the business, and you can put together explosives better than any demolition expert. Without your technical know-how, I would never have been able to complete the Capello job."

"But I want to kill people," he says. "Up close, like you."

"Murder isn't something to aspire to."

He stares up at me, his blue eyes hardening. "You were doing it when you were younger than me."

"I had no choice."

Miko looks away, his jaw twitching. "Maybe if I killed my stepfather like you did, I'd be a hitman like you."

My head pounds. Miko already knows my story. It's not so different from his. We both had reckless mothers and abusive stepfathers, but I had a younger sister to protect. When I found that bastard on top of her, I grabbed his gun and shot him in the temple.

He didn't die immediately. I left him to spend hours lying in a pool of his blood, gasping for air. When my mother finally sobered up, she called her cousin Anton and screamed at him to take me away.

Anton taught me never to miss. We practiced with paint pellets at first, and one day, without telling me, he switched the blanks to bullets.

That's how I became Anton's protégé and then his successor.

"You're right," I say. "Shooting my stepfather was my first step to becoming a murderer. But I don't want the same life for you."

"Isn't that my decision?" he asks.

"Something happens to a person once they've made their first kill," I say. "I don't regret what I did to save my sister, but murdering strangers for money changes you, and not for the better."

His posture slumps, and he stares straight ahead at the computer. "I just want to be useful."

I place a hand on his shoulder. "If you want to work full time in the firm as an analyst, I can make that happen."

The corner of his lips lifts into a smile. "You could?"

I nod. "Murder isn't the only way to help us. If you're that keen to learn how to use a gun, I can take you for target practice."

"Sure," Miko says, his eyes bright. "I want to be able to give back."

"We've had this conversation before," I say, giving his

shoulder a squeeze. "The only thing I want from you is to be happy."

He dips his head, his smile widening, and his cheeks turning pink. "I... Uh, finished the research you wanted on Capello's guards. He's been paying them out of the same account for decades, so I found the names of the recipients and cross-referenced their information with public records and with photos I downloaded from the DMV."

"Can you filter the ones who were in his employment from six years ago until today?"

All traces of the shy young man vanish, replaced by the confident professional. "There's twenty-four. Three are in prison, five died in the past five years, and seven died during our explosions."

I nod. "Making twelve left alive?"

"Yeah."

"Send me files on all twenty-four and identify the deceased."

He makes a few clicks. "Done."

"Excellent work."

"Got a minute to play a game?" he asks.

My gaze flicks down to my phone. I'm tempted to check on Seraphine, but I shake my head. "Not tonight, Miko. Got my hands full."

"Another time?" he asks, his voice flat.

"Definitely." I rise to my feet and give him a pat on the back. "One more thing. Rita got a call from someone who wants a hit on the lone gunman who killed Capello."

His head whips up. "Seriously?"

"He's willing to pay a mill for the job."

His jaw drops. "I hope she said no."

"I accepted the mission," I reply with a smirk. "As soon

as the deposit clears, do what you can to research the person who wants me dead."

"Of course," Miko says, his voice trembling.

"Don't worry. I plan on eliminating this new client before he knows what's coming. Now, get some rest."

I walk out of his apartment faster than normal, eager to know how Seraphine is coping with her punishment.

NINETEEN

SERAPHINE

I've been grinding against this mattress for the last ten minutes, trying something—anything—to create a little friction. All I've managed is to build myself up to a heightened state of arousal that quickly fades.

Tears prick the corners of my eyes. Leroi got me so worked up with that spanking, and the way his fingers skimmed so close to where I needed him most was maddening.

I knew he was special, knew he could be the one to give me my first orgasm. What I didn't know was the extent of his cruelty. I felt his thick erection pressed into my side as he spanked my ass, but he kept it in his pants. Other men would have escalated, but Leroi remained so cool and in control, even though my body begged him for more.

He's unreachable, yet I've never felt this way for any man. I'm beginning to rethink whether I want to be trained by him. Right now, all I want to do is make him scream. Or bleed.

Did he really expect me to hand over the last of my weapons?

I roll my hips, my mind replaying those gentle caresses in between the stinging slaps. No one has ever touched me in a way that didn't make my skin crawl, let alone deliver such pleasure. They usually just stick their fingers where they're not wanted, but Leroi teased me to a fever pitch and left me here to simmer.

Sweat breaks out across my skin. I've been trying to work myself up to an orgasm and all I'm getting is frustration. He could have at least left me with my hands tied around my front.

"Bastard," I sob, envisioning the pretty patterns I'll carve into his skin.

The door swings open, and I freeze.

"Who's a bastard?" asks a deep voice that makes my spine tingle and my clit pulse.

I turn my head, finding Leroi standing in the doorway, still dressed in black. He tilts his head, his gaze assessing.

"You left me here to suffer." I twist my body to the side.

He closes the distance, and heat blooms across my cheeks. How long was he standing behind the door, listening to me trying—and failing—to get some pleasure?

Before I can say anything else, he takes my shoulder and turns me onto my back. The new position stretches my arms underneath me and my back arches, displaying my tightened pert nipples. Leroi quirks a brow, "I left you here to learn a lesson, and it seems like you haven't."

"I'm sorry," I whisper.

He raises his brows. "For?"

"I lied about hiding weapons." My throat dries, and I swallow hard. "And for disobeying when you told me to stay in my room."

"Is that all?" he asks, still stern.

"And for calling you a bastard," I murmur.

He draws back. "Turn around."

My heart beats so hard its vibrations reach my core. I roll onto my front, all the while trying to keep eye contact. Maybe if I'm convincing enough, he'll accept my apology and finish what he started.

He crouches by the bed, but instead of reaching for my ass, he slides his fingers through my hair. His touch is gentle, soothing, and warmer than expected, considering I'm being punished. My lips part with a gasp. What is he doing?

Just as I'm about to ask, he trails his fingers down my back, setting my skin alight. I exhale a breathy sigh, my core clenching in anticipation. As he reaches the base of my spine, my legs part, a silent invitation for him to rub circles around my clit.

"Still wet?" he asks, his voice hoarse.

"Yes, sir."

I meet his eyes, and they're even darker than before. My gaze trails down his muscular body and settles on the bulge straining against his pants. He's hard for me, and that gives me courage to speak.

"Please, touch me," I say.

"What makes you think you deserve a reward?" he asks.

The words dry up in my throat.

"I'm going to ask you once, and I want you to tell me the truth. Have you hidden any more weapons?"

"Yes," I confess before I can stop myself.

Without another word, he unfastens the buckles of my wrist binder, eases one arm out of the leather shackle, and massages around my shoulder. I melt into his touch. I hadn't realized the strain I was under until he released the restraints. Next, he frees the other arm and repeats the soothing ministration on my tight muscles.

But there's one more muscle that's still in need of his attention.

As he helps me up to sitting, I press my chest against his and whisper, "I'm sorry. Please, sir. Touch me."

He cups my face in his large hands. "You took your punishment very well, but I don't want to train you into thinking that disobedience is acceptable. Do you understand?"

I shake my head.

"Obedience and good behavior are rewarded." He slides the pad of his thumb over my cheekbone, a warm trail follows his touch, and my skin tingles. "Bad girls who don't follow the rules go to bed with spanked asses and no orgasms."

I whimper at the unfairness, even as heat flickers between my legs. "But I told you about my past. Isn't that worth a reward?"

He stares into my eyes, looking for me to answer that question for myself.

"What if I gave you all the weapons I'm hiding?"

"That would be a start on making amends." He steps back, giving me space.

I walk to the ensuite, lift the lid off the toilet tank, and pull out two knives I took from the dead men. By the time I turn back, Leroi is already standing in the doorway.

"Is that the last of them?" he asks.

"Yes, including the gun I left on the table."

He nods. "Apology accepted. Put on some clothes and join me for dinner."

The next morning, I'm in front of the chopping board, slicing through every item in Leroi's refrigerator. All the sharp blades are gone, and all I have is a dull table knife. Stacks of vegetables pile on the counter, looking like they've fallen victim to a slasher.

I sat through an entire meal last night and ate everything on my plate, thinking that he would lead me back to the bedroom and give me an orgasm for my good behavior. At the end of the evening, he gathered up all my weapons, locked them in his armory, told me to get some sleep, and left me there. Alone and unsatisfied.

My finger aches from the heavy duty slicing. The only thing keeping me going is imagining each vegetable I hack up as one of Leroi's body parts.

"What are you doing?" he asks.

I whirl around, finding him leaning against the doorframe, shirtless and in a pair of gray sweatpants. My gaze wanders down the planes of his chest, over the V-shaped muscles at his hips, before resting on the outline of his penis bulging through the fabric.

It's long and thick and perfectly shaped with a bulbous crown. My breath quickens and my fingers close around the table knife. Heat pools between my legs, and I swallow. By the time I tear my gaze back to his face, he's raising a brow.

Right. He asked a question.

"There's nothing to eat, so I had to cut these vegetables."

The corners of his lips twitch. "Do you answer every question with an accusation?"

"Maybe if you'd given me what I wanted last night, I wouldn't have to imagine these vegetables were you." I pick up a zucchini and start slicing it.

He steps closer, and his nearness makes my skin break out in a sweat. I clutch the knife and straighten.

"I have something for you." He reaches around me for a wok and places it on the stove, then he opens the refrigerator and retrieves a bottle of oil.

"What are you doing?" I ask.

"Making breakfast with the proceeds of your massacre." He pours a splash of liquid into the wok and turns on the flame before giving my chopped vegetables a pointed glance. "Is there anything in there I should know about?"

It takes a second for his comment to fully register, and my cheeks burn. He won't let me forget about that time I sliced through that man's dick.

"I wasn't..." I shake my head, refusing to be flustered. "That depends on what kind of meat you keep in your fridge."

Leroi snorts. It's the gentlest of sounds, his expression unchanged, and I can't help but feel a thrill at having amused him. He reaches for the cut vegetables and throws them into the wok, creating an explosion of sizzling aromas.

He flicks his head toward the refrigerator. "Get a box of eggs, some soy sauce, and start cracking them into the mixture."

I do as he says, not quite believing I'm making an omelet in a strange apartment and with a hitman who hasn't laid a hand on me apart from a spanking, even though he's seen me naked.

Leroi directs me to add some herbs to the bubbling mixture of eggs and vegetables, and the kitchen fills with the scent of cooking.

It's so surreal that for a minute, I wonder if I'm trapped in a fever dream, still trapped in the basement. I can't believe I'm free. Dad is dead and so are his bastard sons, but somehow it's true. Yet I can't even enjoy this moment because it's been ages since I saw any footage of Gabriel.

"What's wrong?" Leroi asks.

"I'm thinking of my brother."

"We can look through the leads I've gathered while we eat."

"You've found something?" I ask.

He nods. "Miko gathered photos of every guard who worked for Capello in the past six years. You should recognize some of them from the night they assaulted your mother."

My shoulders stiffen, my skin breaks out in goosebumps, despite the kitchen's heat. I hold my face into a neutral mask and ask, "What about Pietro?"

"The man who took you to your grandmother?" Leroi asks with a frown.

"No, our driver was Felix. Pietro worked for the twins. He's the one who drove me to my assignments."

He tilts his head. "Assignments?"

I feel myself pale, every ounce of blood draining from my face and racing toward my frantically beating heart. My spine stiffens, and my empty stomach twists into knots. I'm not supposed to tell anyone what Dad and the twins used me for.

TWENTY

LEROI

Seraphine bows her head, hiding her face. I wait for her to elaborate on these assignments, but she remains silent. Now is the perfect opportunity to find out more about Anton's methods without revealing I know the identity of her trainer.

Turning off the stove, I place my fingers beneath her chin and lift her face so our eyes meet. Even then, she drops her gaze as if she can't bear the weight of her shame.

"May I have some chocolate?" she asks. It's a poor attempt to change the subject.

"I don't have any. I'm allergic."

"Oh." She shuffles on her feet, clutching both hands to her chest.

"After breakfast, you will tell me what you mean."

Her eyes widen. "You're going to let me eat?"

"Withholding food was used to control you in that basement?"

She nods.

"I will never hold food over you as a reward or punishment. Is that understood?" I wait for her to nod again before continuing. "Now, fill two glasses with orange juice and take them and some silverware out to the balcony."

Seraphine scurries off to do as I ask, and I divide the omelet into two portions, my chest tightening with the urge to give her every ounce of my protection. I can't stop thinking of the videos Miko showed me of powerful men being set up by Capello to perform career-damaging acts in front of cameras.

Did they force Seraphine to put their targets in compromising positions? How could Anton have put a girl into a situation so reprehensible? No women or children. That was the code.

I take the plates through the living room to find her sitting outside at the balcony table with her head still bowed. The morning sun illuminates her hair with a golden halo, making her look even more angelic with the rest of her features in shadow. Ignoring the ache in my heart, I set the plate in front of her.

"Eat."

She stares down at the omelet, her shoulders hunching. Her posture turns rigid, as though she can't believe I'm allowing her to eat, despite her withholding information.

I slide into the seat opposite. "We won't talk about these assignments until after you've eaten."

Her tension eases, and she picks up her knife and fork. We eat in silence, but I feel her gaze on me as I chew. I update her on what we've found out about Gabriel, and she leans forward to soak in my words without making eye contact.

Each time I glance up, she dips her head, her cheeks flaming. It's hard to reconcile this timid creature with the little devil who held me at knifepoint while grinding on my cock. Or perhaps she's remembering last night when she begged and pleaded for my touch.

My cock stirs at the memory of her writhing on my lap, her pussy dripping with arousal. I clench the cutlery, trying to force away that image. Our arrangement is not about my desires. Its only purpose is her training. To tame her impulses so she's no longer destined for the electric chair. Besides, whatever she's going to reveal next will be traumatic.

The distant rumble of traffic far below us is the only sound as we eat the rest of our breakfast. At this time of the year, Beaumont is crammed with tourists that fill the city with traffic and crowds. Up here in the penthouse, it's quiet enough for a man to gather his thoughts.

I had planned on training Seraphine using Anton's methods, but her situation is far more complex than mine ever was. I was never forced to follow Anton's instructions, and I saw the man as a role model. Any reminder of my mentor might send her into a darker space. And from what I gather from yesterday's conversation, she's had no closure.

Seraphine never had a chance to face her abusers because I killed Capello and his sons. Anton is alive and well, but I can't hand over a father figure for her to execute. Without him to clean up after the death of my stepfather, the state of New Alderney might have tried me in court as an adult and given me life imprisonment or the electric chair.

I owe Anton my life, but does that mean I should protect a predator?

Minutes later, she's demolished her omelet and finished the last of her juice. I take her plate and set it to one side.

"Tell me about these assignments." It's not a request, but she hesitates.

Stiffening, she clenching her hands into fists. "I can't say."

"Can't or won't?" I ask, my voice gentle.

"You'll make me leave again."

"Seraphine."

Her head snaps up, but she still doesn't meet my gaze.

"Whatever they forced you to do wasn't your fault. Do you understand?" I ask.

She clamps her eyes shut as if trying to block out the world. Her breath catches as she gasps for air. Every muscle in her body trembles in double time to the rapid rise and fall of her chest. She's on the verge of a panic attack.

Sympathy twists my gut as I watch her struggle. I can understand her overwhelming sense of dread. I've never had sexual contact with anyone I assassinated. Dealing with Miko was a hundred times easier. At least we had some common ground.

"Let's try something different," I say.

———

I take Seraphine up to the rooftop terrace, an open space with panoramic views of the city. The morning sun shines down on us from a clear blue sky, drenching us in soft light. Concrete flower beds and potted shrubs break up the expanse, turning the space into an oasis of color and fragrance.

I guide her to a shaded corner of paving stones that Miko calls the chill-out zone and lower myself onto the thick mat that's built into the floor. After indicating for her to sit cross-legged in front of me, I begin.

"Meditation is a technique that has helped me with facing the past. It's helpful for discipline."

She sits forward, her pretty features furrowing into a frown. "You think I can't control myself?"

I raise both brows. "What do you think?"

Her lips pinch into a thin line and the rest of her features tighten into a scowl. "I know what it's like to want to lash out and drain a bastard's life with your hands, but that won't find you Gabriel."

"And meditation will?"

"Staying calm and detached can make the difference between success or failure."

She raises a shoulder, still not convinced.

"Close your eyes," I say.

When she obeys, I talk her through a guided breathing exercise to help her focus on the movement of air through her body. It's a repeat of the meditation CD Anton made me listen to every morning while I was his apprentice.

Seraphine's features remain pinched, as though she's annoyed and thinks we're wasting time meditating when we should be hitting the streets. She's oblivious to the fact that she's spiraling toward being a serial killer.

Hell, I still don't understand why she stabbed a man in the eye for talking shit, but then, this is the same young woman who murdered eight men when only one of them needed to die.

The world doesn't take kindly to serial killers even if they started out blameless. The state of New Alderney won't care that she was twisted and bent and corrupted until her knee-jerk reaction to stress turned deadly. Those who failed to protect a minor are more likely to condemn her for not rising above her abuse, even though such a feat would be impossible. She's full of righteous anger, but she's lacking self-control.

By the time the breathing exercise is over, her posture

and face have relaxed. It's going to take more than one session of meditation to calm her mind, let alone soothe her spirit. I hope to hell that wiping out every man who assaulted her mother will give her the peace she needs to lead a murder-free life.

"Well done," I say. "We'll do this every day until the habit becomes ingrained."

She opens her eyes and nods.

"How does that feel?"

"Better," she sighs.

"Are you ready to tell me about these assignments?" I ask.

She bows her head. "What if you decide you don't want to help me?"

My breath hitches. Compared to the poker massacre, what could she find so terrible? When she cringes, I remember that Anton trained her as a Lolita assassin. I don't need to read the Vladimir Nabokov book to guess what the hell that entailed.

"Come here." I beckon her over.

After a moment of hesitation, she shuffles across the mat, so we're sitting so closely that I feel the heat of her smaller body.

"Would you prefer to tell me while on my lap?" I ask.

She crawls into my arms and sinks into my embrace. I tighten my grip and dip my head, inhaling her strawberry-scented shampoo.

My heart aches. Having her pressed against me is an unexpected comfort. I want to press a kiss on her temple and whisper that everything will be alright, but I stay silent. No matter how much I want to protect Seraphine, it's impossible to give protection from her inner darkness.

"Talk." My stomach twists into a knot of dread, thinking about what she will reveal.

Her situation was horrifying when it only involved the Capellos. Knowing that Anton is in the mix is like a knife to the heart.

TWENTY-ONE

SERAPHINE

I thought sitting on Leroi's lap with my back resting on his chest would be calming. It's anything but. Anxiety tightens the lining of my stomach, turning the omelet I just ate into lead bricks. I'm not so frightened about Leroi's reaction. He's a killer just like me, but I am worried he'll think I'm damaged beyond repair.

"Seraphine." His deep voice vibrates up and down my spine. "Nothing you could say would make me turn away from you. No matter how bad it is, I'll still be here."

He tightens his arms around my middle, creating a cocoon of trust. Maybe he's right. He didn't shoot me through the skull when I held a knife to his throat, and he didn't even get angry when my second blade could have sliced through his shaft.

Closing my eyes, I lean back against Leroi's strong chest and fall into a sense of calm. If I'm going to admit to what I've done, then facing away from Leroi is the best way to do it.

"Start where you left off," I say. "Your driver took you to see your grandmother."

"Alright." I lick my lips. "Things got worse when Dad came to Nanna's house with the same bodyguards. They took her away in one car, and I rode in the back with Dad."

"Where was your brother?" he asks.

"Staying the night at his girlfriend's," I rasp.

"What did Capello say?"

"Dad told me that Mom was dead along with my real father, and that I would have to repay him for every penny he wasted thinking I was his daughter."

Leroi's breathing is deep and even, just like the relaxation exercise. When he doesn't speak, I continue.

"The twins were waiting for me in the basement," I say, my voice hitching. "They must have spent the day getting things prepared because the door had already been secured with a fingerprint lock."

I pause, my breath mirroring Leroi's, and try to relax in the warmth of his embrace. It's impossible as the muscles around my lungs tighten, making it difficult to exhale.

"Was this the first time you'd met Samson and Gregor?" Leroi asks.

"Yes," I say with a sigh. "Dad called me their little sister, but he talked about me like I was a dog that needed to be fed and watered. He said that if they couldn't take care of their new pet, he would hand me over to someone more deserving. And then..."

Beneath me, Leroi goes perfectly still.

The words wither on my tongue and turn to ashes. I can't talk about how they waited for Dad to leave before forcing me to strip or how Gregor mocked my body and said I wasn't worth his time.

My head bows. "You already know the rest."

"When did they install the chip?" Leroi asks.

"After they realized the collar wouldn't be enough."

"And when did they fit the collar?"

I blow out a breath and fix my gaze on the clouds, wishing I could float away like them, and hoping he won't freak out. "The first week, I bit a chunk out of Samson's dick. Gregor came back the next day with a collar and called me an animal, but after that Samson was never the same."

"What do you mean?" Leroi asks.

"The bite became infected and Samson got a fever. By the time someone forced him to see the doctor, it was too late."

"Was it amputated?"

"I think so," I pause, lost in the memory. "Samson never pulled out his dick on me after that."

Leroi hesitates. "What happened next?"

"They beat and starved me until I was so weak that I stopped moving. Dad eventually found out, and they offered me another way to pay him back."

"Which was?"

"To kill three people in exchange for them freeing Nanna, Gabriel, and myself."

"How did he expect a sixteen-year-old girl to do something so dangerous?"

"He brought in a handler to train me," I tell him. "I didn't want to do it, but I was so hungry and just wanted the pain and the electric shocks to end."

Leroi's chest deflates with a sigh. "This... handler. What did he do?"

"He made sure I was eating right and forced me to exercise. He warned the twins to back off because I needed to look pretty and healthy to be a convincing assassin."

His body stiffens. "What else?"

I raise a shoulder. "He made me practice with syringes over and over, with my hands behind my back, tied above my head, and in all kinds of awkward positions. I had to learn human anatomy, pressure points, and where to plunge a knife."

He relaxes as though relieved. Was he expecting worse?

"After five months, the handler said I was ready, and that's when I got the chip."

"So you wouldn't escape," he says, his voice flat. "Even though they were holding what was left of your family captive?"

My head bows, and I rest my chin on my breastbone. Of all the shit I've been through in the past five years, that was the worst. Until then, I was fighting to stay alive. If the police raided Dad's house, I could explain that they were the bad guys, and I was the victim. If I'd been thinking straight, maybe I wouldn't have been so gullible.

"It was a trick," I tell him.

"What do you mean?"

"The first man I killed was really important. I didn't know until afterward, when the handler left a note with his name, saying that everyone would come after my head if I ever told anyone."

"What was his name?" I ask.

I shake my head. There's no way a man like Leroi won't recognize the name. Even if Dad didn't talk about him all the time, his name was everywhere around town. The man I injected with poison owned a hotel, a casino, and a shipping company.

"Seraphine, I won't be able to protect you unless I know who might want you dead."

"His name was Enzo," I rasp. "Enzo Montesano."

Leroi stops breathing.

My stomach plummets. This is it. This is the moment Leroi decides I'm too much of a burden. He'll cast me out without even offering me the apartment next door.

"Did you know him?"

"He was my uncle."

The words hit like an icy fist, and I lurch forward, trying to spring out of Leroi's lap. His arms tighten around my waist, holding me in place. I wriggle, my heart beating in triple time to Leroi's gentle thrum, but he's too strong.

Shit. I knew talking about the assignments would be trouble, but I never thought Leroi would be connected to anyone I killed. At any moment, he could wrap a hand around my throat and crush my windpipe, but his hold remains on my waist, gathering me back into his lap.

"You must hate me," I whisper.

"I don't," he murmurs, his breath feathering my ear. "It's not your fault. Capello and his sons risked your life by sending you to him as an assassin."

"But he was your uncle."

"Who would never have gotten into that position if he didn't mess with an underage girl," he growls. "Were you hurt?"

I gulp, and it feels like swallowing lead. "N-not really."

"What does that mean?"

"He died. Killing him means that nothing he did to me counted."

I'm still trembling when his grip loosens. Leroi is right about his uncle and all the others I killed. They deserved to die because they were predators. I should apologize for his loss, but I'm not sorry.

"Are you still going to help me?" I ask, my words halting.

"Yes."

"Why, when I killed your uncle?"

Leroi sighs. "I can overlook a whole lot of shit. Rape isn't one of them. Messing with underage girls is unforgivable. You cleansed the world of one more monster."

"But the handler said that Enzo Montesano's men would be looking for me." I trail off, letting him fill in the gaps.

"Everyone thought he died of a heart attack. There was no mention of a girl."

"I injected him with poison and smothered him with a pillow."

Leroi pauses. "Are you sure he didn't hurt you?"

"Not any more than the others."

"There were others."

My breath shallows, and shame settles in my stomach like a stone. After that night, I was trapped. The twins told me I was the most wanted person in New Alderney and I had to keep killing if I wanted their protection.

"Every few months, they'd send me to kill some man. I had to memorize his face and the pictures of his associates. They didn't even free Gabriel because now I owed them for protecting me from Enzo Montesano's sons."

"Shit," he hisses.

"I'm glad they're dead, but I wish I was the one who had killed them."

"Yeah." He tightens his arms around me. "So do I. That's why I plan on helping you take down every guard who worked with Capello to destroy your family."

My eyelids flutter shut, and I melt against his broad chest. For the first time since I arrived in Leroi's apartment, I feel a sense of peace and hope. Peace, knowing that Leroi will help me slay my demons. Hope at the thought he might help me to be normal, like him.

I've never felt so at ease with a man, but I'm not stupid. Men are as changeable as the weather. One moment, you're basking in the sunshine of their love, thinking it's going to be warm forever, then it only takes one dark cloud or a gust of wind can ruin things forever. In the space of twenty-four hours, I went from being Dad's sweet princess to the chew toy of his psychopathic twins.

Leroi's generosity has an expiry date. I have to make sure to leave him or kill him before he changes his mind. Because he eventually will. I can't really trust anyone.

"You did well this morning," he whispers against my ear. "And your rewards are mounting up."

His words don't spark any kind of excitement. My eyes open, and I gaze around the rooftop garden, the flowers I once thought vibrant, now dull. All this talk about my past has left me wrung out and drained.

The only way to feel right again is to spill blood.

"Can I see the pictures you gathered of the guards?" I ask.

Leroi helps me to my feet and guides me to a wooden bench where he takes out his phone. With a few taps, he brings up the photos.

The first few faces are unfamiliar and not the ones that haunt my dreams. I'm about to lose hope of ever finding those bastards when I meet a pair of cornflower-blue eyes set within cruel, angular features. They belong to a blond man I last saw lying on the floor of Dad's office with his throat slit.

"That's him," I whisper.

Leroi pauses. "Who?"

"Dad says he was my real father."

"Raphael Orlando?"

"I only knew him as Raphael," I mutter. "He was our guard, but he never talked to me."

Leroi doesn't speak, instead he lets me stare at the photo for as long as I want. Raphael looks nothing like me, apart from the hair and eyes. Dad was dark-haired with green eyes. He always said I got my looks from Mom, but now, I'm not so sure.

"Do you think he knew?" I ask.

"Your mother certainly did," Leroi says.

I tear my gaze off Raphael's picture to meet Leroi's deep brown eyes. "What makes you think that?"

"Raphael is the name of an archangel, as is Gabriel, and your name is suspiciously close to the word seraphim. The affair probably started before your brother was born."

My jaw clenches. I had thought the same during my darkest days, when I lay starving and shivering, cursing everyone for my predicament. How could Dad punish Mom's infidelity when he already had a wife and family?

"Do you think she told Raphael?" I ask.

"It would have been obvious," Leroi says, mirroring my thoughts. "All of Capello's children were dark-haired and green-eyed. Raphael probably kept his distance because he suspected you were his."

I nod, my throat constricting. So, it wasn't just one father figure who rejected me, but two. Raphael could have taken us and ran but he chose to stay and was killed for it.

"How was any of this my fault?"

"It wasn't," he replies.

The backs of my eyes burn. Not with grief or unshed tears, but with the pit of resentment that's simmered in my veins since my life turned to shit.

"They were selfish," I rasp.

Mom and Raphael risked everything for their affair, and now they're dead. Dead and gone, like the girl I used to be. Raphael had to have known Dad was a monster, but I can't believe they ignored the risks that came with crossing him.

I swipe past Raphael's picture to another photo I don't recognize, but stop at the next. Dark brown eyes stare out from craggy features that have haunted my nightmares since the beginning of my imprisonment.

"You recognize him?" Leroi asks.

"He's the one who wrapped his hands around Mom's throat," I say through clenched teeth.

"Julio Catania," Leroi replies. "He's still alive and still living in New Alderney."

"Let's go after him now." I move to get up, but he wraps his large hand around mine.

Leroi exhales. "He's not going anywhere, and we still have to search through the rest of the photos."

I give him a sharp nod, my fingers itching to draw blood.

Finally, we're making some progress.

TWENTY-TWO

SERAPHINE

We spent the rest of the morning looking through pictures of Dad's employees. It's easy to remember the ones I want to kill because they feature prominently in my recurrent nightmares.

Sometimes, I'm not peeping through the gap in the door, I'm inside the room, screaming at them to stop. Other times, Dad grabs me and hands me over to his guards.

After so much time in captivity or in the company of perverts, my brain has filled in the gaps so the dreams are as vivid as real life.

In the end, we only find four viable targets out of the seven men who attacked Mom: Julio Catania, Paolo Rochas, Mike Ferante, and Edoardo Barone. Two others were killed when Leroi detonated explosions around the mansion, while another died last year.

I hope they're suffering in hell along with Dad and the twins because any death that isn't the result of slow torture is far too quick.

We also found the twins' driver, Pietro Fiori, who took

me to and from my assignments. I'm not sure if I want him dead. He never once threatened to detonate my chip with the remote, and there were times when he got out of the car to carry me into the back seat because I'd been injured. But then, he knew I was a prisoner but failed to help. Leroi suspects Pietro might know where Dad has hidden Gabriel. I'm not so sure, but that won't stop me from slicing pieces of his flesh until he screams something useful.

While new sofas are being delivered to replace the blood-soaked ones that were disposed of, I pass time coloring in pages from the book I bought from Wonderland.

When I get bored with filling in the lines, I pull out the blank notebook and draw a picture of Leroi sitting in the full lotus position with his hands resting on his knees. His eyes are closed in meditation, and empty thought bubbles rise from his head.

My lips curl into a smile. Beside him, I draw myself, mirroring his pose, except my thought bubbles contain screaming faces and knives dripping with blood. After coloring my hair with the yellow felt tip, I tilt my head and examine my work.

Leroi thinks that killing the men on my list will cleanse my thoughts. That after the last man is dead, I'll no longer be haunted by my past, but I'm not sure that's true. I add little red droplets to my thought bubbles and make them drip into my hands.

Afterward, Leroi takes me across town to a high-rise building overlooking the ocean.

"Is this where Pietro lives?" I ask as we exit the car.

"We're visiting an associate who will make you look less like yourself." Leroi places a hand on the small of my back and leads me up a paved walkway to the building's entrance.

I shrug him off. "Why are we wasting time on disguises? Gabriel needs us now."

Leroi's steps halt. He turns to face me, his eyes sharpening. "How many men did the Capello's force you to kill?"

"Why do you want to know?" I ask.

"Humor me."

My fists clench. Can't he see the situation is urgent? We spent all morning eating, meditating, and getting deliveries. Now that we're ready to get started, he wants to add one more useless task. I shoot him a glare, still not understanding why he wants to know my kill count.

"Don't know," I mutter.

"Guess." His stare intensifies until my skin begins to itch.

Teaming up with Leroi was a mistake. Each time he's on the verge of giving me what I want, he withdraws. Now that we have a lead on Pietro, he wants to make a detour. This is just like how he got me so close to my first orgasm last night and then tied my wrists behind my back to leave me aching.

The weight of his glare is suffocating, but I refuse to cower. Leroi's eyes are too dark, too penetrating. It's like he's peering under my skin and looking into the ugly void.

My nostrils flare. The urge to claw at him spreads across my flesh like wildfire, but I force my hands behind my back. As soon as I find Gabriel and kill those men, I'll hollow Leroi's eyes until he's crying blood.

For now, I'll be civil and remind him of what's really important.

"Gabriel could be all alone without food or water—"

"I asked you a question, Seraphine," he says.

"Maybe twenty. I lost count."

"Twenty or more deaths under similar circumstances, with each man last seen with an angelic little blonde."

"So?" I snap.

He raises a brow as though the conclusion is obvious. "The only reason there isn't a manhunt for you is because Capello suppressed any investigations with the shit-ton of dirt he had on the police."

My lips tighten. "I don't have time for this. We need to find Gabriel."

"The only reason the relatives and associates of the men you killed haven't found you is because Capello kept you in a basement."

"What's your point?"

"Your appearance is too distinctive. Eventually, someone will recognize you as the girl who was seen on the arm of multiple dead men and word will spread. Finding Gabriel will be the least of your worries if you become a target."

Oh... I hadn't thought of that. Tearing my gaze away from Leroi's, I walk toward the building's entrance.

"Besides, Fiori will disappear if word gets out that he's being hunted by a little blonde angel," Leroi adds.

I scoff. "You should see what I did to the last man who called me that."

"Don't tell me you stabbed him in the eye." He opens a door that leads to a huge art deco hallway.

"I electrocuted him in the bathtub."

"Bullshit." He strides down the corridor. "Most circuits are designed to shut off power if there's any risk of electrocution."

"Then why did he die twitching?"

We cross a black-and-white tiled hallway of ebony walls adorned with paintings of flapper girls. I have to walk fast to keep up with his long strides. At the elevator, he glances down at me, his gaze skeptical.

"Did you drug him first?" He presses the call button.

"Why do you ask?"

"Did you?" The elevator doors open, but he doesn't step inside. "Well, did you?"

Walking in, I mutter, "He would have jumped out of the tub otherwise."

Leroi snorts.

I whirl around. "What?"

He selects the eleventh floor. "If he was convulsing, then it was an overdose. The poison you injected your target with killed him, not the electricity."

"You don't know that." I cross my arms. "Anyway, why are you so bothered by all the minor details?"

"Because you're reckless. The toaster you threw into the man's bath would have attracted attention, or at least started a fire. You also could have gotten yourself electrocuted."

"Hairdryer," I mutter.

"What?"

"I threw a hairdryer into his bath. The toaster oven would have needed an extension lead, and it was too far away."

Leroi shakes his head. "You must have a guardian angel because anyone else in your position would have gotten caught."

The elevator doors open, and we step out into a hallway lined with black doors. Leroi takes a right turn and leads us to the apartment at the very end. Before he gets a chance to ring the bell, the door swings open, revealing a tall, thin man wearing a pink kimono and a flesh-colored wig cap. He's blessed with a natural beauty, high cheekbones, a pert nose, and thick, dark lashes that don't need makeup.

His gaze passes over Leroi and lands straight on me. "This is the girl?"

Leroi nods. "Can you help her?"

"What's your name, sweetheart?" the man asks with a broad grin.

"You don't need to know." Leroi shoves his way inside, making the thinner man stumble backward with a shriek. "This is Farfalla. Don't hurt him."

Farfalla steps aside and lets me in. I cast him a wary glance, but his eyes only radiate warmth.

My gaze lands on an indigo velvet sofa that takes center stage of his apartment, adorned with silver throw pillows. The walls are painted cream, and the artwork is so colorful that my eyes hurt. Fashion sketches hang beside magazine covers in gilded frames and three-dimensional paintings.

A jazz instrumental fills the room, along with faint hints of incense. Vague memories of art lessons rise to the surface, but I shove them back. I'm no longer the carefree girl who took cookery and art classes at an expensive private school.

Leroi walks through the colorful space as though he's seen it all before and leans against a wall. "We need a subtle disguise that will make her look less—"

"Angelic?" Farfalla asks with a raised brow.

My lips thin. "Don't call me that."

Farfalla's gaze snaps to Leroi's, and something unspoken exchanges between them. I take another look at the man, wondering if there's more to him than his harmless appearance.

He gazes down at me, his features softening. "If you want to look less distinctive, you'll need heavier makeup, darker hair, and a change in eye color."

"Is that really necessary?" I ask.

"Yes," Leroi says.

Farfalla leads me into a dressing room illuminated by a vanity mirror surrounded by lightbulbs. Clothes racks take up most of the walls, each displaying an array of feminine costumes. It's obvious that he's some kind of performer. A sink sits in the corner beside a wall-mounted hood dryer and chair, where there's already a box of store-bought hair dye.

Leroi slips a stopper beneath the door to keep it wedged open. I try not to bristle that he doesn't trust me alone with his friend and instead focus on Farfalla.

He tilts his head, his gaze wistful. "It's almost a shame to dye such lovely hair."

"Then darken it with coffee," I say.

Both men stare down at me like I've said something crazy.

I raise a shoulder. Whenever Dad was away on long business trips, Mom used to experiment with her hair. Sometimes, she would go lighter with lemon juice or chamomile, other times, she would change her shade of blonde to something warmer.

Being her guinea pig in those hair experiments was fun. Mom was always a different person when Dad wasn't around. She wore different clothes and went out to meet girlfriends.

I used to love helping her choose her outfits and wished she would invite these glamorous female friends over to the house for coffee. Her excuse was always the same. These women were old money. They lived in the illustrious Alderney Hills and wouldn't care to visit a house in Queen's Gardens. She'd just blow me a kiss and leave with Raphael the bodyguard and not return until the next day or the day after.

It took her death and my imprisonment to work out that these 'ladies' nights' were a sham. Casting aside the bitterness, I zone back into the conversation and ask, "Don't you know about natural hair remedies?"

Farfalla grins. "Leroi can brew the rounds of coffee. While we're waiting for the pigment to darken your hair, I'll teach you how to apply makeup and fit your contact lenses."

The thought of playing dress-up while Gabriel is festering in a darkened room makes my throat thicken with so much guilt that my breath stalls. I hate that Leroi has a point. All my missions were carefully planned so I would meet the target with few witnesses. Even if I was spotted, it was only briefly.

The twins worked out my exit routes and always had Pietro waiting to drive me away. I escaped mostly unscathed. A disguise might allow me to move about without anyone connecting me to former missions.

Leroi heads toward a kitchen area behind the sofa and opens and closes cupboards without complaint. This man isn't like my captors. He lets me talk to people and we've been outside every day. He hasn't taken advantage of me, unlike every man I've met since Dad handed me to the twins. When he disappears out of sight, my chest tightens until he returns with a coffeepot.

My jaw clenches. I can't grow too attached. For sixteen years, I was Dad's princess, until he decided that I wasn't. Leroi might be the most attractive and interesting man I've met in my entire existence. He might even be my perfect match, but that doesn't mean he won't stab me in the back.

Which is why I plan to stab him first.

TWENTY-THREE

LEROI

I lean against the living room wall, watching Farfalla teach Seraphine how to contour her eyes. She looks so at ease with Farfalla that it's hard to believe the trauma she's suffered.

It's hard to tear my gaze away from her when she's so vibrant and happy. She's so mesmerized by the process that her posture relaxes as she applies pigment with a makeup brush. When Farfalla places a hand on Seraphine's shoulder, I stiffen, expecting the worst. But she glances up at Farfalla and smiles. It's the same radiant expression she gave the redhead at Wonderland. Maybe that's because she doesn't see either of them as a threat.

Yet another glimpse of the mystery that is Seraphine.

I could spend all morning staring at this girl applying makeup, but the Capello job has more loose ends than a rag rug. If Seraphine is ever going to have a normal life, I need to fasten them tighter than a garotte.

Our first lead is Pietro Fiori, the driver assigned to the Capello twins who also took Seraphine to and from her murderous missions. According to Miko's research, he lives alone in a house close to Capello's estate. I expect he's probably enjoying a few days of paid leave, thanks to the death of his employers.

I glance down at my phone and fire up one of the many surveillance cameras Miko and I set up to observe Capello's movements. Construction workers have already cleared the rubble from our explosions and are rebuilding the damaged wing. Some of their vehicles are parked a street away from our target, so we will have to be careful when extracting Fiori. Too many witnesses.

A text from Miko appears on the screen.

Tracked the deposit from an offshore account linked to the Di Marco Law Group.

My eyes narrow, and I wait for Miko to elaborate.

The next text contains a hyperlink that leads to a page on the New Alderney Times with the headline: OPENING DAY OF HOTEL MARISOL

A photo appears of Frederic and Marisol Capello holding a ribbon beside a gray-haired man in his late sixties in the foyer of a luxury hotel. The caption reads: *Frederic Capello and Di Marco Law Group Chairman, Joseph Di Marco, at the opening day of Hotel Marisol.*

Another link appears, which leads to a page that announces the engagement of Joseph Di Marco's daughter to Samson Capello. My brows rise. I wonder how Samson explained his rotted penis to his fiancée.

I send a message back to Miko.

Great work. Are you sure the funds came from Joseph Di Marco directly? How about someone else in the firm?

He replies immediately, likely expecting my question:
Working on it.

Miko and I work our way through everyone in the Di

Marco Law Group who might be powerful enough to have access to the funds to pay for a hit, but find no one else but its chairman. Joseph Di Marco is the only lawyer in the firm with strong ties to the Capello family. He has no partners and even his senior employees don't appear to be connected to any major families in the underworld.

This leaves me with two options: kill the old man or present him with the dead body of someone convincing enough and with enough connections to have pulled off the massacre.

"What do you think?" Farfalla's voice cuts through my thoughts.

I glance up from the phone to lock gazes with Seraphine and have to take a second look.

Her hair is now a tantalizing brown with tawny high-lights that betray no trace of her previous blonde. It's a stark contrast to her delicate porcelain features, which now appear sharper, seductive, sophisticated.

My breath hitches. Without meaning to, I close the distance between us for a closer look.

Her new eye color isn't just brown. It's a warm copper with flecks of gold that glimmer in the light. It's like gazing into the depths of a fire and wanting to be consumed by the flames.

Damn it. This girl is turning me into a fucking poet. I need to stop looking at her, but I'm enthralled.

"Don't tell me I can't work miracles," Farfalla says, his voice dousing the flames of my fascination.

I blink away the vision of her to regain focus. "You look older."

Seraphine tilts her head, wanting me to elaborate.

Farfalla gasps. "You can't say that to a lady!"

"It's not..." I clear my throat. "It's a compliment."

The corners of Seraphine's lips lift into the tiniest of smiles, twisting the frayed fibers of my heart. I shake my head and cast off the strange ache.

What does it matter if Seraphine only shows her happiness to Farfalla and the girl at Wonderland? She doesn't need to get entangled with another killer. I'm a reminder of the life she needs to leave. As soon as she finds her brother and avenges her mother's assault, I'll set her free to start the life she deserves.

The drive across Beaumont to Queen's Gardens is silent. Half the properties in the exclusive gated community are mansions hidden behind acres of land and tall trees. The smaller buildings assigned to staff and security are well within the gates, but far enough away to be hidden from the main house.

A man as paranoid as Frederic Cappello makes his non-essential employees live beyond his gates, and that's where we'll find Pietro Fiori.

I glance at Seraphine through the rearview mirror, trying to decipher what she's thinking. She's eerily calm for someone who is approaching the location of her captivity. It's disturbing. Even if they only transported her in and out of the mansion at night, she should be feeling something.

"Are you alright?" I ask.

"I'm fine," she replies, her voice emotionless and flat.

She isn't, but I don't know her well enough to decipher her blank state or lack of body language. I won't push, either. At least not now, while I'm half distracted by driving.

Seraphine's unpredictability is only charming when she's half-naked over my lap and getting a well-deserved spanking.

"We lived in a house like this," she says.

"You and your brother?"

She nods. "And Mom. She always told us Dad was away on business, but he had a second family. Do you think she knew?"

"Do you want the truth?"

"You're going to say she must have known."

"Frederic Capello was one of New Alderney's most prominent businessmen. It would be impossible for her not to have known he was married."

"Right," she rasps.

We fall silent for several minutes, passing tall hedges, walls of conifers, and the ornate iron gates until we reach the outskirts of the Cappello estate. If there was something I could say to ease her mind, I would say it, but nothing could ever compensate for the torment she suffered after Capello's betrayal.

As a small fleet of construction vans pass, it occurs to me to ask, "Was your mother's house also in Queen's Gardens?"

When she doesn't reply, I glance at her through the rearview mirror again. Her eyes are closed, showcasing thick, black lashes and smokey lids, and her red lips pursed.

Is she meditating?

After exhaling a long breath through her nostrils, she says, "Yes."

"Fuck," I growl.

"I should have known Dad had a second family," she mutters.

"How?" I ask. "If you lived behind one of these gates, I expect your life was sheltered."

Her shoulders rise toward her ears. "Mom and Dad didn't allow me to use the internet, and we had limited access at school, but maybe I could have—"

"Don't blame yourself," I say. "You were a child."

She glances out of the window and blows out a long breath. "Right."

We reach the Capello estate's front gates, which are wide open to let in construction vehicles. At the far end of the drive, is a glimpse of the building work.

If Di Marco is hiring assassins to take out his buddy's killer, is he also the one responsible for ordering the repairs? It's possible that he's readying the family home for its new owner—the Cappello daughter Roman wanted me to kill.

Around the corner is a street of smaller houses, where we'll find the man who drove Seraphine to and from her missions. Since he knew about her, it's possible that he also knows about Gabriel.

"I've already looked up Fiori's vehicle," I tell her. "We're going to place a tracker on it and watch his movements. If he leaves Queen's Gardens, we'll know."

"Why don't we break into his house and torture him for information?" she asks.

"It's broad daylight, and security in this neighborhood would have doubled since I killed an entire houseful of people. We can't risk getting spotted."

She falls silent for several beats. I wait for her to argue that I'm being too cautious, but she asks, "Okay, what's the plan, then?"

"We wait for him to leave this district and follow him to a less guarded area," I say. "Once he's alone, we'll pull him over and get the information we need."

"Or we can snatch him off the street." She raises a hand and points to a figure carrying a hose toward a car.

Before I can tell her to stick with my plan, the door is open, and she's jumping out into the street.

Fuck.

TWENTY-FOUR

LEROI

Seraphine charges toward the man holding the hose, her newly darkened hair swinging behind her like a war banner. The man, who I can only assume is Pietro Fiori, glances in her direction for a few shocked seconds before dropping his hose and making a run for it.

I grind my teeth, shut off the engine, and reach for a lightweight mask. Disguises can only do so much to hide a person's true appearance. If this man has been ferrying Seraphine to and from her missions, then I'm certain he knows to be wary of the tiny, harmless-looking young woman.

By the time I slip the mask over my head, Fiori is already halfway to reaching the entrance to his house.

Seraphine is quick on her feet, but at five feet nothing, her petite legs can't keep up with the long strides of a man running from a furious assassin. I catch up to Fiori in a few fast strides and slam him into his front door.

He's six-two, with the soft build of a man who doesn't

work out to compensate for spending all day behind the wheel of a vehicle.

"Who are you?" Fiori pushes back against my weight.

I pull out a gun and press it into his temple. "Make a sound, and you're dead."

He sucks in a breath through his teeth, his body trembling.

"What are you doing?" Seraphine hisses from my side. "He's mine."

Fiori shudders. "Oh my god, oh my god. You're alive."

Ignoring them both, I unhook the gun's safety, producing a click that makes him stiffen with a noisy gasp.

"What did I say about making a noise?" I snarl.

Fiori swallows, his head darting toward Seraphine. "Please, don't kill me," he whispers. "I was only doing my job."

My brows rise. I'm the one with a gun to his head and outweigh him by at least fifty pounds, yet he's begging Seraphine for mercy? Interesting.

"Do you live alone?" I ask, already knowing the answer.

He nods furiously.

"Open the door and let us inside," I say. "Answer our questions and nobody gets hurt."

With shaking fingers, he unlocks the door of his house, letting out a cloud of nicotine. Keeping my gun to his head and an arm around his shoulders, I push him forward. Seraphine slips in behind us and closes the door.

We step into a small, tidy living space combined with a kitchenette, with nicotine-stained walls unadorned with art or photos. The only prominent feature is a flat-screen TV mounted on the wall.

"I thought we were going to drag him to the car." Pouting, Seraphine walks into view, making Fiori flinch.

"Well, I'd planned on attaching a tracker to his exhaust and catching up with him in an area less populated by Capello's associates, but you decided to act alone." My grip on Fiori tightens. "Since we're here, let's get the information and get out."

The man shrinks into my chest, his breath coming in panicked gasps. "Keep her away from me. Please."

My gaze darts down to Seraphine's scowl. No matter how many times I look at her, I can't see what's so frightening. After all, I'm the one holding the gun.

"Where's Gabriel?" she asks.

He recoils so closely into me that the pounding of his heart vibrates against my ribs. "W-who? I don't know what you're talking about."

I press the gun harder into his temple. "Don't lie to us."

"Please. I swear, I've never heard of him."

Seraphine glances around the room before striding to the kitchenette. I follow her gaze to a magnetic strip on the wall, holding a set of knives. Instead of approaching them, she opens up cupboard after cupboard before extracting a bottle of lighter fluid.

Fiori whimpers.

"It's in your best interest to answer my questions before she gets creative," I mutter.

"Where did they keep my brother?" Seraphine asks with a scowl.

"I swear, I don't know who that is!" Fiori cries, his voice rising several octaves.

When Seraphine brings the fluid to a pack of cigarettes and lighter at a low table, my stomach forms a knot. If I don't get this guy to talk, Seraphine might start a fire that will attract unwanted attention.

"Did any of your employers order you to make regular deliveries to an address?" I ask.

"Wh-what kind?"

"Food."

"N-no," he shakes his head.

"Not even monthly?"

"The twins drove their own cars. They only called me when they needed me to pick them up from bars and clubs when they were too fucked up to function."

"What else did you do for them?"

"I..." He swallows, turns to Seraphine, and shivers. "I drove her around."

In a much smaller voice, he adds, "She's a killer."

"You had to know they were holding her brother hostage," I snarl. "Didn't you question why someone so young would assassinate dangerous men?"

"They said she was a psycho."

Seraphine splashes the lighter fluid onto the man, hitting me with several droplets. My heart jumps, and a bolt of excitement surges straight to my balls.

Fuck.

No part of me finds being burned alive while clinging onto another man arousing, but my libido thinks anything Seraphine does is a sexual wonder.

"See?" Fiori screams. "I heard she sucked one of them down to the root, bit it off and swallowed it so there would be nothing to reattach. She's crazy."

Seraphine picks up the cigarette lighter, and my dick stirs. I have never in my entire thirty-four years of existence been erect in such close proximity to another man, yet this woman's antics has my dick in a death grip.

"Stay still," I growl, pushing him back to the wall when

Fiori presses his skinny ass so close to my crotch that it's torn between hardening or shriveling.

"They were controlling her through her brother," I snarl. "Tell me what you know about that."

He shakes his head. "They never mentioned a brother, and neither did she. There was only a remote and a chip."

My jaw clenches. He sounds so convincing that if I hadn't seen footage of an emaciated man tied to a chair, I would believe every word.

She flicks the lighter, creating a spark.

"Who else might know about the brother?" I ask.

"I don't know!" His voice becomes shrill.

"Can I burn him now?" Seraphine asks, her voice quickening with impatience.

"Not unless you want to be put to bed with another spanked ass and no orgasm." I adjust my grip around his shoulders to form a chokehold and snarl into his ear, "You're not doing yourself any favors. Give us some names. Tell us what you heard while working for those bastards."

Seraphine flicks the lighter again, this time bringing up a flame. For entirely different reasons, both Fiori and I moan.

"Alright." He wails and trembles. "The twins worked for old man Capello, and he had mistresses all over New Alderney. Maybe the brother lives at one of the places he visited."

"Who would know these addresses?" I ask.

"Bruno Capello." He gulps. "He's Mr. Capello's driver, a third cousin once or twice removed."

"Where do we find him?"

"His house is inside the gates."

Shit.

Seraphine flicks the lighter again and steps closer. "Call him."

"No!" Fiori raises a hand and produces a tiny flick knife. "Stay back."

I hiss through my teeth. How the fuck did I miss that weapon? My gun presses into his temple. "Drop it."

Seraphine rushes forward and reaches for the blade. Before I can order her back, Fiori slashes her palm.

She falls back with a yelp.

My stomach plummets to the floor. My gaze locks onto the blood pooling in her palm. Every barrier I erected over the years to contain my fury disintegrate into nothingness in the presence of her pain.

He hurt Seraphine.

He made her bleed.

My vision fogs with red rage. Rage at letting Seraphine get hurt. Rage at the powerless boy I once was who couldn't stop my bastard stepfather from hurting the two women I was supposed to protect. It clouds my senses, grips my throat, and fills my lungs until I can't breathe.

Fiori gasps. "I'm sorry. It was a reflex. I didn't mean to—"

I tighten my arm around his neck and lift him off his feet. His face turns crimson, and he stares up at me through bulging eyes.

"I can't breathe," he rasps.

"That's the point," I growl.

Fiori wriggles, writhes, and retches for air. I barely notice his struggles because I'm transfixed at the sight of Seraphine's fascination with her bleeding palm.

She gazes down at the blood, her lips parted, her chest rising and falling with rapid breaths. Pink stains her cheeks the way it did when she talked about wanting to have an orgasm.

Seconds pass, and the man continues to fight against my choke hold. Seraphine gazes up at me through those artificially colored eyes and all I want to do is tear off her disguise. I want to see her–not the facade. I want to witness the softening of her features as I end her pain.

Fiori stops struggling and falls limp, his death pushing away the bloody haze. I release my grip around his throat, twist his neck, and let him fall to the floor with a heavy thud.

"Seraphine," I say.

She offers me her wounded palm, her eyes bright. Blood spills from her fingers and down her arm, dripping DNA onto the floor.

I take her wrist. "Let me take care of it."

"Wait." She drops into a crouch and picks up Fiori's dagger. "If he had a knife all along, why didn't he use it earlier?"

"He was waiting for the right moment."

I guide her to the kitchenette, to the first aid box in the corner by the stove. After lifting her onto the counter and opening the kit, I hold her hand under a stream of running water.

"Why are you washing it away?" she asks, her voice breathy.

"You like blood?" I ask with a smirk.

She grins, her eyes sparkling. "It's beautiful."

So, Seraphine smiles at Farfalla, at the woman at the fetish store, and at blood. Interesting. I pat the wound dry with a wipe, only for it to start bleeding again. The cut isn't deep enough to need stitches, so I apply some ointment, gauze and medical tape.

She watches me work with rapt attention, her cheeks still flushed.

"Next time a man comes at you with a knife, don't run toward its blade," I say.

"Alright," she grumbles.

Her delicate fingers close around mine in a grip so tight that my heartbeat doubles. I'm about to ask if she also likes pain when something cool lands on my throat.

It's Fiori's knife.

TWENTY-FIVE

SERAPHINE

Leroi has such beautiful veins. When he's angry, they stand out against his skin like little rivers of blue. If I look close enough, I can almost see the hot rush of blood as it disappears beneath his mask.

I press the dagger's blunt edge into his jugular, but he grabs my wrist. Warmth pools in my core, and the pulse between my legs pounds to the rapid beat of my heart.

"What do you think you're doing?" he asks.

My gaze snaps to meet his eyes. They're dark pools that draw me in, daring me to run the blade across his neck and slice his throat. Heat radiates from his fingers into my skin, electrifying the blood coursing through my veins. He squeezes, the sudden pain pulling me back to awareness, but this time, I don't drop the knife.

"Leroi?" I whisper.

"Are you alright?" he asks, his brows a deep furrow.

"No."

He glances to my wounded hand and back into my face. "What do you need?"

I want to see why the blood beneath those veins colors his flesh that unusual shade of blue. I want to nick his skin and find out if the liquid beneath it is vermilion or crimson or magenta, but most of all, I want to clear my head.

Somewhere on the edge of my awareness, I know Pietro gave us another lead, but the last few moments are replaying on an endless loop. Leroi just flew into a protective rage because of a little cut. He strangled Pietro to death because he hurt me, and then he tended my wounds.

Men don't protect women. They only stake their claim. They almost never care if a woman gets hurt unless it's out of some twisted sense of ownership, but Leroi just did the unexpected. Could he be different? The only way I'll know is if I get a peek at what's running in his veins.

"Seraphine." He moves my hand and the knife away from his neck.

"Yes?"

"Tell me what you need," he says, his voice so deep that the muscles of my core constrict.

Shifting on the kitchen counter, I sweep my gaze up his muscular chest. "Touch me."

"What?" He pulls off his mask.

"You said I was racking up the rewards," I whisper. "I want my reward. I want my orgasm."

His nostrils flare. "Bleeding turns you on?"

"Not when it's my blood," I say.

"Then what?"

My throat tightens, and I swallow hard. "I liked it when you killed Pietro."

His pupils dilate, and the hand encircling my wrist tightens. Without another word, he plucks Pietro's dagger from my fingers and cleans it with some antiseptic wipes.

My breath quickens. "Let me do it."

"What do you think I'm going to do?"

"Cut yourself for me," I reply, my voice breathy. "Let me see all that lovely blood."

He chuckles, the sound carrying no warmth. "Is that what you want, little Seraphine?"

"More than anything."

"Even more than that orgasm?"

I nod.

"My blood wasn't part of our bargain," he says. "But since you like blades so much, I'll give you a choice. Do you want to come on my fingers or the knife?"

"The knife," I reply instead of asking what he means.

Leroi steps back. "Take off your panties."

Without hesitating, I lean to the side and ease down my underwear and leggings in one swift movement. Leroi slips off my shoes and pulls the garments down to the floor.

He parts my thighs and stares down at my bare legs and exposed pussy. I tremble with anticipation, feeling exposed, and more vulnerable and needy than I was when he spanked me.

"You're so wet," he says. "Is that for me, little angel?"

"Yes," I whisper.

The pad of his thumb brushes a slow circle over my inner thigh. "Is that sweet little pussy aching for me?"

I nod, my eyes squeezing shut.

"Look at me or I'll stop," he commands.

My eyes snap open, and I'm once again transfixed by the intensity of his stare.

"Good girl."

Even though it's irrational, a part of me preens at his praise. A cool draft wafts over my exposed flesh, and I shiver, my nipples tightening into stiff peaks. I'm a kaleidoscope of conflicting emotions, ranging from arousal to terror. Leroi could slice me open with that dagger he just cleaned, and I would still ache for more.

"Does that turn you on?" he asks, tracing the blade along my inner thigh, cooling my heated flesh. "Do you like it when this blade is so close to cutting slices off your pink little pussy?"

"Yes," I whisper, biting down on my bottom lip. All sensation races to my core and the intensity of his stare makes me grow wetter.

"Yes, what?" His voice hardens.

"Yes, sir."

He slides the cold blade over my wet folds until it's hovering just below my clit. My muscles tighten in anticipation. I don't know if he's going to give me pain or pleasure, but I need to feel something more than this desperate ache. The flat metal glides over my clit, leaving me panting, trembling, and desperate for more.

When he pulls back the dagger, my throat vibrates with a disappointed whimper.

"You want more?" he asks.

"Please, sir." My voice cracks.

"Spread your legs. Show me how much you want it."

I place a palm on each knee and push my thighs so far apart that cool air hits my overheated flesh. This should be embarrassing, but I've never wanted anything more.

"Just like that," he says. "Now, be a good little girl and stay still."

He flips the knife around and presses the handle against my clit. The metal's intricate designs send delicious thrills straight through my core.

Adrenaline races through my veins, making me feel alive for the first time in an eternity. I'm so focused on what he's doing with the knife that all thoughts of revenge fade into the background.

"Oh god," I moan.

"Not god," Leroi growls. "Say my name."

"Leroi."

He grazes the textured head around my clit, making it swell to the point of bursting. "Once more, angel."

"Fuck," I groan. "L-Leroi."

"That's my girl."

Somewhere on the outer reaches of my subconscious, pleasure bubbles up at the thought of being Leroi's anything. I don't dwell on that for long as the metal handle's up-and-down moments push me to the brink.

Pressure builds up behind my clit, and the muscles of my core tighten. Getting pleasured by the hilt of the same dagger used to cut me open and make me bleed is even more intense than getting spanked.

I glance up at Leroi. His face hasn't changed since he caught me reaching for his jugular.

"You look so pretty down there, writhing against this knife," he says. "And look at the mess you're making on the kitchen counter."

My gaze drops to the tiny pool of fluid gathering on the dark surface, and I flush. That can't be all from me because I almost never get aroused. I shake my head, not wanting to admit that something like a knife could get me so excited.

"Don't deny it," Leroi growls. "You love it when I rub your clit with the hilt of a knife. Admit it."

I nod, my heart beating faster.

"Use your words," he says.

"I love it."

"And?"

"And I want more," I say through panting breaths.

My clit feels like a raw nerve, every stroke pushing me to desperate precipices of pleasure. Just as I'm about to explode, the hilt slides down my folds. The sudden absence of the metal is almost too much, and I'm left panting. I cry out but stop when the thick metal circles my opening.

Fuck. Leroi isn't going to—

"Will you take this hilt like a good girl?" he asks.

"Please!" I buck my hips, wanting it, needing it, aching for him to fuck me with the knife.

"Open wider, angel," he says.

I part my thighs as far as they'll go, and he pushes the hilt into my opening. It's thicker than a man's finger, but cool compared to my needy heat. The swirling patterns of the metal press against my inner walls as he moves it in and out. I clamp around it, adjusting to the pleasant intrusion.

Leroi stands so close I can feel the heat of his body radiating through his clothes. Each time he thrusts inward with the hilt, the pad of his thumb grazes my clit. and his chest brushes against my peaked and desperate nipples.

"Yes," I rasp. "More."

"Look at how well you take the knife. See how much you coat it with your juices."

He uses his other hand to grasp the hair at the nape of my neck, forcing me to look down between my thighs and I moan. He's right. The metal is glistening with my fluids. My clit has swelled to twice its usual size and is so red that I swear it will burst. Each time his thumb even gets close, he detonates tiny explosions of ecstasy.

"Fuck. You look so pretty when you're taking this dagger. Pretty enough to draw blood."

My legs tremble, and I throw back my head, letting it hit the wall tiles. Pleasure builds and builds until I'm so close to climaxing that I can barely breathe. If Leroi pulls back like he did during the spanking, one of us will die.

He leans even closer and growls. "Come for me, little angel."

The muscles of my core clamp around the hilt, and my clit swells to the point of agony before he swipes it once more with his thumb. I explode in a powerful orgasm that throws me back against the kitchen counter.

I shudder and gasp, my entire body convulsing as I ride out wave after wave of pleasure. It spirals through my veins, infuses every nerve ending with sparks. I've never felt anything so intense. These all-encompassing sensations burn through my memories, my thoughts, my very being. Ecstasy and awe battle through my senses until I lose myself in the climax.

Leroi's whispered words of encouragement hover on the edge of my awareness until the orgasm subsides, and I'm left trembling and panting with aftershocks. Then he eases the dagger out and pulls me into his chest.

I melt against his larger body, the last vestiges of my orgasm still sizzling across my senses. His arms tighten around my shoulders, keeping me from splintering.

"Leroi," I rasp.

My throat thickens, and the backs of my eyes sting. I suspected Leroi might be the man to give me my first taste of pleasure, but never dared to hope it would be so intense. I'm breathing so hard that it feels like every pent-up emotion forms a bottleneck at the tops of my lungs. There are no words to describe this euphoria. Part of me feels like I'm orbiting our joined bodies and the other part thinks I'm dreaming because there's no way a man could make me feel so good with just his hands and a dagger.

Leroi's lips graze my temple, but I want them to graze

my mouth. I would follow this man into hell for another taste of this pleasure.

"You did so well, angel," he murmurs.

"That was amazing," I say through panting breaths, my body entirely boneless.

Leroi sets the dagger aside and returns his hand between my legs.

"What are you doing?" I ask, my eyes half-lidded.

"We're not finished."

I'm so relaxed that I don't even flinch when he slides in two thick fingers that open me up with a delicious stretch. He moves them in and out in time with the steady beat of my heart, driving me higher and higher until I'm clinging to his shoulders with both hands.

"Leroi?" I moan.

"You're going to give me one more."

His thumb finds my clit a second time, and he works me back into another pleasurable peak. I'm panting so hard that my throat dries and my voice goes hoarse. Two orgasms should be impossible, but Leroi makes me soar higher and higher until I'm nothing but a quivering mess.

"That's it," he murmurs into my ear. "Let it go."

My pussy is still clenching and spasming around his fingers when my body builds up to a second climax that makes me cry out. It's more intense than the first, with spasms so powerful that they border on pain.

I cling to his shoulders as my orgasm burns me into ashes floating on the breeze. When I come back down, I'm slumped against Leroi's chest with his large hand rubbing circles over my back.

"Good girl," he murmurs. "You were so beautiful, coming apart at my command."

My eyes flutter closed, and I relax into his embrace. He

showers me with encouragement and praise, but I'm not naïve. This moment is too perfect to be real. Girls whose fathers condemn them to lives of death and degradation don't get rescued by white nights.

The first orgasm filled my head with clouds. The second has given me perfect clarity. Leroi might appear protective and caring, but he's still a man. Sure, he's better looking and is more skilled than most, but that just means he's better at hiding his true intentions.

I'm going to enjoy this blissful moment while it lasts and be ready for him when his mask slips.

TWENTY-SIX

LEROI

Hours later, I'm standing beside Miko in the firm's private shooting range, teaching him how to use a firearm, but I can't stop thinking about my encounter with Seraphine.

She stands on the far side of the range, clad in a protective face shield and a large pair of earmuffs. Despite the distance, her sweet scent still lingers in my nostrils, and her soft cries still haunt my ears. My balls ache from the release I denied myself as she came apart in my arms.

After she came down from her orgasm, I set her on her feet and wiped her DNA from the crime scene. Though there's no amount of bleach that could scour my mind of the image of her coming apart for me on that knife.

I disposed of Fiori's body with a raging hard on. Seraphine stared at the side of my face the entire journey back and neither of us said a word. I thought I could give her what she wanted and remain detached, but there are so many dimensions to Seraphine that she's not so easy to dismiss.

She's a killer like me–a kindred spirit with a darkness that rivals mine. Not only that, but she's beautiful, resourceful, and full of surprises. She could have set me on fire with that fluid, and my body was aroused at the very thought of succumbing to her flames. No woman's unpredictability has ever aroused me like hers.

If I had known she would be so alluring, I would have refused this unconventional agreement. Being within ten feet of her is an exercise in restraint.

I gaze at her out of the corner of my eye. Her stance is good. Posture straight, eyes focused, yet she still misses the target by over a foot. She's frustrated, and I can't blame her.

Capello's driver was our best chance of finding Gabriel, but he died in the explosions I detonated while escaping the mansion. His closest relative, who he might have confided in about Gabriel's whereabouts, is a cousin who Seraphine murdered during the poker massacre.

From the tight set of her shoulders, it looks like she's finally considering the consequences of her actions. Pointing this out right now would be callous.

"What do you think?" Miko's voice drifts through my ear plugs.

I turn my attention back to his target. It's littered with holes and he hasn't missed a shot.

"Nice job," I reply with a smile. "You're a natural."

Miko grins, his freckled cheeks turning pink. "Thanks. Real guns are even better than video games."

"Except in real life, your opponents don't always stand still."

"And I can get hurt," he says with a nod. "I'm not stupid."

I give him a clap on the back. "Never said you were, but there's more to contract killing than shooting."

Miko glances over at Seraphine, his brows pinching. "I bet you're not saying that to her."

From the nervous glances he's casting Seraphine, he suspects she was a participant in one of Capello's blackmail videos. My hand tightens around his shoulder, and he pulls off his earmuffs to look me full in the face. At nineteen, Miko is mature enough to know there's a difference between their situations, yet he's choosing to regress into the boy I brought home.

"Seraphine is on the other end of the spectrum," I say, my voice low. "I'm teaching her self-control."

Miko glances at the other end of the range, where she's still shooting at her target with a single-mindedness that borders on obsession. His Adam's apple bobs up and down before he looks back at me and gripes, "What if she can't learn it?"

"She will."

"Is she the reason Don's clean-up crew—"

"Miko," I snap.

"What?"

"The less you know about this, the better."

His gaze darts to her again and then back to me. "Alright."

I nod. "Can you spare me your talents for a few hours tonight?"

His eyes sparkle, and his features light up in a grin. "What are we doing?"

"It's time I visited Joseph Di Marco. Since he's behind the hit on the lone gunman responsible for the Capello murders, maybe he'll share some information before I put a bullet through his head."

———

Infiltrating Di Marco's mansion is easy, even though he also lives in the gated community of Queen's Gardens. It helps that attorneys don't usually require guards that work in shifts. After Miko disabled the security system, I slipped through an open window and made my way to the master bedroom. I almost regret leaving Seraphine behind, but I couldn't afford a repeat of her earlier impulsiveness.

Joseph Di Marco is gray-haired, in his early seventies, and looks every bit his age in his flannel pajamas. The only things that belie his elderly appearance are the pistol beneath his pillow and the twenty-something blonde slumbering beside him, who is most definitely not his wife.

I pocket the firearm, pull out a syringe, and inject her with 50 mg of ketamine. That should keep her asleep until long after Di Marco's body has cooled.

By the time I turn my attention back to the old man, he's already awake and staring at me through wide eyes.

I take a seat on the edge of the bed. "Good evening, Mr. Di Marco."

He reaches for the landline on his bedside table, pulls the receiver to his ear, taps on the hook switch over and over, before realizing it's dead and then drops it.

"What do you want?" he croaks and pulls himself up to sit. "If it's money—"

"Where is Gabriel Capello?"

"Who?" he asks through ragged breaths.

"Five years ago, Frederic discovered his mistress was cheating with her bodyguard. You must have heard about it. He slit the guard's throat, ordered his men to gang rape the woman, and then abducted the son and daughter."

His features flicker with recognition before forming a blank mask. "I don't know what you're talking about."

"Where did he put the son?"

He shakes his head.

"Capello is dead, as is the rest of his family. Who are you trying to protect?"

Di Marco's chest rises and falls with rapid breaths, and sweat gathers over his brow. He swallows over and over, his eyes searching the darkness for an answer.

I extract his gun and point it between his eyes. "Tell me what you know or you'll die slowly."

He flinches. "I never learned the boy's name, but I'm sure you're talking about the donor."

"What?"

"Fred had a liver transplant around that time." He swallows again. "When I visited him at the hospital, he was already drinking champagne. I asked if that alcohol was wise so soon after having major surgery, but he bragged about having the perfect donor."

"Who?" I ask, already knowing the answer. Capello discovered Seraphine wasn't his biological daughter because he had tested her and her brother because he needed a new liver. Looks like Gabriel was his perfect match.

"He didn't give me any details, and I didn't ask. I assumed it was a black market deal."

"Go on," I growl.

His shoulders sag, and the rest of his posture slumps. "Fred had another transplant two years ago. I asked if the liver came from his perfect donor, and he said yes."

"What else did he say?" I ask, my throat tightening.

"That it only took around two months for a liver to fully regenerate after donating." Di Marco glances away. "And there was an endless supply."

"Where is the donor?"

"I don't know." He bows his head.

"Capello didn't trust his lawyer and future in-law?"

"Fred wouldn't hand such powerful information to anyone. Not even his most trusted confidante."

"Then why did you put a hit out on the gunman who killed him?" I ask.

Di Marco's head snaps up. "That was you?"

"Answer my question."

He raises his chin, his eyes hardening. "You're going to kill me anyway."

I aim the gun to his shoulder and squeeze the trigger. Di Marco cries out and raises both arms in a full-body flinch.

"Speak," I say.

"Fuck you," he growls through clenched teeth.

I fire three shots, each one hitting a limb. He jerks, screams, and shudders. "You don't want to be stubborn. Tell me why you offered a million to kill the assassin, and I'll let you live."

"Bullshit." He coughs, his eyes glistening. "Either way, I'm dead."

He's right. By now, he's probably deduced that he hired the wrong firm to find the lone gunman. I don't intend to let him survive for long enough to correct his mistake.

"Then talk, and I'll put you out of your misery. Why put out that hit when the Capello family is dead?"

Di Marco's face contorts with a mixture of agony and animosity. His breathing labors, even though I haven't yet hit anything vital.

"If I'm not talking, it's because I'm buying time," he says, his voice strained. "My security company would know the moment you cut the telephone lines. In a moment, the police will arrive with reinforcements."

I close my eyes and focus on the wail of distant sirens. Joseph Di Marco is playing a dangerous game of chicken, and it looks like the old bastard is winning.

"If you leave now, you might escape before they arrive," he says through labored breaths.

My jaw clenches.

He's withholding a vital piece of information, but what?

"Leroi," Miko hisses through my earpiece. "The police are heading toward us."

There's no time to torture him for answers. The stubborn old bastard is ready to die with his secret. If we can find the hospital that performed the liver transplant, then maybe we can find the donor, and with any luck, it will lead us to Gabriel.

He falls back on his pillows and gasps. "You won't get away with this."

I shoot him through the head, turn on my heel, and exit the master bedroom.

This breakthrough is exactly what I need to soothe the awkwardness between me and Seraphine.

TWENTY-SEVEN

SERAPHINE

I sit on my heels in my bedroom with felt-tip pens spread all over the desk. The picture I drew of Leroi needs more red. I draw gashes down his neck and two down the lines of his chest. His mouth is open in a silent scream as blood pours over the bed and stains the sheets.

Slicing him open in picture form isn't enough. I need him to bleed.

Leroi made me feel so alive this morning when he fucked me with Pietro's dagger. For those blissful moments, I felt loved, protected, pleasured. He gave me my first orgasm, then another so powerful that my vision went black.

And when he pulled me into his chest, my mind fell quiet. I was finally at peace and where I belonged.

Then he pulled away.

All the way back. Leaving me in a void of silence.

It's been years since I felt so rejected. Discarded.

He led me out of Pietro's house without a word, as though what we'd done together had been a mistake. Maybe he hadn't meant to kill Pietro in a murderous rage for hurting me, or he was having regrets. Regrets about getting close to a girl he thinks is tainted.

Leroi barely spoke to me at the firing range. My vision was so clouded with rage that I couldn't hit the target. He stayed huddled close to Miko, looking like they were plotting how to send me away.

My fingers grip the felt-tip pen so tightly the plastic snaps. This feels like Dad all over again. One minute, I'm his angel. The next, I'm nothing more than a disposable toy. Leroi's compliments and praise ring through my ears like an alarm that won't stop, no matter how many red slashes I make across his lying mouth.

I squeeze my eyes shut and toss the notebook to the headboard, where it lands with a soft thud. Drawing his demise won't calm my mind and neither will moping in this room.

Replacing the broken felt-tip pen for the knife I took from Pietro's kitchen. I slide off the chair and walk out into the apartment.

I'll just have to slice something open and imagine it's Leroi.

By now, the sun has set, casting the living room in gloom. I walk past the floor-to-ceiling windows, taking in the nighttime view of Beaumont city.

Leroi is out there, probably wining and dining a tall brunette. If it's not Rosalind with her fake pregnancy, then it will be Monica, the nosey therapist. If he's stupid enough to bring her back to our apartment, he'll wake up on a mattress soaked with her blood and a knife to his throat.

I fling open the kitchen door, turn on the light, and glance at the counter. The block of knives is still missing. I shrug at his attempt to keep them from me, it doesn't matter since I took another from Pietro's kitchen after Leroi turned cold and pretended I didn't exist.

The refrigerator has been restocked with enough vegetables to last a month. I gather an armful and set them on the counter, then return to select a pack of steak.

I slice the meat into tiny strips, imagining them as Leroi's misshapen heart. It's cold and dry with only the tiniest bit of moisture, but the real thing would stain my fingers with blood.

Once I've cut through the steak, I move onto a cabbage the size of his head. The satisfying crunch of the knife slicing through its thick leaves feels like carving his skull.

It wasn't always like this. Before Dad turned into a backstabbing psychopath, I used to help our cook, Bianca, in the kitchen. She taught me how to hold a knife, to cut vegetables without slicing my fingers, and a host of useful kitchen skills. Looking back at my childhood, it seems the only real parental love I received was from the domestic staff.

I hope Dad didn't kill our driver, Felix, for taking me to Nanna's house or Bianca for being his wife. All they ever tried to do was help, but if he could so easily order those men to violate Mom before snuffing out her life, imprison Gabriel, and turn me into an assassin, then he could murder an innocent old couple.

At the click of a door opening, I stiffen, my hackles rising. It snicks shut, but only one set of footsteps approaches. I slide the knife under a kitchen towel and turn my back to the counter.

Leroi leans against the doorway, his arm resting on the top of the frame. He gazes down at me through half-lidded eyes, reminding me of a predator who's already eaten his fill.

"You're still up," he says, his voice low.

My fingers twitch toward the knife. "Where have you been?"

"Following an interesting lead," he says.

A breath catches in my throat. "About Gabriel?"

He nods.

All traces of rejection and resentment fade into the background at the thought of getting closer to finding my brother. I push off the counter and close the distance between us. "Why didn't you bring me along?"

"It was too dangerous," he says.

"I can take care of myself," I reply.

He places both hands on my shoulders and stares down at me with those impossibly dark eyes. "You're impulsive. You lack control. We were supposed to place a tracker on Fiori's car and leave. Instead, you charged at him, and we had to improvise."

"That's why you're shutting me out?" I step out of his grasp.

He sighs as though he finds our conversation tiresome. "Tonight's mission required zero margin for error. If anything went wrong, we'd have two targets on our backs."

"But—"

"Seraphine," he says, his voice sharper than any knife. "You don't see what I see."

"And what's that?"

"The bigger picture, and that's not your fault. For the past five years, your world was narrowed into captivity, killing, and abuse."

His honesty makes my throat tighten and the backs of my eyes sting. "There's no need to be so rude."

"You're the strongest young woman I know, but the

things that happened to you have stunted your maturity and given you a deep distrust of men."

I part my lips to protest, but he speaks first.

"Including me, but I understand."

Resentment simmers in my belly, building up in intensity until I'm on the verge of slicing him open and painting the kitchen floor with his insides. He's so uptight and always in control. Control over information, control his emotions, control over every aspect of my quest to save my brother and avenge Mom. Pushing my resentment aside, I make a mental note to draw this image in my notebook.

"What did you find out about Gabriel?" I ask.

He glances away.

My heart plummets to my stomach. "What is it?"

"Your brother was..." He inhales a deep breath as though trying to find the right words. "He was hospitalized two years ago, but he made a fast recovery."

"What happened? Where is he now?"

He shakes his head. "It was a routine procedure. Miko is checking through the records of every hospital in and within driving distance of New Alderney. We'll find him."

Hope flickers in my chest, but it's only a tiny spark which fades. Leroi is planning on getting rid of me after he's found Gabriel. He admitted as much the night we'd buried that bastard I castrated in the woods, but I don't want to replace Leroi with my brother. I don't want to have to choose between them. I want them both.

"Do you promise?"

He cups the side of my face, his eyes softening. "I promise."

Some of the tension leaves my shoulders, and I lean into his touch. "You'll like Gabriel," I murmur. "He's just like Miko."

Leroi strokes my hair, sending pleasant shivers down my scalp. "It's late. You should go to bed."

"Can I sleep with you? Pietro died, and I can't be in that room alone."

Leroi's face stills. "You slept well enough in there after you killed Billy Blue and all the others. Why would Fiori's death make a difference?"

"Because I witnessed his murder," I whisper. "They don't count when I do it."

He studies my expression for a few long seconds, his jaw clenching. "Go to bed."

"But—"

"Now."

I dig my heels into the floor.

His eyes darken, and he steps so close that the air between us crackles with electricity. "Go. To. Bed."

Maybe what I said about being too traumatized to sleep was bullshit, but there's still something between us that's keeping me awake. I take a step backward toward the counter, my skin tingling. "If you want me to leave the kitchen, you'll apologize."

He raises a brow. "Explain."

"You paid that bucket of bleach more attention than me. You walked away from me at Pietro's house. Then you acted like it was my fault that Dad's driver's cousin was dead—"

"Because you killed him—"

"And then you ignored me in the shooting range and spent all your time with Miko," I say, my voice rising.

He rubs the spot between his brows. I know by now it's his way of saying he's tired of dealing with me. "Seraphine," he says, his voice measured. "Miko and I were planning tonight's mission."

My jaw tenses. We could have planned it together, but

he left me out on purpose, and I know why. We were getting along perfectly until he fucked me with that knife and then gave me that second orgasm. My back stiffens at the memory of him gazing down at his wet fingers, his face a blank mask, his erection strained through his pants. His body wants me, but he doesn't want to get involved with someone so tainted by abuse.

"I didn't think you were the kind of man who got squeamish after giving a girl an orgasm." Taking another step backward toward the counter, I seek comfort from my new knife. Leroi stalks after me, his irises turning black.

I'm trapped between his much larger body and a hard surface, and the pulse between my legs won't stop throbbing. Leroi cages me with both hands on the counter and leans in.

"Don't test me, little Seraphine," he growls.

"What are you going to do?" I ask, my heart pounding. "Spank me?"

His eyes flash. "Lose the sass before I do something you'll regret."

My breath hitches.

I can't wait to see what he'll do next.

TWENTY-EIGHT

LEROI

Defiance blazes in Seraphine's cornflower blue eyes, and I'm glad to see the flames. It's a change from the sullen girl who stopped communicating with me in the shooting range.

She's right. I shut down after her second orgasm, but I had to pull back. Since we left Fiori's, I've been haunted by her panting breaths and her delectably sweet scent.

Everything about her draws me in, and it had taken every effort not to fuck her on that kitchen counter into a third climax.

"You owe me an apology," she snaps.

"And I told you to lose the attitude." Wrapping a hand around her throat, I run the pad of my thumb over the line of her jaw, where her skin is the softest velvet.

Her pupils dilate, and her full lips part with a gasp. Seraphine is so beautiful and breakable that all I want to do is lean in for a kiss. "Drop the attitude, angel. If anyone needs to apologize, it's you."

This little brat is testing my limits. I can't forget that

beneath her pretty exterior is an untamed serial killer. I'm playing with fire, knowing that I'll get burned, yet I can't resist the heat.

She rears back. "What for?"

"Jumping out of the car without permission and letting Fiori know you were alive. He could have raised the alarm. The little stunt you pulled with the lighter fluid could have set us all alight."

She scowls, her chin rising. "You're exaggerating. Gabriel can't afford to wait around while we follow your convoluted plans."

At the reminder of her brother, any excitement I had about taming Seraphine dwindles, and my gaze falters. I can't let her think that her only living family member is being held in an unknown basement with no food or water. Hell, I'm already keeping enough secrets from her.

"What?" she asks.

"Your brother is safe," I say, my grip on her neck loosening.

"How would you know that?" She clutches at my forearm.

"It's something Joseph Di Marco said," I mutter.

"Tell me." Her fingers tighten around my wrist.

I exhale. "Di Marco said that Gabriel donated part of his liver to Capello."

She gasps, her eyes widening, her bottom lip trembling, and her palm presses against my chest. "That's not true. Gabriel wouldn't. He's terrified of needles—"

"I don't think your brother really had a choice," I mutter.

"We have to find him." She shoves hard, trying to push me backward, but I cup her cheek.

"Miko is already searching all hospitals in the area," I

say. "We'll find your brother. Right now, you have to trust that he's safe."

"How, when they've taken his liver?" she wails.

"Seraphine." I place both hands on her shoulders and squeeze hard enough to recapture her attention. When her gaze meets mine again, I continue. "The surgeon would have taken a piece of Gabriel's liver to give to Capello. After a few weeks, it regenerates to its original size."

Her brows pull together, and she gazes up at me with glistening eyes. "Are you sure?"

"Positive." I slide my fingers through her silken strands and cradle the back of her head. "I'm telling you this because Capello wanted to keep Gabriel alive and well for future transplants."

"More?"

I nod, my throat clogging with regret. If I'd known, I would have kept that bastard alive for long enough to extract the stolen liver. "There was a second transplant two years ago, but Gabriel would have already recovered from that. He's safe now. We just need to find him."

Her eyes flutter shut, and she flops forward, her head leaning against my chest. I wrap an arm around her shoulders. Seraphine spent five years forced to murder men because her mother cheated on a cheater. Her brother paid the price with his liver, not once, but twice, because his father is a bastard.

The underworld is a cesspool of backstabbers, killers, and sorry motherfuckers who would sell their own grandmothers to fuel their personal demons. Despite this, I've never heard of two innocent people suffering so much for the sins of their parents.

She draws back, her gaze meeting mine, and whines, "Are you going to make me leave?"

"No." I brush a dark strand off her face. "You'll stay here with me until we find your brother."

Her face pinches. "What if he's still sick?"

"Then we'll take care of him until he can take care of you both. Even after that, I'll still be there for you."

She blinks, and a tear slides down her cheek. "How can we ever repay you?"

I lean down and press a kiss on her forehead. "Work with me to control your impulses to kill, and we'll call it even."

"What if I can't?" she asks, her eyes glimmering.

"Then you'll work out a way to do it without getting caught, restricting your kills to only those who deserve to die."

She wraps her hand around mine and squeezes. I bring her knuckles to my lips and sigh. "I won't give up on you, Seraphine. I promise."

She gulps. "And you'll stop holding back information?"

"Alright."

My stomach twists at the half-truth. Anton trained me in the art of murder, and he put that collar around her neck and the chip under her skin. It's exactly how he trains his dogs and he allowed Capello to do the same to a sixteen-year-old girl. It's hard to reconcile the man I know with the man that helped create this version of her.

"Thank you," she murmurs, her shoulders relaxing. "Can I ask for something else?"

"Anything," I rasp.

"Don't lock me up anymore. Sometimes, it feels like I'm still a prisoner."

Guilt grips my chest so tightly that I feel the sting of its claws at the back of my throat. "You're not my captive."

"Then let me go out on the balcony or the terrace by

myself," she says, her voice breaking. "I'm cooped up in here, and it's driving me crazy."

My jaw tightens. "And if you hurt yourself again?"

"I won't," she rasps.

"Or hurt someone else?"

She shakes her head. "I've learned my lesson."

Those mesmerizing blue eyes shine with innocence, sincerity, and a vulnerability that ignites my instincts to possess, protect, and provide. My mouth drifts close to her pink lips with an urge to comfort her with a kiss, even though somewhere deep in my psyche, my last shred of decency screams at me to stop.

I jerk my head to the side and force myself to look away. Seraphine draws me in with whatever allure she used to make men drop their guard. Even if I have enough resolve to not take advantage of her, she's still a dangerous young woman capable of unpredictable acts of violence.

"Please," she whispers. "I won't let you down."

The desperation in her voice pulls at my frayed heart-strings. She just wants a little freedom. I'm not Capello or his bastard sons. Who am I to keep her cooped up in this apartment?

My gaze wanders over her shoulder to the pile of steak cut into neat strips. How the hell did she manage that with just a table knife?

"Seraphine," I say, my voice sharpening.

"What?"

"Have you been hiding weapons again?" I turn to look her full in the face.

Her eyes widen, and her lips part to form a perfect O. "No."

I turn her around. "Then where did you get the knife?"

Her arm twitches toward a kitchen towel concealing a

long knife, but I grab its hilt before she can even reach the counter.

With any other woman, my behavior would be irrational and controlling, but Seraphine near any weapon is like playing Russian roulette with a fully loaded gun.

She glances at the blade, her breath quickening. I can't tell if it's out of fear or excitement, but the sight of her looking so flustered makes my balls tighten.

Seraphine is a tornado in a Tiffany box. You never know what to find in that pretty little package.

"Answer my question," I snarl.

"I found it," she blurts, her pretty features crumpling. "Pietro had so many knives, and I took one. I wasn't planning on using it to hurt anyone. When you're not around, I get all these horrible thoughts and then all the memories pour in and I don't know if it's a dream and I'm still stuck in the basement because you're not there to tell me I'm safe. Cutting things up is the only thing that helps."

Her words continue in a stream that becomes more jumbled with each passing moment. I let her continue until tears are rolling down her cheeks.

"Seraphine," I say.

"What?" she rasps.

"If you agree to go to bed right now, I won't say anything about the knife."

She stares up at me, her eyes wide with disbelief. After several heartbeats, her shoulders sag and she nods.

I can't tell if I'm taming Seraphine or if she's taming me.

TWENTY-NINE

SERAPHINE

I don't understand what just happened. First Leroi is making my skin heat and my core throb. Then he's annoying again, and now I'm being put to bed like I'm fragile and he's agreeing to everything I ask for.

Well, not everything.

He refused to let me into his room and didn't believe me when I said I couldn't sleep, which wasn't even a complete lie. How am I supposed to relax when he's plotting to kick me out on the street? Or at least I thought he was.

After tucking me in so tightly that I can't move my arms, Leroi strokes my hair. The warmth of his fingers seeps into my skin and soothes my nerves. I don't remember the last time someone touched me with so much care. Mom was always too busy to check in on me, and Gabriel acted like I was a pest. Whenever Dad was home, he always sat at my bedside and kissed me goodnight.

Tears well in my eyes and threaten to spill over. I'm no longer that little girl. My hands are saturated with blood, my soul is stained with gore, and I've been tainted by more men than I want to admit. But the way Leroi takes care of me awakens something in my heart I thought was long gone.

Maybe I still have a chance at being normal. Leroi is a killer, just like me, but he knows how to tread the line between darkness and light. He's worth keeping alive, at least until he stabs me in the back.

My eyelids flutter close, and I let the warmth of his touch lull me to sleep. For the first time in over half a decade, I no longer feel so alone. This time when I sleep, there are no nightmares, not even a flashback. It's as though Leroi has chased them all away with his imposing presence.

The next thing I know, I'm awakened by the scent of fried meat. Sunlight streams through my closed eyelids, Leroi's cocoon of sheets still holding me in a warm embrace. It takes several tries to slide out of bed, but when I do, I feel awake and refreshed. When I emerge from my room, I find Leroi stepping out of the balcony, dressed in a white shirt unbuttoned to the sternum.

My gaze lingers on the muscles of his chest and travels up his strong neck to the vein pulsing at the base of his jaw.

He catches me staring and raises a brow. I drop my gaze, my cheeks heating.

"Steak and eggs hash," he says.

My head snaps up. "What?"

He flicks his head toward the balcony before walking back to the kitchen. "I made breakfast."

Leroi emerges seconds later, carrying two iron skillets. The first contains a frittata of potatoes and cabbage, while the second holds sizzling strips of steak, sliced peppers, and cherry tomatoes. The aroma fills the living room, and my stomach growls.

"Are those the vegetables I cut?" I ask.

He smirks. "You make a great little prep chef."

A smile tugs at the corners of my lips, and I shuffle on my feet. No one apart from Bianca has ever acknowledged my knife skills before, even though I took years of cooking classes at that preppy private school.

"Come." Leroi steps into the balcony. "I've made enough for both of us."

He sets the skillet on the table and heaps a large portion of frittata and steak on my plate, while I pour the juice. With the delicious aromas floating around us and the sun warming my skin, it feels like I'm part of a family. A twisted family of killers, but it's still a hundred times better than what I had before.

"I thought about what you asked for last night," he says.

My mind dials back to our conversation. "About Gabriel?"

He shakes his head. "Miko is still searching. He's ruled out Beaumont Central and Simon's Memorial Hospital and is casting his search wider."

"Oh."

I take a bite of steak and find it seasoned to perfection. Maybe Leroi's about to let me sleep in his room?

"You said you wanted more freedom."

My shoulders sag. "I'm not moving to the apartment next door."

"Not that," he says. "Now that you've changed your appearance, there's nothing stopping you from going out and exploring the city on your own."

I choke on my mouthful of steak and grab a glass of juice to wash it down. Leroi gives me a gentle pat on the back.

"Really? I can leave anytime I want?" I ask.

His eyes soften. "Just be careful not to carry out any revenge missions. You may still be a target."

I give him an eager nod, not quite believing he'll let me explore the outside world. As soon as I finish eating, I rush to the bedroom, jump in the shower, and sift through my new clothes. I settle for a pair of leggings and a pink t-shirt that no longer suit my new coloring. After putting on the contact lenses the way Farfalla taught me, I slip on a pair of sneakers and step out.

Leroi is already waiting for me by the door.

My steps falter. "Are you coming with me?"

He raises a shoulder. "You're going to need money. I thought I'd tag along until you get your own card."

I give him a shy smile and a nod. This almost feels like a date. I try to push that thought away, but the prospect of walking around town with Leroi still makes my heart race.

He holds open the front door and gestures for me to step out.

"Um..." I clear my throat and smooth back a lock of hair. "Will there be a reward if I don't kill anyone?"

He quirks a brow, the corners of his lips lifting. "What would you like?"

"A kiss," I rasp.

"Why?"

Butterflies flutter in my stomach, and my gaze lingers on his lips. Kissing was part of my training. It was a way to distract a man before injecting him with poison, but it always turned my stomach. A kiss with Leroi would be different. Leroi would take his time and make sure I enjoyed it.

"There weren't any boys at my prep school and Dad wouldn't let me date." I shrug. "I just want to know what it would be like to be kissed by someone I liked."

His face falls. "That's not on the table, Seraphine."

My cheeks flush, and I duck my head, my insides

squirming. What was I thinking? Of course he doesn't want to kiss a girl like me. I'm just an assassin who had to seduce men to stay alive. He's probably still freaked out by that bastard I castrated.

"Sorry," I mumble, my gaze fixed on my feet.

Leroi lifts my chin, forcing our eyes to meet. "Don't apologize. I can give you any other reward within my limits—"

"It's alright." I pull away from his hold. "Let's go."

As we step out into the hallway and head toward the elevator, the apartment next door opens. Miko pokes his head out and grins.

"Hey, where are you guys off to?" he asks, his eyes flickering over my outfit.

Leroi steps forward, blocking me from Miko's view. "A walk around town."

"Really? Seraphine's going out already?"

I peek out from behind Leroi's shoulder. "What's wrong with that?"

He holds out his palms. "Nothing, nothing at all. It's just... I thought you'd be working on something, that's all. And you're looking good, by the way."

Miko disappears behind his door, and Leroi places an arm around my shoulders.

"What was that about?" I whisper.

Leroi shakes his head and walks us to the elevator. Neither of us speaks until we step out of the building and into the sunny street.

Traffic rumbles around us, and the streets are bustling with pedestrians. I shrink into Leroi's side, feeling exposed without the cover of night. The last time we went out hadn't been so nerve-wracking, although I suppose that was before Leroi made me realize that my actions have consequences.

It's crazy that I didn't appreciate how much work went into a mission until after spending time with a professional hitman. Even crazier to think someone could be searching for a girl who fits my description. It's a wonder that I've survived this long.

Leroi brings his head down to my ear and murmurs, "Miko wants to be like us."

"He wants to kill people?" I whisper back.

He nods.

"Are you going to help him?" I ask.

"I'll make sure he learns to use a gun, but I won't teach him how to kill unless it's in self-defense."

"How long has he worked for you?"

My gaze darts to a chocolatier's window display, where a mini fountain surrounded by truffles spurts a cascade of sticky, sweet, deliciousness. My mouth waters and I swipe my tongue over dry lips.

"Miko isn't an employee," Leroi replies. "I picked him up on a job nearly six years ago, the same way I did with you."

We stroll down a sidewalk lined with offices and apartment buildings, the air filled with the sounds of horns and chatter. Some of the tension in my posture relaxes, knowing that Leroi won't teach Miko to be like us. I want Leroi's attention all for myself.

As we cross the road and enter the park through tall, iron gates, I turn to Leroi and ask, "Are you teaching me to be an assassin?"

"No," he replies, his voice tightening as we continue down a tree-lined sidewalk.

"Why not?"

He glances down at me and grimaces. "Because you're not cut out for the job."

I bristle, my hackles rising, every instinct rushing to defend my abilities. "How can you say that when I've been doing it since I was sixteen?"

"You're too emotional, too impulsive," he counts off. "You act on instinct instead of logic. You don't detach yourself from your targets."

I scowl, my lips tightening. "Are you calling me sloppy?"

He stops abruptly and grabs my shoulders. "You should never have been dragged into this line of work." His words are so soft I have to lean closer to hear them. "You were a child, already traumatized by what happened to your mother. Then the only father you knew handed you over to a pair of psychopaths."

I drop my gaze to our feet.

He leans closer. "Capello and his sons threatened the people you loved and forced you to murder for them."

A tight band of anger wraps around my ribs, turning my breath shallow. None of this is news to me. I don't understand the point of rehashing a wrong I can never put right.

"Why are you telling me this?" I ask, already knowing that none of this is even my responsibility.

"Because being a good assassin isn't a badge of honor. It's the mark of a person devoid of a soul. I don't want you to lose what's left of your humanity."

"What about the guards who killed Mom?" I scrape out. "Are you going to tell me I should be the bigger person and forgive them?"

"Absolutely not." He squeezes my shoulders. "You're going to kill those four bastards and wipe them off your conscience. Then you're going to spit on Capello's grave and never look back."

I nod, the pressure easing off my lungs.

"That's why I won't teach you to be an assassin," he says, his grip on my shoulders loosening. "But I will teach you self-control."

My chest fills with a mix of conflicting emotions. Relief that I might have a life outside of murdering and maiming. A life without trauma. There's also a part of me that enjoys working side by side with Leroi, even when he's being persnickety. A lump forms in the back of my throat, and I swallow.

"What about you?" I ask.

He cocks his head.

"Will you continue being an assassin?"

A flicker of something crosses his features, but it's too quick for me to process, let alone identify. "It's too late for me. I've been in this business for so long that I don't know how to be anything else."

I meet his dark gaze, not knowing how to respond because I can't imagine myself never wanting to gouge out a man's eyes for looking at me for too long or fantasizing about what Leroi would look like covered in blood.

What hope do I have of breaking free from my bloodlust if a man as normal as him won't even try?

Before I can voice my thoughts, he wraps an arm around my shoulder. "Let's get you some ice cream. Afterward, I can tell you what I've planned for tonight."

THIRTY

LEROI

We sit side by side on a wooden bench watching the ducks circling the lake and I catch a glimpse of Seraphine from my peripheral. The sight of her licking her cone like it's a cock has mine instantly hard and jealous.

This was definitely a mistake.

No matter where I turn my head, I'm painfully aware of how her tongue swirls around its rounded crown. If my attention strays too far from her ministrations, then her pleasured moans are there to remind my libido that she's a siren sent to pull me into her allure, torturing me with pleasure and drowning me in desire.

It's torture.

I clear my throat, shake off my inappropriate thoughts, and shift in my seat. Seraphine is my... charge? protégée? A disturbed young woman I swore to protect?

I can't become like every man who ever abused her by allowing myself to think about her as a sexual object. Fuck knows she's suffered enough.

"So good," she says, her voice breathy.

My mind drifts back to the morning she rocked back and forth on my shaft with one blade pressed to my throat and another at the base of my dick. I hadn't known where to look with her nipples erect and protruding through her shirt. Had she known what she was doing when she threatened me with castration and death? Or am I just a sick bastard who can't resist her twisted charms?

"You're not having any?" she says.

"I don't like sweet things," I mutter, my gaze fixed on a swan swimming toward a tight gaggle of ducks.

"You're missing out." she hums. "I could lick this cone all day."

Her words are delivered with an inflection so flirtatious that I tear my gaze away from the impending waterfowl fight to look Seraphine full in the face. She's no longer licking the ice cream; she sits and stares up at me through half-lidded eyes.

My eyes track the movement over her tongue darting out to lick her bottom lip, and I bite back a moan.

She's doing this on purpose.

Little vixen.

Despite appearances, Seraphine isn't a sweet, innocent girl. Anton trained her to become a Lolita assassin, and I'm not sure I can stomach what that entailed.

But one thing is for certain: Seraphine knows exactly what she's doing. The only question is why. I'm already helping her find Gabriel and the men she needs to kill to erase her demons. I didn't pull her out of that basement for my own sick pleasure, so there's no need for the sexualized charade.

Her eyes flutter closed. "Hmmmm."

"Stop that," I snap.

"Stop what?" Her eyes open comically wide, confirming my suspicions.

A woman pushing a stroller walks by, accompanied by a gaggle of kids under the age of five. They pause in front of us to watch the swan being chased off by the ducks.

I lean into Seraphine and growl in her ear, "Tease me like this again, and I'll restrain your arms again and bring you to the brink of orgasm again and again and again until you pass out from frustration."

The air thickens, despite the breeze blowing in from across the lake. Seraphine shivers, her artificially darkened eyes dilating and she looks me straight in the eye.

"Is that a promise?" She gives the rounded tip of her cone a long, languid lick.

My cock stirs, and I grab a newspaper off the bench and place it on my lap. Thankfully, the family has moved on and can't see the evidence of my arousal.

Little brat.

"It's a warning," I say, my jaw clenching.

She smirks, thinking she's won this round. I can't help but wonder if this was a technique she used to lure her targets. Only the most heinous of predators would approach a young girl enjoying her ice cream. I'm determined not to be one of them.

Her soft moan as she takes another lick of her cone makes my balls ache. I clamp a hand on her shoulder and pull her close.

"Don't mess with me. That bullshit doesn't work. I still remember what you did to Samson and Billy Blue."

Her smirk fades, leaving her looking so murderous a shudder travels down my spine.

"They deserved it."

"I agree."

Any man who forces his way into the mouth of an unwilling victim is begging to have it bitten off.

Seraphine glances down at her cone and grimaces. "I don't want it anymore."

I rise off the bench. "Come. I want to take you somewhere you can get prepared for tonight."

She tosses the cone into the bank of the lake, attracting the attention of the swan, who races toward the sugary treat with a pair of ducks in hot pursuit.

"Are we scratching off a name from my list?" she asks, sounding hopeful.

"I thought we could alternate between murder and training you out of your murderous impulses."

She cocks her head. "Huh?"

I steer her down a path that leads to another of the park's many exits. "One of your triggers is men touching you inappropriately."

"So?"

"We're going to work on how to defend yourself against grabby assholes without cutting or gouging body parts."

She scowls. "They shouldn't touch me in the first place."

"No, but unfortunately, the State of New Alderney doesn't agree with your brand of justice," I say. "Your task tonight is to survive a night in a club without ending up in jail."

Seraphine falls silent, although her expression is still mutinous. I glare down at her, and she looks away.

"I can't do this," she says.

"How did you keep your urges at bay during missions?"

"That was different." She shrugs.

"How?"

"The first year and a half, someone was always nearby

to activate the chip if I strayed from the plan." She runs her fingers through her coffee-darkened hair.

My gaze drops to the bandage plastered behind her ear, and I shudder. Anton used to call this schedule of punishments and rewards operant conditioning, except he used it to train dogs. When they learned to perform a task, they would get a treat. When they fucked up, the electric collar.

"And the later years?" I ask.

She dips her head, a curtain of brown hair falling over her face. "Some men harassed me while I was on missions, but I banked the anger."

My steps slow, and I take her arm. "What does that mean?"

Seraphine jerks her head to the side. "If someone touched me, I just took it. I didn't react because I would save my rage for their boss or whoever was the target."

"So, instead of lashing out, you used the anger as fuel to complete your mission?"

Her features harden. "I can control myself, but it's like turning on the heat to a pressure cooker. My anger will build and build and build until I release everything in a huge explosion."

Fuck.

This explains why she didn't stop killing after castrating Billy Blue and why she stabbed that bum in the eye at the gas station.

I release her arm.

Anton would advise me to put Seraphine down as a mad dog, but he was one of the bastards responsible for breaking her psyche.

"What happens when you explode?" I ask.

"It depends on what's available." She raises both shoulders. "If there's a knife, I'll keep going until I'm satisfied.

Sometimes, I like to experiment, like that time with the hair dryer."

"And afterward?"

"The pressure goes away, and I feel like shit because the twins will either punish me for making a mess or starve Gabriel."

Which explains why she never ran. Even if she could get out of the range of the remotes that activated her tracker, Seraphine was bound by her imprisoned brother.

"You can bite, kick, scratch, slap and scream to get through the night," I say, my voice soft. "But you can't use weapons unless it's in self-defense."

"How will I know the difference?" she asks.

"If he inflicts pain, tries to carry you off, threatens your life, or pulls out a weapon of his own, that's self-defense. Understand?"

She nods. "What if he says something creepy?"

"Then do what you can to get away from him and find me."

Her lips tighten, presumably with disapproval.

"Try it tonight," I say. If you succeed in the exercise, you can choose your reward."

Her eyes light up, and her lips part, reminding me of when she asked for a kiss.

"Within limits," I add. At her frown, I ask, "Deal?"

"Whatever," she huffs, sounding half a decade younger.

I shake my head and continue toward the park's wrought-iron gates. Seraphine is a deadly little handful, but I'm determined to use every method at my disposal to quench her thirst for blood. For her sake, I hope my training works.

THIRTY-ONE

LEROI

Seraphine and I walk the few blocks from the park to the boutique Rosalind used to rave about before she became so bothersome. According to her, its owner sources the best nightclub attire.

After warning her on the walk here that there would be consequences for bad behavior, Seraphine and the sales clerk disappear behind the fitting room door to try on a handful of dresses.

My phone buzzes with an incoming call. It's Rita, the firm's coordinator and customer service woman.

"The client is getting impatient and wants to know if you've made progress tracking down the Capello killer," she says before I have a chance to say hello.

A corner of my mouth lifts into a smile. Joseph Di Marco already got the answer to that question right before I shot him between the eyes.

"Still working on it," I say to placate her. "Is there anything else?"

She huffs. "That's not good enough. What exactly should I tell him when he calls back in ten minutes?"

Wait.

What?

My gaze darts toward the fitting room. There are no blood-curdling screams or suspicious red liquid seeping through the door, so I proceed toward the exit.

I step outside into the street, letting the rumble of traffic muffle my side of the conversation. If Joseph Di Marco wasn't the man who commissioned the hit on the Capello killer, then who did?

Every high-ranking member of Frederic Capello's organization would have benefitted from the death of their boss. I can't see who would waste money on avenging the worthless bastard.

"When did the client call?" I ask, my brows hitching.

"Just now." Her voice is hard. "He was extremely agitated."

Not surprising, if he just discovered that Capello's lawyer was murdered. Who else was close enough to the family to want to avenge their deaths? The illegitimate daughter? I shake off that thought. Roman said she was a visual artist and implied that she'd lived apart from her father. It couldn't be her.

It could be Samson's fiancé, Joseph Di Marco's daughter. She might have convinced her father to put out the hit, but how much can a woman love a psychopath with a rotted dick? I shake off that idea. Rita said the client was male.

"So, what should I tell him?" Rita asks.

"One of my informants recognized a contract killer walking through the Capello Casino a week before the murders," I lie, hoping it would satisfy her and the mystery client. "I'm following up on leads to find out who hired him."

Rita's exhaled relief eases a little of my tension. "Good. I'll tell him."

"Let the client know the assassin will need a lot of persuasion to release those details. It'll take time to track someone who doesn't want to be found."

"Alright."

I hang up, my jaw clenching so hard that my molars grind. That bullshit I just rattled off might just buy me enough time to find this mystery client and kill him before he gets tired of waiting and contracts a rival firm to find out who murdered the Capello family.

After a cursory glance through the boutique's window and finding no sign of Seraphine and any ensuing mayhem, I send a text to Miko.

Di Marco transferred funds on behalf of the real client. Monitor Rita's phone and find out who just called her. Client plans on calling her back in a few minutes.

Miko sends a shocked emoji, followed by:

Shit. OK.

I rub at my temple. There's nothing left to do but wait for Miko to work his magic. Any preemptive murders might lead to getting caught. I can take care of myself, but I need to protect Miko and Seraphine.

When I don't hear from Miko in the next few moments, I assume he's busy hacking the phone records to trace whoever's about to call Rita. I return to the store just in time to find the door to the fitting room swinging open.

Seraphine steps out clad in a gold mini dress that show-cases her slender legs. The fabric gathers around the breasts, accentuating her cleavage, and cinches at her tiny waist. Her sandals are heeled, with two golden straps holding her pretty little feet to the shoe leather.

My breath catches in my throat at the sight of her radiance. Her contact lenses reflect the gold material, creating an effect I can only describe as otherworldly. If she's the sun, then I'm Icarus, flying close for a kiss of her gleaming rays. She looks like a fallen angel, the kind that lures men to their deaths.

I should know better than to succumb to her fatal allure.

"What do you think?" She turns in a slow circle, giving me the full view of her delicate curves.

Without meaning to, my eyes trace every inch of her body before settling on her face. Not even the knowledge that she would blind a man for looking at her the wrong way could stop me from being awestruck by her beauty.

"Leroi?" she asks, her gaze fixed on mine.

"You look perfect," I reply, my voice rough.

She steps toward me, her hips swaying. I force my eyes on hers, but they keep wandering down to her neckline. It takes every effort to remember that Seraphine isn't like other women. Every move, every glance, every inch of her being, was crafted to ensnare my soul.

"Perfect for what?" she asks.

My heart races, but I keep my features in a blank mask. I lean down and whisper close to her ear, "Perfect for attracting every horny fucker with eyes."

"What if they're rude?"

"If anyone gets too close, I'll be the one gouging out the eyeballs."

She glances at me through the mirror. "Really?"

I nod. "Get dressed. Pick a few more outfits similar to this one, and we'll go back to plan the rest of our week."

Seraphine sashays back to the fitting room. I'm so

mesmerized by the sway of her hips that I don't even think to ask about the missing sales clerk.

Some women are so stunning they can get away with murder. Seraphine is one of them–at least with me. But I'm not so captivated by her beauty to believe it's enough to guarantee her survival if she ever gets caught by the law. That's why I can't allow myself to get distracted.

My phone buzzes, and I glance at the screen. It's a message from Miko.

I tracked the calls to Rita's phone to a digital SIM that's already deactivated. Whoever Di Marco helped to pay for that job knows what they're doing.

Shit.

Most clients aren't so tech savvy.

He sends another message:

What should I do next?

That's an excellent question. If I don't eliminate this Capello sympathizer, I risk losing everything, including the two people I most want to protect.

After thinking the matter through, I type out a response:

Find the funeral home. Whoever's so invested in avenging the Capello family would have visited them.

As an afterthought, I add:

And hack into Di Marco's daughter's phone in case she's connected to the hit.

I slip my device into my pocket, hoping Miko can find the man who wants me dead before he figures out I killed his precious Capellos. Something about his persistence tells me he won't be satisfied with only my death.

THIRTY-TWO

SERAPHINE

My heart pounds so loudly that it muffles the music as we approach the entrance of the familiar establishment. Leroi's hand on the small of my back is the only thing keeping me upright as the guard lets us through the doors of the Phoenix Nightclub.

He doesn't know this is where it all began. I came to this club, followed by that awful handler, to murder Enzo Montesano, the most powerful criminal in New Alderney. Leroi's uncle and my first kill.

I haven't told him the importance of this place because I want to face my demons. If I can get through tonight without killing or maiming anyone, then maybe I'll be normal for Gabriel... and for Leroi.

"Are you alright?" He slides my jacket off my shoulders and hands it to the coat check attendant.

My insides are quaking too much for me to speak and I don't want my voice to tremble, so I gaze into his dark eyes and nod.

He leans down and whispers in my ear, "You're going to

be fine. I'll be right here the entire night, watching your back."

His words are a balm on my frayed nerves and infuse me with the confidence I need to face the evening. Squaring my shoulders, I stare straight ahead into the dimly lit space, taking in the flashing lights and the sea of bodies jumping to the music. My nose fills with the mingled scents of dry ice and alcohol, giving me the familiar rush of adrenaline that comes before each mission.

The layout has changed in the five years since I was first here. There's now a cordoned-off section on the edge of the nightclub with its own bar. A guard stands at its entrance, making it clear that it's a VIP area, but there's still another door that leads to the room where Montesano's guard served me drugged champagne.

Crowds part for Leroi as we make our way toward the VIP section. I can't help but notice the glances we receive from both sexes. Leroi radiates power and not just because he's tall, muscular, and dressed in a tailored black suit. He stands out with his sharp cheekbones, chiseled jaw, and dark eyes. They're a deadly combination that signals danger and invites desire.

Leroi is so focused on me, he doesn't notice that every woman we pass is eyeing him with various degrees of hunger and awe. It's understandable. Compared to Leroi, every man in the club looks the same.

My skin hasn't stopped tingling since I stepped out of the fitting room wearing this dress. It's more revealing than the pastel ones I wore during my missions. Those were designed to make me look younger, innocent, more vulnerable. Tonight's the first time I've been allowed to go out with my dark hair and makeup, and I almost feel like a new woman.

After winding our way through the crowd, we finally reach the VIP section, and the guard steps aside to let us through. Leroi guides me to a table with a great view of the dance floor. As soon as we sit, the man behind the bar rushes forward with a menu.

"Whiskey on the rocks and..." He turns to me.

"Champagne," I say.

"Make that a Sprite," Leroi says.

As the waiter hurries back to the bar, I turn to Leroi with a scowl.

"I can handle my liquor," I say.

He raises a brow.

I lean into his side, keeping my voice quieter than the music. "My handler trained me to handle syringes in any physical state, including inebriation."

Leroi shifts in his seat, his features pinching.

"What?" I snap, still stinging at the reminder of how he once called my electrocution story bullshit. Leroi acts like I'm feral, as though I didn't endure six months of intensive and painful training.

"You don't believe me?" I ask.

"It's not that," he mutters.

"Then what?"

"I want you to stay sober tonight and not take any chances."

He doesn't elaborate on why he doesn't want me drinking, so I brush it off as one of his controlling quirks, like the way he made me meditate before we left and repeat a bunch of affirmations.

The waiter returns with our drinks. I sip from my glass and pretend it's champagne. One benefit of being irritated with Leroi is that my heart is no longer pounding. He has a way of erasing even the worst anxiety. The music is so loud that its bass makes my bones vibrate.

I straighten in my seat and survey the people on the dancefloor. Right now, I feel confident, poised, and because I'm sitting beside Leroi, powerful. It's a change from the first time I was here when I'd struggled with the thought of killing. Now, murder is infused in my blood.

Leroi's gaze burns the side of my face. I turn to meet his dark eyes and say, "Let's dance."

The corner of his lips lift. "Go right ahead."

"Come with me." I stand up and hold out my hand.

He snorts. "I don't dance."

I roll my eyes. "What's the point of going to a club just to sit around and drink?"

He lounges back in his seat and sweeps a hand toward the dance floor. "You dance. I'll watch."

With a huff, I turn on my heel and walk out of the VIP section to where everyone is dancing. The music is thumping with a tune I heard at the boutique, and I sway in time with the beat.

Leroi's gaze heats my skin, even though I'm trying not to look in his direction. No matter where I turn, he's on the edge of my awareness, a constant presence that's impossible to ignore.

In some ways, he reminds me of the handler Dad hired to train me into becoming a killer. They're both tall, dark, and unsmiling, except the handler didn't have a soul. He was a creep whose eyes I wanted to scoop out with a rusty spoon. Leroi might be a killer, but he has a heart.

A loud burst of giggles on my left catches my attention. I turn to find a group of five women around my age performing the same steps. It's a variation of the Grapevine, a dance so old Mom used to incorporate it into her aerobics routine. I watch them for a few repetitions before joining in.

As I dance, I catch Leroi's eyes again, but his expression is unreadable, though his gaze follows me like a sniper's red dot. I smirk. If he's so worried about what I might do to these women, then maybe he should come to the dance floor for a closer look.

"Hey," the woman closest to me yells over the music. "I like your shoes."

She's tall with a mass of dark curls that remind me of Gregor, the less insane of the twins who wore his hair long.

"Thanks," I shout back. "They came with the dress."

We continue the dance steps and the woman asks me more about my outfit. Her own dress is made of scraps of denim sewn together to mold around her curves. I'm no expert in fashion, but the outfit looks homemade.

The music changes, and I glance toward our table. A man wearing a black leather jacket sits beside him and is looking in our direction. He's dangerous and edgy, and reminds me of some of the men I've had to kill. Leroi is so relaxed around him that it's obvious they're friends or associates.

"What's your name?" shouts the curly-haired woman.

"Sera," I answer. "And you?"

"Emberly," she says. "My friends call me Ember."

Ember introduces me to the other women, whose names I instantly forget. They're a friendly bunch with bright eyes and easy smiles, but I can't help but feel disconnected. Everything about them is light and carefree, while my past is encased in the kind of darkness that can never feel bright.

All I feel for them is a bone-deep envy that makes my ribs ache.

The next time I glance in Leroi's direction, he's

standing and gesturing at that dark-haired woman who barged into our apartment, Rosalind.

I'm about to charge over to the VIP section to handle her, when a pair of arms wrap around my waist and I feel a tiny erection grind into my ass. The hands move to my hips and a deep voice slurs in my ear, "Hey, baby, wanna dance?"

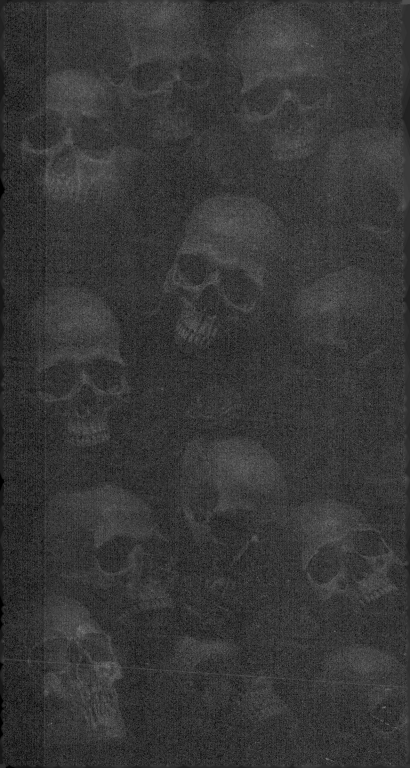

THIRTY-THREE

LEROI

I can't keep my eyes off her, and the way she moves in that golden dress is mesmerizing. With her hair darkened and the makeup, she finally looks her age. Seraphine looks radiant, dancing with the other women as though she belongs with them.

Someone approaches from the side. I rise off my seat and lock gazes with Roman, who grins at me like I'm Santa Claus.

"When the fuck did they let you out?" I wrap an arm around my cousin's shoulders.

"A few hours ago." He slaps me on the back. "I fucking owe you, man."

"We're even." I lower myself back into my armchair.

Roman takes the seat next to mine, his eyes scanning the crowd. "Cesare told me your girlfriend was tall." He nods towards Seraphine. "You got someone new?"

"Sort of."

I shift in the seat. Roman might be my oldest friend and cousin, but I'm not about to open up wounds. He won't take kindly to knowing that Uncle Enzo was taken out by an underage assassin for being a prick who couldn't keep his hands off little girls, and not a heart attack as we'd all been led to believe. Some secrets are best left festering in the grave.

"See that girl dancing with yours?" Roman says.

My gaze darts back to where the sextet still performs the same steps. "Which one?"

"Patchwork denim."

"What about her?"

"That's Emberly Kay."

I turn to look Roman full in the face. "You have got to be fucking joking."

"Benito noticed her the moment she stepped through the doors. That's why I rushed here." Roman's eyes gleam. "I wanted a closer look at Capello's hidden daughter."

My mind stalls for the split second it takes for me to realize he's talking about the woman he wanted me to kill and not Seraphine. While both of them might consider themselves Capello's daughters, only the taller one with the dark curls is his heir.

"What are you planning?" I ask.

He rubs his chin. "I've changed my mind about taking her out."

"Why?"

"Last week, our lawyer set up a meeting with Joe Di Marco." He pauses. "That's Capello's attorney. We wanted to work out a legal way to get back Dad's assets, but that bastard had a will that left everything to her."

"So?"

"I just heard that if she dies, her next of kin is a distant relative with connections to the Galliano family in New Jersey." He shakes his head and grimaces. "Too risky."

"Does she know she's a billionaire?"

He flashes me a grin. "Someone murdered Joe Di Marco before he got a chance to deliver the news."

I nod, my features falling into a mask of indifference. "What's your next move?"

"Emberly Kay, and everything she owns is going to be mine."

"Don't tell me you plan on romancing her out of her fortune," I say with a laugh.

"Watch me."

He claps me on the shoulder and rises, only for his brothers, Cesare and Benito to appear at the other side of the cordon.

I stare at my cousins, wondering what they plan on doing to Emberly after they've divested her of her fortune. Most of Capello's wealth originally belonged to the Montesano family, but Emberly Kay never met Capello and is innocent.

Why am I even thinking about this? I have enough to concern myself with Seraphine.

When the Montesano brothers step aside to let in Rosalind, my lip curls. I glance at the dance floor, where Seraphine and Emberly are deep in conversation, and I turn my gaze back to Rosalind.

She flashes me a smile. "Hey, I want to apologize for coming to your apartment—"

"What did I tell you?" I rise out of my seat.

Her steps falter, and her eyes widen. "You didn't say anything about approaching you in a club."

"It's over. Go fuck someone else."

"Is it because of that blonde bitch?" She glances around, looking for signs of Seraphine.

"This is your last warning," I growl. "Get lost."

Rosalind raises a hand. I don't know if she wants to slap me or claw out my eyes, but I grab her wrist and spin her around. When she presses her ass into my crotch, I realize my mistake. Rosalind is the sort of woman who wants any kind of attention, particularly if it's negative or painful. I should have known better to react.

Movement out of the corner of my eye pulls my attention to the dance floor. Some asshole has grabbed Seraphine from behind and is grinding his crotch into her ass. She struggles against his hold, but that only encourages him to grip her by the hips.

The sight of that bastard with his hands on her ignites a spark of fury that has me shoving Rosalind to one side and storming toward the dance floor. Hasn't Seraphine suffered enough at the hands of psychopaths? She doesn't need to endure this grabby sociopath.

"What the hell?" The look on his face when I grab him by the neck is almost comical.

"Come with me." I drag him off the dance floor.

Rosalind trots after us, but Cesare encircles her waist. If I wasn't so incensed by the asshole who touched Seraphine, I might warn Cesare to be careful with Rosalind, since she's a snoop, a stalker and a reporter. I shelve that thought and haul the groper out through a fire exit.

Cool air wafts over my senses, but it does nothing to lower the temperature of my blood. It reaches a boiling point when the other man falls onto the ground with a yell. Discipline and common sense tell me that the danger has passed. I should return to the club and watch over Seraphine, but my baser instincts scream at me to make this guy pay.

He scrambles to his hands and knees, but a kick in the gut brings him back on his belly.

"What the fuck do you want from me?" he yells.

"That girl you touched is mine," I snarl.

"I-I didn't know," he stammers. "She was dancing like she wanted the attention—"

"She wasn't." I press my foot into the back of his neck, making him whimper.

The training Anton drummed into my head tells me to back off now before I do something that will attract the wrong attention. I've already neutralized the threat, and killing a man in an alleyway is both reckless and a waste of clean up resources.

But I think of Seraphine, kept in that basement and blackmailed to enter clubs like this to murder predatory targets. How many times did she force herself to endure the touch of assholes who only saw her as an object to grope and fuck?

The asshole grabs my heel, attempting to push my foot off his neck. Bile rises to the back of my throat. I pull out my pistol and attach a silencer to its barrel.

"What are you doing?" His voice rises several octaves.

"Making sure you never touch her again."

The man's eyes widen, and his breath comes in ragged pants. "You've got to be kidding me. It was only a dance. I didn't hurt her. She was asking for it." He thrashes. "God, please. Do you want money? Take my wallet."

Blood roars between my ears, muffling the sound of his begging. A crimson haze creeps along the edges of my vision, crowding out everything else apart from this worthless piece of vermin. How many times did Seraphine beg for mercy before her mind shattered? How many times did she replay the rape and murder of her mother?

The questions spin around, along with images of the

collar, the chip, the chain attached to the wall. I press the silencer against his temple and pull the trigger.

He falls limp, and then my mind falls silent.

A breeze blows down the alley, cooling the outer layer of my skin. I stare down at the unmoving body, and blink away the red fog of rage.

What the fuck was that?

The last time I lost control like that, I was fourteen, finding my stepfather on top of my little sister.

After that, Anton trained me out of my impulsiveness. I've meditated, wrestled down my emotions to nothingness, and executed over a hundred and fifty kills. This short time I've spent with Seraphine has unraveled the tight hold I've placed over my restraint.

Shit.

If I don't rein in these feelings brewing toward Seraphine, I'm going to get us both killed.

I detach the silencer, shove the pistol back in its holster and spit at the corpse lying at my feet. The longer I stand out here, the more time I'm leaving Seraphine exposed to some other asshole who finds her irresistible.

After dragging him behind a dumpster, I send Don a quick text and forward the location on Google Maps. He messages back with a thumbs up, and I reenter the club, hoping to fuck that Seraphine hasn't gotten herself into trouble.

THIRTY-FOUR

SERAPHINE

I'm about to follow Leroi and the creep he's dragging off the dance floor when a small hand grabs my shoulder.

"That guy is friends with the owners," Ember yells over the music. "Let him deal with the creep."

My brows pinch. "You know them?"

She flicks her head. "My roommate recognized them."

"Come on." She tugs my arm and pulls me toward her friends.

I dart my gaze across the dance floor. Leroi has already disappeared into the crowd. I catch a glimpse of Rosalind being manhandled by a man similar to the one who was talking to Leroi and hope he's escorting her to the door.

Maybe Ember has a point. Leroi wanted me to get through tonight without murdering or maiming, and rushing after that guy with a broken bottle might jeopardize my reward.

Heat pools between my thighs at the thought of him giving me another orgasm, so I turn back to join Ember and her friends. The music is faster, and they've started a new sequence of steps. It takes two rounds for me to pick up the pattern before I'm dancing.

Assholes gather around our group like vultures, making my skin itch. One of them approaches and wraps an arm around my waist, and my heart rate spikes.

"Hey, babe," he murmurs, setting my hackles soaring.

My gut churns with a cocktail of agitation, nausea, and resentment. For a split second, I imagine it's me being held down by those guards and not Mom. Then the pressure inside me explodes.

I whirl around in time to the music and elbow him in the gut with enough strength to make him double over, his face turning a putrid shade of red. The jackals watching us erupt into cheers.

"Don't touch me," I yell over the noise.

The man steps back with both hands raised. "Sorry, sorry."

I glare in his direction until he disappears into the throng. When I turn back, Ember and her friends are grinning. Some of the tension drains from my body, and I exhale a trembling breath.

Shit. I did it.

My chest fills with warm triumph. I stood up for myself without shedding blood, and I may have even earned a bit of respect from Ember and her friends.

When we continue dancing, my steps are lighter, and I'm smiling so hard my cheeks ache. More women join the circle, and for a moment, I imagine I'm just like everyone else—normal and carefree. The only thing that would make this better is if Leroi were here to witness my victory.

The music slows, and a few of the girls in our group break off to slow dance with men. My skin tingles with the sense of being watched by someone more powerful and significant than any of the onlookers, and when I turn around, I lock eyes with Leroi.

My heart thuds with anticipation. Even at twenty feet away, Leroi stands out amongst the crowd. It's not just that he's taller and more muscular, it's the way he carries himself. He commands attention and respect, his presence so imposing that all other men fade into the background.

A few women on the dance floor turn to move in his direction, their movements more exaggerated, trying to attract his attention, but their efforts are wasted. Leroi looks at me like we are the only two people here, and everyone else has ceased to exist.

His gaze is so intense that it lands on my skin with a lingering caress. Warmth rises to my cheeks, and my steps falter. Frozen, I'm caught in his sight. Predator and prey. All my attention centered on him.

I want him to take me away from the crowd and back to our apartment. I want him to pull me into his bedroom and kiss me breathless. I want him to growl filthy words in my ear and taste me until I come apart on his tongue. Most of all, I want him by my side as we step over the bones of my enemies and rescue Gabriel.

The crowd parts as he stalks across the dance floor toward me. With each approaching step, my heart races harder, faster, until its vibrations reach my core. When he reaches me, I'm sure that I've stopped breathing because the edges of my vision blur and all that's left is Leroi and the music.

He takes my hand, pulls me into his chest, and wraps an arm around my waist. I suck in a shuddering breath when he leans in, his lips a mere inch away from mine.

Instead of kissing me, he murmurs into my ear, "I saw what you did to that red-faced bastard. I'm so proud of you."

My heart swells. I scramble for the right words, but nothing comes to mind.

"I thought you said you didn't dance," I say with a smile.

His deep chuckle tickles my skin. "I don't."

"Then what do you call this?"

He pulls back and gazes down with the tiniest hint of a smile. "A congratulatory hug."

"In time to the music?"

He smirks. "I didn't say I couldn't dance. But I'll make an exception for you."

Enchanted, I stare into his fathomless eyes, my heartbeat drowning out the music. We continue swaying to the music, locked in a connection I never knew existed.

The worst part about my imprisonment was the absolute power they held over me when they took Gabriel hostage. As long as they hid where they were keeping my brother, I couldn't see a future for either of us.

I certainly never saw myself dancing with a man like Leroi.

He doesn't recoil from me for being a killer. Instead, he's more concerned that I might get caught. He's kind and strong and considerate. He's the only man who's ever shown me the true meaning of pleasure.

"Let's go home," he says.

Home. The word fills me with giddy warmth. When I nod, the arm around my waist slides toward my hand, and he intertwines our fingers.

I turn to say goodbye to Ember, but she's already deep in conversation with an older man. They both look acquainted with each other, so I turn back to Leroi.

"Ready?" he asks.

"Let's go."

Leroi leads me to the edge of the dance floor. I take one last glance over my shoulder at Ember to wave goodbye, but she's waving her arms at the man as though trying to make a point.

"What happened to that guy?" I ask as we walk to the cloakroom to collect our jackets.

He doesn't reply.

"Leroi?" I place a hand on his bicep.

He stares straight ahead, a muscle in his jaw flexing.

My gaze drops to a glistening speck of liquid on his shoe. As he accepts our jackets, the light catches and I tilt my head, squinting to get a closer look. It's thick, viscous, crimson.

It's blood.

I straighten, my eyes widening, my mind putting together the clues.

Leroi's narrow. "That man was a threat. He won't be bothering anyone again."

I'm reeling on my feet as he slips my jacket over my shoulders. Not because he murdered a creep who deserved to die, but because Leroi broke the rules.

He wraps an arm around my waist and pulls me into his side, his features a stony mask. That man Leroi killed wasn't dangerous or even significant—just a regular lecherous asshole.

"Leroi?" I whisper as we walk to the exit.

"Don't ask," he growls.

My throat dries. This is the third man he's murdered to protect me. The first was the one I stabbed at the gas station. He garrotted that one so he wouldn't reveal anything about me to the police. The second was Pietro. Leroi snapped his neck for slashing my palm. Now, he's killed that creep for grinding on my ass.

I stare at his handsome profile, wondering why he's been taking such risks when he's always so controlled.

Could he... like me?

We step out into the street, and a pair of green eyes meet mine. It only takes a second for them to widen with recognition, and I jerk my head to the side.

It's Samson.

Samson Fucking Capello.

The more psychotic of the twins, whom Leroi said was dead.

THIRTY-FIVE

LEROI

Thank fuck Seraphine dropped that line of questioning because I'm a hypocrite. Every day, I chastise her for being careless and impulsive, yet I'm the one who's racking up the kills. I can't explain it. It's not something I want to admit, but my little murderess is seeping under my skin and burrowing her sweet way into my heart.

I couldn't stand the thought of anyone else touching her but me, let alone that worthless opportunist. Seraphine is mine. I swore to protect her from the evils of the world. Myself included.

If I don't keep this fixation with her under control, the mystery Capello sympathizer will be the least of our worries.

Seraphine clings to my arm with both hands, squeezing so tightly that I stare down at her and frown. She can't still be angry about that asshole?

"Hurry to the car," she whispers. "Please."

I've done this job long enough to know the signs of someone sensing danger, and her fear is unmistakable.

Picking up my pace, I hover a hand on my holster. "What's wrong?"

"Later."

We're inside the car in an instant. I start the engine, pull out, and don't speak until we're halfway down the road.

"Talk to me," I say.

"Are you sure you killed every member of the Capello family?" she asks.

My eyes narrow. Maybe I should have pulled her out of that group of girls and informed her of the identity of her new dance companion, but she was having so much fun. I didn't have the heart to ruin her night.

"I went through each room, taking out every guest staying in the mansion. There's going to be a few cousins or illegitimate children left over, but I got everyone who counted. Why?"

She releases a shaky breath. "I just saw Samson."

My hands grip the steering wheel. "Capello?"

When she doesn't answer, I glance over to the passenger side. She sits forward with her head bowed, her darkened hair hiding her face.

"Are you sure?" I ask.

"I saw that face nearly every day the past five years," she replies, her voice hoarse. "I also know the difference between Gregor and Samson."

Fuck.

That wasn't my question, but she's unknowingly given me an answer and solved the mystery behind the Capello sympathizer who hired me to take out the lone gunman. It also explains who Joseph Di Marco was trying to protect.

Samson Capello.

How the hell is he still alive?

Pressure builds up behind my eyes like a kettle. I squint

through the windshield at the road ahead and mentally retrace my steps.

"The second Capello son I killed was sleeping face-down on the bed. I shot him in the back of the head."

"Did you turn him around?"

"I didn't take the chance after having trouble with the first one." My jaw tightens. "Nobody could survive a gunshot at such close range."

"But if he was staying the night with his fiancée..."

She doesn't need to complete her sentence because I'm already coming to the same conclusion. Samson must have gone home with Di Marco's daughter or somewhere else, and let one of the guests use his room. Until now, he's been lying low and working with his father's lawyer to take out a contract on the man who killed his family.

"Did he see you?" I ask through clenched teeth.

"He looked right at my face," she replies.

My gut clenches. "Did he recognize you?"

"I don't know," she murmurs. "Maybe. I glanced over my shoulder at him, but he was already halfway down the road."

Reaching across the front seat, I grip her shoulder. "We'll figure this out. I'll keep you safe."

A barely perceptible nod is her only response, but I can't blame her lack of trust. After all, I assured her that the people keeping her prisoner were all dead. Now one of them not only survived, but knows she's thriving.

I don't remember ever having left a job with so many loose ends. Samson Capello and all the resources that come with his organization are going to be difficult to navigate.

———

Hours later, I'm still at her bedside, stroking her silken hair. It's my way of assuring her she's safe. As soon as I'm certain she's peacefully asleep, I walk next door to Miko's apartment. He's usually up until the ass-crack of dawn, so I know he'll be awake.

Miko lets me in with a grin. "Ready for that game?"

I run a hand through my hair. "No time."

His face falls. "What's happened?"

"Samson Capello is alive."

"You're joking."

"Seraphine saw him when we were leaving the club."

Miko shakes his head. "But you killed both twins."

I give him a shortened version of my mistaken identity theory, and he curses. "Nobody visited the funeral house except Joseph Di Marco and his daughter," he says. "If one of the twins had been there, I would have seen it in the security footage."

"I expect he's been keeping a low profile to make sure whoever killed his family didn't know he's still alive."

"What are you going to do?" Miko walks across the room and settles behind one of his monitors.

Lowering myself into the gaming chair next to his, I exhale a long breath. "Finish the job I started."

"What about Seraphine?" he asks.

"We're going to work our way through Capello's bodyguards. At least one of them will lead us to Samson's whereabouts."

"I could hack into the nightclub's security feed," Miko says.

"He only walked past the entrance, but you can see if the camera caught anything."

I pick up my phone. It's time to inform the Montesano brothers of this new development. Wiping out the Capello family wasn't just about getting Roman off death row. They also wanted to claw back the empire Frederic Capello stole from their father.

"Any word on Gabriel?" I ask.

He looks up from his screen. "Are you sure you still want me looking for the brother? If Samson's out there, putting out hits on your head—"

"Gabriel is the only leverage he has over Seraphine," I say. "There's no telling what she might do if Samson makes her choose between her brother's survival or slitting my throat."

Miko shudders. "Alright. I'll keep digging."

Benito is the first to reply with a string of expletives, followed by a list of Samson's usual haunts. I doubt that the last legitimate Capello will be out in the open again after being recognized.

Roman doesn't text back, and neither does Cesare. I expect Roman is busy trying to romance Emberly Kay out of her inheritance. Cesare? I shake my head. Let's just say that Rosalind won't have any complaints.

"I searched all hospitals within a hundred-mile radius of New Alderney," Miko says, breaking me from my thoughts. "There was no trace of anyone with the name of Capello, Capelli, or any other variation, beginning with CAPE having had a liver transplant."

"So he used another fake name?"

"That's what I thought, so I searched all liver transplants with live donors and narrowed them down by gender, age, and ethnicity."

"And?"

"Thirty-four."

"Any way to find out which patients are repeat transplants?"

He shakes his head. "None, but if he used a different fake name—"

"And a different date of birth." I rub my chin.

"I'll keep looking. Once I find Capello's transplant information, then I'll be able to locate information on the donor."

I'm about to make another suggestion when my phone rings. It's Rita, sounding snippy. "The client just called with a description of a man he thinks is the shooter."

Fuck.

"Do you know what he said?" she asks.

I don't reply because Rita is already on a roll.

"That the man was last seen escorting his sister into a black BMW and even gave me the license plate number. He wants to know why he's making more progress than trained professionals."

I exhale the longest breath. "We're not a detective agency, and if he already knew the identity of the killer, why didn't he provide that information?"

"Don't you think I asked him that?" she answers with a huff. "He's considering passing those details to another agency."

I swallow back a curse. "Tell him we'll send details of the car's owner during working hours. If we can ID the lone gunman, he'll be dead before the close of business tomorrow."

"Alright," she says, sounding less harried. "We've also had a few more inquiries, but all the junior agents are busy with assignments."

"Turn them down. I'm busy chasing down this mysterious gunman."

"Anton never refused work, no matter how busy the firm got," she says.

"Anton is retired."

I don't know her well enough to explain what's really happening. She's loyal to Anton, and Anton is Seraphine's former handler.

"Fine. I'll wait for the client to call back." Rita hangs up.

My nostrils flare. Samson Capello has the nerve to refer to Seraphine as his sister. Men don't exploit and assault their female relatives or keep them chained to the walls like dogs, they protect them.

At the thought of my sister, my heartstrings twang with a pang of regret. Regret at the looks of combined horror on their faces when I shot her attacker in the head.

When Anton took me away, he also helped my family move to another state. I tracked them down, but they refused to speak to me or even acknowledge my presence. I lost them forever because I could no longer stand by and let them get hurt by that bastard.

Seraphine isn't like them. She doesn't recoil at the prospect of death and violence. She thrives on it, perhaps a little too much, but she's the only person I know whose soul is both as pure as it is tainted.

Rising to my feet, I head to the door. I'll protect Seraphine from her enemies and anyone else who wishes her harm. And that starts now by grabbing one of the bastards who helped kill her mother.

THIRTY-SIX

SERAPHINE

I can't eat, can't sleep, can't think of anything but Samson being alive.

If he believes I'm connected to his family's deaths, then he might finally carry out his threat to kill my brother. Samson could be interrogating Gabriel right now or making him suffer in revenge for his grief.

Thoughts like this swirl around in my head, adding to images of Dad ripping out Gabriel's liver over and over in a Promethean punishment for Mom's cheating. I lie as still as death, trying to erase my mind, but it's like trying to fight the wind.

Leroi stands in the doorway of my bedroom. I can feel his eyes on me, but I refuse to acknowledge his presence. He was supposed to have killed the entire family and now the most psychotic of them still lives. I don't know how I feel about him right now. He helped me escape from the basement and I want to be mad at him, but I can't find it in myself to feel furious.

Samson was awful enough before I bit through his penis

and made it rot. If Dad and Gregor hadn't been there to control his anger, he would have tortured me slowly until I begged for death.

With a sigh, Leroi retreats from my room and shuts the door.

My eyes snap open, and I stare into the dark. Tomorrow, I need to convince Leroi to let me hunt Samson. Every moment Samson spends alive is a risk to Gabriel's continued survival.

Hours pass, and the sky changes from black to indigo to blue before the morning sun shines in my eyes. I lie on my back, all traces of enjoyment from the nightclub forgotten, as I work out a way to get to Samson.

It's difficult since Leroi has reverted into overprotective mode and scrubbed his home of weapons sharper than a table knife. The front door is locked, and the apartment is too high up for me to climb down from the balcony. He probably thinks I'll try to escape to find Samson.

Being so dependent on Leroi makes my skin itch. He moves too slowly and makes too little progress. We should be out there, kicking down doors, smashing heads, and blowing up buildings to hunt down Samson, the guards who assaulted Mom, and whoever's keeping Gabriel hostage.

The door opens, and Leroi fills the doorway, dressed for action in a black hoodie and dark jeans. I sit up, my heart pounding.

"We can't just sit around waiting," I say, my voice tight. "Samson is out there, probably torturing Gabriel. We need to find—"

"Come with me." He disappears into the living room.

"Where are we going?" I scramble out of bed.

"I've tracked down one of your leads." He strides to the front door. "He's waiting for us downstairs."

My heart skips several beats as I follow Leroi out of the apartment, down the elevator, and to the basement parking lot. He leads me outside to a courtyard lined with dumpsters, where an armored truck awaits, similar to the one he and Miko used to drive away from the mansion.

Leroi unlocks its side door and gestures for me to step inside. Its interior is dark, save for a stream of light coming in from an upper vent that reflects against walls and floors covered in a transparent plastic wrap.

A heavy-set man wearing blue boxers, a sleeveless shirt, and a black hood over his head sits tied to a chair in the back.

"Who is this?" I ask.

Leroi steps in behind me and shuts the door. "See for yourself."

My pulse quickens with anticipation. I already know this isn't Samson. The bound man is older, hairier, and fatter.

I snatch off the hood and stare into the unconscious face of the bastards who haunt my dreams. Julio Catania, the man who pinned Mom down to Dad's desk, wrapped his meaty hands around her throat, and pounded into her until she fell limp.

My ears fill with the remembered shouts from that night, Mom's cries for mercy, my bumbling cowardice, the way I sobbed into the phone, begging 911 for help.

"Where did you find him?" I whisper.

"It took a lot of digging and a few favors, but we tracked him down to a summer house that belonged to his sister," Leroi says, his voice low. "I drove down and collected him while you were asleep."

"Is he drugged?"

"I knocked him out with a punch," Leroi replies.

Drawing back my arm, I deliver a slap so hard that it echoes across the enclosed space. Julio's head snaps to the side and he grimaces.

"What the..." he slurs, his eyes squeezing shut.

I deliver another blow, this time the sting travels up to my elbow.

Julio glares at me, his eyes burning. I can already tell he doesn't recognize me because he's still calm. He doesn't realize he won't leave this truck alive. Yet.

"I've thought about you every day for the past five years."

His eyes widen, confirming my suspicions. He doesn't even look like he recalls what he did that terrible night. Maybe he's lost track of the many women he's assaulted and murdered.

"Who are you?" he asks.

"You don't remember?" I lean closer, my blood set to boil.

The pulse between my ears pounds so hard that I can barely hear the man's rapid breaths. Grinding my molars, I trace a finger down his cheek, enjoying how he recoils.

"Do you remember Evangeline?" I ask, my throat constricting.

Recognition flashes across Julio's features, followed by wide-eyed horror. He struggles against his restraints and rocks back and forth, trying to knock aside his chair.

I bare my teeth. "I've thought about a hundred different ways to repay you for what you did to her."

"It wasn't me." He shakes his head. "I was under orders. Frederic—"

"Is dead, and you're here to take both sets of punishments."

Julio's gaze darts to Leroi, although I'm not sure

whether it's out of some sense of male solidarity or if he's delusional and desperate. Leroi wouldn't lift a finger to help him after all the trouble he went to tracking down the bastard rapists.

Leroi clears his throat. "You might consider bartering his life for information."

My head whips around, and I glare at Leroi, who's standing by a table in the truck's corner. Is he taking Julio's side?

He opens up a wooden box containing a display of knives, followed by a tool kit crammed full of orange-handled implements. "If Mr. Catania chooses not to redeem himself, there's plenty here that will make him talk."

I study Leroi's features, wondering if this is some kind of game. Even if Julio handed me Gabriel's address and the key to his cell, I would still give him a painful death. I shake off that thought. Leroi is probably reminding me not to kill that bastard before I extract some intel.

"What do you want to know?" Julio asks, his voice rising.

Leroi nods, giving me the go-ahead to start.

"Where's Gabriel?" I ask.

His features fall slack. "Who?"

"Evangeline's son," I snap, my pulse pounding, my patience fraying into thin threads. "My brother. The man being used as a liver donor."

Julio's chest rises and falls like a set of bellows. "I swear to god, Frederic didn't tell me. I thought he got that liver on the black market—"

"Liar." I deliver another slap, this one hurting my hand even worse than the second.

Leroi clears his throat again, and it's a reminder that I

don't need to use my hands. Not when I have two sets of weapons.

Turning on my heel, I walk to the table. Leroi steps aside, giving me the space to peruse the implements of torture.

If Julio can't lead me to Gabriel or even Samson, then I'll force him to tell me who might have that information. After that, I'll slay the first of my demons.

THIRTY-SEVEN

LEROI

I lean against the wall of the truck with my arms folded across my chest. The space behind the apartment block is deserted six days out of seven, and the vehicle we're in is completely sound-proofed. Seraphine can torture this man to her heart's content without the risk of being disturbed.

The first instrument she snatches off the table is a paring knife, one of the few Anton recommends for precision work. Julio Catania stares with wide-eyed horror as she runs the flat of the blade up and down his flushed cheeks. He's sweating and shaking under her scrutiny.

"You're going to tell me what you know about my brother, or I'll slice off your iris."

He squeezes his eyes shut and sobs. "That night Frederic punished Evangeline, he sent out two pairs of guards to fetch the son and daughter—"

"Which guards?" she asks.

"It was five years ago," he yells. "I don't remember."

"Try."

She presses the tip of its blade into his eye socket,

drawing out a bead of blood. As it runs down his cheek, my mind sinks back to the time she pinned me to the mattress and held me at knifepoint.

My cock stirs at the memory, and I groan. I'm not a masochist or in any way submissive, but I can't help but marvel at the thought of her taking what she wants from me at knifepoint.

I close my eyes, pushing aside the thought of what else she might have taken that morning, and focus on the moment. The consequences will be dire for both of us if we don't find Gabriel and Samson Capello.

Catania screams, and my eyes snap open. She's carved a line from the corner of his lip to his cheekbone in a sick parody of a smile.

"You held her down and laughed as you choked out her life," she says, her voice raw. "You all laughed."

My breath quickens, as does my pulse. There's nothing I despise more than a man who overpowers a woman and disregards her humanity.

Catania jerks his head away. "The guards he sent after the son were Ferrante and Rochas. The pair who were supposed to get the daughter came back ten minutes later to say she was gone."

Seraphine's gaze darts to mine, and I nod. Mike Ferrante and Paolo Rochas are already on the list of people we need to see, but I'll bump them up to the top.

"What do you know about Samson?" she asks.

"He's dead, along with the others."

"I saw him yesterday." She walks behind him and grabs his neck in a choke hold.

Catania shakes his head from side to side. "You're wrong. When I got to the house the day after the shooting, there were twelve body bags. One of them was labeled Samson Capello."

"Then someone lied." She positions the knife at the other corner of his mouth and slices upward, completing the grotesque grin.

With blood streaming from the base of his eye socket like tears and both sides of his mouth smeared with blood, Catania looks like a broken clown.

Artistic.

I rub my chin. How many lies is he prepared to tell for his new boss? All clues point to Samson being alive, starting with the mystery client who wants me dead and ending with Seraphine seeing him outside the club. There's no other explanation.

"Who identified the bodies?" she asks.

I nod. Whoever lied about Samson being among the corpses must have colluded with him to form the pretense that he was dead. I'm impressed that Seraphine is keeping a cool head during the interrogation, even if her methods are unconventional.

He coughs, spraying blood across the floor. "Rochas said he walked around and found the family murdered in their beds."

Paolo Rochas moves to the very top of our list.

Seraphine asks a few more questions, mostly rephrasing her previous inquiries to see if Catania's answers change, but they don't. Eventually, she tilts her head. "Is that every-thing you know about Samson and Gabriel?"

"I swear it. On my daughter's life."

"Then I hope she'll appreciate that I'm getting rid of one more rapist," she says, her lip curling.

His eyes widen. "But I've told you all I know—"

"It's time to pay for what you did to Evangeline."

"She was a whore," Catania yells. "Evangeline was fucking Raphael the entire time she was with Frederic. She only got was what coming—"

Seraphine plunges the knife into his gut, twisting his words into an anguished howl. "Now, you know what it feels like to be penetrated against your will."

Blood spills down Catania's belly and soaks into his pants. The vehicle's walls tremble with his screams. She shoves the knife in and out of the same spot over and over in rhythmic thrusts.

A shiver runs down my spine and settles in my balls. If she wanted him dead, she would have chosen a longer knife or stabbed a vital organ. She's showing him what it's like to be violated.

"Stop," he rasps. "I'll tell you everything."

Seraphine pauses, mid-thrust. "Go on."

"Samson is alive," he slurs, barely able to form the words through his pain. "I haven't seen him since Frederic's birthday party. He's keeping a low profile until the people responsible for killing the family are dead."

I turn my attention to Seraphine, who asks, "Where is he staying?"

"It was his fiancée's house at first," he says through panting breaths. "But after they got to her father, he moved somewhere else and didn't say."

What?

Miko and I didn't pick up any signs of Samson at Joseph Di Marco's house unless he was staying in the servant's quarters or in a building on the grounds.

"Put down the knife," Catania sobs. "I'll do anything. I'll even go back to them for you and spy."

She returns the paring knife to the table, making me frown. Surely she doesn't believe this asshole? Her fingers hover over the tools, pausing briefly at the spirit level before she picks up a claw hammer and the measuring tape.

"You like choking women while fucking them," she says, her voice flat.

"What?" He shakes his head. "I-I don't—"

She swings the claw hammer and connects it with Catania's nose, eliciting a howl that spikes my pulse. Blood explodes from the wound and splatters across her beautiful face.

My balls tighten at her elegant display of violence, and my cock pushes painfully against my zipper. I can't believe I ever criticized her methods. Seraphine is an artist.

Instead of swinging once more, she walks behind Catania and loops the measuring tape around his neck.

"This is what it feels like to be choked," she snarls, her voice menacing.

As she tugs on the tape, Catania's eyes widen. I step forward to get a closer look. I've seen garrotes made of wire or rope or even neckties, but never one fashioned out of something so mundane. She twists it around her hand, pulling it even higher around his neck.

Catania wheezes and gasps, his face turning a deep shade of red that matches the blood still weeping from his injuries. His breaths become labored, his eyes bulge, and he thrashes within his restraints.

"Take it, whore," Seraphine yells over the sounds of his screams. "Take it all."

With her free hand, she jams the hammer's handle into his stab wound, making me groan. I have never seen someone so small and innocent commit such a violent act of justice.

Seraphine's cheeks are flushed the way they were when we were in the fetish store. Without the contact lenses, her eyes are blue and bright, giving me glimpses of the insanity that dwells within her soul. It's creative, spontaneous, and thrilling. My breath quickens, and I regret not being awake during her poker massacre.

She's an avenging angel, bathed with righteousness and blood. An avenging angel I am aching to taste.

I've never been more aroused.

Catania's gaze meets mine in a silent plea for mercy, but I'm so mesmerized by Seraphine's ability to improvise that I can't even muster up the words to tell him he brought this punishment onto himself.

Because he did.

He should have refused Capello's depraved order, but he followed it out of a desire to degrade Evangeline. I wouldn't be surprised if he'd already harbored sick thoughts about Seraphine's mother, and that moment was the culmination of his twisted dreams. Now, he's being violated and strangled by a beautiful woman.

What a way to die.

Possessiveness overwhelms my thoughts at the sight of Seraphine violating another man. I want to be the one who makes her blood run hot, the one to take her to the brink of pleasure.

Catania falls limp. I can't tell if he's dead or just unconscious, but I don't care.

I push off the wall and stalk toward Seraphine, who gazes up at me with defiance.

My cock throbs with the need to own her, claim her, make her mine, but I swore to myself that I wouldn't get involved.

No kissing.

No penetrative sex.

That was our arrangement.

"I made another mess," she says, her voice husky.

"You did." I cup the side of her face.

She lowers her lashes, her breath coming in shallow pants as though she finds my touch electrifying. When she raises her gaze to meet mine again, her eyes spark with desire. They're a silent plea for me to take control.

Shit.

I should send her back to the apartment, wait until my blood is cooled, or even walk away. I should distract her with the mention of Gabriel.

But I can't.

I can't focus on anything but Seraphine's hunger.

There's a darkness to her that draws me in so deeply that I lose all notions of good intentions.

My thumb brushes over her bottom lip, making her shiver. She takes another step closer until we're breathing the same air. When she presses against me and brings her mouth closer to mine, my resolve not to get involved crumbles.

It's just one kiss. Just one taste.

"Fuck it."

I lean down and press my lips to hers, and instantly regret it. Kissing Seraphine is like finding home. As I pull back, she loops the tape measure around the back of my neck and holds me in place.

THIRTY-EIGHT

SERAPHINE

Leroi's lips deliver a warmth that goes straight to my heart and a zing that shoots straight to my core. As he draws back, I tighten my grip on my makeshift garrote, not wanting the kiss to end.

"Seraphine," he groans against my lips.

"Don't stop." I kiss him back, pressing my body against his.

He resists, and for a moment I wonder if he'll break through the tape measure I looped around his neck and tell me he only meant to give me a congratulatory peck until I tighten my grip and slip my tongue between his lips.

Leroi advances even closer, his sculpted body radiating a delicious heat. His fingers curl into my hair with a possessive grip that makes my breath catch. His heart thumps against my chest as his tongue twists around mine. He's tasting me, exploring me, driving me to the edge of ecstasy.

I'm burning up, consumed by Leroi's kiss. I press my hips against his thigh, aching for a deeper connection. I lose myself in his overwhelming presence, until the voices, the images, and the emotions from that night fade back into the recesses of my consciousness.

Leroi is my peace of mind, and his presence is my tranquility. He's the most exciting man I've ever encountered. The heat of this kiss burns through my barriers and ignites the flames of my desire. I want more. I want him.

The tape measure slips from my fingers, and I explore his body. Every ridge, every crease, every contour of his shoulders, pecs, and abs, feels exactly as I'd imagined. Hard as stone yet beneath his clothes lies the heat of his blood.

But he's wearing too much.

My pulse quickens, and warmth pools low in my belly. I need to take off all the layers of clothing and slide beneath his skin. As my fingers curl into the fabric of his shirt, he takes my wrists in his firm grasp and pins them behind my back.

"What do you want from me?" His voice is barely a whisper, yet delivers a thrill that makes my thighs clench.

The answer rises to the back of my throat. I want to be accepted. I want to be protected. I want to be loved. I picture a future of us working together as assassins, ridding the world of those who deserve to die.

"Everything," I moan. "You. I want you."

Leroi pulls back, robbing me of his heat. When he stares down to meet my gaze, his dark eyes burn like embers. Breathing hard through parted lips, he rasps out the words, "Are you sure?"

Sure is an understatement. If he doesn't continue this kiss, I swear I'm going to die.

"Please," I whisper.

He crushes his lips back to mine, this time with his arms holding our bodies so closely that I melt. This kiss is hungrier, deeper, more urgent, and I wrap my arms around his neck and cling onto him as a lifeline.

Because that's how I see Leroi.

He's my rescuer, my teacher, my protector, my *every-thing*. In all the years I festered in captivity, grieving over losing Nanna, I never thought I would meet a man who would serve me retribution.

"You're so beautiful." Leroi's kisses travel down my neck, each press of his lips sending sparks across my skin. "My avenging angel."

He slides his fingers beneath my t-shirt, caressing my bare skin until I'm gasping.

"You're wearing too much," he growls into my skin.

"Then take it off."

He yanks it over my head and tosses it to one side. The blood soaking through the fabric of my shirt cools, making my skin tighten into goosebumps. Leroi's eyes widen when he realizes I'm not wearing a bra.

"Fuck, Seraphine," he groans, his eyes darken. "Are these nipples stiff for me?"

I nod. "What are you going to do about them?"

Nostrils flaring, he raises a hand and rolls my nipple between his thumb and forefinger. I gasp as pleasure skitters down my spine and settles between my legs, but when he takes my nipple into his mouth, my knees buckle.

Leroi holds me steady, not seeming to care that I'm bathed in Julio Catania's blood. Maybe despite all his nagging about my lack of self-control, he's secretly like me and gets excited at the sight of carnage. I can't dwell on that for long because he scoops me into his arms, lifting me off my feet.

"What are you doing?" I whisper.

"You're covered in that bastard's blood," he growls, his

voice filled with warmth. "I'm going to get you nice and clean."

"Does that include an orgasm?" I ask.

His broad smile makes my stomach erupt with butterflies. "Is that what you want?"

"Please."

He carries me across the armored truck, his footsteps crackling over the plastic wrap. At the end, closest to the driver's cab, is a set of doors that I thought were closets, but one of them is a tiny wet room.

It's the most compact thing I've ever seen, yet there's enough space for both of us, even when he closes the door.

I lean against the plastic wall, my heart racing, the muscles of my pussy clenching and releasing in anticipation of his touch. Leroi sits me down on a small bench, giving me a close-up view of the bulge in his pants.

My pulse quickens, but there's none of the usual violence or rage that comes every time I come into contact with a penis. It's different with Leroi. He might get aroused like other men, but his erection isn't imposing. He doesn't pull it out and demand satisfaction. It's just one reason I find him so intriguing.

He kneels between my parted legs, pulls off my shoes, exposing my feet. His fingers trail up my calves, leaving a trail of raised flesh in his wake and it makes my breath hitch. I shiver, but it's not from the chill. The way he massages my legs sends electric pulses straight to my core.

"Lift your hips for me, angel," he growls.

Right now, I would do anything he asked.

I raise my ass off the bench, letting him pull down my panties and pajama bottoms in one swift motion. He pushes my knees apart, his gaze going straight between my legs.

He groans, "Your pretty little pussy is soaked."

I bite down on my bottom lip, my breath quickening. No one has ever called that part of my body pretty. At least no one I didn't later kill.

Leroi kisses the sensitive skin on my inner thigh. I gasp, my legs jerking further apart. As his tongue glides higher, I grip the edges of the bench, my hips rising toward his mouth.

Last time, he fucked me with the handle of the knife and made me climax with his fingers. Is he going to use his tongue? I stare down between my spread legs, noting that Julio's blood has spread down my thighs.

His hot breath fans my folds, making me tremble. Until I met Leroi, I never thought being with a man would be so exciting. My pulse quickens at the thought of him wanting to taste me when I'm covered in the blood of my enemies.

He swipes his tongue up my slit and makes a slow circle around my clit. Sensation floods my core, and my hips jerk.

"Stay still or I'll stop sucking your sweet cunt," he says, his voice a low rumble.

I try to obey, but it's nearly impossible in this state of frenzy. There are too many firsts: my first consensual kiss, my first kill from the list of men on my list, and this, the first time a man has pleasured me with his tongue.

Leroi moves his hands up my thighs, gripping them tightly so I can't move. I lean back against the shower wall with my eyes squeezed shut against the onslaught of pleasure.

"You taste so good, angel." He swirls his tongue around my clit faster, building the intensity until I'm sweating and panting on the bench. I grip his shoulders, my fingers clawing at his shirt.

How am I naked again while he's completely clothed? Why does pleasure with him only go one way? I want to touch him. I want to explore the hard lines of his body with my hands, followed by my tongue. The pressure rises to a crescendo, and my eyes roll to the back of my head. At this rate, I'm going to explode.

The muscles of my thighs tighten around his head, trapping him in place. A keening sound traps in the back of my throat. I never want this moment to end.

"I've got you, angel," he says. "Let go."

My lips part, and I try to speak, but all I can manage are moans. Every lick, every swirl of his tongue makes me more sensitive and I lose myself in his touch.

I'm trembling, panting, so close to my orgasm that I can almost taste it in the back of my throat. Leroi clamps his lips around my clit and sucks, crumbling the last of my resistance, and an orgasm tumbles through me like a demolition ball.

"Leroi!" I cry out as I disintegrate into a thousand pieces, my entire body convulsing around his tongue.

He continues flicking, licking, and sucking, drawing out my orgasm until I collapse boneless against the shower wall. I'm too weak to move and too exhausted to speak. All I can do is slump there and bask in the afterglow.

My mind is quiet, and my entire world condenses into this single moment that I never want to end. Leroi raises his head and gazes up at me, his dark eyes gleaming.

"Good girl," he says. "That was quite the show."

Heat rises to my cheeks and spreads down my chest. I should probably close my legs or something, but I'm too relaxed to care.

As Leroi rises to grab hold of the shower head, my gaze drops to the bulge in his pants. It's a perfect imprint of that thick erection I sat on when I threatened him in his bed.

I want to see it.

I want to run my tongue along that thick crown and make him lose control.

Raising a hand, I reach for the button of his pants, but he grabs my wrist. "No."

My gaze snaps to his eyes. "What?"

His fingers grip so tightly that I'm sure he'll leave bruises. "You heard me," he snarls and turns on the hot spray. "No."

My stomach drops. Is this another rejection?

THIRTY-NINE

LEROI

Seraphine gazes up at me, her lips parted with shock. Water cascades down her hair, plastering it over her pretty face.

When I release her wrist, she clutches an arm over her breasts.

"Why?" she whispers, her huge blue eyes glistening, her features twisting with disappointment and anguish.

I tear my gaze away. "We agreed I would reward you with orgasms and that we wouldn't cross any of my boundaries."

"But you kissed me."

"That was a mistake."

She flinches, and my chest aches with guilt. I can only add to her trauma.

"That came out wrong," I mutter. "What I meant to say is that I can't take advantage of you."

"What if I want it?" she asks in a small voice.

"How can you even be sure?"

"What?"

I turn to look her full in the face. It's wet from the shower and I can't tell if she's crying.

"You're still a captive." She shakes her head and parts her lips to speak, but I raise a finger. "You are. Keeping you locked up in my apartment without sharp objects is confinement."

She scowls and I cup her cheek, forcing her to meet my eyes.

"You can't make that decision while I'm the one holding all the power. Ask me again when everyone on your list is dead and you've found Gabriel. If you still want me, I'll be waiting."

I step out of the shower and close the door, leaving Seraphine to get clean. After texting Don to collect the truck, I open a duffle bag containing a change of clothes.

My balls ache, and I'm still harder than ever. The thought of her wanting me is intoxicating, even though I know it's wrong. She's too young, too vulnerable, too confounded by Stockholm syndrome to make an informed decision. No matter how much I want her, I have to resist her. It's for her own good.

And my own.

Seraphine has spent the past five years as a Lolita assassin. She's become a killer, and has paired with seduction and sex. The only thing I can do for her is redirect those urges. The last thing I want is to sleep with Seraphine and wake up eyeless, castrated, and carved a new orifice.

That shit is hot when she does it to some deserving asshole. Not so arousing when that mayhem is directed at me.

Unlike most men who have crossed her path, I'm going to set boundaries, even if that earns her hatred.

_____

She's sullen for the rest of the day and barely speaks when I take her to the park. Miko meets us at the shooting range, and she glares at us from the corner, barely participating when Miko updates us on his research on Samson's whereabouts.

I've fucked up.

The last time Seraphine was this quiet was her first day, when she wouldn't speak unless the subject was about Gabriel. She's interpreted my refusal to exploit her sexuality as a rejection and can't see that this situation is a double-edged dilemma.

If I give her what she wants, then I'm no better than the monsters she's trying to kill. When they're all slain, she'll come to her senses and add me to the list. But if I deny her, then I'm a bastard who breaks her heart.

Better to be thought of as a heartless bastard than for an avenging angel to tear out a vital organ. Or cut one off.

Later, she can't even muster the enthusiasm to take out her fury on innocent vegetables and hides in her room, refusing to eat. I stare at her closed door, wondering what the hell I need to do to make things right.

I could abduct Paolo Rochas? He covered up that Samson wasn't dead, and is probably our best chance at finding the surviving Capello twin alive.

If there's enough time, I could pick up Mike Ferrante. Thanks to Catania's knife-point confession, we have two priority targets from the list of Capello's surviving guards.

While Seraphine is moping in her room, I venture to the apartment next door and pick up Miko, who is more than enthusiastic to help on another mission.

Paolo Rochas has leased a Lexus from Capello's Car

Rentals, which Miko has tracked down to a brothel in the east end of town. We park across the street and wait, armed with a tranquilizer gun and a plan.

Once Rochas leaves, Miko takes the shot, rendering the bastard unconscious. We load him in our car and head for an empty warehouse the firm owns on the outskirts of town. Underneath the building is a soundproofed basement, where we secure him to a chair bolted to the concrete floor.

"Should we wake him up?" Miko asks.

I place a hand on his shoulder. "This one belongs to Seraphine."

He stiffens. "But she isn't here."

"I'll bring her tomorrow, after breakfast."

He bows his head but remains silent. I give his shoulder a squeeze. "If you're so determined to enter my line of work, then you should start by reading about assassinations."

"But Seraphine gets to torture and interrogate people after a week?" he asks. "I've been with you for years."

"And you're the best support guy a hitman could have." I wrap an arm around his shoulder and steer him toward the exit.

"I want more."

"Seraphine is an experienced killer with a worthy vendetta. The men we're hunting are her quest, not ours."

Miko's posture sags, but he follows me out of the warehouse and back into the car. He's sullen and unusually quiet on the drive home and buries himself in his phone. I keep my gaze on the road, wondering where the hell I went wrong with this boy.

"What brought on this change?" I ask.

"Huh?"

"Your interest in becoming an assassin coincided with the Capello job."

Miko shifts in his seat. "I don't want to be behind the scenes anymore. It's got nothing to do with Seraphine."

"Really." My voice is flat.

He runs his fingers through his hair. "You've been so busy with her."

I inhale a deep breath. "Her situation is fresh, and it's a lot more complicated than yours. With Samson Capello still living, we have to focus on taking him out before he becomes an even bigger threat."

"You're right." He bows his head. "I just... I want to help."

"The work you're doing for me means more than you can imagine. I rely on you to find information that others can't. When this situation is over, we'll have plenty of time for extra training, if that's what you want."

Miko nods. "Thanks. I won't let you down."

"I know."

We drive back to the apartment in a comfortable silence, but I can tell something between us has shifted. Miko has turned from the self-sufficient young man who matured under my care to a boy who needs my attention. The way he's going about it is all wrong though. Once the situation with Seraphine eases off, I'll ask him again if he wants to follow in my footsteps. I suspect the answer will be no.

I walk Miko to the apartment next door and thank him for his help. He's eager to go inside and doesn't linger. But as I approach my door, I hear an anguished scream. And it's coming from deep inside my unit.

Shit.

My hand reaches for my gun.

FORTY

SERAPHINE

A mistake?

A MISTAKE?

Sex was part of our agreement. Why the hell is Leroi changing his mind? This morning, he gave me the most romantic gift—Julio Catania tied up in tight knots, ready to suffer for his sins.

Leroi even presented me with a set of tools and a box of shiny new knives. Killing Julio was supposed to be part of my training. He was a demon I needed to slay to get my mind straight. I performed the task to perfection, and I earned my reward.

I didn't ask for a kiss, but he gave me one. He broke his own rule, whispered all those words of affection, and gave me more pleasure than I thought was humanly possible. He called me beautiful, all but told me I was special, and when I came apart under his tongue and wanted more, he said no.

No more for me. Nothing for him and no explanation that made any sense. No renegotiation of the boundaries he crossed, and no apology. He just said he'd made a mistake.

All that other bullshit he said about waiting for me was just his way of stalling.

Now, he's disappeared from the apartment and left me alone to stew on his rejection. My skin itches so much that my cotton sheets feel like sandpaper, and my clothes feel like the ropes Gregor and Samson used to keep me restrained.

That's why I'm sitting between his silk sheets with my back propped up against his silk pillow.

I want to scream, but there's no one to scream at. I want to slash things, but Leroi has hidden the knives. Instead, I'm drawing all the things I would do to Leroi if I got the chance.

In one picture, he's on his knees in the shower, but it's spraying blood. After he licked my pussy, I cut his throat, and blood pours down his sculpted chest and onto my feet, swirling down the drain.

In the second picture, he's standing up in the shower with his erection pointing toward my mouth. I wrap the yellow tape measure around his shaft and balls, then I open my mouth to reveal jagged rows of teeth, like a great white shark.

He cries fat, blue tears, and a speech bubble pops out of his mouth where he begs for mercy. My forked tongue lolls out like a snake and laps up the white droplets dripping from his slit.

In the final picture, Leroi lies on a four-poster bed with his arms secured to the posts. He's naked, of course, and fully erect. I'm walking toward him with a claw hammer and telling him to choose between loving me and getting a new hole in his body.

The final portrait is of me, sitting on a throne with my blonde hair styled like a crown, Leroi is on his knees, sucking my toes. I don't bother to color it in because my eyes are growing heavy. There are only so many hours a person can stay furious. Besides, my red pen is running dry. Bled out like the men I've killed.

All I wanted was an apology and an explanation that makes sense. Was that too much to ask? Leroi makes up the rules as he goes along, and I can't keep up. He's warm, he's cold, he's horny, he's aloof. My quest for vengeance is hard enough without having to navigate his mood swings.

I slip my notebook under the pillow, slide down the sheets, and close my eyes. Now that I've taken the edge off my anger, I can sleep.

Killing Julio eased a weight off my mind. I finally feel like I'm making progress, even though the list of people I want to kill has increased by one more. When I wake up tomorrow, I'll ask Leroi what we're going to do about Samson.

Samson is out there somewhere, looking for me. There's no Gregor to tell him to calm down and no Dad threatening to break him if he damages his asset. Samson can now hurt me in all the ways he's always wanted with no one holding him back.

That's why we need to kill him first.

I drift into slumber, my mind processing my first revenge kill. One down. Four to go. Their faces drift in and out of my consciousness. Julio's is red and twisted with agony, while the guards who attacked Mom all share the same smug masks.

They crowd around her, cheering as she's pinned to the desk and violated. Dad stands on the other side, holding her face between his large hands. He's yelling at her for being a cheating whore.

I'm trembling behind the door to his office, my gaze

fixed on Mom. Can't Dad see that she's being raped? I rush forward to stop them, but Raphael's corpse blocks my way.

Blood still oozes from his cut throat. He stares up at me and rasps, "Help her."

The red liquid rises from the floor, engulfs my bare feet, and glues my soles to the ground. I can't move backward or forward. I can't even close my eyes.

Dad orders a man with a black ponytail forward. He flips Mom onto her belly and enters her with one thrust. Behind him is Julio, but nobody notices him standing in the corner with blood oozing out of a stomach wound.

I turn back to Dad, who's no longer the father I knew. He used to call Mom and me his princesses and explained that we were the reason he worked so hard. Now, he's a monster ordering his men to go harder, deeper, faster.

Mom screams again, and Dad orders a curly-haired man to fill her mouth. I break free, my feet moving me away from the scene and down the hallway. As I round the corner, large hands grab my shoulders, and I scream.

It's a dream.

It's a dream.

"Wake up," a voice yells. "It's a dream."

Fathomless black eyes stare into mine with an intensity that sends shivers down my spine. I raise my hands and try to claw out his eyes, but he's too fast, too strong. Before I know it, he's pinned me to the silk sheets, yelling at me to wake up.

It takes a few heartbeats for my mind to catch up. I'm already awake.

"Leroi?" I rasp.

He pulls me into his chest. "You were having a nightmare."

As I draw back, Leroi props me up against his side. I

glance around the darkened room, my heart still pounding hard enough to muffle the roar of my blood.

"Oh," I say through ragged breaths.

Leroi draws back and stares down at me from the other side of the bed. "Are you alright?"

"I was dreaming about the last time I saw Mom," I murmur. "It was so vivid."

He exhales a long breath. "Was it because I let you confront Julio Catania?"

"No. Maybe. I don't know." I scoot across the mattress and lean against his larger body, trying to convince myself that it was a dream. "Seeing him this morning brought back a lot of details I'd forgotten."

Leroi wraps an arm around my shoulder and pulls me even closer. "Do you want to talk about it?"

"No."

"Let me rephrase," he says. "You need to talk about it."

"Why?" I pull back and stare into his profile. "I don't want you to judge me."

"For what?"

I shake my head.

"Seraphine," he says, his voice hardening. "If you want me to help you control impulses, then I need to understand what's going on in your mind. Did killing Catania make you feel better or worse?"

I bite down on my bottom lip. "It changed the dream."

"How so?"

"Julio was the only one who wasn't attacking Mom because I killed him."

"That's a good sign." He moves his hand to my cheek and cups my face. His eyes are so intense that I'm drawn in, and my pulse slows. "It shows that you're taking control of your demons."

My throat thickens. "What about the ones I can't kill? Dad was holding her down, barking orders at the others. I can't ever slay him because he's already dead."

Leroi's gaze falters from mine for a second, as though he regrets not leaving Dad alive. "We'll work something out. Let's focus on the ones we can hunt."

Nodding, I lean against his chest and exhale a long sigh. He presses a soft kiss on my forehead. "The road to progress isn't always smooth. You've come a long way from the girl I pulled out of the basement, and I'm proud of your progress."

His words send a wave of warmth through my chest, and I tuck my head under my chin. I almost feel bad for those pictures I drew of him, but not completely.

"We'll get through this," he murmurs. "Together."

"Hmmmm." I burrow into his side.

"But there's one thing I need to know," he says into my hair.

"What's that?"

"What are you doing in my bed, naked?"

FORTY-ONE

LEROI

Seraphine gapes up at me, her lips parted, and her eyes wide. Even though the lights are dim, I can still see her cheeks darkening with a blush.

"Wh-what?" she whispers.

I raise my brows, expecting her to say she sleepwalked or was lying here in wait to ambush me for refusing her advances, but her face crumples.

"Every time I close my eyes, I see my past. I couldn't sleep last night after Pietro, and I needed to rest." She shudders. "I had nowhere else to go."

"And the clothes?"

"My skin started crawling after Julio." She bows her head. "The only thing I could tolerate were your silk sheets."

I can't even tell if this is bullshit because I don't know how she's still functioning after five years of captivity, murder, and abuse. Anyone else might turn to substances to cope, but Seraphine's strength is incredible.

"Do you want to take a break from the killing?" I ask.

Paolo Rochas is waiting for her beneath the warehouse. I don't want to keep him without water for too long. A weak, dehydrated hostage isn't the most coherent.

"No." She clutches my shirt.

"I could interrogate them myself and—"

"No," she shrieks. "I need to slay all the ones that are left alive. It's the only way."

"Only way to do what?"

"Only two things kept me going when I was in the basement. The first was the hope of getting to make them scream. The second was chocolate."

"Chocolate?"

She nods. "I've always wanted my own chocolate fountain."

My head throbs. Such a simple request, but I'm deathly allergic. I can't afford to go near it and lose my edge. "Fine. I won't leave you out."

"Where did you go?" she asks. "You were gone for hours."

Guilt claws at my frayed heartstrings. "I was hunting Paolo Rochas."

"Did you kill him?"

"No." I toe off my shoes and scoot down the bed, so Seraphine can adjust to an easier angle. "We put him somewhere safe, where he can't escape."

She exhales, her smaller body relaxing against mine. "Did you take Miko?"

"He's the one who tracks them down. It's faster if he comes along on missions."

Seraphine falls silent, her breathing slowing. I shift on the mattress, trying to make myself comfortable because she doesn't plan on letting me go. It's best to sleep beside her fully-clothed because the thought of her naked body against my skin sends my libido in a dangerous direction.

"Leroi?"

"What?"

"Stop leaving me behind. I can't be alone with my thoughts."

My chest constricts. I press another kiss on her temple. "Alright."

"Thank you," she says, her voice barely a whisper.

I don't reply. If I had taken the time to turn over the man I shot in Samson's bedroom, I would have known he was still alive. The outcome might have still been the same, but there's a chance that I could have caught Samson while he was hiding out at his fiancée's house.

My jaw clenches at the memory of sneaking into Joseph Di Marco's bedroom, completely oblivious that Samson was close by. Now, I've driven him underground. It's only a matter of time before he realizes that the hitman he hired to take out his family's murderer is one and the same.

I clear my thoughts and force myself into a meditative state. If I can't fall asleep, then I may as well put my mind to rest. Seraphine can't confront another of those guards who assaulted her mother without some kind of intervention. Even if she claims she's unaffected by these killings, it's only a matter of time before she breaks.

I'll protect her from the ghosts of her past, and I'll protect her from danger, even if that danger is herself.

———

Hours later, sunlight warms my closed eyelids, and strawberry shampoo tickles my nostrils. A soft hand slides over my bare chest. It rubs slow circles on one pec before moving onto the other. The gentle touches pull me out of sleep, and I'm aware that the hand is sliding down my abs.

I'm still in that state between sleep and wakefulness when a finger circles my belly button before traveling down the trail of hair that leads to my aching cock.

This is entirely inappropriate, and there's a five percent chance that this is just a dream. Too relaxed to move, I cling to those small odds.

Less than twenty-four hours ago, I kissed her without permission then I buried my face between her thighs and ate that sweet pussy until she came apart on my tongue.

If she wants to touch my chest, I won't complain.

My morning erection is strangled by the tightness of my boxers and jeans. Each gentle stroke she makes on my skin infuses my veins with an electric current.

Her fingers skim lower, awakening the last shreds of my morality. This is wrong. I should stop her before she escalates. I should end this pretense of slumber before I become trapped beneath her with another knife to my balls.

"Let me take off your pants," she whispers, her fingers brushing over the fine hairs on my abdomen. "Please?"

"Behave yourself," I growl.

She pulls back her hand.

I crack open an eye.

She lies wedged against my side, still naked. My shirt is missing, presumably tossed on the floor.

"Is this what you do to people while they're asleep?" I ask with a raised brow. "Undress them?"

She scowls. "You said I could."

I scoff.

"How do you think I took off that long-sleeved shirt? You helped."

My brows pull together. Seraphine isn't strong enough

to roll me over, raise my arms above my head, and remove my shirt without my cooperation, but I would have remembered undressing for her.

"I asked for permission," she adds, sounding petulant.

That sounds oddly familiar. She did ask to take off my pants, and she stopped when I didn't agree. Groaning, I run my fingers through my hair, not believing there's a part of me that wants her to get me naked.

"What was your end game?" I ask.

"What do you mean?"

"If I had let you pull down my pants, what would have come next?"

She hesitates.

I turn around to look her full in the face.

She shrinks back, her cheeks flushed, the pretty pink shade spreading down her neck and across her breasts. Fuck. She looks so sweet and vulnerable that I feel like a dog for letting her sleep in my bed.

Questions burn in the back of my mind, but they're all inappropriate. I want to know if she had a boyfriend before she became a captive, but it's none of my goddamned business. She was a child, and anything that happened after that wasn't with her consent.

Despite knowing this, I ask anyway, "Am I the first man you've gotten close to that you haven't wanted to kill?"

"Who says I don't want to kill you?" she asks with a huff. "You're always blowing hot and cold, then breaking your own rules. It's infuriating."

I hold back a smile and keep my features even. "Want to say that again?"

"What?" she asks, sounding petulant.

My brow hikes even further to my hairline.

She looks away, her cheeks still flushed. "Nothing."

I crack my neck, roll my shoulders, and remind myself that Seraphine isn't a brat in the truest sense. She's experienced more trauma than I can even comprehend. If she's acting up, I have to treat her with compassion.

And a firm hand.

She shifts on the mattress, her fingers twisting around each other to form knots. "You're the first man I've ever wanted." She takes a deep breath and stares up at the ceiling. "Before you, I'd never been attracted to anyone."

My breath hitches.

She turns to me and asks, "Is that wrong?"

"It's normal to have feelings for someone who pulled you out of a terrible situation," I say, my words measured. "I'm also helping you learn to control your impulses, making me a teacher, but I'm still holding you captive."

She huffs a bitter laugh. "I haven't got hero worship syndrome, teacher's pet syndrome, or Stockholm syndrome. Can't you just accept that I think you're hot and you give me orgasms?"

Pressure builds up between my eyes and I curl my hands into fists. She's making some excellent points. "Seraphine," I say with a sigh. "It's just a crush. I'm the only man you've met in half a decade who hasn't tried to abuse you."

"How do you explain your near constant erections?"

My jaw clenches. She's got me there.

"I know you want me, too." She shifts on the mattress and closes the distance between us. "I've seen the way you look at me and all the things you say when you're giving me my rewards. You want me, too."

"That's irrelevant," I growl.

"Why?"

"If I gave into every intrusive thought or desire, I would never have survived past the age of twenty-five."

Her eyes harden. "Is it because I killed your friends?"

"Of course not." I pinch the bridge of my nose.

"Then why not?"

"Time is running out. If Samson works out your location and who you're hiding with, he'll rally every Capello enforcer and lieutenant to our door. You need to forget about fucking me and focus on finding that bastard before he can pull together a plan of attack."

Her nostrils flare, and she jerks away.

I use the lull in our conversation to slip out of the bed. "We're going to train today before our meeting with Paolo Rochas. When I return from the shower, I expect to see you dressed."

Seraphine remains silent as I head toward the bathroom. I make a mental note to ask Miko if he's got any more leads on the location of Gabriel. Seraphine needs more than closure. She needs love. Only, that's something I can't provide.

FORTY-TWO

SERAPHINE

My blood simmers. I sit up on the bed and glare at the defined muscles between his shoulder blades. How the hell can anyone be so ridiculously controlled? He just admitted to wanting me, yet he's refusing to do anything about his attraction.

If he wasn't so alert, I would rush him from behind and grab him by the throat. That's the frustrating thing about being small. The only way I can defeat a man like Leroi is with the element of surprise, but he's always ready.

"Hey," I snap.

Leroi pauses, turns his head, but doesn't look me in the eye. He's probably just expanding his peripheral vision or something just as tactical.

"What?" he asks.

"I still don't understand why I can't kiss you, but you can kiss me whenever you feel like it, and I don't get why you can touch me, but I can't touch you."

He finally turns around, his lips parting to speak.

"That's your choice," I say before he can repeat himself.

"But why do you always leave me behind?"

His brow forms a deep V that accentuates the angles of his face. At this time of the morning, sunlight filters through the window, bathing the contours of his muscles in light and shadow. He looks sharp and sculpted, like a living statue, dipped in bronze.

My gaze wanders to the carotid artery protruding on his neck. I want to run my tongue over it to feel the pulse of his blood.

"You need to work on your impulsiveness," he says.

"What does that mean?"

"Pietro Fiori's home was within view of the Capello mansion. Our plan was to put a tracker on his car and ambush him once he left Queen's Gardens, but what did you do?"

My jaw clenches at the memory of rushing out of the car to confront Pietro. It took a second for him to recognize me as the girl he drove to and from missions before he bolted.

"What's your point?" I snap. "Blame that disguise, not me. Besides, we got what we wanted, didn't we?"

He advances on me, his nostrils flaring. "You charged at him! There's no disguise that would have worked to cover your murderous intent."

I swing my legs off the bed and stand with my fists balled, ready for a fight. Leroi stops so close to me I can feel the heat of his skin. My stomach butterflies flutter. I've never seen someone radiate so much power and strength.

He flashes his teeth. "If he had screamed, every Capello sympathizer in the vicinity would have known that the man who killed their employer was close. We would have been surrounded in seconds."

"So, what?" I raise my chin, refusing to see his point.

"You don't think before you act," he snarls. "That's why I leave you behind. How did you stay controlled enough to perform so many assassinations without getting yourself killed?"

"They were just pictures on a screen, not people I wanted dead," I snap back. "And don't change the subject."

He huffs a laugh, but the sound carries no warmth, and his eyes narrow into slits. "You little brat."

"What was the point of saving me and helping me get revenge if you keep me locked up like some kind of damsel?" I resist the urge to stamp my foot. "It's not giving me any closure."

Leroi's eyes soften, and the tightness of his muscles relaxes. He reaches out and cups the side of my face, his thumb tracing a gentle line across my cheekbone.

"You want to hunt?" he asks, his voice less harsh.

I nod.

"Stalking your prey requires patience, control, and stealth. If you rush at your targets like you did with Pietro, you will get yourself killed."

"It won't happen again," I say.

"It's why I plan on training you out of your reckless-ness." Leroi drops his hand and steps away, pulling back his warmth.

My heart drops at the absence of his touch. He thinks I'm a liability just because I'm not cold and contained like him?

"Do you regret saving me?" I ask.

"Of course not," he says, his features a blank mask.

"Because you act like I'm a burden sent to ruin your life of perfection and control."

The corner of his lips lifts into a tiny smile, and his hands slide to my shoulders. "You're brave, determined, and strong. I don't know anyone who could survive what you did and still be standing."

My cheeks heat without my permission, and I glance away. Compliments like that are like honeyed poison, and remind me of Dad. He made me feel like I was the light of his life. At least until the moment he thrust me into a life of darkness.

Men spout bullshit every day. I heard it on missions, in the twins snarled threats, even in the cold compliments of the handler. They say whatever is needed to get what they want, then they spit you out the moment you're not needed.

"Seraphine," he says. "Look at me."

"What's your endgame?" I ask.

"What do you mean?"

"You have to be helping me for a reason. What is it?" I fold my arms over my chest.

He stares down at me for several heartbeats until my insides twist and squirm. I hold his gaze, my features hardening. If he thinks I'll cower, he can guess again. I've suffered far worse than a man's scrutiny.

Leroi rubs his brow. "Any man who mistreats women and children deserves to die painfully, but killing them isn't enough. These bastards live rent-free through the minds of their victims, and I can't tolerate that."

"What does that mean?"

"I want to erase the memory of what Capello and the others did to you, so all parts of them die," he says.

My breath shallows. "That's all?"

"What do you mean?"

"Did my dad hurt you, too?"

He shakes his head. "I never knew the man."

"Then why do you feel so strongly about this?"

An emotion flashes across his features. I can't tell if it's discomfort or indecision, but he closes his eyes and exhales. When he opens them again, it's with a look of determination that makes me straighten.

"When I was nine, my mother married a police officer who started beating her shortly after. I tried to stop it, but I was too small, too weak. It went on for years, but she wouldn't leave. One day, I found the bastard on top of my sister and something inside me snapped."

"What did you do?" I whisper.

"I shot him in the head."

I nod. "Good."

He glances away. "But he refused to die. My sister and mother were horrified and looked at me like I was a monster."

My lips part with a gasp. "But you saved them."

The laugh he gives me is bitter. "There was blood all over the carpet and bits of brains on the wall. That bastard clung onto life like a demon, filling my sister's room with his ragged breaths. It was a fucking mess."

"What happened next?"

"My mother called her cousin. He finished off my step-father, cleaned up the scene of the crime, and took me."

I flinch, my jaw dropping. "Why?"

"They said the state of New Alderney would have tried me as an adult for murdering a police officer," he replies, his voice laced with bitterness. "I had to disappear."

"For how long?"

A muscle flexes in his jaw. "Forever." At my frown, he adds, "I tracked my mother and sister down to California when I turned eighteen, and they were horrified. they wanted nothing to do with me."

"Why?"

"They said only a psychopath could kill someone so

brutally." He shakes his head as though he still can't believe what he heard. "My mother said the bastard had his faults, and I never gave him the benefit of the doubt. According to her, what I saw was a misunderstanding."

"B-but didn't your sister speak up for you?"

He grimaces. "She agreed with my mother, but what else explains why a man would pin down a half-naked girl and expose his penis?"

My lips part with a gasp. "Unbelievable."

"They both had to pack up everything and leave town," he snarls. "They said I ruined everything and that he was a good provider."

"What?"

"As if putting food on the table and paying the bills justifies what he did," he says through clenched teeth.

I rest my head on his chest. "Is that why you saved me?"

"No matter what they say, I will always eliminate anyone who hurts women and children," he growls. "And when I found you, I wanted to erase every trace of Capello, including the version that lived in your trauma."

Sliding both hands up his pecs, I tilt my head and meet his gaze. There's no pain in his eyes, only fury. Leroi's backstory explains so much, especially why he's so controlled and hates mistakes. I don't understand his family's ingratitude.

It's disgusting.

"If you came to me on that night five years ago and killed those men, I wouldn't have been horrified," I murmur. "I would have worshiped you like a god."

Leroi's eyes widen, and his face falls extraordinarily still. Without another word, he turns around and stalks into the bathroom, leaving me wondering what on earth I said wrong now.

360

FORTY-THREE

LEROI

Like a *god?*

I stand in the shower beneath the hot spray, letting the water wash away my turmoil of conflicting thoughts. Only three women know the full story, yet Seraphine is the only one who didn't stare at me with looks of anger or horror.

When Anton arrived on the scene, he thought I was pitiful for not completing the job. Mom and sister had been yelling at me for nearly an hour, asking how I could have done something so horrific. Their words faded into the background because every ounce of my attention was on the bastard bleeding out on the floor.

Each rasp of his breath grated on my eardrums and frayed my nerves. I would have finished him if I'd been alone, but I couldn't move forward with two women screaming as if I was a cold-hearted murderer instead of a loving brother and son trying to protect them.

I pick up the shampoo and work it through my hair, my thoughts traveling back to Seraphine's words. She said she would have worshipped me if I had killed the men who raped her mother. It's a peculiar way to put it, but it beats being seen as a monster. In her eyes, I'm a hero.

But she'd be wrong.

Heroes are patient and soft. Heroes are gentle. Heroes don't grab women by the throat and fuck them until it hurts. Heroes also don't lust after the women they're supposed to save. Seraphine needs a man who will take it easy and slow, not one who will be demanding and rough.

Someone who isn't me.

She has suffered enough at the hands of other men. Taking off the leash I've placed over myself will only add to her trauma.

My cock chooses that moment to stiffen. With a grunt, I jerk the taps to cold, and the icy spray douses the flames of my arousal. Seraphine is not a natural submissive. She's broken and innocent and sweet. She doesn't realize my calm facade is the cage I use to contain desires that could trigger her killer instincts.

The thought of her coming at me with a blade heats my blood, and my erection swells at the memory of how she ground against me. Dipping my head beneath the cold water, I swallow a groan and focus on putting an end to this insanity before I find myself in too deep.

I rinse off, cut the water, and step out of the shower, resigning myself to the fact that I'll never be the man Seraphine needs or deserves.

She's gone by the time I step into my room, presumably getting dressed as ordered. After slipping on a new outfit, I walk out of my room to get a start on breakfast.

A soft giggle makes my gaze snap to the far side of the dining table, where Seraphine sits beside Miko wearing only my shirt. They're pressed up against each other, hunched over the screen of a computer tablet.

She perches on the chair with one bare leg pulled up close to her chest, her heel balanced on the edge of the seat. As Miko's gaze bounces from his tablet to her exposed thigh, my jaw clenches. Seraphine has no right to invite men into my apartment while she's naked.

"This one decapitates the zombie," Miko points at something on his screen.

She double-taps and squeals. "What else can I do?"

"You can set them on fire," Miko replies with a shy smile.

"Let me try." Her movement causes the collar of my shirt to slip and reveal her shoulder.

When Miko's gaze hones in on her creamy skin, it takes every molecule of self-control not to rip them apart. Pressure gathers in my temples, escalating with each pounding beat of my heart. Keeping a tight control over my rage, I cross the room and slam both palms on the table.

They jerk apart. Miko flushes, while Seraphine gazes up at me with a familiar look of defiance.

"Hey man, I knocked and Sera let me in," Miko says.

Sera?

I meet Seraphine's huge blue eyes. There's no sign of the vulnerable girl who confronted me in my bedroom. She's more like the one I caught splattered in blood and cutting the penis of her enemy into wafer-thin slices.

Now is not the time to deal with her brand of chaos.

"Why are you here?" I ask Miko.

"He's going to teach me to be a hacker," Seraphine says, her eyes bright.

I ignore her taunting and focus on Miko, who shifts in his seat. "I found the hospital they used for the first transplant, it's in New Jersey. The live donor was a man with a birth date that would have made him eighteen at the time, and the address given is a condo in Queen's Gardens around the corner owned by Joseph Di Marco."

"His lawyer knew?" I ask, all traces of possessiveness fading.

"What are you waiting for?" I say to Seraphine. "Get dressed, and let's go."

"Miko said it burned down in a fire, and the building is still being rebuilt."

"Shit." I pinch the bridge of my nose and turn my attention back to Miko. "Any leads on the second surgery?"

"Still working on it." He raises a shoulder. "I've set a macro to search for the fake dates of birth across all hospitals in the United States. It's only a matter of time before we find them."

I nod. "Great work."

Miko rises off his seat, and Seraphine tries to hand him the tablet.

"Keep it," he says, his cheeks darkening.

"Thank you." She lowers her lashes and smiles.

Miko takes one last look at her body before turning toward the door. I can't even blame him—Seraphine is both beautiful and age-appropriate. To a nineteen-year-old virgin, she's the sophisticated older woman next door.

Seraphine would devour poor Miko and leave him in pieces.

I wait in silence until he leaves. As soon as the door swings shut, I advance on Seraphine and yank her up by the arm.

"Not a word." I march her out through the balcony and up the iron steps that lead to the roof terrace.

Traffic rumbles from below, the sound muffled by the fury pounding through my veins. Beaumont city stretches out beyond the railings, its skyscrapers bathed in morning light. I release my grip on her arm and glare down into Seraphine's blank features.

"What do you think you're doing?" I hiss.

Her eyes widen with false surprise. "What do you mean?"

"Miko is off-limits," I snarl. "He's a good kid, and I won't have you leading him on."

She tilts her head and gazes up at me through her thick, blonde lashes. "I wasn't—"

"Cut the bullshit," I snarl. "If you're pissed about this morning, take it up with me. Don't drag Miko into this. He's too young for your games."

Seraphine's nostrils flare. When her lips part with a denial, I close the distance between us and wrap a hand around her throat.

Her eyes widen, and she gasps, her chest heaving. Her nipples protrude through the fabric of her borrowed shirt, even though it's a warm morning.

A flush blooms across her cheeks, and her pupils dilate. As her pulse races beneath my fingers, my blood heats with desire. Damn this woman. Even when she's getting on my nerves, she still manages to make me feral.

"Stop acting like a jealous boyfriend," she says. "It was just a conversation."

My fingers tighten around her throat, eliciting a whimper. I lean in close and press my lips to her ear. "You've spent five years luring men to their deaths. Five years of knowing what to say and how to position yourself to attract their attention. Miko is a child. He doesn't deserve your manipulation."

She jerks back, her eyes narrowing into sharp slits, and her pretty features tighten with undisguised hatred. She's probably imagining a thousand ways of orchestrating my demise—I already saw some of her drawings. The little devil made sure to label her victim, so there was no mistake that she fantasizes about my mutilation.

"You don't want me," she says, her voice breathy. "You don't want me to have Miko. What do you want?"

An excellent question.

I want Seraphine writhing beneath me, her gorgeous face twisted in a medley of pleasure and pain. I want her screams in my ears, her skin marked with my touch and erasing the memories of all those bastards in her past. I want her mind, her body, her soul.

The thought comes unbidden and unwelcome. I force it back, but the effort is futile. Seraphine is still there, pressed against me, with her heart pounding and her gaze searing into mine.

I've never felt this level of desire for a woman. She's innocent yet devious, vulnerable yet strong. It's an intoxicating combination that makes me forget my own rules.

"What do I want?" I snarl.

Her eyes darken, and she draws so close that our lips almost touch. The hand around her neck loosens, and I brush the pad of my thumb over her delicate jaw.

"I want to save you, Seraphine. I want to tame those deadly instincts so you can lead the life you deserve."

My hand moves of its own accord down the curve of her neck, the slope of her shoulders, and the swell of her hip. I realize what the fuck I'm doing and snatch it away.

"If you hurt Miko, I will end you. Is that understood?"

She nods, her lips quivering.

"Good." I step away, wishing I'd made her get dressed before this confrontation. "Now, sit on the mat and let's start some breathing exercises."

Seraphine studies me for several moments before

turning away without a word. I stare after her and ignore the pang of regret. It would be selfish and dangerous to give into desires she isn't equipped enough to handle.

I didn't rescue her from one monster to deliver her to another. She must never find out what lies beneath my tight facade of control.

FORTY-FOUR

SERAPHINE

Leroi makes me meditate on the rooftop terrace for hours. It's my unspoken punishment for getting close to his precious little Miko.

When I complain about being hungry, he brings me breakfast bars and juice. When I say I can't concentrate, he grabs the sides of my head and makes me recite mantras that block out all thoughts of killing him.

He's infuriating.

I wasn't even trying to flirt with Miko. Well, not much anyway. Just enough to let Leroi know I had options and wouldn't wait for him to grow a set of balls. Half the time, he treats me like I'm a fragile little virgin. Other times, he's giving me part of what I want and making me feel bad about it.

He's handsome, dangerous, protective—everything a girl could ever need, yet he refuses to act on his attraction. He's a tease.

I see the way his gaze lingers on my lips and wanders down my body and in the thick erection he gets whenever I come too close. Then the moment I turn my sights to another man, he turns into an asshole. He wants me. No matter what he says.

If I can't use Miko to make Leroi jealous, I'll just find someone else.

"Seraphine."

His sharp voice pulls me out of my musings and I open my eyes. Leroi sits opposite me on the mat with his hands resting on his crossed legs. His expression is unreadable, but my skin burns under the heat of his glower.

Swallowing, I sit straighter. "Yes?"

"You weren't following the breathing exercises," he says.

I raise both shoulders. "I was thinking."

"About?"

"An apology," I say before I can stop myself.

He tilts his head, motioning for me to elaborate.

"I should have gotten dressed the moment I let Miko in. It was wrong of me to make him think I was interested."

He studies me for several moments before asking, "And?"

"And I'm sorry."

"I accept." Leroi rises from his sitting position and offers me a hand. "But you need to learn to control your impulses. Part of that includes thinking before you act."

With a nod, I take his hand and let him pull me up. I'm not sorry for trying to make Leroi jealous, but it was shitty of me to use Miko. He deactivated my collar, and without all his research, we wouldn't have made half as much progress in my quest.

Leroi takes me downstairs so I can get dressed and then serves a brunch of a Spanish tortilla with a huge green salad. Afterward, we go to one of his apartments on the floor below. Thick black mats carpet the floor and mirrors cover an entire wall.

My gaze wanders across an array of free weights, exercise machines, and punching bags on stands. "What is this place?"

"This is where Miko and I exercise when it's raining." Leroi gestures around the room. "And it's where you'll build lean muscle and burn off some of your excess energy."

"But I'm not energetic."

He turns to me with his brow raised.

I stare back. The handler Dad hired to train me provided a cross trainer machine so I could get enough cardio while still chained to the wall, and he also made me do body weight exercises. If I didn't perform my quota of reps, he activated the collar. The thought of that creepy old guy making another girl exercise braless makes me want to electrocute his eyes until they explode into sparks.

Leroi takes my shoulder and walks me to a punching bag on a stand. "Wait here."

He disappears into a room and emerges with two pairs of boxing gloves.

"Put these on." He shoves them into my hands. How did he know my size? "I'm going to teach you to punch. Whenever you're feeling frustrated, I want you to come down here and work out your aggression."

I slip on the gloves, and Leroi stands back, watching me smash my fists into the bag. I imagine pummeling Dad in the liver and making him cry for mercy. Dad morphs into Gregor, and then Gregor morphs into Samson. I'm so focused on revenge that the rest of the room disappears.

"You've got a good right hook," Leroi says, jerking me out of my trance. "You need to work on your left."

He stands behind me, adjusts my posture, and demonstrates the technique. The heat of his body envelopes mine, and the space fills with his masculine scent. Whatever he says disappears into the ether because all I can concentrate on is his presence.

"Now, try again," he says.

I throw a punch with my left and glance at Leroi for approval. He shakes his head and returns to guide my movements. This time, when I try again, he gives me an approving nod.

"Good girl."

The praise hits me straight in the clit, my cheeks flare with heat, and all my blood travels to the needy spot between my legs. Leroi folds his arms across his chest and gives me a look that communicates that he knows exactly what I'm thinking.

"Are you sure you don't have excess energy?" he asks.

Scowling, I punch the bag again, imagining it's him. What a dick.

"Did you adopt Miko?"

I deliver an uppercut to his imaginary face. In my mind's eye, punching bag Leroi staggers backward at the force of my blow.

"No. Family isn't always built on blood," he says.

My gaze darts to the real Leroi before I return my attention to the bag. "What does that mean?"

"He asked me to take him away from his situation."

A breath catches in the back of my throat. "Was he like me?"

Leroi's features harden. "He wasn't a prisoner, but he was in a bad place. I couldn't refuse his request for help."

"Why not?"

"Because when I was in a worse position, someone also took care of me."

I nod, my throat thickening, my mind already conjuring up the scene of a boy standing over a dying man with a gun, the room spattered in blood. Leroi's mentor would have strode in, strong and imposing and dressed in black, exactly as Leroi looked in the basement. The backs of my eyes sting, and I think of anything to change the subject.

"Did you teach Miko to be a hacker?" I try a high kick that makes the bag swing.

Leroi chuckles. "He came with computer skills. I only paid for the equipment to help hone his talent."

"You really care about him, don't you?"

"Of course. He's like a little brother."

I pause, my fist stilling on the bag. The implications of his words wrap around my throat with a leathery grip. If rescuing a younger person while on a job makes them family, does that explain why Leroi keeps pushing me away?

Without looking in his direction, I ask, "Does that make me your little sister?"

"No," Leroi replies. "You're something else."

"What?"

He places a gloved hand on my shoulder and lowers his lips to my ear. "Keep punching."

My hackles rise. I deliver a flurry of jabs to the bag, resisting the urge to bite back with a retort. The imaginary version of Leroi reels back from each hit, while the real one watches on in my periphery.

"This would be so much more satisfying if I had a knife," I say from between clenched teeth.

"Still frustrated?" he asks.

"Yeah." My left fist slams into the bag. "Punching bags don't bleed."

He huffs a laugh. "Are you feeling murdery?"

"That isn't even a word," I say with a scowl and deliver a right hook.

Leroi places both hands on my shoulders. "Cool down, drink some water, and come with me. If it's blood you want, I have exactly what you need."

FORTY-FIVE

LEROI

It's early evening by the time we arrive at the outskirts of Beaumont City. Seraphine slept for most of the journey, exhausted from a day of vigorous training. I'd meant to teach her a lesson, and it worked. After the training session, she didn't think of demanding her usual reward.

The last vestiges of sunlight color the sky a vibrant shade of red, reminding me of the poker night bloodbath. I glance across the passenger seat and smile at my innocent little serial killer. She's curled up with her feet on the seat, and her head is resting against the window.

She looks like an angel. A dark angel. A fallen angel. An avenging angel. My angel. I want to brush the coffee-colored strands off her face, but she'd cut through at my already fraying resistance.

I didn't like the way she used Miko to make me jealous even though it partially worked. I can't deny that I have feelings for her, but there are reasons why she's off-limits.

She's exactly the kind of woman who knocks me off kilter. Getting involved with her means losing control.

For one rage-fueled minute, I saw Miko as competition. I should never have agreed to training her with orgasms, but it's too late to renege on our agreement.

After pulling in outside the warehouse, I turn off the engine, climb out, and walk around to open her door.

"Wake up." I slide my fingers through her strawberry-scented hair.

Her eyes flutter open. "Are we there already?"

"Can you handle seeing Paolo Rochas so soon after the last one?"

All traces of sleepiness vanish, and her blue eyes sharpen into slits. She unbuckles her seatbelt and scoots out of the car and squares her shoulders. "Where is he?"

The walk through the abandoned building is silent, save for her furious breaths. In no time, we're through the doorway of the room where I deposited Rochas.

My nostrils twitch at the mingled scents of urine, sweat, and ass. I step aside, letting Seraphine stride in. Rochas sleeps with his head resting on his chest, his features obscured by a mop of greasy black hair. Both the chair he's slumped on and the floor beneath it are covered in a film of yellow liquid.

Seraphine rushes forward, but I grab her shoulder. "Wait."

"What for?" she snarls.

I walk to the sink at the corner of the room, attach a hose to the tap, and spray both the floor and Rochas with cold water. The man wakes up with a noisy jerk and rocks backward in the chair bolted to the floor.

"What the fuck?" Rochas screams, his head jerking to the side.

"What is this place?" she asks.

"An interrogation room the firm uses from time to

time." I keep hold of her shoulder until the water turns clear and disappears into a grate built into the concrete floor.

"Who are you?" His voice becomes shrill.

"Now, can I go?"

I turn off the water. "Remember to ask about Gabriel and Samson."

She rushes forward and punches him hard across the face. His head snaps back with a guttural yell. Her second punch makes his nose gush with blood.

I grin, my chest swelling with pride. She's a fast learner. Her technique has improved since last night with Julio Catania.

"Who are you?" he growls.

"I'm the one asking the questions," she snaps. "Where's Gabriel Capello?"

"Who?"

I shake my head. It's always the same with these assholes. They play stupid until you really deliver the pain. I open the cupboards beside the sink to remove a toolbox and a roll of knives.

"Seraphine." I lay them on a worktop.

"Thanks." She leaves Rochas and studies the implements. "Do you have anything that runs on electricity?"

My mind skips to the story she once told me about the hair dryer in the bathtub, and I lean into her and say, "You will not fuck up my circuits."

She shakes her head. "It's nothing like that. What do you have?"

With a sigh, I open up a second cupboard, extract the power tools, and place them on the counter. Seraphine reaches for the drill, but I grab her wrist.

"What are you planning?" I ask.

"He just needs some encouragement," she replies with a dainty shrug.

"Do you even know how to use a power drill?"

She studies it for several moments before pressing on the trigger and activating its motor. "Yes, but where's the thingy?"

"The drill bit?"

"Yeah, that."

If his screams are any indication, Rochas can tell Seraphine has never used a power tool in her life and that she doesn't know what the fuck she's doing. He rocks back and forth on his seat, trying to break free, but his effort is futile.

"What do you want to know?" he yells. "I'll tell you. I'll give you anything. Just call off that bitch and her drill."

I attach a 1/16 inch drill bit to the device and hand it back to Seraphine.

Rochas hyperventilates at the sight of Seraphine holding the drill. "You're not even giving me a chance to talk."

"Then talk," she says, her voice cold.

My breath quickens. Something about watching her take charge of another man is exhilarating. Maybe it's her tiny stature, maybe it's the knowledge that she's snatching back her power, but I can't take my eyes off Seraphine and her drill.

"What do you want to know first?" he rasps.

"Where's Gabriel Capello?"

He swallows hard, his eyes on Seraphine. "Last time I saw him was five, six years ago when the boss told me to collect him from a girlfriend's place."

I nod. So far, this matches up with her version of events.

"Where did you take him?"

"An apartment somewhere in Queen's Gardens." He coughs. "That's the last I heard of him, I swear."

"Someone else must have been keeping an eye on Gabriel," she says.

Rochas shakes his head from side to side. "If there was, then it's nobody I know. We talked about that crazy scene for months after, wanting to know what happened next."

My lip curls at the euphemism. A man ordering his guards to humiliate and gang rape the mother of his children is no 'scene', especially when Rochas was one of its eager participants.

"What does that mean?" she snaps.

He flinches. "N-nothing. The night me and Mike took Gabriel was... different."

"Oh," Seraphine asks. "How so?"

"Just a gang bang. The boss punished one of his mistresses for stepping out on him, and the boys all got a piece."

Seraphine's features twist into a rictus of rage at the understatement, and my stomach somersaults. I rush forward and grab her arm before she plunges the drill into his skull.

"Wait." I pull her backward. "What can you tell me about Samson Capello's location?"

"He's dead," Rochas says, his voice strangled.

"Catania told me you walked through the Capello house and identified the bodies."

"Th-that's right," he says.

"Then you must have found one of the twins lying face-down."

"I did."

"Did you turn him over?" I ask.

He flinches. "What?"

"How did you know Samson was dead?"

Seraphine revs the drill's motor, and the sound makes him flinch.

I lean into Rochas, my voice lowering. "You realize you're not leaving this room alive?" He squeezes his eyes shut, and I continue. "Samson isn't coming to save you and neither are your colleagues. You have a choice to die with a bullet through your brain or I'll let my lovely little apprentice open up your skull with her drill."

Rochas sobs, his face crumpling in resignation. "The dead guy was some distant cousin whose car wouldn't start. He must have known Sam was staying the night somewhere else and used his bed."

"Was that so hard? Now tell us where we can find him."

"Last thing I heard, he left town and is hiding out until the man who killed his family is dead." He swallows. "I swear to god. That's all I know. Sam said he'd hired two firms to track down the killers, but—"

"Which ones?"

"I don't know!" he cries.

I step back. It doesn't matter. One of them is the firm I inherited from Anton. The other firm will waste time looking for non-existent clues. All the vehicles I use are leased using counterfeit IDs and fake number plates. I haven't been arrested for so much as a parking ticket, so any DNA evidence they find at the scene of the crime won't get traced back to me.

"Alright," I turn to Seraphine. "Your turn."

Rochas glares at me, his eyes wide. "What about the bullet you promised me?"

"There's one more loose end," I say as I back toward the counter. "But I'll let my little apprentice refresh your memory."

Seraphine advances on Rochas, baring her teeth. What's left of her self restraint melts away, leaving her eyes blazing with fury.

I lean back, fold my arms across my chest, and enjoy the show. No matter how aroused I get at the sight of her demolishing this man, no matter how much my cock aches for release, and no matter how much Seraphine begs me to stretch the limits of her reward, I'll stay strong and not cross any more boundaries.

FORTY-SIX

SERAPHINE

Paolo Rochas is as hideous as I remember. His pock-marked face and greasy hair frequented my nightmares of the night he and the others assaulted Mom.

My hatred for him is so strong that my sinuses are filled with the scent of his blood.

"What are you going to do with that drill?" he screams.

"Doesn't feel so good to be powerless, does it, Paolo?" I hiss through my teeth.

He flinches. "What?"

"You talk about that night so casually, like the most important thing that happened was getting into a car and abducting Gabriel."

His eyes dart toward Leroi, who's giving me space to exact my revenge. My lip curls. Does this scumbag think Leroi will come to the rescue just because they're both men?

"Do you remember Evangeline Capello?"

He swallows, shakes his head, squeezes his eyes shut.

"You should, considering how you choked her with that hideous thing between your legs. What did you say to her?"

His breath hitches, and his body seizes with shudders. I rev up the drill's motor, making him flinch sideways. He was so arrogant when Dad ordered him to silence her, so proud to open his fly and shove his filthy penis down her throat.

"You don't get to zone out." I slap his cheek. "Open your eyes or I'll drill a hole through their lids."

His eyes pop open, his features contorting with anguish. "That wasn't me. It was someone else—"

"Don't lie." I hold the drill bit an inch away from his face and press the trigger with a few warning revs.

He jerks backward and screams. "I was under orders. If I didn't do it, I would have ended up dead on the floor like Raphael."

Another lie. My throat clogs with guilt, but I swallow it back. None of this was my fault. I need to focus on the men responsible for Mom's brutal murder.

"You like it, whore?" I say with a sneer. "You like choking on this huge dick?"

His eyes flash with recognition. "I'm sorry," he croaks. "I wanted nothing to do with what happened to Evangeline, but I had no choice."

"Show me."

He stiffens, his eyes widening.

"I want to see if it's as big as you boast."

"Seraphine," Leroi cautions from behind me.

I ignore him. If I can't use Miko to make him jealous, then I'll take advantage of Paolo's last moments. Paolo swallows, his Adam's apple bobbing up and down. I want to shove the drill bit into the lump to make him choke, but I save that thought for later.

"My hands are tied," he whispers. "If you want to see my dick, you have to pull it out."

I return the drill to the counter, my gaze falling on the roll of knives. They're all too big for what I have planned for Paolo, so I look through the tool set, and decide on a box cutter with a curved handle.

Leroi grabs my forearm, then leans into me and growls, "What the hell do you think you're doing?"

"Don't interfere with my revenge," I hiss.

He squeezes hard enough to punctuate his point. "Behave yourself."

"Are you taking his side?" I look him full in the face.

Leroi's eyes are dark pits of fury, his jaw clenched tight. He doesn't answer because that would mean telling the truth about how he really feels. Leroi is too stubborn to admit he wants me.

He releases my arm, and I turn back to Paolo with a smirk. Paolo's breath comes in short, sharp gasps, and his face is a mask of terror. I step closer, my lips curved into a smile.

"That night, you were touching yourself through your pants, aching for your turn with Mom."

His Adam's apple bobs.

I press the box cutter to his fly. "Now, it's my turn with you."

"Don't do this," he croaks. "Please."

My head tilts. "You remembered. Those are the exact words Mom said before you shoved that filthy thing down her throat."

I don't wait for his response because I'm already slicing through the fabric of his jeans. Paolo flinches and hisses as my blade nicks his skin.

"Oops, sorry." I raise a shoulder. "I hope this doesn't affect the quality of your erection."

"You're crazy."

I reach into the gaping hole and grab his penis. It's soft and limp and pitifully small. "What's this?"

He jerks his head to the side. "Please, no."

My fingers tighten around his flesh until he screams at me to stop. I tug and squeeze, trying to make him harden, but all I achieve are more agonized cries.

"This isn't going to work," I mutter, my fingers loosening. "Not like this."

Paolo flops forward and groans, but it's far too early for him to feel relief.

Leroi's glare burns the side of my face as I return to the counter to pick up the drill. The weight of his disapproval pushes down on my shoulders, but I ignore him and his double standards.

"You're probably one of those guys who can't get off unless he's in a position of power," I say.

Paolo shakes his head from side to side.

"So if you close your eyes and listen to the drill at its highest setting, you can imagine you've trapped a screaming woman."

"You're sick," he rasps.

"At least I'm honest enough to admit it."

I pull the trigger again, and press the bottom of the drill to his penis, letting the vibrations do their work. Paolo's screams mingle with the whine of the drill, creating a horrifying medley.

Tears stream down his greasy face as he writhes and spasms in his seat. My gaze bounces from his pained features to his burgeoning erection, the pulse between my thighs quickening.

"For the love of god," he cries. "Please, stop."

"Where was your god when you were forcing yourself down her throat? You should have thought of that before."

Paolo's penis lengthens and thickens until it's over four times its original size. I release the trigger, my eyes widening.

"Wow," I whisper. "You're a grower, not a shower?"

"Seraphine," Leroi growls.

"It's pretty big for a filthy old man."

Paolo sobs.

I snap my teeth.

"No," he cries.

A laugh bubbles from my chest. "Don't worry. I won't put it in my mouth."

I can almost hear Leroi's sigh of relief, but I'm more concerned about giving Paolo what he deserves. With one hand, I grip his erection.

"Impressive," I whisper, loud enough for Leroi's benefit. "You're so thick that my fingers aren't touching."

Paolo stiffens, his entire body trembling.

I stroke his shaft with a slow and reverent touch.

"Please, stop," he whispers.

Leroi grumbles but doesn't interfere.

Turning around the drill, I aim the bit at Paolo's slit. He twists and screams, finally seeming to understand his fate.

"I'm so glad you're so long and thick, otherwise this won't work."

Paolo's legs jerk, but they're fastened to the chair. He raises his hips, but they're also strapped down. No matter how much he thrashes, he can't escape the drill.

The motor is off when I position the bit against his slit, yet he cries as though it were still on. I insert about an inch before I meet resistance, but one gentle press of the trigger is all it takes to deepen the penetration.

Vibrations reverberate through my fingers, and blood cascades over my skin, but it's nothing compared to how my ears ring with his screams. Revenge on Paolo satisfies nearly all my senses.

I savor this moment of absolute power.

All those years ago when I hid behind the door of Dad's office, I never imagined I'd have such satisfying revenge. I want to send this pretty picture to the girl I once was to let her know the ordeal she's about to suffer won't last forever.

"That's it," I say, mirroring the words in my dream. "Take it. Take it all like a good little whore."

The drill burrows further into his shaft, and by the time it's all the way in, Paolo's screams fall quiet.

He's probably gone into shock.

I pull the drill in and out of his deflating erection, in time to the thrusts that haunt my dreams. It's still surging with blood that soaks his jeans and spreads over the floor.

A gunshot rings through my ears, interrupting my revelry.

When I glance up, Paolo has a hole in the center of his forehead.

Before I can even protest, strong hands grab my shoulders and spin me around. Leroi glares down at me, his eyes still blazing. His lips flatten across his teeth, and every vein on his temple bulges. My gaze travels down to the arteries protruding from his neck, and I moan.

"You touched his cock," he snarls.

Just as I think he's about to chastise me, his lips crash onto mine in a punishing kiss.

FORTY-SEVEN

LEROI

What the fuck is she doing? I was looking forward to watching her drill through his heart, but when she started flirting with that bastard, realization sliced through me with a blade.

She's trying to make me jealous.

This is her response to threatening her about manipulating Miko. I grind my teeth, my eyes narrowing as she runs those delicate little fingers over another man's shaft.

I pull out my gun.

Paolo Rochas is about to die.

"Seraphine," I growl.

She ignores me, but I catch a hint of her smirk as she aims the drill at the head of his cock.

My jaw drops. Is she going to—

The drill bit slides into his urethra, tearing apart the flesh. Rochas screams, and the sound goes straight to my balls.

I can't look away.

As she turns on the motor, my gut twists with horror

and my cock fills with arousal. I've watched some freaky shit, but the sight of a beautiful woman destroying another man's junk makes me so hard I'm lightheaded.

My breath quickens, and I'm torn between putting a bullet through the man's head and tearing into Seraphine.

What the fuck have I unleashed?

I used to think Seraphine was an avenging angel, but she's a beautiful little devil sent to tempt me into the depths of depravity. And I'll follow her into all seven circles of hell.

Blood splatters across her face and neck, coating her in crimson, though it doesn't break her from her euphoric haze. She fucks the shaft with slow, sensual strokes, using the oozing red liquid as a lubricant. Seraphine is so lost in her pleasure, she doesn't notice that Rochas has stopped screaming.

The sight of her in her rapture heats my blood with raging desire. It should be me that makes her smile, and gives her this level of ecstasy, not the suffering of that greasy bastard.

His erection is barely deflated by the time she stands, even though blood continues to spurt from the deep cavity that she drilled.

I'm impressed with her precision, even more impressed at how she's manipulated me to a point beyond reason. After slaying my rival, I cross the room, grab her arm, whirl her around. The blood roaring in my ears drowns out all thought and reason. She's burrowed so deeply under my skin that I may as well be her puppet.

The thought of losing control ignites a burst of fury, and I kiss her hard and fast. My fingers twine through her hair and twist at the roots with a grip that makes her gasp.

When I break the kiss, she gazes up at me, her pupils so dilated that her irises are tiny rings of blue. The blood spattering across her pretty face makes her look feral and only adds to her allure.

Her lips lift with an unspoken challenge, and every instinct in my soul roars at me to tame this little demon and make her mine. But if I steal a second kiss, I won't be able to stop.

"I flirted with him," she says. "What are you going to do about it?"

I should step away, resist her allure, but lust fogs my vision until I no longer see sense.

"Damn it."

My mouth descends on her parted lips, and I devour her with uncontrollable hunger. I slide my tongue into her welcoming warmth and groan as the drill drops to the concrete floor with a crash.

My one remaining survival instinct that isn't completely under her spell warns me that she still has the box cutter, but I'm too enraptured by Seraphine to care.

She kisses back, her tongue twisting around mine, her arm clinging so tightly around my neck that I wonder if she's trying to cut off my air. I lift her off her feet and walk her to the nearest wall.

"Is this what you want?" I growl into her kiss.

"Yes," she whispers, her legs encircling my waist.

I'm lost in the taste of her on my tongue, in the feel of her body pressed against mine, in the blissful madness of her depravity. I want to own this beautiful creature, tame her, consume her, claim her so deeply that she never wants to touch another man but me.

Seraphine is my drug and I'm ready to overdose.

The box cutter falls to the ground with a clang, and Seraphine grinds her pussy against my aching cock.

"Please," she whispers.

"Tell me what you want."

"I need you inside me."

"Fuck," I groan.

Her nails dig into my neck, and the pain pushes away the fog of lust. Alarm bells ring through my ears, warning that I'm about to cross a dangerous line behind which I can never retreat.

"Seraphine," I groan. "I don't want to be another guy that hurts you."

"You won't be," she says through panting breaths. "I want this. I want you."

"Fuck. You don't understand. I'm not right for you. The way I fuck is rough, painful, wild. I can't promise I won't get carried away and do something I regret."

She grabs my face with her bloody hands. "I don't want gentle," she says through clenched teeth. "I want you to take me, to make me feel alive. Please. I trust you."

"Why?" I growl.

"Because you're strong, you're intense, and dangerous. You're the only man I've ever wanted. There's something about you I can't resist."

None of those reasons form a viable base for trust, but her words are the spark that ignites the flames of my libido. They flicker and burn through my resistance until I cave into temptation.

I want her exposed and writhing beneath me, but I can't take off her clothes when I have her pinned to the wall, so I take a step back and set her on her feet.

Slumping against the wall, she stares up at me, her eyes glazed with lust. Her lips are red and swollen, only adding to her deadly allure.

I pick up the box cutter and make tiny slices through the straps of her tank top and down the waistband of her leggings, making sure to cut through her panties. There's no time to get her naked. I'm too consumed with the need to pound into her sweet pussy.

She pants, her lips curling into a smile that makes my heart roar with triumph.

But it's not enough.

I want to be the one who makes her face light up with rapture.

I lift Seraphine off her feet again and push her back up against the wall. She grips my shoulders so tightly I know it will leave marks and I don't care.

Resting the backs of her legs over my forearms, I reach for the hole I made in her panties and rip it open wider. My fingers meet folds so slick with moisture that I can't help but groan.

"Dirty girl," I growl into her ear. "Did drilling through that bastard's shaft get you so wet, or is that arousal for me?"

She trembles. "I kept thinking about you watching me touch him. I wanted to make you mad."

"It worked." I nip at her earlobe, and she gasps.

Seraphine likes pain in specific amounts. I could tell that much from the way she reacted to the nipple clamps.

My cock aches, feeling on the verge of exploding, but my protective instincts force me to make sure she's mentally and physically ready. I rub her clit, making her buck against my hand and moan.

"You like that, don't you?" I ask, my voice rough. "You like it when I play with your clit?"

"Yes," she whispers.

"Do you want more?"

"Please," she whispers and grips my shoulders even tighter as I caress her bud with gentle strokes. Her hips move against my hands, and my nostrils fill with the heady scent of arousal.

My baser instincts scream at me to take her, to bury my cock into her tight heat and fuck her until she's mine. I rein back those urges, reminding myself that this might be her first time having consensual sex.

Sliding two fingers into her entrance, I trail kisses all along her neck and chest. The pad of my thumb brushes against her clit, making her keen.

"That's right, angel," I growl in her ear. "You're making such pretty noises for me."

Curling my fingers, I stroke her walls, pushing her higher and higher until her nails are digging into the skin on the back of my neck and she's panting against my ear.

She wraps her legs around my hips, making my cock push painfully against my fly. It's desperate, aching, straining to break. I pull down my zipper, and it springs free.

"Is this what you want?" I rasp.

"Yes," she whispers. "God yes."

"Remember, you asked for this," I growl. "If it gets too much, you're going to use a safe word."

"Red to stop and yellow to slow down?" she asks through ragged breaths.

It takes a second of me wondering how the fuck she would know something like that until I remember our trip to the Wonderland fetish store. She must have read one of the books the sales clerk convinced her to add to the cart.

"Got it." I pick up the pace of my strokes, my cock thickening as her walls clench around my digits. When they quiver with the telltale twitches of orgasm, I press my lips against her ear.

"Let go, angel. Come all over my fingers like a good girl."

Her breath hitches, and her back arches. I circle her clit with my thumb, and within seconds, she's screaming my name. She convulses and jerks, her pussy closing in around my fingers with tight spasms that force all my blood to rush to my cock.

Shit.

I haven't even fucked her yet, haven't claimed her, but in that moment I make a silent vow: I will never let her go.

FORTY-EIGHT

SERAPHINE

I'm clinging to Leroi's neck with my back pressed against the wall, my ankles locked around his hips. Every inch of me still convulsing from the orgasm he gave me with his fingers. I clench around his thick digits, wanting more, needing it, but they remain still.

His chest heaves against mine and his hot breath fans against the side of my face. His grip around my legs loosens as if he wants to put me back on my feet.

"We're not finished," I murmur against his neck.

"Still not satisfied, angel?"

"No."

"Tell me what you need."

My lips tighten. I already told him at least a hundred times. Does he want me to beg? Probably, considering I flirted with Miko and then complimented Paolo's greasy dick.

"Fuck me," I say.

His fingers withdraw from my pussy, and I groan at the sudden emptiness. My stomach sinks, and I wonder if this is going to be anything like the spanking where he built me up into a frenzy and left me writhing on my belly, crying for release.

When he lines the bulbous head of his cock against my entrance, my breath catches, and all doubts evaporate under the heat of our combined arousal.

"What do you say?" he growls.

I want to say 'now', but that will only prolong my torment. If humbling myself will get me the pleasure I want from Leroi, then I'll say whatever he needs.

"Please fuck me and make me come..." The chaotic part of me adds with a smirk, "If you can."

His snarl makes the fine hairs on the back of my neck stand on end, and my insides quiver with anticipation.

With one hard thrust, he pushes inside me so deeply, I can feel him in the back of my throat.

Pleasure explodes across my nerve endings, bringing back echoes of my fading orgasm. I gasp, a strangled scream stretching my vocal chords.

He's big. His girth far exceeds Paolo's and I'm not sure my pussy could accommodate his full length. My walls twitch and expand around him, but before I can adjust to his size, he pulls out and re enters me with another snap of his hips.

"You're mine," he says, his voice dangerously low. "Who do you belong to?"

"L-Leroi," I reply with a whimper.

"Good girl. See how well you're gripping my cock? That's your cunt inviting me in, welcoming its new owner."

My heart flutters. I can't get enough of his filthy words.

I buck my hips, pushing up against him as his strokes become harder, deeper, faster. My limbs tremble, and my breath comes in shallow pants that barely graze the tops of my lungs. He fucks into me with all his strength, and I dig my nails into his shoulders and squeeze my eyes shut, unable to do anything to withstand the overwhelming pleasure.

"Look at me while I fuck your tight pussy," he says.

I can't.

It's too much.

I've never felt such immense pleasure. A lightning storm of ecstasy surges through my nervous system, burning the girl I was into ashes. All that's left of me is a creature reborn from his acceptance, eager to break free.

"Do you want me to stop?" he asks.

"Never."

"Open your eyes, angel. I won't ask you again."

I crack open one eye and then another, and meet his fathomless depths. Leroi's features are wild with lust, his jaw clenched tight as he groans.

He pounds into me with renewed strength, each thrust slamming me harder and harder against the wall.

Leroi thought my traumatic past meant that I couldn't take him, but I can. I haven't just consented with him, he's made me fight for this much intimacy, starting from when he helped me escape the basement. I've wanted this from the moment I straddled his hips and pointed that knife to his throat. Maybe even before then.

"You're so beautiful when you're squeezing my cock with your pussy."

My muscles tighten around his length.

"That's it, angel. Take what you need." He grips my hips and pounds into me until I'm gasping for air.

Each thrust of his hips delivers sensations so intense that I'm lost in a whirlpool of ecstasy. My muscles quake. My breath shallows. Pressure builds up in my pelvis, and my orgasm is so close that I can almost taste it. My walls quiver around his shaft, and my lashes flutter.

"Eyes on me. I want to see you come."

Leroi pounds into me with a hard thrust that fills my vision with fireworks. I cry out, my muscles closing so tightly around his length that his thrusts become quick and shallow.

"Just like that," he groans. "Take it all."

"Leroi," I moan through gasps.

"I know, angel. I know." He grabs the side of my face, and our gazes lock.

"Now, scream for me," he growls and picks up speed, pounding into me with abandon.

I release a choked cry.

"That's it baby," he croons. "Let me hear you come."

Wave after wave of pleasure crashes through my senses, and I yell his name. Throughout the orgasm, I claw his back, my muscles tightening and contracting around his impossibly thick shaft.

Leroi's thrusts quicken and become erratic, pushing me higher and higher. His breathing grows hot and heavy, and his gaze penetrates mine with an intensity that fills my entire vision. With a full body shudder, he lets out a guttural moan, his release filling my pussy with warmth.

"Mine," he growls.

Arching my back, I push against him and squeeze around his length, trying to milk every last drop of his pleasure. His grip tightens on my hips and we stay locked together, his head resting against my temple, our hearts pounding in unison.

Tears sting the backs of my eyes as we breathe the same air. Until this moment, I never noticed I had a void, but this has filled my heart to bursting. I've never felt so connected to another human being. We're so close that our souls touch.

Dozens of men have tried to make me their possession, but Leroi is the only one who has ventured beyond my looks and welcomed my darkness. It almost feels like a bond of unconditional acceptance.

He's nothing like the others.

Nothing like the targets who picked me up at parties or nightclubs. Nothing like the bastards who saw a young girl they picked up off the street and wanted to exploit for their own sick pleasures. Nothing like the vermin I killed.

I bask in his presence, feeling a strange sense of completion that verges on pain. I never want this moment to end. My mind is as still as the night's sky, its darkness lit up by twinkling stars. A bright full moon casts a velvet hue over my spirit, and I know deep in my heart that it's coming from Leroi.

My pulse slows, my breath evens, and my muscles melt into bliss.

Leroi draws back a few inches to give me space, but he never lets go of the side of my face. Instead, he gazes into my eyes as though he wants to connect to my soul.

Finally, he breaks the silence and says, "Now that I've had you, I can't ever let you go. You're mine, Seraphine. Every beautiful piece of you."

My heart swells, infusing the rest of my body with giddy warmth. His words wrap my broken pieces in a cocoon of safety and love.

"Yours," I whisper, meaning every word. "And you're mine."

Nodding, he smiles and presses a soft kiss on my lips. It's chaste and brief and carries a heart full of emotions.

Leroi truly accepts all of me, including the parts that are twisted and dark.

I'm no longer alone.

I finally belong.

I rest my head against his shoulder and let my eyes flutter shut. This thing between us feels real. So heartwarmingly real. So heartbreakingly real.

Despite what he's said, I'm not naïve enough to stake my life on words uttered in the heat of the moment. Men will say anything to get what they want, even if that's something as simple as adulation. They can be perfectly protective and loving until they're not.

But I can hope.

I can dream.

Can't I?

FORTY-NINE

LEROI

Kissing Seraphine is like tasting the finest, most exquisite wine. She's delicate and sweet, yet there's an edge of something dark to her that resonates with my twisted soul. She's intoxicating.

Fucking Seraphine, being enveloped in her tight heat, and eliciting those sweet whimpers is like coming home. She's a perfect balance of decadence and innocence that I've never seen in another, let alone in a woman so beautiful.

I'm powerless to resist her.

Pulling back, I gaze into her eyes, and they sparkle with an emotion that mirrors mine. It's as if she's truly seeing me and accepting the monster, and I'm the only person in the world that matters.

Her cheeks are flushed and still smeared with another man's blood. Strands of damp hair frame her face, clinging to her forehead and neck, she's more beautiful than ever before.

My heart swells with a heady mix of tenderness and

protectiveness. I can't remember feeling so close to anyone since before my family's rejection. Seraphine would never recoil if I killed to protect her; she would worship me like a god. It only proves that she's my perfect match, created only for me.

"Are you alright?" I ask.

She smiles, her expression blissful. "Never better."

Placing another kiss on her swollen lips, I moan, "You belong to me. Body, mind, and blood."

"Forever?" she whispers.

Forever has never sounded so sweet. "That's right."

Tightening my grip around her legs, I step back from the wall and walk across the room. We pass Rochas, whose corpse sits slumped in the chair, his lower half drenched in blood, forming a thick pool on the concrete.

The corner of my lips lifts into a smirk. He's a mutilated reminder of what happens when someone crosses what's mine.

I pick up the bag of clean clothes I left on the counter and turn on the sprinkler.

"What's that for?" she asks, her voice light.

"To clean up this mess. Dried blood is a bitch to get out of the floors."

She giggles. "You care more about the state of the floors than you did about your dead poker friends."

I open the security door, step out into the hallway, and pause for the automatic lights. As they flicker on, I meet her huge, blue eyes. "That morning, when I woke up, seeing them all dead, the first thing I thought about was you."

Her lips part with a gasp. "What do you mean?"

"I thought someone had broken in to steal you back. The thought of you being taken... It made me murderous."

She pauses for several heartbeats before raising trembling fingers to the side of my face. "You cared for me even back then?"

"From the moment I saw you in the dark," I say, my voice choked.

Seraphine cranes her neck to reach my lips, and I meet her halfway in a kiss that feels like salvation and hope. I thought fucking her hard and fast against the wall might break her, but it's only brought us closer.

We're kindred spirits, bonded by blood. I want to keep Seraphine at my side forever because she gives my life a new meaning. When she's near, I'm no longer the outcast on the fringes of the criminal underground, but a man with a purpose.

I carry her to the bathroom, a functional white room with a large soaking tub. After placing Seraphine on its edge, I drop the bag of clothes on the floor and turn on the taps.

She glances around the tiled space. "Why does an inter-rogation room need a bath?"

"I had the tub installed once I took over the firm. Some-times, even a hitman needs a little rest and relaxation between torturing hardened motherfuckers for information."

Her tank top has already gathered around her waist from when I cut its straps, revealing beautiful, firm breasts, tipped with rosy pink nipples. I reach out and circle each areola with my fingertips, making her shiver.

"You're so fucking beautiful, especially when you're covered in blood."

She glances down at her breasts and smiles. "You like the spatters?"

"I like the flesh beneath them more, but the blood makes you look like an avenging angelic warrior."

I kneel at her feet and pull off her shoes and socks, revealing her dainty little feet. After pressing kisses on each arch, I reach up and slide her leggings down her hips.

Blood covers her belly, her thighs and even the thatch of blonde curls that cover her pussy. Steam rises from the bathtub behind her, creating a faint halo around her body. Maybe I'm drunk on adrenaline and desire, but she looks truly celestial.

I shake my head. "What a dirty little angel you are, covered in another man's blood."

"It doesn't count when it's the blood of my enemies," she says with a smirk. "Are you going to wash it off?"

"I'm going to do more than wash you," I growl.

Seraphine watches me undress with a hunger that would make another man blush. Her lips part each time I remove an item of clothing, making my cock swell to the point of pain. By the time I stand before her in just my boxers, she's panting.

"Let me." She reaches for the waistband, her eyes blazing with blue fire.

My heart pounds so hard that its reverberations make my cock throb, and a shiver runs down my spine and settles in my balls. She might be tiny and unarmed, but I've seen the damage this woman can do to a penis.

It's then I realize I just fucked a former Lolita assassin who still hasn't overcome her compulsive urges to maim and kill. She will use any weapon necessary to castrate a man, including her teeth.

Letting her near that part of my anatomy is like placing it in a steel trap and hoping it won't get snapped.

But I do it anyway.

Cold sweat breaks out across my skin as she runs her delicate fingers along the waistband of my boxers. As she takes hold of the elastic, she gazes up at me through those huge, cornflower blue eyes.

Her stare is filled with incandescent heat, but I can't tell if that's a good thing or a portent of doom.

My cock, that stupid motherfucker, swells at the prospect of Seraphine's teeth sinking into its flesh. I inhale a deep, shuddering breath, the hairs on the back of my neck rising.

It's not like I mistrust Seraphine. Her needs are simple. She wants to find her brother, get revenge on the men who raped and murdered her mother, and make sure that Samson is in broken pieces, six-feet underground.

And she wants me.

She slides down my boxers, inch by painstakingly slow inch, until the crown of my cock springs free.

Her eyes widen. "Wow," she says, her voice breathy. "So big."

From any other woman, those words would be a compliment. I can't stop thinking about how she sliced Billy Blue's severed penis like it was salami.

I clear my throat. "That time you bit through Samson's cock."

"Yes?" she whispers.

"What happened to the rest of it?"

"I chewed it." She shrugs and pulls down my boxers, exposing even more of my shaft.

My knees tremble. Seraphine is taking her sweet time and I'm not sure how much of this suspense I can take.

"Why?" I rasp.

"So there would be nothing to sew back."

She pulls the waistband around my hips, finally freeing my balls. After weighing them in her hands, she runs the pads of her fingers along the underside of my sac, igniting my nervous system with a lightning storm of sensations.

Heaven help me.

Hell, come to my rescue.

I need to concentrate in case something inside her snaps and she turns me into a bitter eunuch.

"Did you swallow?" I ask with a gulp.

She lowers her lashes, wraps her fingers around the base of my shaft, and makes slow, up-and-down strokes. Her non-answer is an answer in itself, but I still have to ask.

"Seraphine?"

Her gaze snaps up to meet mine, and my heart slams against its cage.

"I swallowed as much as I could before Gregor charged in and knocked me unconscious. Are you going to continue asking questions, or do you want this blow job?"

FIFTY

SERAPHINE

Leroi is being uptight, and he won't stop ruining the moment with his constant questions. What difference does it make? I had to defend myself from Samson. The psychopath got what he deserved.

A network of thick veins runs vertically along the underside of his shaft, which branch out into smaller diagonal and horizontal vessels. Leroi's cock is a thing of beauty, much like the man himself.

Precum beads on its bulbous crown, making my mouth water for a taste. I wonder which is saltier, his cum or his blood. I want to taste them both.

Just as I'm about to run my tongue along the mouthwatering vein running up Leroi's shaft, he takes hold of my face and forces me to look into his eyes.

"Seraphine?"

I let out an exasperated sigh. "What?"

"Get in the bath."

"Don't you want a blow job?" I ask, my mouth drifting toward his cock.

Groaning, he steps back and out of the reach of my mouth. "That's a lesson for another time."

My lips tighten, and I push back a surge of irritation. He's a control freak and a perfectionist, but I suppose that's part of his charm. It takes a man with that level of discipline and restraint to sneak past all those guards into the Capello mansion and murder the entire shitty family. I can't even blame him for Samson being alive because I spent five years with the twins and only managed one major victory.

With a reluctant sigh, I rise off the edge of the bathtub. Leroi climbs in first, takes my hand, and lowers us down to sit, so I'm resting on his lap with my back against his chest.

His thick erection nestles between my ass cheeks. I give my hips a little wiggle, and he releases a throaty moan.

"Behave," he growls, his voice thick with arousal.

When he grabs my thighs to hold me still, I settle back with a giggle.

"Yes, sir."

"Say that again," he says, his deep voice vibrating against my back.

"Yes, sir," I repeat, my voice softening with mock submission. Reaching behind my back, I wrap my fingers around his shaft. "Anything you want."

Leroi groans. "That's my naughty little angel."

He places soft kisses on the side of my face, all the while rubbing off the blood with his wet hands. The water is warm, but it's nothing compared to the heat of his touch.

"You took my cock so well," he says. "Are you sore?"

The muscles of my pussy clamp. "Just a little. It's more like an ache from being stretched."

"Is that what you like? Being stretched open?"

"Only by you."

His hand drops.

"What's wrong?"

"Are you sure you're alright?" he asks.

"Of course. Why are you even asking?"

He lets out one of those long, frustrated sighs that are usually accompanied with pinching the bridge of his nose or rubbing the patch of skin between his temples. I pretend not to notice. If Leroi has hangups about sex, then he needs to do it more, not less.

"Seraphine," he says.

"Leroi." I mimic his tone.

"You can't erase years of abuse with a few brutal murders."

"Why not?" I glare straight ahead.

"You're impossible."

I raise my shoulders, not feeling the slightest bit murdery. Leroi doesn't understand that his presence is everything I need.

He wraps his arms around me and plants a soft kiss on the tender spot behind my ear, over the scar from my chip. Shivers skitter across my skin, making my nipples tighten.

"Do that again," I whisper.

"This?" He kisses it again.

My muscles relax. "Yeah," I say with a long exhale. "Your touch is all I need to erase my past."

His second sigh is quieter, sounding a little more resigned. I reach for his large hand and intertwine our fingers.

"It wasn't that bad," I say softly.

Leroi doesn't respond. Either he wants me to elaborate or he thinks I'm lying.

"I suppose the first few weeks were the worst. It was terrible, really, but that's so far in the past, it's barely worth mentioning."

"Yet you still have nightmares about what happened to your mother."

I stiffen. "That's different."

"How?"

"It just is."

"Seraphine."

The hands running over my skin still, and I grind my teeth.

"What's the point of rehashing the past? I'm over it."

"You gouged out a man's eyes for... How did you put it? Being rude?"

"I was still upset about the man who came to my room," I mutter.

He pulls me into a hug that feels like swaddling, but I tense under his grip. Is this where he insists that I see another therapist? My lips purse, ready to refuse.

"I'm sorry for letting you stay in the apartment when I had company. I should have ignored your wishes and carried you over to Miko's, where you would have been safe."

My eyelids flutter shut, and I relax back into his embrace. "That's alright," I murmur. "I got over that pretty quickly, too."

"Murdering the man who assaulted you is understandable, but you didn't stop there. You need a healthier outlet."

"I have you." It sounds harsher than it was meant to. I reach behind my back again to take hold of his erection, but he grabs my wrist.

"You're avoiding the topic." His voice is even, but the words sharpen.

My hands curl into fists. I pull at my arms, trying to break out of Leroi's grip, but he's too strong. Even when I jerk my head backward to smash the back of my head into his nose, he's already two steps ahead.

"Let go of me," I snap.

"So you can derail this conversation?" He scoffs. "You claim to be unaffected by what happened to you in that basement, but your actions say otherwise."

"Are you judging me for Paolo?" I jerk my elbow backward, trying to snap his ribs.

"No." He pulls my arms out of reach. "But I can't help you if I don't know what you've suffered."

My eyes sting, mostly out of frustration because he's caught me at my most vulnerable. I'm naked, without weapons, and positioned so I can't use my nails and teeth.

"Let go of me," I say, my voice straining. "Please."

"Not until you tell me something."

"I already told you about Samson's dick. What more do you want to know?"

"Did the abuse stop?"

"Yes?"

He exhales a sharp breath. "You don't sound so sure."

"Well he couldn't exactly rape me without a dick, could he?" I snap.

"What about Gregor?"

"He never touched me like that, even though he acted like he did."

"What does that mean?"

"I'd hear him tell Samson that I was a worthless fuck or too loose. It was all excuses."

"Was he gay?"

I shake my head, squeezing my eyes shut. In some ways, Gregor was worse than Samson, because he wasn't like the average man who only thought with his dick. "I don't know.

Maybe? He only cared about hurling insults and sending me out on missions."

Leroi kisses the side of my face. "Thank you for telling me."

I don't relax because this interrogation isn't over. He's still gripping my wrists.

"How long did the sexual abuse last?"

I bow my head. "A few weeks. Dad was the one who took me to the basement, saying that I was an impostor who owed him."

"For what?"

"All the money he'd spent on me since I was born."

Leroi makes a disgruntled sound.

"Yeah. He said since Mom was dead, I had to work off her debt." I say, my voice barely more than a whisper. "He left me down there for hours with no food and water until I was weak and feverish. That's when he brought the twins and introduced me as their new toy."

Leroi hisses through his teeth. "They just accepted that?"

"Gregor laughed and said no, but Dad insisted. He said they could do whatever they wanted, but they couldn't leave any permanent marks."

When Leroi doesn't react, I continue. "Gregor rejected me at first, saying that little girls weren't his type and he didn't want Samson's sloppy seconds, so it was just me and Samson until he made the mistake of forcing me to give him a blow job."

"That's when you bit him?"

I nod. "It was worth it at the time because Samson didn't touch me like that again."

Leroi relaxes a little before asking, "What happened next?"

424

"The twins beat me up, then left me to starve and fester until Dad came charging in, screaming about me ruining his son. By then, I was too weak to care. I thought he was going to throttle me until Gregor stopped him."

"Why?" Leroi asks.

"I didn't understand what was happening until I woke up one day drenched in cold water. There was a new man in my room. He said he was there to train me. That I was going to learn to kill to pay off Mom's debts."

Leroi's breath hitches. "Who was he?"

"Gregor called him Anton."

FIFTY-ONE

LEROI

My stomach clenches at the reminder that Anton, the man responsible for saving me from my deadliest mistake, turned an innocent young woman into a killer.

Not even a woman.

Seraphine had been a mere girl. Traumatized, imprisoned, grief-stricken, and subjected to sexual assaults, she was at her most vulnerable and had no means of self-defense.

I force breaths in and out of my lungs, my heart pounding so hard that I'm sure she can feel my body tensing with alarm. I want to believe it's a different Anton from a different organization; anything other than what I know is true. He called the day after my massacre at the Capello mansion, asking about Seraphine. His missing Lolita assassin.

There's no denying the facts. Anton turned Seraphine into the sickest form of honey-trap. An underage girl sent to seduce and murder perverts.

My grip on her wrists loosens, and I take a few deep

breaths before forcing myself to speak. "What did he do to you?"

"The first thing he did was attach a remote-control collar that delivered electric shocks," she pauses, and her breath slows. "He said it's how he trained all his bitches."

The rest of her account is eerily familiar to my own training, minus the schedule of reward and punishment. Anton was firm and fair, but I had been an eager student. After failing to kill my stepfather, I was determined never to make the same mistake. As a sixteen-year-old girl suffering abuse and trauma, Seraphine would have been terrified.

"There was a lot of calisthenics, some cardio, knife skills, and practicing with syringes." She sighs, her weight pressing against my chest. "Was your training similar?"

"Not nearly so brutal," I murmur. "I also learned explosives and how to use guns."

"What was your trainer like?" she asks.

My throat thickens. Do I tell her we were both inducted by the same man? Seraphine reacted so terribly when I mentioned that the first target she killed was my uncle. How would she react if she discovered that the man who trained her like a dog had treated me like a son?

Knots of apprehension twist in my gut, blazing an agonizing path to the back of my throat. "That's a difficult question."

"Why?"

"I grew up without a permanent father figure, and my trainer stepped into the role the moment he cleaned up my dying stepfather and moved me into his home."

She hums. "Sounds nice."

Inhaling deeply, I push past my unease. "He was tough, but exactly what I needed at that stage of my life."

Seraphine shifts on my lap, so we're sitting face to face

with her straddling my legs. My heart sinks, and all traces of my erection vanish. Wet streaks mar the blood smeared on her cheeks. She looks like she's been crying.

I straighten, my face a mask of composure. "What those people did to you was unforgivable," I say, my voice thickening. "But I swear, every one of them that's still alive will suffer."

Guilt strikes my heart at the thought of killing Anton, even if he was responsible for the corruption of an innocent young girl. I have so many fond memories of the man and not just from our early days.

Every few months, I take Miko to his place by the lake for a few days of fishing and relaxation. It's a cruel discovery that the man who taught Miko to light a campfire also taught Seraphine to kill.

I clench my jaw, steel my emotions, and focus on how desperately I need to protect Seraphine.

Her eyes soften, and she nods. "We need to find Samson before he gets to Gabriel."

At the change in subject, my chest loosens with relief, and I'm finally able to offer her a smile. "Along the way, we'll gather up the other two guards on your list.

She nods. "Can I sleep in your bed tonight?"

"Of course."

She lowers her eyes and curls in on herself. "There's one more thing I need to ask."

"Anything."

"When you're hunting those men, don't leave me behind." Her lips tighten. "I know you called me impulsive, but I'm trying. Sometimes, I keep things so bottled up that I don't know something is wrong until I explode."

My throat constricts, and I can only nod. "Does that

explain why you bolted out of the car when you saw Pietro Fiore outside, washing his car?"

"He knew I was being forced under the threat of the chip. He knew and said nothing. Did nothing. Acted like it was all part of the job," she says, her voice bitter.

"Is there anyone else you want to kill?"

She tilts her head, her lips curving into a smile.

"Anyone apart from me?"

I squeeze her around the middle, making her double over and squeal. Warmth spreads across my chest at the sound of her girlish laughter, and my nose fills with her strawberry scent. Who would have thought Seraphine was ticklish?

"Maybe Anton," she says.

Instantly, a lump forms in my gut, dread pooling in its place as I think of what Anton might have done to Seraphine. "Did he... touch you?"

She's silent, her features remaining still. The dread twists, expands, and takes on a new form that sinks its claws into my stomach and threatens to tear at my heart.

She shakes her head. "Not really."

I school my features into a mask of calm, even though my heart thuds so hard that its cage rattles. Through ragged, shallow breaths, I ask, "What does that mean?"

Seraphine glances to the side. "It was nothing like it was with Samson."

Steam rises from the bathtub, and the air thickens with anticipation. It closes in on me on all sides and squeezes tight. My breath stills as I await her reply, and the silence bears down on us until my ears ring, making me force down a wave of frustration.

Why is she hesitating?

What did Anton do to her that was too terrible to even mention?

I swallow over and over, trying to digest the notion that Anton could be a worse predator than Samson. Because there's a selfish, twisted part of myself that wonders if I'm the same. I knew she was damaged, knew she'd been abused, yet I fucked her against the wall after she tortured a rapist.

"You can tell me anything," I say. "They'll be no judgment, no matter what."

I keep my voice even and my gaze soft, despite the anger and hatred burning through my veins, despite the overwhelming helplessness of knowing that the man I called a mentor is a monster.

She lowers her lashes. "He never touched me, not in a way that was inappropriate, but he..."

"Seraphine, what did he do?"

She swallows. "He said I had to learn to attract men and look innocent and harmless so they could drop their guard."

Hesitating, I wait for her to continue.

"I had to exercise naked, and he would get really close to adjust my form." A shudder runs through her bones, sending ripples through the bathwater. "Sometimes, I could feel his breath on my skin. Do you think that's why I stabbed that man at the gas station in the eye?"

"It's possible." My words are choked.

What Seraphine describes isn't just sexual abuse, it's psychological torture. Being forced to assume vulnerable positions and never knowing when Anton's control might snap is the worst kind of mind fuck.

"He also ordered me to change into cute little outfits while he watched. Sometimes I had to dance."

My jaw clenches.

That sick bastard.

"When Samson brought him in, he'd stand back and do nothing while Samson used the collar to make me humiliate myself with sex toys. When he was with Gregor, he just stared at me while I was training in a way that made my skin crawl." She shakes her head. "It's so difficult to describe—"

"I believe you."

Her eyes widen. "You do?"

"Even if they didn't rape you, it was still abuse. They were evil men, and when we catch up with them, they will die horribly."

She wraps her arms around my neck and pulls me into a tight hug that I don't deserve. If Seraphine knew that I owed my life to Anton, she would leave me without a second thought.

Or maybe she would snap. She isn't healed enough to take care of herself and doesn't have the resources to find Gabriel.

Then she'd be out there alone and vulnerable, killing people until either the police caught up with her. Or Samson.

She must never know my secret.

FIFTY-TWO

SERAPHINE

Leroi has barely said a word to me since he lifted me out of the bath and dried every inch of my body with fluffy towels. Then we returned to the interrogation room to switch off the sprinkler, and Leroi dragged Paolo's corpse to a disposal chute without explaining what would happen next.

I lean against the car door watching his profile, my mind replaying our conversation, trying to figure out the reason for this prolonged silence. It's impossible to pinpoint the part that disturbed him the most. Maybe it was when I took advantage of the afterglow and asked to sleep in his bed?

"Leroi?" I murmur.

The corners of his lips tighten. "What?"

"Did I say something wrong?"

"Of course not." His voice is harsh and betrays his words.

"Then is this about what I did to Paolo?"

He gives his head a tight shake.

My heart sinks. At this rate, I'll never get an answer. I

pull my gaze away from Leroi and stare out into the darkened highway.

Sex with Leroi was the single most pleasurable experience of my entire existence. Climaxing with him inside me was ten times more intense than his fingers, tongue, or the hilt of a dagger. It was like connecting with another human being and looking into their soul. He was no longer only a mysterious stranger I was desperate to conquer, he was my other half that wanted me as much as I wanted him.

We connected at a level deeper than anything I've ever known, looked into each other's eyes and saw compatible spirits. Time stood still when he was fucking me hard and fast. I had no traumatic past, no uncertain future, no hunger for blood or revenge. He placed me completely in the moment. He had been my pleasure, my solace, my peace.

And the reverent way he washed the blood off every inch of my skin afterward melted my heart. I rested against his chest, trusting him without reservations until he started with the questions.

Swallowing hard, I steal a glance at Leroi as we continue to the end of the hallway. A muscle in his jaw clenches as though he can't stand the feel of my stare.

I would ask him what's wrong again, but he'd never reveal his innermost thoughts.

The rest of the journey home is just as quiet, with Leroi giving me one-word answers. Maybe he's already having second thoughts.

He unlocks his door and lets me inside without a word, then tosses the bag he brought to one side and turns toward me, looking like he's about to announce that sex was a mistake.

Before he even gets the chance to say the words, I hurry across the living room and open my door.

"Seraphine?"

I let it swing shut and lean against the wood, using my body as a barricade.

A few moments later, Leroi knocks. It's a gentle tap on the wood that vibrates against my back and not the fist pounding I expected.

"Are you alright?" he asks.

"Go away," I say.

He hesitates.

My breath catches. I want him to force the door open, pick me off the floor and demand answers, but that would assume he even wants me to stay.

I bend my neck and rest my head on my bent knees, my heart thudding with trepidation. Any minute now, he'll explain that what we did together was a mistake and that it must never happen again.

But he doesn't.

Instead, he releases a long sigh, and his footsteps retreat toward his bedroom. When his door opens and shuts, I close my eyes and let out my own breath of relief.

I took advantage of Leroi and made him break his rule about having sex, and now he regrets it. There's no crew on standby to clean up this mess. Somehow, I need to figure out a way to make this right.

———

Hours later, when the first rays of light dance across my eyelids, I rise off the floor and take a hot shower to soothe my aching muscles. It isn't the first time I've spent the night on a floor, but I've never slept sitting up with my back against a solid surface.

I cast a wistful glance at Leroi's door as I cross the living room and enter the kitchen, only to find the block of chef's knives on the counter.

My stomach drops.

Does this mean he doesn't expect me to stay? I shake off that thought. It's time to think positive. Maybe this is a test, and he's waiting for me in his bedroom with a gun beneath his pillow.

He probably expects me to sneak into his room and try to slice his throat.

But he'd be wrong.

I'll prove to Leroi that I can use kitchen knives for their intended purpose. Then he'll see that I'm no longer the disturbed girl he pulled out of that basement and that I've changed into a woman worthy of his love.

Then he'll think again about sending me away.

When I open the refrigerator, it's full of phallic shaped vegetables and nine-inch salamis. Ignoring the obvious trap, I grab an onion and slice it into thin pieces, then do the same with a bell pepper, tomatoes, mushrooms, herbs, and bacon. Leroi likes high-protein breakfasts, so I'll make us a frittata.

After beating the eggs and mixing them with herbs and spices, I pour it into an oven dish, add the chopped ingredients, and make a start on the coffee.

As the frittata cooks, and the kitchen fills with delicious aromas, the door opens. I step away from the knives and walk to the coffeemaker, my heart pounding.

"I didn't know you could cook," Leroi says from behind. "I thought you only chopped."

I turn around, my features schooled into a mask of indifference. "Our cook taught me how to make a few dishes."

He crosses the tiled floor and pulls me into a hug. "What happened last night?"

My heart skips several beats. He missed me? Closing my eyes, I lean against this hard chest and savor his embrace. Had I misinterpreted his silence? I inhale his sandalwood scent. He wants me now, so does what happened last night even matter?

Yes, it does, because he's blowing hot and cold.

I draw out of the hug to look him full in the face. "You went silent. You either got what you wanted and no longer needed me, or decided you'd made another mistake. So, I left you alone."

He winces. "I was... processing."

"Processing what? The sex?"

"Not that." He glances away. "I couldn't get certain aspects of your story out of my mind."

My eyes narrow. Nothing about my past should be news to Leroi. He's seen first-hand that I kill and castrate men, yet the only thing he ever complained about was the mess and something about getting caught.

"Which parts?" I ask. "It's not like didn't tell you anything you didn't already suspect."

"You're right," he rasps. "I'm sorry. I won't shut you out like that again."

My eyes narrow. His apology is genuine enough, but his actions don't match his words.

Leroi cups the side of my face, bringing my attention back to him.

"I mean it," he murmurs. "From this moment, I will include you in everything."

Just as I'm about to answer, the doorbell rings.

Leroi's face hardens. "Someone's here."

I give him a blank look.

"All my allies know to call first or use a specific knock."

My eyes widen. "Oh."

The doorbell rings again, only this time more insistently.

Leroi's gaze darts to the block of knives, and he pulls out a gun. "Arm yourself and hide in a blind spot. Whatever you do, don't leave this kitchen."

FIFTY-THREE

LEROI

Whoever is at the door knows I'm at home because the doorbell is now on a continuous ring. I walk out of the kitchen, pick up my phone, and check on the security camera app. Surprise, surprise, they've placed a finger over the lens.

I grind my teeth and reach beneath the dining table, where I've hidden a silencer. After extracting it from the duct tape, I attach it to the gun.

The ringing continues, accompanied by thudding. Whoever's on the other side of the door can't be a professional killer. They're creating enough ruckus to give their target time to arm themselves or be halfway down a fire exit.

This is probably Rosalind, trying for another hookup after getting dumped by Cesare. It's a pity because they'd be a match made in Hell. She loves it hard and rough and degrading while he... Let's just say Cesare can give her all that and more.

I position myself away from the door and yell, "Who's there?"

"Where is she?" screeches an unfamiliar female voice.

"You're going to have to give me a clue," I say.

"Rosalind," she yells. "What have you done to my sister?"

My brow raises. Rosalind didn't mention having any siblings, though I suppose there was a limit to what she could say with her mouth stuffed with a gag.

"She's not here," I say.

"So, you admit to knowing her?"

"I admitted to there being no one here by the name of Rosalind," I say.

The woman behind the door sobs. "That's it. I'm calling the police."

Fuck.

I dart my gaze toward the kitchen door. This time, Seraphine isn't peeking through the gap. Maybe she's learned her lesson about following orders.

"Take your finger off the camera lens," I say.

The woman doesn't answer, hopefully not because she's calling the cops, and I glance at the app to find a petite girl with features similar to Rosalind.

She's not much taller than Seraphine and wears a sweatshirt that says Tourgis Academy. After checking through the camera app that there's no one else in the hall-way, I open the door a crack and resist the urge to pull her inside.

I promised Seraphine that no one would enter this apartment without her permission.

The girl rushes at me. "Where's my sister?"

"I don't have her." I hold her back with my arm. "Try looking for her somewhere else."

"Don't lie to me. Rosa texted me a few nights ago from the Phoenix, saying she was going back to your apartment."

My lips tighten. It's awfully presumptuous of Rosalind to assume I would take her back after the bullshit she pulled at my doorstep. Even more audacious that she thought I would choose her over Seraphine.

I would slam the door in this girl's face, but I don't need the extra attention from the police. She looks young, excitable, and exactly the type who would cry to the cops if I grabbed her by the throat with a warning never to return.

Fucking Rosalind. Her pregnancy stunt had been bad enough. Now, she's sharing my home address with her next of kin.

"Your sister isn't here. She never was."

The girl's face crumples. "Then where is she?"

"Retrace her steps. Find out where she was when you last heard from her and start from there."

She shuffles on her feet, gazing up at me like I have more answers. And she'd be right. The last person I saw her with was Cesare, but I'm not about to throw my cousin under the police bus.

"That's the best I can give you," I say. "Now, if you don't mind, I'd like you to leave. My girlfriend and I are about to have breakfast."

The girl's gaze drops, and she rubs the back of her neck. "Are you sure that's all you know?"

I exhale a sharp breath, mostly out of frustration.

I'm not completely heartless, and the girl reminds me a little of my sister. If Rosalind has holed up with Cesare and has forgotten to call to say she's alive, then I can tell my cousin to remind her to send a text.

"Do you have a number?" I ask.

As she pulls down the strap of her backpack and reaches inside, my fingers twitch toward my gun. Instead of extracting a weapon, she produces a sheet of paper with her name and number already written multiple times. She tears off a strip and I take it with a nod, glancing down to find that she's called Miranda.

"I'll call you if I hear anything," I say before closing the door.

"Thank you," she says from the other side.

Stepping back from the doorway, I watch her leave via the app. Twinges of guilt prick at the frayed edges of my conscience. Rosalind may be a manipulative liar, but I could have been less of an asshole to her sister.

I return to the kitchen to find that Seraphine has already plated her breakfast and is picking through a delicious-looking concoction of eggs, bacon, and vegetables.

"You lied about not knowing Rosalind," she says without looking up.

"She was just a random hookup who got overly attached."

"Is that what I am to you?" she asks. "Just a random hookup?"

"What do you think?" I ask back.

Her lips part, but she doesn't speak, so I close the distance. "Do you think I bring random hookups into my home for days, clean up their murders, hunt down their enemies and provide safe and soundproof spaces for them to get their revenge?"

She glances to the side.

"Look at me, Seraphine."

When she doesn't move, I hold her chin and force her to meet my gaze.

Seraphine stares up at me, her eyes blazing.

"You are not a random hook up," I say. "What we did together last night was everything. I've never met a woman I find so completely captivating, and I never will again. You're it, Seraphine. It doesn't get more perfect than you."

She bows her head, not seeming to believe me.

"Hey, I would raze the world to ashes if it meant keeping you safe."

Her eyes shine, and her chest rises and falls with rapid breaths. "Then why were you being so cold?"

My gaze falters. Now's not the time to tell her. There's no predicting how she'll react so soon after that reminder of Rosalind.

She'd ask when I worked out that Anton was her trainer, and I'd have to admit that it was the day after I brought her to the apartment. Then she would worry that I'd hand her over to Anton the same way Capello handed her over to the twins.

I can't tell her until Anton is dead.

Hell, even if I wanted to explain that the reason for my silence was I'd been thinking of murdering the only man that's ever been a father to me, I can't form the words.

"Sorry," I rasp. "I was working through my rage. Hearing about what you suffered made me feel powerless. I wanted to travel back to before it all started and burst into Capello's mansion with guns blazing."

The corners of her mouth lift into a sad smile. "You already kind of did."

"Five years too late," I say, my laugh bitter.

"You came, and that's all that matters."

The morning sun shines through the kitchen window, illuminating her hair, making her look vulnerable and small. I want to raise every man who ever hurt her from the dead so she can destroy them one by one. I want to help her reclaim her power. I want to protect her from the evils of the world. But all I can do for now is hold her close and never let her go.

I pull her into my chest. "No one will ever hurt you again," I say, meaning every word. "I will burn down the entire state of New Alderney before anyone lays a finger on you again."

Seraphine wraps her arms around my middle and tucks her head beneath my chin. "I believe you," she whispers. "You're the hero I dreamed about in the dark."

We hold each other in the middle of the kitchen for several minutes, our hearts beating in unison. I close my eyes, savoring Seraphine's sweet warmth, and everything else fades into insignificance. She's the only thing that matters.

I want to give Seraphine everything she never had: protection, love, and a future free from fear. I'll erase all traces of Anton, help her find the last two men on her list, and hand her Samson Capello's bound and twitching body so she can send him to hell in a hundred bloody pieces.

But first, I need to call Cesare, ask him what the fuck he did to Rosalind, and give him a heads up that a determined girl with the cops on speed dial is hunting down her missing sister.

FIFTY-FOUR

SERAPHINE

Leroi orders me to pack my things so we can move to the apartment directly below. He's been paranoid since Rosalind's sister visited and acted like she was going to call the police.

I could ask why he didn't just tell that girl he last saw Rosalind at the club, but I'm too caught up by his admission.

He finds me captivating. Perfect. He wants to protect me with his life. My heart flutters a thousand times a second. It feels like I'm living in the epilogue of a fairy tale where the hero helps the damsel get revenge on all the villains.

Packing only takes a few minutes and before I know it, Leroi is escorting me to the apartment containing all the gym equipment. As I walk around the machines' perimeter to move my things to the spare bedroom, he places a hand on my shoulder.

"Put your things in the master suite."

Heat rises to my cheeks, hopeful that he wants me to sleep in his bed.

Strong arms wrap around my middle, and he pulls me into his chest. "I can't bear the thought of you being in another room." he growls in my ear. "From now on, you're with me."

"Alright," I whisper, my breath coming in shallow pants.

With an arm around my shoulders, he guides me into a room identical to the one upstairs, with the same gray decor, king-sized bed, walk-in closet, and door that leads to a bathroom.

"Why do you have a replica bedroom?" I ask.

"It pays to take precautions. If that girl sends the police looking for me upstairs, they'll find an unoccupied apartment. The firm also has properties in other locations across the state."

"Do you think she will?"

Leroi walks to the window, lowers himself on a brown leather sofa, and pulls me down onto his lap. "That all depends on if Rosalind is still with my cousin."

I nod, remembering Leroi talking to some dark-haired men at the club who looked a little similar. He pulls out his phone and sends a text to a man in his contacts called Cesare.

The first one Leroi sends says:
What's going on with Rosalind?

Three dots appear immediately, but we wait several seconds for Cesare to reply.

You knew and didn't say???
WTAF?

My brows crease. "What are you talking about?"

He chuckles. "It's our shorthand."

Leroi places soft kisses on my neck, distracting me from his phone. Each press of his lips sends tingles across my skin, and I squirm on his lap.

With a groan, Leroi wraps an arm around my waist and traces his fingers over the skin above the waistband of my shorts. I whimper, and he smiles against my neck.

He brushes his hand between my legs, and fire rushes through my skin.

"You like that?" he rasps, his breath hot against my ear. "You like it when I stroke your hungry little pussy?"

"Yes," I moan, my muscles clenching at the building pressure. "I want more."

"Greedy girl."

He continues exploring me over the cotton until he finds my sensitive bundle of nerves. Shivers of pleasure course up and down my spine, and I arch into his fingers with a moan.

"Let me touch it. Let me feel your bare cunt," he says.

"Oh, god." I squeeze my eyes shut.

His phone buzzes, but neither of us pay attention to Cesare's response. Instead, Leroi's fingers move off my clothed clit to where the hem of my shorts gapes open at my inner thigh.

"Seraphine," he growls, his fingers circling a sensitive spot on my thigh inches away from my crotch. "Let me in."

"Please."

He slides his fingers beneath the fabric to the outer edge of my pussy. My hips jerk, and my legs twitch at the contact.

"So wet. Is that all for me?"

I gulp. "Y-yes."

"You're such a good girl. Always so ready for my fingers or cock."

Leroi makes slow, tortuous circles over my clit until my mind goes blank and my eyes roll to the back of my head.

His hot mouth travels down the column of my neck with gentle nips and kisses that set my skin alight.

Heat sears into every inch of my flesh, but it's nothing compared to how he's turned my core into a molten furnace. I'm so feverish with want that my breath comes in short gasps.

If he stops, I might just bite through his jugular.

Leroi's erection presses into my ass, and I swear I can feel its veins and ridges. His hips move with shallow thrusts as he rolls my nipple between his thumb and forefinger in time with the circling over my clit.

I'm so close to losing control of my senses. My ears ring, my hips roll in counterpoint to his fingers, and all my limbs go taut.

"Come for me, angel," he whispers, his fingers gathering speed. "Let me have it all."

"N-not yet." I shake my head from side to side, not wanting this to end.

"You have until a count of three or I'll stop."

My breath hitches. I'm not ready.

"One," Leroi growls, his breath warm against my neck.

Oh, fuck.

He increases the pressure, his fingers making up-and-down strokes. The pleasure builds, sharpens, and twists into a tight coil.

"Two."

I groan, my body trembling with the effort of holding back. I'm clinging to this moment of perfect bliss.

"Two and a half," he growls. "Now."

When his fingers tighten around my nipple, my body interprets the sudden pain as the highest form of ecstasy. An orgasm rips through me like a tsunami, sweeping me into an ocean of pure rapture.

"Leroi," I cry.

The entire room washes away, leaving me panting hard and clinging to Leroi like he's my lifeboat. He holds me tight as I ride out the waves of pleasure, my body shaking with each delicious ripple.

"You were so beautiful, angel, coming apart in my fingers."

As I finally come back to reality, I rest my head against Leroi's shoulder and sigh.

He kisses the top of my head. "Good girl."

"That was incredible." I whisper, my heart still pounding with enough force to wake the dead.

Leroi pulls away just enough to look into my eyes. He brushes a strand of hair off my face and gazes down at me with a tenderness that makes my heart soar.

His phone buzzes once more.

With a groan, he gropes around the sofa and picks it up. A second later, his muscles tighten. "Shit."

"What's happened?" I ask, my eyes still half-lidded, my mind still drowsy with bliss.

"It's Rosalind. My cousin took her back home, and she tried to inject him with poison."

I sit up, my eyes widening. "Wait—what?"

"He knocked her unconscious, opened her purse, and found a bunch of syringes. He used her Face ID to open her phone and found pictures of the Montesano brothers. And me."

My breath catches. "Don't tell me she's like me?"

"No," he mutters. "Rosalind is a *paid* assassin."

FIFTY-FIVE

SERAPHINE

Leroi wanted me to stay behind while he dealt with the Rosalind situation, but I insisted he bring me, reminding him of his promise to not leave me behind. He tried to argue that it's not the same, but I can't sit in his apartment, fretting about another hitman running around wanting to kill him and his family, when maybe there's something I can do to help.

After throwing on some clothes, I put in my colored contacts and we head across town to Alderney Hills. This district is fancier than Queen's Garden, with every street lined with dense juniper trees that shield its mega-mansions from prying eyes. I remember Mom calling this the old money part of the city because it's where the original settlers built their homes. It's also the location of the Montesano estate.

Leroi's jaw is set, and his grip on the steering wheel is so hard, his knuckles are white. Tension raises his shoulders, and the veins on his temple stand on end. I reach over to the driver's seat to offer some comfort, but he barely responds.

As we drive through streets that wind upward through a conifer-covered hill, my stomach coils with dread. I'm about to meet the sons of my first target, Enzo Montesano.

"Will they recognize me?" I whisper, a shudder running down my spine.

The guard who served me drugged champagne would have remembered laying me on that bed, and there might have even been cameras.

He shakes his head. "We all thought Uncle Enzo died of a heart attack. Even if they suspected he was murdered, you're no longer a blonde-haired, blue-eyed little girl."

I nod, but it does nothing to ease my churning stomach.

Finally, we reach the top of the hill, which has been flattened to create an estate surrounded by a wall of tightly packed conifers. We stop at a tall iron gate manned by armored guards and Leroi winds down the window.

A man in a visor peers in, his gaze assessing Leroi before lingering on me. My breath stills, and I sit straighter in my seat.

"Who's the girl?" the man asks.

"She's with me," Leroi growls.

"Let them in," says a voice from the guard's walkie-talkie.

We pass enough men to form a small army, and submit to a few more security checks before we finally pull up to a mansion that looks built for a Roman senator. It's a huge, white villa that's half covered in ivy with a palazzo-style front porch of marble pillars. Coming here reminds me of how Dad used to rant about how Enzo Montesano thought he owned New Alderney.

Leroi gets out and opens my door, snapping me out of my thoughts. I don't understand why my mind is dredging up such old memories.

We walk hand in hand up stone steps that lead to a set of double doors, passing armed men who acknowledge Leroi's presence.

I recognize the man waiting in the hallway from the nightclub. Up close, he looks a little like Leroi, with the same piercing dark eyes, olive skin, and broad shoulders. This has to be one of the Montesano brothers. His features are harsher than Leroi's, as though he's lived a harder life, and under his shirt are glimpses of tattoos.

"Bringing a girlfriend?" He arches a brow in my direction.

"Apprentice," Leroi replies.

"Like Miko?" He turns to me, his gaze sharpening and becoming more critical.

This man is nothing like his father. He was a greasy and lecherous old man who deserved to die. He's the kind of predator more interested in shooting a woman through the head than placing a hand up her skirt.

I straighten, my face forming a blank mask even though my stomach trembles at the thought of him recognizing me as the woman who killed his father.

"I'm nothing like Miko," I say. "I like to get my hands dirty."

He cracks a smile.

"This asshole is Roman," Leroi says. "He's the oldest brother."

With a nod, Roman turns on his heel, expecting us to follow. "Cesare's still in the middle of interrogating the assassin, but I can tell you what we've found out so far."

Now that I'm no longer under Roman's scrutiny, all the tension leaves my lungs in an outward breath. Leroi tucks me under his arm as we walk alongside the oldest Montesano brother through a house that looks more like a museum.

The entrance hall is four times the height of a regular mansion with a glass atrium that floods the space with natural sunlight. We walk through white marble arches, passing busts of people who look like Leroi and Roman.

I finally get the meaning of old money. It's a level of class and sophistication that would have eluded a man like Dad. He never had an interest in art, and the only beautiful possessions he ever valued were his women. It's obvious that the Montesano family has held power for generations.

"Did Leroi tell you this is where he grew up?" Roman asks from Leroi's other side.

"No?" I glance up at Leroi's profile, wondering if this was where he shot his stepfather.

"Until I was ten," Leroi says with a wistful smile. "Then my mother moved us out after my dad died."

The men fall silent, and I can tell they're both thinking about the past. Leroi's grip around my shoulders tightens, and I wrap an arm around his back and give him a gentle squeeze.

I can't help thinking how shitty it is that parents' actions can vastly affect the lives of their children. Dad burned with jealousy over Enzo Montesano, so he arranged his death and framed his oldest son for a crime he didn't commit. And he used me as a killer to pay off Mom's debt because she slept with our bodyguard.

A door to our left opens and a wild-eyed woman steps out with messed up hair, wearing a silk kimono covered in white dust. Behind her is a mass of broken furniture, glass shards, and smashed vases. I catch a glimpse of slashed paintings and heavy curtains hanging off their rods in tatters.

Our eyes meet, and I do a double take. Isn't that the one I danced next to at the nightclub?

Her lips part. "Sera?"

"Ember?"

"Are you friends?" Roman asks her.

Ember scowls. "Fuck off!"

Before I can even process what's happening, she slams the door. As Leroi pulls me away, I hear glass smashing against the wall.

Roman chuckles. "Emberly has a volatile temper, but that comes with being a talented artist."

I glance over my shoulder, back toward the door where Ember disappeared. What on earth is going on in this mansion? It's like a reunion from the nightclub. Ember didn't exactly look like she was here against her will. If she was, she wouldn't have shut herself up in that room and she certainly wouldn't smash up expensive-looking antiques.

My mind is still reeling when we reach a room that doesn't match the rest of the mansion, a gentleman's study with brown leather furniture and lined with ebony book-shelves. Daylight floods in through floor-to-ceiling windows that overlook manicured gardens and a set of stone steps that lead to an enormous pool.

When Roman shuts the door and guides us to sit at the sofas by the window, Leroi asks, "What are we dealing with?"

"How did you not suspect that the woman you were fucking was an agent for a rival firm?"

"Not all hitmen come in male packages," Leroi drawls. "Besides, I wasn't her target."

"What makes you think that?"

"The only thing she tried to kill me with was her whining. It's likely that she was using me to get close to you or gathering intel."

"Shit."

Leroi shrugs. "You, of all people, should know how far your enemies will go to take you down."

Roman threads his fingers through his curls and sighs. "Shit. You're right."

My gaze bounces from one man to the other, and I wonder if they're talking about how Roman got framed for murder. I clear my throat. "Who is Rosalind's client?"

"Capello," Roman mutters.

"Did she say?" Leroi asks.

"Cesare got her to admit it. Now he's working on getting her to name specifics." He walks to a drinks cabinet, pours a glass of amber liquid, and holds it up as an offering.

Leroi waves him off. "I doubt that she's even a key player. Some agents infiltrate their target's household or friend group before a large job. That's what I did for my last one."

The corners of Roman's lips pinch, as though he disapproves of Leroi even referring to murdering the Capello family. It's a good sign for me because it proves he doesn't suspect my association with them.

"Benito tells me that Rosalind was a regular at the club. Cesare got her to confess to working with a few others to identify every close associate of my brothers."

Leroi nods. "Capello must have been planning a massacre months before he died."

Roman grunts. "Probably wanted to finish the job he started when he got me locked up."

I shuffle on my feet, my skin crawling at the reminder that Dad was universally evil and not just to me. The worst thing is that I never saw him coming.

"How long have you known Rosalind?" I ask.

"Three, four months," Leroi mutters.

"The real issue is getting the firm to call off the hit," Roman says. "I need to find Rosalind's handler and persuade him that attacking anyone connected to the Montesano family is a deadly mistake."

Leroi reaches into his pocket and extracts a scrap of paper. "Take this."

Roman's brow furrows. "What is it?"

"Rosalind's sister came by my apartment this morning, thinking she was with me. You can use that family association to persuade Rosalind to talk."

Roman reaches for the number, but Leroi pulls back. "Promise you won't hurt the girl?"

He frowns. "How old?"

"That's not the point. She's innocent."

"I won't fuck with her. Neither will Cesare nor Benito, but Rosalind doesn't need to know that."

"Fine."

"It had better work." Roman takes the paper and examines its contents. "Otherwise Samson Capello's survival will be the least of our problems. If we can't call off that hit, there'll be a full-scale war."

FIFTY-SIX

LEROI

I navigate the twisting roads of Alderney Hills, gripping the steering wheel tightly enough to wear out its leather. What I thought would be a simple massacre to save my cousin from death row is turning out to be a complicated web of twists and betrayals.

Killing Frederic Capello when I did only slowed down a conspiracy to assassinate Benito, Cesare, and everyone else who's loyal to the Montesano brothers, including myself.

The thought that Rosalind got close to me to gather intel on my extended family is maddening. I didn't even see her coming. Everything about her screamed that she was just a clingy sub.

Seraphine's stare burns the side of my face.

She wants explanations, but I don't have the heart to tell her that the wild woman who was smashing up the Montesano heirlooms is Capello's illegitimate daughter related by blood. I'm still trying to figure out how to break the news that the creepy handler who twisted her into a serial killer is my father figure.

My jaw clenches. This is a shit storm.

"What are you thinking?" she asks.

"We need to speed up the schedule," I mutter. "If this hit on the Montesano family doesn't get canceled, we're all screwed."

"You're tense."

I snort. "You think?"

Her hand slides over my thigh, but the touch is far from soothing. As her fingers make a slow ascent toward my crotch, all sensation rushes to my second brain.

"What are you doing?" I ask, trying to focus on the sharp angle ahead that leads to a steep drop.

"You think too much. I want to help."

Seraphine's fingers slide over my hardening cock to my zipper. Forcing my attention back onto the road, I exhale a shaky breath.

"And you think too little," I reply.

Seraphine pulls down the zipper. My stomach clenches, and I suck in a sharp breath. I should tell her to stop, but I'm torn between the danger of distraction and the promise of pleasure.

Her fingers slide into my fly, her blunt nails grazing my expanding shaft. Adrenaline courses through my veins and anticipation tightens my balls as she grips me by the root and pumps.

Fuck.

"I don't understand why you're so stressed," she replies. "Roman will pick up Rosalind's sister and get the information he needs to stop the assassins."

"It's not that simple," I reply with a groan. "If Rosalind holds out—"

"She won't."

I want to squeeze my eyes shut, savor her gentle strokes, but a truck barreling around the bend sends my mind crashing back to the road.

"How can you be so sure Rosalind will talk?" I ask.

"I overheard how worried Miranda was when Rosalind didn't come home. If Rosalind loves her sister as much as she loves her, then she'll give Roman and Cesare the information they need."

She strokes the pad of her thumb over my slit and smears precum across my crown.

My hips jerk, and I clench my teeth. "Maybe."

"No doubt about it," she says, her hand making twisting movements over my cock head. "I could have escaped the twins any time. The only thing that kept me staying was Gabriel."

The momentary reminder of how those bastards fooled her into remaining their prisoner makes me deflate. Her fingers close in around my shaft like a vise, and she punctuates each word with a powerful tug. Electricity zips up and down my spine. I glance toward the passenger seat to check that she's alright, but her eyes are closed.

"If I'd known Dad was using Gabriel as his regenerating liver bank, I would have escaped," she snarls through clenched teeth. "Mom was already dead, and so was Nanna. All I had left was my brother, and I had no idea Dad was invested in keeping him alive."

"Seraphine," I say with a gasp. "Slow down."

Pain and pleasure mingle with an impending sense of alarm as I navigate a hairpin turn. Sweat breaks out across my brow, my palms, the soles of my feet. She's so lost in her resentment that she doesn't hear my warnings to stop.

Shit.

Only Seraphine could combine handjobs with horror.

I lose track of what she's saying. It's a maelstrom of words and memories and murder.

"Seraphine," I say, my voice strained. "Calm down. Take a deep breath. You're safe now."

She pours all her pent-up rage into her ministrations, and my poor cock doesn't know whether to shrivel or spurt. Her hand moves faster and faster around my shaft, and I can barely keep my eyes on the road.

At this rate, she's going to get us both killed.

I make another sharp turn, nearly clipping the side mirror as she continues the sweet torture. Her soft hand combined with the angry strokes are pushing me toward a dangerous precipice. Literally.

An orgasm builds up in my balls, and I'm seconds away from losing control. I clench my jaw, trying to keep it together, trying to stop myself from exploding across the dashboard.

"I'm not your enemy," I yell over her words.

Sweat prickles across my forehead and my breath comes in short pants. No matter what I say, Seraphine shows no signs of slowing down.

The engine roars as I round another bend and I have to swerve around an asshole speeding toward us. Adrenaline punches me in the gut and the fine hairs on the back of my hair stand on end.

"Seraphine," I bark. "Listen to me. We'll crash if you don't slow down!"

This handjob from hell has gone too far.

I grab her wrist, but this only makes the situation worse. Her grip tightens, with blunt nails digging into my sensitive flesh. Lightning strikes my every nerve, charging up my senses with liquid fire. We're going to crash, and she's going to die before she even completes her revenge.

Tingles spread across my groin with an intensity that turns my vision white. I slam on the brakes, and scream, only it's too late. I swerve, but the bumper hits something solid and detonates the airbags.

Seraphine doesn't react but continues to pump the life force out of my shaft, making me lose energy at an exponential rate. My cock pulses, throbs, and convulses to the beat of my frantic heart. I spurt once into the airbags, twice, three, four times, and then I lose count.

Seraphine continues milking me until my soul flees my body and every ounce of cum escapes my balls until I'm gasping and groaning with every stroke.

"Feel better?" her voice cuts through my post-orgasmic cardiac arrest.

I crack open an eye and glare at her through a cloud of airbag dust.

She stares up at me through those wide, innocent eyes, not looking like she almost just killed me with her hand.

My head rolls back. I'm still panting so hard that it takes several heartbeats to form words. "As soon as I've caught my breath, you're going to get punished."

Her cheeks turn pink. "Okay."

Okay?

My eyes narrow. It almost looks like Seraphine nearly got us killed on purpose to earn a punishment. I'm going to spank that ass so raw she'll be sleeping on her belly for a week.

FIFTY-SEVEN

SERAPHINE

I don't like it when Leroi broods, which is most of the time. He's always so preoccupied with irrelevant details, when he should enjoy the fact that he's free. This was the only way I could think of to distract him from brooding.

The only sounds left when he turns off the engine are the hiss of airbags and my ragged breaths. His gaze bores into me with an intensity that makes my heart flip and my fingers release the seat belt.

Now, I'm wondering about this punishment.

Leroi shoves down his airbag, his nostrils flaring, his black eyes burning so hot that my skin tingles from the reflected heat. I haven't seen him this angry, not even when I got blood all over his apartment and he slapped my sandwich out of my hands.

Prickles skitter down my spine and settle between my legs, making my core clench. It's a strange mix of anticipation and fear that makes me wonder if I pushed him too far.

"Do you remember your safe words?" he asks, his voice cold.

"Yes, why?" I ask.

He pushes down my airbag, filling my vision with a puff of powder. "Because this punishment is going to hurt."

The pulse between my legs throbs in time to the beat of my pounding heart. I don't know if I'm scared or aroused, but I know I'm ready.

Before he can make his move, I grab for the car handle and swing open the door. "You'll have to catch me first."

"Seraphine," Leroi growls.

I bolt into the trees, my heart thudding in my ears. Leroi curses and yells at me to come back, but I don't even bother to spare him a glance.

Shrubs and tree trunks blur as I race further away from the road, making sure not to run a straight path. Leroi will probably waste time locking his car before giving chase, so I have to take advantage of this opening.

"You have a count of five before I catch you," he roars from the direction of the road. One."

Every inch of my skin skitters with excited tingles, and my nostrils fill with the mingled scents of pine and damp earth. I can't remember the last time I ran through the woods, but the feel of branches brushing my arms and twigs snapping underfoot is exhilarating.

"Two."

Brambles tug at my clothes, but I keep running. Leroi's voice grows fainter and fainter until all I can hear is the pounding of my heart and the roar of blood between my ears.

"Three."

My heart soars. I have never felt so free.

"Four." There's so much distance between us that I'm sure it's my imagination. Even when I think I hear him say five.

I like Leroi. A lot. He's the only man who makes me feel safe and warm and protected. He's the only one who looks beyond the surface and sees who I am and doesn't recoil or attack. I like the way his veins bulge when he's agitated and the way he makes my toes curl with his kisses. I like his temper, his possessiveness, and his intensity. I even like his punishments.

The canopy thickens, letting in dappled sunlight. Up ahead, I catch glimpses of a tall brick wall covered in ivy. I run away from it, not wanting to get too close to the estate.

Movement in the corner of my eye makes my heart flip. It's Leroi, charging through the trees like the terminator.

With a squeal, I pick up my pace, duck behind a tall shrub, and catch my foot on a creeping vine. I tumble forward and land on my hands and knees.

Shit.

Scrambling to my feet, I try to ignore Leroi's footsteps thundering from behind, but every fine hair on the back of my neck stands alert.

He's going to catch me.

This is the first time I've enjoyed feeling like prey.

I run faster, dodging low branches and leaping over fallen trunks. My heart pounds, my lungs burn, but the adrenaline pumping through my veins keeps my limbs light.

All those years of exercise machines in the basement have finally paid off. I'm outrunning Leroi.

Strong arms wrap around my waist and lift me off my feet. I scream, my legs cycling uselessly in the air.

Leroi's hot breath tickles my neck. "Bad girl," he growls. "Now your punishment's about to get a lot worse."

My pussy clenches with anticipation as both his arms encircle my middle, pulling me against his broad chest.

"Get off." I shove my elbows back, but he only tightens his grip.

So I spin around and knee him in the balls.

Leroi snarls. "You're about to learn what happens to naughty little brats."

His threat leaves my mouth dry and my core quivering. I try to wrestle free, but it's futile. He's too strong. I'm powerless, but for once, it feels good.

"Tell me your safe words."

He carries me through the trees, further away from the wall until we're heading back toward the road.

"Red to stop and yellow to slow down," I say between ragged breaths.

"Good," he says, his voice deep and rough. "I'm going to fuck your tight little cunt so hard your legs will tremble for a week."

He punctuates the word by tugging on my shirt, ripping through the fabric like paper. Cool air swirls over my exposed chest, contrasting with the way my pussy floods with heat. My clit throbs. I can't believe how much I want that to happen.

When we reach a grassy patch beneath a tree with wide, twisting branches, he sets me down on my hands and knees. My torn shirt pools around my waist, leaving me completely exposed. Every inch of my skin shivers with anticipation and my nipples tighten into hard peaks.

"No bra?" he growls.

Leroi drops to the ground with me and presses his chest against my back. He pinches my nipple, triggering an explosion of pleasure and pain.

His other hand tugs down my panties and leggings in a sharp movement that has me gasping.

"I'm going to fuck you like an animal," he snarls in my

ear. "Pound your perfect little pussy into the dirt until you scream. Would you like that, my fallen angel?"

I shiver, my nipples tingling against the dry grass.

He grabs an ass cheek and exposes my puckered hole, triggering a spike of emotion. It's a mix of arousal and alarm that has me kicking backward and breaking free.

"Seraphine," he hisses.

I'm already on my feet, running, and pulling up my leggings. If Leroi wants me, he'll have to work for it. My feet pound against the ground, the sound of his frustration echoing in my ears. I've just made my punishment worse, and I don't care.

My breasts bounce, and my veins course with undiluted exhilaration. The breeze blows through my hair and caresses my skin. This is the freedom I hadn't dared to dream of in that basement. Having the choice to run half naked through the woods, pursued by a man who wants to give me orgasms.

Flying past the trees, I barely register each slap of the branches against my bare skin. A tall shrub stands twenty feet straight ahead, it's thick enough to create a hiding spot. I'm almost within reaching distance as Leroi tackles me to the ground. My arms shoot out to break my fall, but he's on top of me in an instant.

He flips me onto my back and pins my wrists above my head. Sunlight filters in through the trees, coloring the ends of his black hair a bright shade of mahogany. The shadows cast his eyes in darkness, making them look even more intense.

"You think you can escape me, angel?" he asks in a low growl.

"Let go of me." I raise my pelvis, trying to buck him off,

but he's too heavy. Even twisting to the side is difficult, with him straddling my hips.

He leans down and says in a low voice, "You're in a world of trouble. Now, I'm going to make you beg."

As he sinks his blunt teeth into my neck, my pussy responds with a rush of wetness and heat.

I'm helpless.

For the first time in my existence, I'm aroused at a man having me at his mercy. I can't wait to find out what he'll do next.

FIFTY-EIGHT

SERAPHINE

I'm on my back, thrashing, kicking, and struggling, but Leroi's dominance over my body is absolute. He glares down at me like the vengeful god of lust, his features switching between anger and arousal.

"Your ass is going to regret that," he says, his mouth so close to mine that his minty breath warms my lips. "You're too fond of pushing my buttons."

"No, I'm not." I jerk my neck forward to deliver a head butt, which only makes him draw back.

"Liar," he says, his grip around my wrists tightening. "I'll bet that sweet little pussy is soaked."

All the self-defense moves the handler drilled into me are useless against Leroi. It's as though he anticipates my every move. His free hand slides down to my waistband and yanks down my leggings, then he slides his fingers into my panties and finds my slick folds.

"Dirty girl. You're soaked. You love being hunted," he says, his voice rough and low.

I shake my head, my clit swelling, my hips jerking to

create more friction, but he pulls his hand away. I groan with frustration.

"Oh. Did you think I would make your punishment pleasant, angel?" he croons, his teeth closing in on my earlobe and delivering another burst of pleasure and pain.

Before I can even respond, he drags me across the dry grass to a fallen log, and flips me over it onto my stomach. My breath catches, and I crawl on my hands, trying to get away, but the flat of his palm lands on my right ass cheek with a hard slap.

The sting races through my buttocks and settles into my clit. I cry out, the top half of my body collapsing onto the dry ground.

"Little brats who run away from their punishments get extra hard spankings." He places a hand between my shoulder blades. "Now, count them."

Shivers run down my spine. I part my thighs, remembering my first punishment when he spanked my ass and rubbed my clit and made me beg and cry for more. I want more of that.

"One," I rasp, my voice trembling.

He delivers another hard slap to the same buttock, and I cry out, my hips arching.

"Two!" I scream, my fingers closing in around the grass.

This punishment is different. There are no light strokes or caresses, no mercy or restraint. It's more pain than pleasure, but the intensity of each spank builds as I count and by the time he reaches six, my eyes water.

The spanks come in a steady rhythm, each one a little harder than the last. Clenching my teeth, I press my cheek into the log's rough bark, my legs trembling, my walls convulsing with need. I'm lost in a sea of agony and ecstasy, with arousal trickling down my inner thighs.

He stops after the tenth, leaving me breathless. The breeze barely cools my burning ass cheeks, but it's nothing compared to my pulsing clit. It aches so desperately with need that it feels fit to burst.

I try to rise off the log, but I'm desperate and weak. If he doesn't fuck me this instant, I'm going to die.

Leroi's thick fingers slide into my soaking pussy, filling the air with obscene wet sounds. "Fuck," he growls. "You're dripping. You love getting stripped naked and spanked out in the open."

I swallow hard, my hips quivering. "No."

His harsh laugh makes my hair stand on end. He pulls his fingers out, making me gasp at the loss.

"Don't lie to me, little Seraphine. You like hurting men and making them bleed, but nothing gets your cunt wetter than a hard spanking."

The cheeks on my face burn hotter than my ass. I want to shake my head and deny the accusation, but I want his touch more.

"Yes," I whisper, barely able to form the words. "But I need you inside me now."

"Not until you've learned your lesson. When I give you an order, you obey."

I grind my teeth. "Why didn't you just say red?"

"Because I'm the one in charge," he snarls.

I know that, but I love getting Leroi so riled up and aroused that he forgets himself.

His fingers circle my clit, making it swell to nearly twice its size before pushing at my entrance. "What do you say?" he asks. "Are you going to be an obedient little girl who gets her wet cunt filled with my cock, or a disobedient one who gets to sit in the car with a hungry pussy?"

I'm tempted to push him further, but the need for release is overcoming.

When he pulls back his fingers, my heart drops into the log. He wouldn't leave me like this?

"An obedient one," I say with a whimper.

"That's my girl."

Leroi pushes his finger past my opening and searches around until he finds a spot that sends a jolt of arousal through my nervous system, and my legs go rigid. My eyes squeeze shut. This feels amazing. He massages it with gentle strokes until my vision fills with stars.

"You like it when I stroke your g-spot?" he asks.

"Yes," I moan.

The digit stills. "Fuck my finger."

"Wh-What?"

"If you want that orgasm, you're going to take it."

My breath comes in shallow pants, my mind reels, and it takes a second to realize that he's asking me to push back on his digit. I bite my lip and move my hips back and forth, trying to create a little friction.

"Dirty little angel," he grunts. "You'll take it however you can get it, even when you're covered in dirt, lying on a filthy log."

My muscles clench around his finger, and I shift, trying to position it exactly where I need it most. Sweat breaks out across my skin and I buck harder. This isn't working. I need more.

"More" I say through gasping breaths. "Please."

"Beg. Tell me how much you want it."

"Please, give it to me," I cry. "Give me two fingers."

"What do you say?"

Frustration burns through my chest and up to the back of my throat. I already said yes. What more does he want?

The need brimming inside me is a flame that sears through my soul.

Leroi wants to be in charge. He probably wants me to act more submissive. I'll play along, for now, until I get my orgasm. After that, I'll go back to being my own woman.

"Please give me two fingers, sir."

The pressure between my shoulder blades lifts, and he pulls out the first digit. As he positions two at my entrance, I add, "And please fuck me with your huge cock, master."

His deep growl vibrates against my back, telling me he's pleased. When two thick digits stretch me open, I moan. This is exactly what I need... For now.

Leroi doesn't move them, but it doesn't matter. I roll my hips, finding a rhythm and movement I need to put pressure on my sensitive spot.

"Just like that," he rumbles. "Take what you need, my filthy little angel."

"Yes," I cry, my thighs tightening and increasing the pressure on my clit.

"Fuck. You look so good, taking my fingers like they're a cock."

As I fuck myself on his digits, I no longer feel the grass between my fingers, the dirt beneath my knees, or the rough bark on my stomach. I move back and forth, letting his fingers stroke that sensitive spot. My breathing shallows. My lungs burn and my face heats. All that exists now is Leroi and me and the pleasure that builds and builds until my vision goes black.

Heat radiates from my core, and my muscles tighten around his fingers. Molten rapture pools behind my clit, turning my body into a raw nerve. I pant hard through the sensations, feeling my approaching orgasm.

Leroi remains a still presence at my back, his hot breath

fanning one side of my face. "That's it, angel," he rasps. "You're doing so well."

This is the closest I've ever come to climaxing without Leroi's help. His fingers are inside me, but I'm the one doing all the work. He continues encouraging me to move harder, faster, until my body is drenched in sweat.

"You look so pretty when you're taking my fingers," he says. "Now, I want you to come."

The heat inside me intensifies. I whisper, "I-I'll try, sir."

"You have until the count of five, Seraphine. If you don't come all over my fingers before then, I'll spank you again until you can't move."

"Oh, fuck!"

"One."

My hips move faster, and the pressure around my core intensifies. I'm so close that I can almost taste that orgasm. Squeezing my eyes shut, I focus only on the sensations.

"Two."

Leroi wouldn't leave me wanting, even if I fail. Would he?

"Three."

Oh, shit. I think he's serious.

I bite down on my lip and move faster, pushing harder against his fingers. My hands clench into fists, and I imagine myself back in his bedroom with a steak knife pressed to his jugular. Instead of sitting on his thick erection, I'm riding it, my movements making him bleed.

"Four."

As I reach down to taste the blood trickling down his throat, he releases a moan so loud and deep that pushes me over the edge. The pleasure is too intense to hold back and rolls through my body like thunder. I scream, my body convulsing with each lightning strike of pleasure.

It's like being electrocuted, only the current comes from my core and not the collar or the chip and what I'm feeling is ecstasy and not agony. My inner walls spasm around his fingers. The climax is so powerful that I cry out his name.

Finally, I collapse against the log like a pile of burned leaves, my breathing slowing, my muscles satisfied and limp.

Leroi pulls his fingers out of my twitching pussy and pulls me off the log.

He wraps his arms around my waist, holding me tight. "Well done, angel. Your first orgasm that you gave yourself."

I rest my head against his shoulder and close my eyes.

"This isn't over. Not by a long shot," he says. "Get on your hands and knees. I'm going to fuck you until you come even harder."

FIFTY-NINE

LEROI

Seraphine clings to my shoulders and gazes up at me through heavy-lidded eyes. I'm so proud of the way she took charge of her own pleasure and came apart around my fingers.

I hold her close as she catches her breath, seeming too boneless to follow my instructions. There's no sign of the mischievous little devil who jerked my cock to the brink of madness and made me shoot all over the airbags.

If the only way to make her submit is with pleasure, then she's about to get more than she can handle.

Wrapping an arm around her waist, I guide her off my lap and position her on her hands and knees. Her arms tremble, and she drops her head to the ground. Her hair has lightened to a darker shade of blonde and spreads out like a dirty halo.

"You're so beautiful with your ass pointing at the sky," I whisper, my hands tracing the curve of her little red ass. "Now open your legs."

Her knees shuffle further apart, displaying her engorged

clit and glistening pink pussy. I savor the sight for several heartbeats, my cock already hard and straining against my fly.

If she was any other woman, I would pound into that tight heat and fuck her mercilessly until she screamed my name. But this is Seraphine. I need to check in with her after everything she's suffered.

"Tell me what you want," I say, my voice raw with need.

"Please, fuck me," she moans.

Fuck.

"Is that what you want, my filthy little angel? To fill your hungry pussy with my cock?"

She whimpers.

"Use your words."

"Please." Her voice breaks. "Now."

Gripping the base of my shaft, I rub my tip up and down over her clit, dragging it through her wetness, teasing her sweet pussy. The gurgled cry she makes goes straight to my balls.

"I'm going to fuck you hard and deep, then fill you with my cum. You'll take every drop until it's dripping down your legs."

"Leroi, please." She's openly sobbing, her beautiful little body shaking with the force of her need.

No woman has ever cried so prettily for my cock or with so much raw need. I take hold of her hip, press my crown against her slick entrance, and slide in with one deep thrust.

The satisfied groan she makes goes straight to my balls. I lean against her bare back, threading my fingers through the hair at the nape of her neck. The strands feel like silk against my palm, and I grip tight.

Seraphine cries out.

The muscles of her core close in on me with a grip as

strong as her fist. I twist my fingers into her hair, making her whimper.

"Feel how hard you make me?" I growl into her ear.

Her skin is slick with sweat, and she trembles beneath me, chanting her words over and over until they're nothing more than a continuous whine.

"Leroi, please. Leroi, please. Leroi, please."

She picks up speed, and with a harsh sob, rocks backward, taking me in deeper. Fuck. She's pulling pleasure from my cock the way she did with my fingers.

"Say it again," I demand.

She moves her hips back and forth. "Leroi, please fuck me."

"You beg so beautifully for my cock."

It's no exaggeration. Her voice is a siren's song, and I'm entranced.

"You like that, don't you? You love it when I fuck you into submission."

Using her hair as my reins, I draw my hips back and slam back into her with a snap of my hips that makes her howl. I want to ride her to oblivion, claim every delicious inch of her for my own, but not until I get that final word of consent.

"Yes!" she cries.

My thrusts are merciless, deep and fast, but she meets each stroke with the same intensity, creating a friction that makes my eyes roll to the back of my head.

"That's it," I rasp, my lips brushing her neck. "Fuck this cock and take your pleasure."

"Ah, yes," she moans as she pushes back, her wet heat closing in on me with an intensity that makes me shiver.

Sex with Seraphine is like discovering the angel you're fucking is a wanton succubus. No other woman I've slept with fucked back with such enthusiasm, even the ones who boast that they love it rough. It's like heaven conspired to create me the perfect companion to fulfill my every need.

We move together in perfect rhythm, my senses filling with her strawberry scent. I never knew Seraphine could be this passionate about something other than murder and torture. As pleasure coils low in my gut, I imagine our future.

We'll kill every bastard on her list, including Samson, find her brother, and provide him with healthcare. We'll move him into the apartment next door, but Seraphine will stay with me.

No woman has ever matched me so perfectly or ever will. Seraphine has cut a hole through my ribcage and captured my heart. Her pussy spasms, pulling me out of my musings.

"You're mine," I growl.

"Yours," she says through gasping breaths.

The intensity builds and builds. I'm pounding into her, my balls slapping against her flesh, my mind battling through the sensations of her tight walls. My body tenses, and I clench my jaw, trying to hold off an explosive orgasm. She continues thrusting backward, testing me, pushing me, making me teeter on the bring of euphoria, making me lose control.

"Oh god," she moans.

"Come for me, angel," I growl from between clenched teeth.

Her head shakes from within my grip. "You first."

I release my hold on her hips, slide my fingers between her wet folds, and find her clit. With frantic movements, I tap the little bundle of nerves in time to our thrusts until her muscles close so tightly that my movements fall shallow.

"Come for me," I growl. "Now."

"Oh!"

When her muscles quiver and her breaths quicken, I know she's close. I continue the steady rhythm of my fingers and cock, pushing her over the edge. "Seraphine," I snarl. "I told you to come."

She convulses, her muscles clamping around my shaft as though her sadistic little pussy wants to put it off.

The thought of her castrating me with her cunt breaks my self control. I thrust into her once, twice, my balls imploding and expelling a lifetime of release. I come so hard it feels like she's sucking out my soul. She can have it.

"Fuck!" I roar.

Her lower body collapses, and I roll us off the log and to the side. I position her to my front and curl an arm around her waist, holding her tight, never wanting to let her go.

She trembles and squeezes around my shaft.

"Are you cold?" I ask.

She shakes her head.

"Seraphine, what's wrong?"

"That was so..." she replies, her voice thick with unshed tears. "So..."

My breath shallows as I wait for her to complete her sentence. That was the most intense fuck of my life, although I'm sure that's what I said the last time. I've never fucked anyone whose spirit was so closely attuned to mine.

Seraphine doesn't complete her sentence, seeming overcome with the intensity of the moment. I press a kiss on her head.

"It's alright, angel. I know."

"Did you mean what you said?" she asks.

"When?"

"That I was yours?" She gazes up at me, looking even

more vulnerable than she did when I found her in the basement.

My heart swells in my chest. She was off limits for a reason. I never thought someone so innocent and vulnerable belonged with a monster like me, but that was before I saw what was beneath her pretty exterior. Seraphine is more than my perfect match, she gives my life a new meaning. Everything I have endured was to prepare me for Seraphine.

I tighten the embrace. "I meant every fucking word. You're mine, whether you want me or not."

"And you're mine, too?"

"Always."

She swallows hard. "Today was the first time I ever had a chance to run."

I understand her meaning immediately. She's describing the invisible cage the Capellos placed over her mind, making her think her brother would die if she tried to escape.

Those bastards had a fucking nerve. She could have sought help from the police or even from her targets. Making her believe staying with them was the only thing keeping Gabriel alive was sick and twisted.

"You will never have to worry about becoming anyone's captive again," I say with so much conviction that my voice trembles.

"But Samson—"

"Will die, just like those bastards who touched your mother."

"What if he's ready for us?"

"It doesn't matter. We'll find a way, even if it means the two of us sneaking into his hideout through heating ducts." When Seraphine's lips part to ask another question, I add,

"But I'll stand back and let you kill him in the most painful method he deserves."

"Leroi," she whispers, and brings her mouth to mine.

I kiss back, but as I slide my tongue between her lips, the air fills with the sound of gunshots.

SIXTY

SERAPHINE

Leroi helps me scramble to my feet at the first crack of gunfire, and I yank up my leggings and panties. My breath stills. The noise is coming from the direction of the nearest estate, even though I can barely see its walls through the dense trees.

In a blur of synchronized movements, Leroi extracts his pistol, scoops me to his chest and fires back at the shooter in a sprint. Clinging to his shoulders, I glance around for signs of an attacker, but he's moving too quickly through the trees for a clear enough view.

Palpitations thrash through my heart. Both at the prospect of being hit, but at the thought that what Leroi said might be true.

Could he truly belong to me? This devastatingly attractive older man with his perfect life, perfect control? It hardly seems possible.

"Head down," Leroi says, his voice low and urgent.

With a squeak, I tuck my head into his chest. The last

time Leroi carried me like this, it was out of Dad's mansion. Now, he's become more than my rescuer or even my protector. Leroi is my lover.

He zigs zags, using tree trunks as cover until the gunshots finally stop. He keeps hold of his pistol long after the last bullet, but his grip on me relaxes.

"Are you alright?" he asks.

"Fine."

"Looks like we're safe for now," he says, his lips brushing my brow.

"Was that another hitman?"

He hesitates several seconds before answering. "Hard to say."

I look over my shoulder in the direction he's carrying me and find his black SUV parked off the road, right beside a large boulder. Sunlight shines off its polished surface and bounces off the pieces of broken glass strewn across the tarmac.

"What's that?" I point at the shattered glass.

"Smashed headlight." He jogs across the road, flings the passenger side door open, and deposits me into the front seat. The airbags have deflated, coating the car's interior with powder.

After sliding into the driver's side, he pulls out onto the road and drives away with a screech of tires.

I stare at his profile, now knowing better than to distract him while he's speeding through the twisting roads of Alderney Hills. My ass still smarts from the spanking, and my pussy aches from getting pounded.

It's only once we reach a straight stretch that he takes his eyes off the road and turns to meet my gaze. "Are you sure you're alright?"

"Are you?"

He snorts, reaches into the back seat, and tosses a sweater into my lap. "Getting shot at is part of the job. I'm more worried about you."

"It was exciting." I pull the garment over my head and fold back its arms.

Leroi turns to me, his brow raised. "Getting chased through the woods and brutally fucked or escaping an asshole with a gun?"

"All of it," I reply with a shrug. "I was with you, so I knew I'd be safe."

Smirking, he shakes his head and focuses back on the road. "You are something else."

I relax in my seat and watch him drive. The muscles on Leroi's forearms flex as he grips the steering wheel with his large hands. I lick my lips, my gaze wandering back to his profile and to the arteries running down his neck.

My tongue runs along the back of my teeth, wanting to trace each of those large vessels to see if I can taste blood.I'd like to trace the veins on his thick shaft, too.

"When are you going to let me give you a blow job?" I ask.

He chokes, his fingers tightening on the steering wheel. "What?"

"You heard me."

He peers out at me out of the corner of his eye. "Not a chance."

"But I'm really good at it?" I snap my teeth.

He huffs a laugh. "Behave."

I sink into my seat and pout. "You think I'm going to bite it off."

"You may not be able to control yourself," he says, the

corner of Leroi's mouth lifting into a smirk. "My cock is really tasty."

"Now I want to try it even more."

"You're trouble, you know that?" he asks.

"I'm nice!"

He laughs. It's a deep, rich sound that makes my heart flutter. When he glances across the front seat at me, I'm awestruck at the way his smile accentuates his masculine beauty. When he's brooding, the harsh angles of his features are almost intimidating, but when he smiles, it's like the sun coming out after a storm.

"Don't ever change, Seraphine."

My brow furrows. "What does that mean?"

He takes my hand and traces a circle over my skin with his thumb. The heat of his touch makes the butterflies in my stomach take flight.

"You're wonderful just the way you are."

"Even if I'm reckless?"

"It's part of your charm," he murmurs. "Something I didn't appreciate until now."

I shift in my seat. "Maybe remember that the next time you spank me because my ass is raw."

Leroi's chuckle is as addictive as Belgian chocolate. It makes me want to misbehave more often so I can hear it again. He pulls our joined hands up to his lips and presses a kiss against my knuckles.

"After we've found Gabriel, eliminated Samson, and killed the next two men on your list, I'm going to take you somewhere private and show you just how much I appreciate that smart mouth."

He turns off the highway and to a motel that's tucked away from the roadside. It's a single-story building with a pristine white facade and window boxes filled with pink flowers.

"What's this?" I ask.

He reverses into a parking space. "Mike Ferrante lives close by. We'll rest up here and pay him a visit later when his wife starts her shift at the hospital."

My pulse quickens, and my skin tightens at the memory of a sandy-haired man with a bald spot slapping Mom across the face with a part of his anatomy I plan on removing.

"How do you know their schedule?" I ask.

"Miko."

He opens the car door and jogs toward the motel office, leaving me staring at his broad back. All thoughts of the fun we had in the woods evaporates, leaving my mind filled with images of those monsters surrounding Mom. At some point in the future, I plan on finding the ones lucky enough to have died before we could hunt them down and desecrate their graves.

Leroi returns a few minutes later and opens the passenger side door, letting in the sound of traffic and a gust of cool air that snaps me out of my thoughts.

As I climb out, he wraps an arm around my waist and pulls me into his warmth. "Let's get you cleaned up, and then we'll do something about your bruises."

He opens the door to the room. It's cleaner than I would have expected and completely free from the musty odors I always found to linger when I killed targets in hotels in motels. There are two double beds with white sheets, a small kitchenette, and a bathroom.

After pressing a kiss on the top of my head, he darts out through the front door and returns moments later, holding a leather bag. "Let's soak in the whirlpool and then I'll see to the welts on your ass."

I step back, my heart swelling. The last time we had sex, he gave me a bath and wrapped me in towels like I was precious. Now he wants to tend to my wounds.

No one could be this perfect. Can they?

SIXTY-ONE

LEROI

Seraphine is as docile as a kitten as I lower her to the motel's sunken tub and work shampoo through her hair. The coffee dye is fading fast, turning her back into the blonde angel I rescued from the Capello mansion.

Warmth fills my chest as I lose myself in her delicate features. She's no longer the innocent girl I thought she was, but a woman whose darkness surpasses mine.

After getting her clean, I lay her face-down on the bed. Both her perfect little ass cheeks have darkened from the spanking and I apply a thick covering of cooling gel to her heated flesh. When I'm done, she rolls over and wraps her arms around my neck, her eyes shining with light.

It's a combination of gratitude, admiration, and affection that's more than a man like me deserves. If it hadn't been for Capello's twisted attempt to turn her into a killing machine, a mafia princess like Seraphine would never have crossed my path.

She would have graduated from an ivy league college or

married into an influential family, living out her life in luxury and comfort. But here she is, in a motel with me.

I place a kiss on her lips, feeling something inside me shift. Seraphine has become my purpose, and I'd do anything to keep her safe.

"What did you want to do with your life?" I ask.

She shifts on my lap, her hand trailing down my chest. "I used to dream of killing the twins in front of Dad before stabbing him with hot pokers. Why?"

"Before that," I ask.

Her head tilts to the side, and her eyes glaze with a faraway expression, as though she's lost in a memory. "I wanted to study at the Cordon Bleu cooking academy."

"Is that why you learned your knife skills?" I ask.

She rests her head on my shoulder. "I used to help Bianca in the kitchen."

"Your cook?"

"She was married to our driver, Felix. He used to give me driving lessons and was the one who took me to my grandma's house that night..."

She bows her head, too overcome with her memories. I stroke her hair, wishing there was something more I could do to ease her pain. Keeping her safe isn't enough when she's still plagued by the monsters from her past.

Wrapping her legs around my waist, I rise off the bed, pull back the covers, and ease her onto the mattress.

"Stay with me?" She tugs at my arm.

"That was the plan." I slide into bed and gather her in my arms. "Tell me about Bianca."

Seraphine launches into a description of a middle-aged Italian woman who lived in the mansion's servants' wing with her husband. The more she talks, the more obvious it becomes that Bianca was the one who did most of the child rearing.

Her mother, Evangeline, appeared more interested in socializing, shopping sprees than in parenting her two children. And, of course, cheating on Capello with her bodyguard.

"Bianca was so great," she says with a yawn. "She set up a table in the kitchen and let me watch her cook while I did my homework, and she even let me help prep."

I rub circles on her back until her eyelids flutter shut. "Would you like to find her when things go quiet?"

Her entire body stiffens. "I can't."

"What do you mean?"

"If Dad killed Felix for driving me away that night." She raises her head, her pretty features stricken. "If he hurt Bianca—"

"It's alright," I say. "We don't have to look them up."

She relaxes against me, her body still rigid. I continue rubbing slow circles on her back until the tension melts away.

It was naïve of me to think I could hand her over to a therapist to help fix her mind. Seraphine's story is a complicated tangle of secrets, betrayals, and violence. It needs to be unraveled at her pace.

"You're safe with me," I murmur into her hair. "No matter what, I will always protect you and put you first."

She relaxes fully, and her breathing deepens as she drifts off to sleep. I stare down into her streaky blonde hair and swear to myself that no matter what, I will make her future brighter.

Half a day later, we've checked out of the motel and are sitting around the corner from the home of Mike Ferrante. It's the basement condo of a five-story brownstone building in a quiet suburb of Beaumont. According to Miko's intel, his wife is a nurse working two jobs to fund their two children's college education.

Street lights illuminate a quiet block lined with parked cars. I glance across at Seraphine, who sits alert, her knee bouncing. We've already gone through the plan a dozen times, and now she has to wait.

"She's not leaving," she says.

"Miko checked the hospital's schedule," I mutter. "She's probably running late."

Moments later, a blonde woman in scrubs emerges from the steps, carrying a small backpack. She hurries to a silver sedan parked outside and speeds off.

"Let's go," I say.

Seraphine bursts out from the car and hurries down the street. I pick up my bag and follow after her with long strides. She's still impatient, but this is a vast improvement from the last time when she jumped out of a moving car to chase after Pietro Fiori.

By the time I catch up with her, she's already at the bottom of the basement steps with her finger pressed over the bell.

The door flies open, revealing a balding man with a bulbous nose covered with a red rash spreading down its bridge to his cheekbones. He's too busy glaring down at Seraphine to notice me descending his steps, and yells, "What the fuck—"

With well-practiced precision, she stabs Ferrante through the ribs with a syringe, making him stagger backward and drop his gun.

506

I wince, hoping she didn't reach his heart. Seraphine needs closure, not just quick kills.

Mike clutches at his chest with one hand and gasps for air. He kicks out at Seraphine, but she side-steps.

"Bitch," he snarls.

"Don't worry," she says. "It's just a sedative. You'll be awake in a few minutes and then we'll talk."

I step into the condo, close the door behind me, twist the deadlock, and attach the chain. Mrs. Ferrante will be gone for at least eight hours, and we can't leave anything to chance.

"Find the bathroom," I tell her.

She rushes ahead, opening and closing doors until she finds the right one. "Here."

I drag Ferrante across the wooden floorboards into a room of white tiles and an equally pristine suite. Tasteful. I sit him on the toilet seat and handcuff him to the towel rack.

While I'm taping plastic wrap to the floor, Seraphine returns with a nail gun.

I raise a brow.

"You should see all his tools," she says, her cheeks flushed. "He has so many."

"Can you do something for me?" I ask.

"What?"

"Don't touch his cock."

Her brows pinch. "Why not?"

"If you touch him like you did that other guy, I'll put a bullet through his head."

SIXTY-TWO

SERAPHINE

Leroi sounds jealous. It's almost as though the only penis he wants me torturing is his. While he fusses with covering the entire hallway in plastic wrap, I sit on the edge of the bathtub with the nail gun on my lap, watching Mike Ferrante.

Mike has gained weight since I last saw him. He doesn't look so menacing, slumped on a toilet seat with a patch of blood on his t-shirt. The next time I dream of that night, I hope to find him sitting in the corner looking so helpless.

Leroi insisted on placing duct tape around his mouth, so his screams wouldn't disturb the neighbors, and he even provided a notepad and pen in case Mike wants to share some information about Gabriel and Samson. He's so thoughtful.

A murder bag sits on the sink, containing an assortment of knives, tools, syringes, and ammunition. We both know Mike will need some extra persuasion.

He grunts, and his eyelids flicker. I rise off the edge of

the bathtub, expecting to see his terror, but his eyes remain closed.

"Open your eyes," I say.

He doesn't move.

"Wake up, Mike." I kick him in the shin, but he doesn't even flinch, so I press the nail gun into his shoulder and pull the trigger.

Mike's muffled groan infuses my spine with a tingle of excitement. His lids snap open, revealing eyes so bloodshot they might as well be crimson.

He grunts through the duct tape and tries to raise his hips off the toilet seat, but he's taped down with nowhere to go. Swinging his hand not handcuffed to the rail, he finds it's chained to the cuffs and throttles his reach.

I step back, the anticipation making my pulse race.

"You have an hour before the clean-up crew arrives," Leroi says from the doorway.

Mike's head jerks toward the source of the sound, his eyes widening with even more alarm. He makes a noise behind the gag that sounds like, 'What do you want?'

"Why are we on a tight schedule when Mike's wife will be gone for at least eight hours?" I snap.

"You know why."

My lips tighten. I don't want to admit that Leroi has a point. If whoever shot at us earlier is connected to the contract out on the Montesano brothers, then Leroi might also be in danger. That's not even counting what Samson is plotting from the shadows.

"Fine." I turn my attention back to Mike. He's breathing so hard and fast that the red blotches on his face darken to a nasty shade of purple.

"Five years ago, after you and your colleagues raped a

woman by the name of Evangeline, your boss sent you to collect his son. Where did you go?"

He rears back, his head shaking from side to side as though denying any involvement.

"We don't have time to sift through your lies." I press the nail gun to his shoulder and pull the trigger.

Mike howls as much as he can with his mouth taped shut, and my blood sizzles with satisfaction.

"Answer my question or I'll fill you with iron and then pull it out with a magnet."

He shudders.

"Give him the notepad," Leroi says.

I place a spiral-bound book on his lap, pull out the pen and place it into his trembling fingers.

Mike scrawls:

Girlfriend's place.

"Where did you take him afterward?" I ask.

Some apartment in Queen's Gardens.

"Then what?"

He shakes his head.

"That's the last you heard of Gabriel?" I ask.

He gives me a vigorous nod.

I grind my teeth, the pulse in my ears pounding with frustration. It's so loud I can barely think.

My fingers hover over the nail gun's trigger, and I press its barrel into Mike's collarbone. He makes a gibbering sound behind the tape and scribbles something else.

You are the daughter.

"So what?"

They said you ran away.

"And?" I ask

Take off the tape. It's quicker.

"What's he writing?" Leroi asks from the doorway.

"He wants me to ungag him."

Leroi snorts. "He's wasting time, thinking that someone is coming to save him in an hour's time."

I turn back to Mike, my eyes widening. "Is that why you're holding back?"

He shakes his head vigorously, but doesn't write anything else. My veins burn with a twisted sense of curiosity. If there's a chance he knows something... I shake off that thought. Leroi is right. If Mike can speak the answer, he would write it.

"Where did Frederic Capello have his last surgery?" Leroi asks.

Mike scribbles: *Somewhere in Mexico*

My nostrils flare. We hadn't thought of searching overseas. I ask a few more questions about who he brought with him, but Mike reveals that he thought his boss was going overseas to treat an ulcer. It looks like Dad was holding secrets from everyone, including his own guards.

"Let's move onto Samson Capello. Where is he?" I ask.

Mike writes in extra shaky writing: *DEAD*.

"We all know he didn't die." I turn to Leroi. "Hold my gun."

His eyes narrow. "What are you planning?"

"Relax, I'm not going to touch his dick. At least not with my hands."

Mike makes a strangled noise in the back of his throat, and he jots something on the paper. Ignoring him, I walk to the bag of tools perched on the bathroom sink and sort through the tools. No matter what Leroi says, Mike is still one of the monsters that took pleasure in violating Mom. He's one of the reasons memories from that night still haunt my dreams.

There's only one fitting punishment for a rapist. If I can't directly touch his junk, I just need to improvise.

I return to Mike, holding the smallest pair of pliers. He eyes the tool, his breath coming in ragged pants, and then he meets my gaze.

"If I'm satisfied with your answer, I'll let you keep your balls. Where is Samson Capello?"

He writes faster, the words almost blurring together.

In his summer house.

"Where?" I flip the page to a fresh sheet.

After he scrawls down an address, I rip it out and hand it to Leroi. "Can you check on this?"

Leroi disappears down the hallway with the scrap of paper, and I turn back to Mike to ask, "Is there anything else you want to tell me about Samson or Gabriel?"

He shakes his head.

"You're sure?"

Mike nods, his eyes squeezing shut, seeming resigned to his death. After all, he heard Leroi give me an hour to wrap everything up. He probably thinks he's given me all the information I need, so I'll drive a nail through his skull.

He would be wrong.

"Let's move onto the next subject," I say, my voice shaking with rage. "Evangeline."

His eyes snap open, his pupils tiny pinpricks within his light-brown irises. He tries to write something on the notepad, but I snatch it out of his hands.

"She's a what?" I snarl. "A slut, a whore, a cheater who had it coming?"

He shakes his head, his eyes darting around the room, searching for an escape. Mike thrashes within his restraints, looking like he's finally realized his fate isn't to die quickly.

"I watched you all through the crack in the door," I say.

"She was begging, screaming, crying for it to stop, but you all laughed as you took your turns."

He flinches.

I use the pliers to pull down his zipper and return to the sink to extract a larger pair that remind me of crab claws. After cutting through his boxers with a retractable knife, I clamp the plier's jaws on his foreskin and pull out his penis.

Mike's muffled screams are so loud that Leroi charges back to the bathroom with more tape and winds it around his nose.

"But he won't be able to breathe," I say.

Leroi scoffs and returns to the doorway and leans against his frame, holding a TV remote. "He'll survive for long enough."

Mike groans, his face covered in sweat. With most of his face now covered with tape, all I can see are his bloodshot eyes, which stream with tears.

"You slapped my mother across the face with your stinking dick, just to make the others laugh," I yell, loud enough to hear myself over the blaring TV.

He makes a noise behind his gag and gestures at the scrap of paper.

"What?" I snap. "Are you going to tell me she's an undeserving victim because that's not exactly news."

I snatch the nail gun, press its nose into the base of his dick, and squeeze the trigger.

Mike's muffled roars mingle with the sound of the television from the bedroom next door, sounding like it's part of the movie.

"Don't whine." I backhand him across the face with the power tool. "You're the one who joked about nailing her, and now I'm nailing you."

With the help of my pliers, I nail his penis to his thigh,

without so much as touching it. Blood soaks his lap and spreads across the bathroom floor. I shoot nail after nail into his withered dick until the gun's magazine is empty.

"How do you feel?" Leroi asks from the doorway.

I stare at his reflection in the bathroom mirror. "Better, but not satisfied."

"How will you finish him?"

I glance down at the open murder bag and extract the longest screwdriver. "Mike also said something about wanting to screw Mom, so this is only fitting."

By the time I turn back to him, his eyes are closed. No amount of threats will force him to open them, so I jam the screwdriver's sharp edge through his eyelid. With my free hand, I hammer its handle further in until it's sunk deep into his socket.

Blood pours down one side of his face, making pretty trails over the tape. It settles on his shirt with large splotches.

Leroi approaches me from behind and wraps his arms around my waist. His thick erection presses into the small of my back, making me shiver.

"How do you feel, now?"

I turn around in his embrace. "Compared to being chased in the woods, it's a bit of an anti-climax."

He nibbles my neck. "But we've found out two new things. One, Gabriel was forced to donate his liver in Mexico. Two, Samson has a summer house and we have its address." "

"I wish we could have kept him alive to check his facts," I mutter.

"Sorry to have spoiled your fun. Is there anything I can do to help?"

Reaching between our bodies, I trail my fingers over his

length and give him a gentle squeeze, making his breath quicken.

"I want to try the nipple clamps."

SIXTY-THREE

LEROI

I sit on the edge of the mattress, watching Seraphine sleep. Her eyes were drooping by the time Don's clean-up crew arrived to wrap up Mike Ferrante's corpse, place it in their chest freezer, and carry the appliance away. I drove her to the downstairs apartment and tucked her in bed.

Moonlight shines in from the open window, making her pale blonde lashes glow. After everything that's happened in the space of twenty-four hours and beyond, she somehow manages to look peaceful.

It was a long day for both of us, and I couldn't stop thinking about whether it was time to find another location. I sent a text to Cesare to check on his progress with Rosalind, but I'm still waiting for him to reply.

I'm haunted by several things she revealed about her captivity and can't shake off the instinct that I could have done more to help. Anton might have dropped a clue that I missed or Miko and I could have planned the Capello Massacre faster, so I could reach Seraphine earlier.

The thought of her trapped in that basement makes me

want to do something, anything, to ease her pain. If I can't hand her Gabriel on a platter, then maybe I can do something else.

After telling Miko to expand his searches on Capello's liver surgery to hospitals in Mexico, it takes him no time to find the fake profile he used in his previous transplant. The name given for the live donor is Gabe Jenkins, but the blood type, date of birth, and all other details match the donor profile from four years ago.

So now we have a possible alias for Seraphine's brother.

Gabriel has to be alive somewhere. There has to be prescription records or medical bills somewhere that will give us a clue to his location. It's only a matter of time before we reunite Seraphine with her brother.

After placing a kiss on her cheek, I leave the room to make a few phone calls and set up the apartment next door. Tomorrow's going to be another eventful day.

———

Hours later, the first thing I'm aware of when I awaken are soft hands roaming over my chest. I inhale the scent of strawberries and open my eyes to find Seraphine leaning over me with a mischievous grin.

"I've been trying to wake you for hours." She presses her lips against mine.

I run a hand through my hair. "I went to bed late."

"What were you doing?"

"It's a surprise."

Her eyes sparkle. "Tell me."

"Watching you sleep," I say with a smirk.

"What else?" Her hands travel down my abs, which

tighten under her touch, and she trails feather-light kisses on my skin.

As she slides her hand beneath the waistband of my pajama pants, my breath quickens, and my mind rifles through images of the cocks Seraphine has terrorized. Billy Blue's getting sliced into sashimi, Rochas getting drilled through the middle, and Ferrante's that she nailed to his thigh. That's not even counting the ones I didn't witness.

"What are you doing?" I rasp.

"I'm just touching it."

"Why?"

"Because it's mine, and I want to feel you." She leans in and whispers in my ear. "Let me play with it, please?"

"Behave yourself."

She chuckles. "It's so long and thick and veiny. I can't resist it."

Fuck. I'm not the type of man to make a woman beg to touch his cock. Scratch that, I am. But this is Seraphine. The last time she got this close to it, I crashed the car. The time before that, she was holding a knife to my balls.

"What else are you planning on doing with my cock?" I ask.

She wraps her fingers around the base of my shaft. "Maybe take it for a ride?"

I fling an arm over my eyes and groan. "Fuck."

Seraphine tightens her grip and runs the flat of her tongue up the length of my shaft. The way her path meanders tells me she's tracing one of its veins. When she reaches the head, she circles it with her tongue, and my balls tighten.

As much as I want this to continue, coming so soon would ruin Seraphine's surprise. I spent half the night setting up something to make her smile.

"You said you wanted the nipple clamps," I say between panting breaths.

She pauses, mid lick. "Where are they?"

"Come with me."

She gives my cock head a parting lick before releasing it and sitting back on her heels. With a groan, I ease my erection back into my pajama pants and pull myself up.

Seraphine is a picture of blonde debauchery. Her blue eyes are dark with desire. A flush blooms her cheeks as she pants through her parted lips. Sunlight filters through her golden hair, illuminating its ends like a halo of spun gold. My gaze drifts down her pink nightshirt to the erect nipples that are begging for the clamps.

I rise off the bed and offer her my hand. "Come with me."

At this time of the morning, most of the neighbors have already gone to work, so I don't bother with dressing gowns as we walk to the studio apartment next door.

I open the door and let her in first. She takes one step inside and stops abruptly with a loud gasp.

"Leroi." She whirls around, placing both hands on my chest. "What is this?"

Her eyes sparkle with delight, and the flush on her cheeks darkens to a delicious shade of red. My heart warms at her excitement, and I turn her around. "Go inside and take a closer look."

Squealing, Seraphine rushes to the right side of the room, where a four-tier chocolate fountain rumbles on a table, surrounded by an array of fruits and small snacks. On the table, far away from the fountain, are Belgian waffles on a plate and coffee. Next to them is a brand new notebook, one pack of assorted felt-tip pens, and another pack containing varying shades of red.

"Oh, my god." She whirls around with a smile so broad I can't help but return it. "Is this all for me?"

I nod. "You dreamed of having a chocolate fountain. Maybe seeing it will show your subconscious that you're free."

Her breath catches. "But you said you hate chocolate. You're allergic."

"All true," I say, my gaze softening. "But it's a sacrifice I'm willing to make."

I send a silent word of thanks to the twenty-four-hour drugstore for delivering a large quantity of antihistamines before the all-day bakery filled the studio with the rich scent of theobromine.

"How did you arrange it so quickly?"

"That's why I went to bed so late." I walk across the studio and take her hand. "Come on. You need to see the rest."

"But what about the chocolate?" She glances over her shoulder at the fountain.

"Did you think I'd let you gorge yourself on poison without earning the privilege?" I take her to the leather bondage table on the other side of the room.

Seraphine clasps both hands on her cheeks. I'm surprised she didn't notice this before, but that's a testament to the lure of chocolate.

She gapes at a table. It has a leather backrest that can be laid flat or slanted. Its seat is U-shaped, allowing access to the cunt and asshole with adjustable leather stirrups on either side. My cock stirs at the image of Seraphine strapped to the device and pleasured to within an inch of her sanity.

"This is incredible," she says, her voice breathy with awe. "How did you know I liked it?"

"You and the sales clerk spent a lot of time admiring this

beauty." I place a hand on her shoulder. "Take a closer look."

Seraphine walks to the table and trails her fingertips over its smooth leather surfaces. "I can't believe you did all this for me."

I press a kiss on her temple. "You're worth it, and this is only the beginning. Now, take off that nightshirt and get on your knees."

SIXTY-FOUR

SERAPHINE

I'm locked in Leroi's dark gaze, every inch of my skin exploding with sparks. This can't be real. This has to be a dream. No one has ever given me anything I wanted, especially at such a high cost.

Leroi hates chocolate. He won't even allow it in his home, yet he's put together a fountain that's filling the air with the rich scent of cacao. Any minute now, he's going to clutch his throat and collapse.

"Wait," I ask. "How are your eyes not streaming?"

The corner of his lips lifts into a half-smirk. "I took lots of allergy pills."

My breath shallows. "Oh."

I take off my nightshirt, feeling a cool breeze tickle my skin, and sink down onto my knees. My heart gallops around my chest like a wild horse trying to break out of its fence.

Leroi cups my cheek and murmurs, "Good girl. Will you stay still while I bring the blindfold?"

I nod.

He walks to a table beside the leather bondage furniture and picks up the pink cat-eye mask I chose at Wonderland. As he approaches, my gaze drops to the perfect outline of his erection. I'm so lost in the sight of those thick veins protruding through the gray sweatpants, that it comes as a surprise when the blindfold covers my eyes.

"What happens now?" I whisper as he fastens it behind my head.

"I'm going to try out a few toys we bought together, including the clamps. Every time you make a pretty noise, I'll reward you with something from the fountain."

"Can it be chocolate-covered strawberries, please?" I ask.

He chuckles. "Anything you want. Do I need to remind you of your safe words?"

When I shake my head, Leroi helps me to my feet, and we walk a few steps forward. Being blindfolded is new for me, it's different from spending hours in the dark. I'm completely dependent on Leroi and can't see where I'm going, but tiny chinks of light stream through the gaps between the suede and my face, bringing me a sense of security.

The warmth of his hands sinks into my bare skin as he helps me onto the bondage table. I lie back on the butter-soft leather and let Leroi arrange my legs in the stirrups.

"How does that feel?" He strokes my thigh.

"Alright," I whisper as my belly dips with each of his touches. "Is it time for the clamps?"

His thumb and fingers close in around my nipple, detonating sparks of pleasure. My spine arches off the leather backrest and I moan, unable to control my delight.

"Not yet." His hot breath fans against my ear, and his voice is husky and filled with promise. "First, I want you to focus on your breathing. Relax and let go of your thoughts while I adjust the straps."

Ignoring the shivers running down my spine and the wetness gathering in my folds, I inhale a deep breath, just as Leroi taught me in the rooftop garden. He remains close, the heat of his body warming my side as my muscles unwind.

Leroi takes his time exploring my body with his hands and mouth as he fastens each strap. He kisses my nipples, my fingertips, the insides of my knees, and my toes, alternating between giving me pleasure and buckling up the restraints.

I'm lost in the clink of metal, the warm caress of his fingers, and the heat of his mouth on my skin. Each touch intensifies the arousal coiling within me, and pressure builds deep in my core. Before I know it, I'm bound and utterly vulnerable.

The scraping of wood against wood from below makes me think he's pulling the table of toys closer. My anticipation heightens with several shuddering gasps. Something leathery and soft trails over my inner thigh, setting my skin alight. This has to be the suede flogger the sales clerk promised me I would love.

She was right, and I want more.

"Are you ready for the clamps?" he asks.

My nipples harden in response, and I give him an eager nod.

"Good girl." His lips press on my forehead. "I know how much you enjoyed them in the store."

I lick my lips, already knowing I won't be using the safe word.

Leroi places the clamps on each nipple, letting the rubber-covered tips pinch my skin with a delicious amount of pressure. The sensation is an exquisite mix of pain combined with a pleasure that infuses my nerve endings with sparks.

As the cold metal chain attached to the clamps drops on my breast, I groan, my arms jerking involuntarily within their restraints.

"You took that so well." He kisses me on the mouth.

Hungry for more, I part my lips, but he pulls away.

As his footsteps retreat across the room, my heart skips several beats. Is he walking to the fountain? I squeeze my eyes shut behind the mask, focus on the sounds and try to decipher what he's doing, but all I hear is the clink of china and the rumble of the fountain.

"What are you doing?" I ask.

"Preparing a treat for my good girl."

Moments later, Leroi returns, pressing something sticky and warm on my lips. I open my mouth and let in a choco-late-covered strawberry. The sharpness of the fruit mingles with the chocolate's rich creaminess, creating an explosion of flavor that stokes the flames of my excitement.

"How is it?" he asks, his fingers trailing down my neck, heading toward my breasts.

"Better than I imagined," I reply with a moan, although I'm not sure I'm talking about him or the sweet treats.

He picks up the metal chain that connects the two clamps and tugs, setting off an explosion of sensations so powerful that I swear I can see fireworks.

"How's that, sweetheart?"

My hips lift off the leather seat, and I moan.

"You're so perfect," he whispers, his lips grazing my earlobe. "So beautiful, bound and blindfolded, and at my mercy. You should see the way the stirrups spread you open so I can enjoy your dripping pussy."

I whimper at the thought of him moving between my spread legs and pounding me mercilessly until I climax. It will be even better than what we did in the woods yesterday, because I'll be totally helpless to resist him.

"Do you want more?" he asks.

My pussy clenches, needing him to fill me and make this moment complete. "Yes, please."

He tightens some screws at the side of each clamp, increasing the pressure and I gasp and shudder. It's like being branded with bliss. The next time he tugs the chain, the sensations intensify, and I make a high-pitched squeal.

Leroi presses another chocolate-covered strawberry to my lips, and I savor its sticky sweetness. As I swallow, something light and leathery brushes over my breasts.

My spine stiffens, and I release a shuddering moan.

It's the flogger.

"I'm going to whip your pretty pink pussy until it's aching and dripping. If you can take the flogging like a good girl, then I'll fuck you until you come around my cock," he growls, his hot breath tickling my neck.

My stomach flips, and my clit swells as though trying to meet the flogger's touch.

"Do you want it, little Seraphine?"

"Yes, please," I whisper.

Leroi gives the flogger a few experimental swipes against my inner thigh, and I bite my lip to keep from screaming. Every nerve ending sets itself alight with a deadly mix of anticipation and frustration. That's not where I need it.

"You like it when I whip your little cunt?"

"Yes." My voice rises several octaves. I can't believe I'm making such high-pitched whines.

"Filthy little angel," he croons. "My eager little pet."

He gives my pussy a few light flicks with the flogger, sending shivers of pleasure across my skin. Then he moves up, swiping the flogger around my clit, teasing it until I'm arching my hips, begging for more.

The flogger's soft suede tails slide over my clit, making me gasp and writhe. My hips convulse on the leather seat, chasing each of these new sensations.

"More," I cry.

He delivers another flick, sending a surge of pleasure that teeters on the knife-edge of agony and ecstasy. My legs spasm and the rest of my body quivers.

Leroi increases the intensity of his strikes, and I tumble into a void of complete ecstasy. My eyes roll to the back of my head. I can feel the flogger everywhere—in my toes, in my fingers, in my very soul.

My ears fill with Leroi's hot and heavy breaths, the rumble of the chocolate fountain, and the gentle swish of the flogger. Its soft tails also set every nerve ending alight with the most delicious pleasure. I feel the leather on my legs, my arms, my back, and a thin coating of sweat breaks out on my brow.

I inhale the mingled scents of cacao, coffee, and sandalwood and the taste of strawberries and chocolate lingers on my tongue. The only thing missing from this wonderful experience is a toe-curling kiss.

This is no fever dream.

It's real.

I'm free.

I have someone who cares for me so deeply that he would help find Gabriel, kill my enemies, and bring my fantasies to life.

"Stay with me." His deep voice brings me back to the present.

Every stroke brings me closer to the edge until I'm screaming out my pleasure in garbled moans and cries as a tiny crack of the flogger hits my clit.

Leroi makes a low growl that sends tingles down my spine. "Come for me, angel."

His words send me over a precipice, and I scream as I come, my body quaking with the force of my orgasm. Leroi strokes my clit with the flogger as the muscles of my pussy clench and release.

I'm still moaning and panting when his cock lines up to my entrance. My hips jerk, trying to quicken the penetration. I want his tongue in my mouth while he fucks me on this bondage table, and I want it now.

His phone rings, and he draws back. I wait a few breathless seconds, hoping he'll ignore whoever's ringing, but he snaps, "What?"

Whoever's on the other side hesitates for a moment before saying, "I'm sorry about yesterday's breach in security, but an older gentleman is on his way to see you. I asked him to wait to be announced, but he pushed past."

Leroi stiffens.

The man on the other end of the line clears his throat. "He says he's your father."

"Fuck!" he roars.

LEROI

My heart rate kicks up several notches and my jaw tenses to the point of pain. Anton is here and on his way up. If he doesn't find me upstairs, he'll either ask Miko to check the rooftop garden or assume I'm downstairs.

Shit.

I unshackle Seraphine as fast as humanly possible, my heart pounding so hard that I can barely hear her questions. After setting her on her feet, I pull off the blindfold and grab her shoulders.

"Stay here. Don't make a sound." I glare into her eyes. "The man coming upstairs to see me is dangerous."

"But I thought your dad was dead," she says.

"I'll explain later." I break off in a sprint, all traces of my erection gone.

"Leroi?"

"Do as I say!"

It comes out sharper than necessary, but I can't take any chances with Seraphine. If Anton gets one glimpse of her, he'll know she's the innocent girl he trained to be a Lolita assassin. The girl he abused.

I dart out into the hallway and toward the stairs, my gut twisting into agonizing knots, but I ignore the pain and pick up my pace. It's only when I reach the upstairs level and stare into the elevator's opening doors that I realize I'm unarmed.

Damn it.

Anton steps out wearing a black leather vest on top of his usual black shirt and slacks. He's clean-shaven but his salt-and-pepper hair is slicked back in the ponytail he's grown since retirement. It's a demeanor that's always commanded affection and respect, but not today.

I slow my steps, slow my breathing, and smooth my features into a mask of calm.

"Leroi." His voice is deep and smooth, but his eyes are as sharp as ever. "Have I interrupted your workout?"

"What brings you to the city?" I ask.

"Let's talk inside."

My pulse quickens as I open the door to my apartment and let him in, hoping there's nothing lying around to remind me of Seraphine. Sunlight reflects off the newly painted living room walls, making the space suspiciously bright.

Anton steps inside, his gaze wandering from side to side. I stay a step behind him, ready to grab his arm if he tries to reach for a gun. He stops by the dining table and turns to meet my eyes.

"Coffee?" I ask.

"No, thanks."

"Mind if I make some?" I gesture toward the kitchen.

"Go ahead." He lowers himself into a dining chair.

I step into the kitchen, prepare a fresh pot of the special

blend, and open the cupboard beneath the sink where I keep a spare gun. I pull it from where I left it taped to the underside of the cabinet, check the magazine, and slip it into the waistband of my sweatpants.

It's been four months since I last saw Anton. Any warmth I might have toward him is now cold. My mind can't reconcile Seraphine's horrific accounts of abuse with the stoic man who brought me into his home, but there's a fury burning in the pit of my stomach that's threatening to erupt.

My feelings for Seraphine override my loyalty to Anton, but I have to stay cool. Anton never just visits without a reason. If he's come prepared for battle, I can't risk letting my emotions take control. That would risk Seraphine's safety.

The kitchen door opens, and Anton steps in.

"Changed your mind about the coffee?" I reach for a mug.

He snorts.

"Why are you here?" I ask.

Anton leans against the counter. "Rita tells me you're running the business to the ground."

"How did she come to that conclusion?" I ask with a smirk. "Everyone's completing their assignments and the contractors are getting paid on time."

"She exaggerates." He lifts the coffee pot and pours out a steaming cup. "But the question still stands. What are you doing with the business?"

"You'll have to be more specific."

"You're making a mess of the Capello job."

I stiffen, my throat tightening until it hits. He's talking about the million-dollar deposit transferred to the firm from the bank account of Joseph Di Marco. I made the mistake of thinking our mystery client was Capello's lawyer.

"These things take time," I say. "Whoever massacred that family had to be a professional because they didn't leave any clues."

"Yet you didn't once visit the mansion to find them," Anton says.

Shit.

I huff a laugh. "Rita told you that?"

"No, I heard that from Samson Capello."

"Isn't he dead?" I raise a brow.

Anton takes a long sip from the mug, all the while staring at me through those cold, gray eyes. My heart pounds so hard its vibrations fill my ears, but I keep my breath deep and even, the way Anton taught me when I was a boy.

"He's alive, and he's demanding his little sister."

I cock my head to the side. "I thought he only had an identical twin."

"Leroi," he says in his cut-the-bullshit tone. "I know you have Seraphine. The GPS on her collar last registered her at this location."

My lips tighten. There's no point in wasting my breath with denials. Anton must have known the truth from the day he called, informing me that a lone gunman had murdered the Capello family. The question is, why has he taken so long to act?

"You're in contact with Samson?" I ask.

He nods and takes another sip. "Who do you think helped the boys plan out Seraphine's little missions?"

Bile rises to the back of my throat. I would wash the bitterness away with a cup of coffee, but that would mean drinking the special blend.

"Why would you even create something so sick?" I ask.

Anton's lips lift into an icy grin. "I taught you better than to ask such asinine questions."

"Indulge me," I say through clenched teeth.

"Everything I have is because of Frederic Capello. Did you know he was my first regular client?" He takes another sip of coffee. "Assassination is a word-of-mouth business, and he spread the news of my services. I owed that man everything."

"That's why you corrupted an innocent young girl?"

"Don't be sexist," Anton drawls.

"What?" I hiss.

"You were even younger than Seraphine was when I brought you under my wing." He gestures at me with the mug. "Same with Miko."

My nostrils flare. "But I didn't train him to kill."

"Nope, but you took advantage of his skills as a hacker."

I swallow down a response. Anton might think he's making a point, but mine and Miko's situations were different. We both knew what we were stepping into the moment we left home with hitmen. Seraphine was imprisoned in a basement, sexually assaulted, tortured, and trained like a dog. Anton wants me to lose focus arguing, but I won't take the bait.

"Where is Samson Capello?" I ask.

He raises a shoulder. "No idea. Somewhere in hiding."

"And Gabriel Capello? Were you involved in farming an innocent young man for his liver?"

Anton's features harden. "Who told you that?"

"Answer my question."

"Gabriel looks good enough to me. He stays with his mother in that little estate close to Alderney State University."

"Evangeline?"

"That's the one," he says with a nod. "They told Seraphine her mother was dead and Gabriel was a hostage."

"Why?"

His brows rise. "You should know. That little wildcat is impossible to control."

A tense silence stretches out, punctuated only by the ticking of the clock. If Seraphine's mother survived the gang rape and strangling and isn't living as a prisoner, then what is she doing to help her daughter?

"Does Evangeline know what happened to Seraphine?"

He shrugs.

My jaw tightens. "If you knew I had her, why did it take you so long to act?"

Anton sets down his mug. "Samson isn't fit to manage all the Capello empire. He's too erratic and never commanded the same respect as his father and brother. I sat back, wondering if you were going to take Samson out and bring the Montesano family back into power. Instead, you're running around town with Seraphine killing low level grunts."

"Samson is next on our list."

He laughs, the wound carrying no mirth.

My gut tightens. "Are you working with him?" I ask.

He shakes his head. "Never liked the boy. Always fucking things up and bruising the Lolita."

Lolita.

I tamp down a rush of fury and focus on my next move. That contemptuous word erases my last shred of loyalty. It never registered that Anton didn't abuse me because I was a willing participant in my own moral destruction.

Seraphine wasn't.

She fought against her captors with everything she had, including her teeth.

However I look at it, Seraphine and I were both tools that were sharpened to Anton's specifications. It was Seraphine who exposed Anton's true evil. I have to erase him from existence. It's the only way she can truly be free.

"So, you're the only one who knows I have Seraphine?" I ask, keeping my voice light.

"Yeah. Sam's never getting her back. She belongs to me."

Our eyes lock for a tense heartbeat before we both reach for our guns. Anton's reflexes have been dulled by the special blend, so I shoot first.

His eyes widen, he falls to his knees, and his pistol slips from his fingers. A wet patch blooms across his shirt, just over his heart.

He stares up at me, his eyes wide, his mouth opening and closing in a soundless gape. The man I thought I knew was only a facade. Despite my newfound loyalty to Seraphine, my chest twangs with a pang of regret.

This mess needs to be cleared up before she comes upstairs looking for me with a knife.

SIXTY-SIX

SERAPHINE

I lick chocolate off my fingers, trying to calculate the amount of time it would take for Leroi to walk upstairs, tell his father that he's busy, and come back. Five minutes, if they're arguing. Ten, if they've gotten into a conversation.

Concern taints the deliciousness of the Belgian waffle I drenched in melted chocolate, strawberries, bananas, and marshmallows. Much of it is already gone, washed down with gulps of coffee.

My gaze skims Leroi's thoughtful gift of new art supplies, complete with extra red pens to make the blood more vibrant, but I can barely concentrate because he's taking too long. Besides, I thought his dad was dead?

I take another huge bite. If he doesn't return by the time I've finished this waffle and licked the plate clean, I'll sneak upstairs and see if he needs help.

Screw that.

By the time I've chewed and swallowed my mouthful, I'm already upstairs ringing the doorbell holding a metal skewer in one hand and a broken plate in another that I've fashioned into a shank.

Leroi doesn't answer, so I press my ear on the door to listen for any movement. Hearing nothing, I walk to Miko's apartment next door and keep ringing the way Rosalind's sister did yesterday.

Minutes later, the door creaks open. Miko peeks out through puffy eyes, his red hair standing up at all angles.

"Sera?" he croaks. "What's up?"

"Leroi's not answering." I flick my head toward the door. "Do you have a spare key?"

Miko rubs his eyes and yawns. "What? No. Um... you'd better come in."

He shuffles aside, letting me into an apartment that's the polar opposite to Leroi's. It's smaller, with computer equipment stretching over an entire wall, while the others are lined with shelves filled with action figures still in their boxes.

I glance over my shoulder, letting the door swing shut behind me. My fingers close around my makeshift weapons, and I fold my arms over my breasts. I'm only wearing a thin nightshirt, and it's spattered with melted chocolate.

Miko lowers himself into a leather gaming chair with a footrest that's reclined all the way backward. If I wasn't so worried about Leroi, I'd wonder if that was his bed.

"Can you call him?" I ask.

"He's not answering." He stares down at his phone and sighs. "Take a seat."

"No, thanks." I point at the balcony door. "Is there any way I can climb into his apartment from there?"

Miko swings his chair in the direction I'm looking and frowns. "You'd have to smash through the glass partition. What's wrong? I thought you two were joined at the hip?"

"He had a visitor," I say. "The man downstairs said it was his father."

Miko snorts. "You might as well sit down and get comfortable. Anton is a bit of a windbag. They're going to take a while."

My heart skips several beats.

"Anton?"

"Leroi didn't tell you how he became an assassin?"

"He did but..."

Anton is a common enough name, isn't it? I don't know how many older hitmen work in New Alderney, but it's too much of a coincidence. Leroi would have said something if my handler and his mentor were the same man. Wouldn't he?

"Oh!" Miko says, his excitement cutting through my confusion. "I think I found Gabriel."

"Where?" I rush to his side.

He launches into a long, garbled explanation about finding an alias for a live donor who matched Gabriel's credentials in a Mexican hospital and then cross referencing these details, giving Miko an address.

I grab his shoulder. "We should go."

"Shouldn't we wait for Leroi?"

I glance at the door. This mission likely requires a professional. Even if Dad didn't hire guards to keep Gabriel from escaping, he'd use high-end technology to keep him locked up.

But Miko is Leroi's tech guy, and I've seen him handle a gun.

"Call Leroi," I say. "If he doesn't reply, then we'll go without him."

With a nod, Miko taps his phone and puts the call on speaker. It rings twice before Leroi answers.

"I'm busy," he snaps. "Is this urgent?"

"I'm with Seraphine—"

"Stay where you are and keep her busy."

I flinch at the harshness of his words. Fifteen minutes ago, I was the center of his attention. Now, he makes me sound like a nuisance.

Miko frowns at his screen. "He hung up."

"Let's go."

"Don't you want to get dressed first?" He gestures at my nightshirt.

Any other time, I would shrink away. Miko isn't a threat, but I can't stand the thought of a man who isn't Leroi looking at me when I'm barely dressed.

"Do you have anything I can borrow?" I ask.

———

Less than ten minutes later, we're driving down the highway toward an apartment building owned by Dad's lawyer, Joseph Di Marco. The afternoon sun shines through the windshield, making me pull down the brim of my borrowed baseball cap.

On the way, Miko shares his backstory with me. It's similar to Leroi's, except he was an only child that took the brunt of his stepfather's abuse. I nod at the right places to show him I'm listening, while trying to find an opportunity to bring up Anton. I need to know if he and Leroi are connected to the Anton I want to kill.

"Leroi's my hero," Miko says, his voice choked with emotion. "I never had a real dad until I met him."

"He isn't old enough to be your dad," I reply.

He grins. "He's thirty-four and I'm nineteen. Technically, he could have had me when he was fifteen."

"Did you live with him, too?"

"For the first few months, I stayed in his spare room. Leroi got me a therapist, took me out jogging, and taught me how to meditate." He shakes his head and sighs. "He paid for all my online courses, got me whatever I wanted. He's my fucking idol."

"But you work for him, right?"

"I'm a freelancer, but yeah, I do a few jobs for Leroi." He pulls in outside a low-rise apartment building and parks. "If it wasn't for Leroi, I don't think I would have survived my teens."

My throat thickens. All evidence so far points that Leroi found me by coincidence while helping out his cousins. I've even seen one of the Montesano brothers up close. Leroi is a hitman with a heart, he can't be connected to my handler.

Miko leans across to the glove box where a pair of pistols sit amongst a short-blade knife and a computer tablet. "Take one. We could be walking into anything."

I select a gun, and while Miko is distracted, I slip the knife in my pocket and exit the car. My heart hammers in double time to my footsteps as we walk across the lawn that surrounds the building. Gabriel might be inside one of these units, tied to a chair in that darkened room.

For the first six months of my captivity, Samson and Gregor only allowed me to watch him sit there, battered, emaciated, and struggling for breath. The backs of my eyes sting at the thought of how he's going to look after being forced to donate his liver twice.

"Are you alright?" Miko asks.

"Y-yeah." I nod.

He opens the front door. "This has to be nerve-racking. How long has it been since you last saw Gabriel?"

"Five years," I mumble. "Which one is it?"

He points at a unit on the left.

"Hide the gun," he whispers.

My lips tighten. Did Leroi ever tell him that I spent those five years killing dangerous men? Step one of being an assassin is to make sure they don't see you coming. I brush off the annoyance. Miko probably thinks he's being helpful.

We knock on the door, and an auburn-haired woman answers, wearing long pigtails with an even longer, flowing dress. My heart sinks. She doesn't even remotely look capable of holding a man hostage.

"Does Gabe Jenkins live here?" Miko asks.

She smiles. "Gabe moved out a year ago. Do you want his new address?"

Miko and I exchange shocked glances.

New address?

Wait a minute. I thought Gabriel was a prisoner.

SIXTY-SEVEN

LEROI

The doorbell rings and rings, but the deafening pounding of my pulse muffles the sound. My breaths are so shallow that oxygen stops reaching my lungs. My throat thickens as I stare down at Anton's unmoving form.

I linger on his lifeless eyes, my chest constricting with an overwhelming sense of grief and regret.

Grief for the man who saved me from death row and taught me everything he knew about the art of killing. Regret because if he hadn't reached for his gun, I could have waited until he fell unconscious and offered him up to Seraphine as a gift.

I pause, waiting for something else to rise to the surface, but there's nothing more for Anton. Everything I have left is devoted to protecting Seraphine. There's no guilt for the murder of my mentor, but some of the unease I felt about not being able to save Seraphine from her past fades into a sense of satisfaction.

Until now, I hadn't realized how desperately I'd wanted

to participate in the revenge killings. Seraphine is no longer his Lolita. She's mine. My perfect angel.

Since presenting Anton for execution is no longer an option, I'll have to do the next best thing.

I kneel beside his corpse, my jaw tightening at the warm blood seeping through the fabric of my sweatpants. After a quick search of his vest pockets, I extract Anton's phone from the inside pocket and hold it over his face to unlock the device.

Even if he claimed not to know about the liver transplants, he was still one of the bastards who let Seraphine believe Gabriel's life hung in the balance. I'm hoping Anton knows Gabriel or Evangeline's addresses.

I navigate through his contacts, finding phone numbers for both Samson and Evangeline. Miko's distinctive ringtone blares out from my phone and tells the AI assistant to pick up the call.

"I'm busy. Is this urgent?"

Whatever Miko says barely registers. Something about Seraphine disobeying my orders and going upstairs. I order the AI to hang up. If he has Seraphine, then I can put thoughts of her safety aside while I clean up this kill. Anton deserves a burial to make up for what I'm about to do to his body.

He taught me how to keep a cool head in high-pressure situations, and how to move a body without leaving evidence. I'll honor his memory by doing just that.

Stepping around the expanding pool of blood, I walk out of the kitchen and open the armory, where I extract a bag of cat litter and a bone saw.

Guilt punches me in the chest as I sprinkle cat litter over the blood. I didn't offer any to Seraphine when she killed Billy Blue. Instead, I made her clean it up, just like Anton taught me with sponges and a bowl.

Back then, if I hadn't been so concerned about the state of my apartment, I would have realized Seraphine had lashed out like that because she was traumatized.

Once the cat litter has absorbed most of the blood, I roll Anton's body onto a tarp and saw through his neck. The blade grinds against bone and cartilage with a sound that sends shivers down my spine. My mind festers with the intrusive thought that I'm not cleaning up any old target—this is Anton.

Anton, who clothed and fed me when my family cast me out because I couldn't stand watching them get abused. Anton, who understood that I killed out of the need to protect. He was the only father figure I had since mine died and Mother moved us away from Uncle Enzo.

Fuck.

If Uncle Enzo hadn't been a disgusting predator, Seraphine would never have gotten close enough to kill him and Roman might never have spent the past five years on death row.

When Anton's head falls loose from his body, I line a bowl with ice and place it inside, then I make quick work of removing his hands, which I add to the bowl before storing the lot in the refrigerator.

I saw the rest of his body into transportable pieces, and stuff them in black trash bags before moving them into a suitcase. Once all traces of his corpse are dealt with, I pour a bleach solution on the floor and head for the shower.

The hot spray washes away the blood but does nothing to ease the mounting dread about how I plan on explaining this to Seraphine. I'll have to confess my relationship with Anton. Once we've found Gabriel and dealt with Samson, she'll be in a better state of mind and I'll tell her why I never spoke up when she mentioned his name.

Maybe presenting her with his severed head will ease the blow?

Perhaps.

I work strawberry-scented shampoo into my hair and build up a thick lather. That's what I'll do. Hand her Gabriel, Samson, and Anton's heads all at once. She'll be so pleased that she'll overlook my past mistakes.

A laugh bursts from my chest.

If someone had told me I would simp for a tiny blonde, I'd ask what they were smoking. I only ever noticed tall brunettes, which was probably my mistake. Instead of the darkness of their hair, what I should have been looking for was the darkness in their souls.

Seraphine is my perfect match in every way imaginable. She doesn't flinch at the thought that I'm a killer, and she's the only woman I know who keeps me on my toes. I love her unpredictable temperament and her capacity for violence, which outstrips my own.

Now that I have found her, I can't ever give her a reason to leave.

The doorbell rings, interrupting my musings. I rinse the shampoo from my hair, turn off the water, and wrap a towel around my waist.

Seraphine probably got tired of waiting around with Miko and now she wants to come inside. I walk out of the bathroom, through the bedroom, and out into the living room that smells of bleach. At least the kitchen door is closed and the case containing Anton's remains is hidden from view.

The bell rings again, and I hesitate. If she's with Miko, then he would have taught her the special knock.

I walk to the wall, out of the door's line of sight, and into the kitchen. Stepping over kitchen tiles still wet with bleach solution, I pick up the gun.

"Who's there?" I say from the kitchen door.

When bullets pierce through the door, I dive to the ground.

Thank fuck I didn't drop my guard and answer the ring. It was only a matter of time before this place was found by Samson's second team of assassins.

SIXTY-EIGHT

SERAPHINE

The woman rattles off an address that I don't catch, but Miko enters it into his phone and tells me it's a short way across town. I walk on numb legs, my pulse pounding in my ears. All this time, I imagined Gabriel being held in a darkened room just like me, but that couldn't have happened if this woman knew where he moved.

I slide into the front seat of the car and stare at the gun.

What if he escaped, found somewhere to live, and started a new life? My throat tightens at the suggestion that he didn't think that I also needed saving.

"Sera?" Miko asks, breaking through my foggy thoughts. By the exasperation in his voice, it sounds like this isn't the first time he's tried to catch my attention.

"What?"

"Put the gun back in the glove box."

He fires up the engine, and the voice on his phone gives his first direction.

While Miko pulls out, I place the pistol on top of the other one and slide the knife beneath the computer tablet.

"Can I play the zombie game?" I ask.

"Sure," he replies, his eyes on the road. "Passcode is 1677."

With the knife nestled between my thighs and the computer tablet, I enter the numbers and open the photo app. Most of the thumbnails look like porn. I scroll further down to the ones with fully clothed people in them and find one of Leroi sitting on a deck chair with a cooler full of beer.

My lips quirk at the memory of him sitting like that in the dark while I dug a grave, but I don't linger on that memory. Too many weird things are happening at once. Leroi's father figure, who just happens to be named Anton, coming to the apartment, and finding out Gabriel has a forwarding address, has left me reeling.

The next few images are of a fishing trip with Miko and Leroi at various stages throughout the day.

"What are you doing?" Miko asks at a stoplight.

"I forgot which one was the zombie app, so I'm browsing your fishing photos," I say.

"Sure you're looking at the fishing?" he says, his voice hopeful.

He's probably accusing me of salivating over his dick pics. I'm too preoccupied with recent revelations to comment on something so trivial, so I hold up the tablet with a picture of Miko grinning with a fishing rod.

He smiles. "Leroi always takes us out of town to unwind after a big job."

"Where do you go?"

"Anton has a house a few miles out of town by the lake. It's surrounded by woodland, so it feels like you're in the middle of nowhere. He says it's perfect for clearing your mind."

"Is Leroi planning another trip there?" I ask, already

trying to calculate a way to hunt down Anton. "I can't imagine killing the entire Capello family and demolishing one half of their mansion being a small job."

"But it's not finished," he replies with a shrug.

I wait for Miko to say more, but the light changes to green, and he steps on the gas. He wouldn't tell me if there was another reason Leroi wasn't taking his vacation. He wouldn't reveal that Leroi doesn't want me to meet Anton. Miko's too clever. Besides, if I pressed, he would say Leroi still needs to kill Samson.

My gaze drops down to the fishing photos. Some of them are videos and look like they're being shot by a third person and not with the camera held on a tripod. I continue scrolling, desperate to see the face of their companion.

I stop at one photo of a large man with long gray hair streaked with black, but it's shot from behind. It could be Anton the handler, but I can't be sure. He stopped visiting the basement after I completed the Montesano mission.

Shallow breaths escape my lungs as I click on the next video. The man holding the camera points it at Leroi and asks him what he's caught so far. I don't hear Leroi's response because I recognize that gravelly voice. It's him. The handler who put the collar around my neck and forced me into a life of degradation and death.

The next photo is of Anton standing in the middle of the lake, wearing waders and holding up a large fish. I zoom in on the picture with my fingers and examine his face. He's grayer, a little rounder, and smiling, but I could never forget those eyes.

There's no mistaking it.

Leroi is working with Anton.

Anton is the man who completed Leroi's first disastrous kill, cleaned up the crime scene, and saved him from death row. He's the man who trained Leroi to become a professional assassin, the man Leroi considers a father.

I've been such a fool.

All this time, I thought Leroi finding me was a lucky coincidence. All this time, I thought he was the enemy of my enemy. I thought he had taken me in out of the need to pay forward a favor he'd received as a teenager.

But I was wrong.

It all makes sense. Only three people could access that basement: Dad, Gregor, and Samson. If Anton never entered alone and always had to be accompanied by one of the twins, how did Leroi get in? Maybe it took Anton all this time to work out how to break through Dad's security.

My gaze darts to Miko.

He's one of them, too.

Bile rises to the back of my throat, and I swallow back the bitter tang of betrayal. Betrayal would mean Leroi was an ally who stabbed me in the back.

It can't be betrayal when he had a plan from the start. Either he and Anton were working together to acquire me for their firm, or Leroi was training me for Anton as some kind of twisted Father's Day gift.

That's right. I remember how Anton used to leer at me and make me change into those horrible little outfits as part of my training. If he had been alone, he would have done more than just look.

What if sex with Leroi was part of my training?

A shudder runs down my spine.

Step one would be to train me to have sex with men without wanting to kill them. Step two would be to get me addicted to sex. Step three would be sex with Anton.

I reach beneath the computer tablet, my fingers tightening around the hilt of the knife. Every fiber of my being screams at me to plunge it into Miko's neck and then hunt Leroi down to make him pay for his lies. I squeeze my eyes shut, take a deep breath, and force myself to stay calm.

Lashing out won't solve anything. If I stab Miko, they'll know I'm on to them and their plan. They'll be prepared for me, and I'll lose the element of surprise.

I need to be like Leroi and play this smart.

I'll use everything the bastard taught me to survive this trio, use them to eliminate Samson, and escape them with Gabriel.

"Here we are," Miko says.

My head snaps up as he turns into a street of two-story pastel-colored houses set within well-manicured lawns. In the distance, a dark-haired man hugs a blonde woman from behind.

As we drive closer, the man's face comes into focus. It's Leroi.

My heart rate spikes, but then it crashes when I look at the woman he's holding.

Her blonde hair is the exact shade that mine used to be before the coffee dye, and it's styled in a familiar layered bob. I can't make out her features, since she's bowing her head, but something about her looks achingly familiar.

My breath hitches. No. It can't be. When she raises her head, and I catch sight of the blue eyes that have haunted my dreams, only they're streaming with tears and the rest of her face is twisted with anguish.

All the blood drains from my face and into my thrashing heart.

This can't be possible, but it's there before my eyes.

It's Mom.

Mom is alive.

SIXTY-NINE

LEROI

I crawl on my belly to the suitcase stuffed with Anton's remains. If I'm lucky, the assholes behind the door will stop shooting and leave. Based on how they're concentrating their shots at the lock, I'm guessing they're trying to access the apartment.

Let them.

I could use this opportunity to shoot back, maybe hit one of them, but leave myself exposed to the second. Instead, I shuffle backward to the dining room table and extract another gun I left taped beneath the chair.

Sending a silent word of thanks to Anton's body parts for teaching me how to use a gun with both hands, I crouch behind the case and wait for them to break in. Hopefully, they think I'm not shooting back because I'm already dead. I keep my breath slow and even to force my heart rate not to spike.

I need my aim to remain steady.

The next two shots cannot miss.

The first of them enters wearing a mask, his head whipping from side to side. My jaw clenches, and my arms twitch.

Not yet.

As the second one steps into the apartment, I spring up and fire two shots. One intruder falls, another fires back, but I'm already diving behind Anton's remains. The bullets embed themselves in the case.

I take aim again and catch the second assassin in the throat. She drops her gun and falls to the floor.

Shit. Miko had better have barricaded Seraphine in his apartment, because this is far from over. Any worthwhile assassin wouldn't enter enemy territory without backup. Killing these two will have repercussions.

I crawl beneath the dining table toward the balcony door, ease it open, and slip out, just as something falls into the middle of the living room with a *clunk*.

FUCK!

I'm halfway up the stairs when an explosion shakes the walls, sending debris and shards of glass flying. One of the guns slips from my fingers as I clamber up the emergency stairs to the rooftop garden.

For now, the concrete space is empty, but won't stay like that for long. I jog naked across to the roof, having lost my towel some time between now and the first gunshots. I need to get to my phone in the downstairs apartment and check on Miko and Seraphine.

———

After an embarrassing dash down the hallway, I get dressed and log into my backup device that's a clone of the one I hope got destroyed in the explosion. There's already a message from Miko saying he and Seraphine are heading to an address they found for Gabriel.

It's a different location from the one Anton had on his phone for Seraphine's mother, so I decide to split our efforts and head there instead.

Ten minutes later, I'm walking across a front yard and ringing the doorbell of a pastel blue house. The woman who answers is petite and blonde with cornflower blue eyes set within hardened features.

There's no mistaking the family resemblance.

"Evangeline?" I ask.

Her eyes flash, and she tries to slam the door, but I force it open with my shoulder.

Pushing past her, I step into the house. "I'm here about your daughter."

She claps both hands over her mouth and makes a noise in the back of her throat, as if struggling to hold back a scream. Her blue eyes widen, their pupils dilating. "Get out of my house. S-Sera isn't here."

The normal response to someone asking about a daughter who's been missing for five years is to ask questions or show concern.

It almost reminds me of the horror I saw in my mother and sister's eyes when I killed that asshole and then the terror they showed when I tracked them down to where they'd moved. They looked at me like I was a monster. Evangeline stares up at me like I'm her judge and executioner.

I take another step forward, and she backs away and stumbles over a rug.

"But you know where she is, don't you?" I ask.

"Gabriel!" she screams, her voice panicked.

My eyes narrow. If Gabriel lives here, then Evangeline

has to know about the liver transplants. Is she the one holding her son hostage?

Footsteps thunder from upstairs. I turn just in time to find a tall young man charging downstairs with a gun. He glowers at me, his scowl reminding me of a Capello twin.

This isn't right at all.

Neither is the man pointing his pistol at me from the middle of the stairs. He has the signature green eyes and dark brown curls of the Capello family with a lean, healthy build. He looks nothing like the figure Seraphine pointed at on the basement's television screen. That version of her brother was emaciated. This one is slender.

"Are you Gabriel Capello?" I ask.

"Who's asking?"

"A friend of your sister's." I reach into my holster and pull out my gun.

Gabriel's face falls slack. "Sera's alive?" He lowers the gun and descends the stairs, his chest rising and falling with rapid breaths. "Where is she?"

"Safe," I reply.

This is all wrong. Gabriel looks eager to know about his sister's whereabouts, while Evangeline remains guarded. Guarded out of fear and suspicion or guarded because Capello took Seraphine with her consent?

I turn my attention back to Evangeline. "You know what happened to her, don't you?"

She closes her eyes and shudders.

My pulse hammers at the increasing realization that Seraphine's mother might be worse than mine. Two women who turned away from their children, but while mine helped me get away with murder, Seraphine's mother allowed her to be abused and turned into a murderer.

"Mom?" Gabriel's voice cuts through my anger.

"What's he talking about?"

Evangeline shakes her head. "Your father told me to make a choice. He could put a bullet through my head or I could pay him back for all the money he wasted on us."

Gabriel grabs the banister, the rest of his body slumping to the stairs. Having heard Seraphine's story, I'm already one step ahead of him, but I'm curious about how much he knows.

"What did she tell you?" I ask, not moving my gun away from Evangeline.

He swallows, his head bowing. "She said Roman Montesano murdered Sera to hurt Dad."

"And you believed that?" I ask.

He shakes his head. "I-I don't know. He went to jail for killing another woman, so it made sense."

"Your father framed Roman," I reply, my nostrils flaring. "From what your mother says, it looks like Capello gave her an ultimatum. Seraphine's life or hers."

Gabriel raises his head and stares at me through glassy eyes.

"Mom?" His voice trembles.

I glare down at the cowering woman. How is she going to talk her way out of this situation? Who is she going to throw to the sacrificial pyre?

"You don't know what that man did to me." Her voice thickens, and her face contorts into a rictus of agony. "I had no other choice—"

"But to let your daughter suffer for your infidelity?" I growl. "What Capello and his sons punished her for five years solid."

My fingers twitch toward her neck. I want to grab her throat and crush her lies, but out of consideration for Seraphine, I don't.

"You always had a choice. You could have saved your daughter and taken the bullet."

Gabriel rises off the stair, his green eyes widening, all the color draining from his shocked features. "What's he talking about, Mom?"

Evangeline backs toward the door, her body shaking. "He's exaggerating. Your father told me Sera was fine."

"Fine doing what?" The young man's gaze bounces from me to his mother. He raises the gun with a trembling hand and screams, "What the fuck happened to my little sister?"

Evangeline opens the front door and bolts.

Gabriel turns to me, his eyes filling with tears. "What happened to Sera?"

"She can tell you herself." I chase after Evangeline, who's already made it halfway across the lawn surrounding her cozy little house.

Sunlight shines down on her blonde hair, making it glint like fool's gold. Evangeline and Capello were a perfect match, two treacherous souls who treated their children like commodities. One became an organ bank. The other, a weapon.

I catch up with her in a few strides and grab her by the waist.

She stiffens and hisses, "Let go of me."

"Not a chance," I snarl. "You didn't just trade your life for your daughter's. You condemned an angel to five years of hell. Now, you're going to explain this and how you bargained his liver to save your worthless hide to Gabriel."

I turn around, my arms still wrapped around her waist, when pain slices through my back. Releasing Evangeline, I stare into the murderous blue eyes of her daughter.

And she's holding a bloody knife.

SEVENTY

SERAPHINE

Leroi lets go of Mom and looks me full in the face. His eyes are wide, yet he holds his features in that deceptive mask of calm. That's the trouble with Leroi. You don't see the snake beneath the suave exterior until it's wrapped its coils around your throat... or that of your supposedly dead mother.

"Sera—"

I cut off his lies with a knife to the gut that brings him to his knees. Mom clutches her temples and fills my ears with the same screams that are the soundtrack to my nightmares. My stomach lurches. I part my lips to speak, but all that comes out is a dry heave.

My ears ring with a gunshot. A hot knife of pain sears my shoulder. I whirl around, finding Miko standing by the car, holding a pistol.

I should have killed him when I had the chance.

Leroi grabs my wrist and croaks something that gets lost between the roar of blood between my ears and Mom's continuous screams.

Miko charges at me with the pistol. Behind him, the car is still running with the driver's side door open. Memories of that night rise to the surface, only this time they're not a dream. I need to get away. Clear my head. Work out how to win a gunfight when all I have is a blade.

I charge at Miko with the knife. He's so furious that I hurt his precious Leroi that he raises a hand, expecting to grab my throat. At the last moment, I sidestep and slip into the driver's seat of the car.

"Seraphine!" Leroi yells.

It's too late. I slam my foot on the gas pedal, lurch the car forward and clip the vehicle in front. Someone rushes to the passenger door. It's Gabriel, looking nothing like the emaciated figure from the screen.

"Sera," Gabriel rasps.

This is no apparition. This is no picture on a screen. Everything I knew about the state of my family has been an elaborate lie. I speed down the street, tires squealing and engine roaring. Gabriel tries to run after me, but soon disappears from my rearview mirror.

It takes several heartbeats to realize I've stopped breathing before I fill my lungs with air.

Mom is alive.

Gabriel is healthy.

Leroi is working with Anton.

I can't trust anyone, not even myself, because the knife in my heart burns hotter than the bullet wound in my shoulder.

It was all one giant conspiracy. Samson must have hired Anton's firm to assassinate Dad, Gregor, and their inner circle. I must have been part of, if not all, of the payment. Then Anton ordered his second-in-command to handle me. That's where it gets twisted.

Anton knew I found him disgusting, as did Samson, so they ordered Leroi to get close to me and become my new handler.

They'd learned from their past mistakes and knew I would rebel if Leroi trained me with the chip and collar. That's why they set him up as my white knight. They wanted to direct my loyalty to Leroi, which is why he was so generous and kind.

How could I have been so dumb?

Leroi completed the training that Anton couldn't give me, even going so far as to get me to kill the guards closest to Dad, so that Samson could rule the Capello empire without any opposition.

Shit.

I've been nothing but a pawn.

What if the lie started the night Dad's guards attacked Mom? What if it began with Gabriel, whose throat they slit to stop me from learning the truth? I no longer know what to believe.

I drive through the traffic, trying to outrun my thoughts. The bullet wound is a dull ache, pounding in time with my pulse, but it's nothing compared to the hole in my heart. Everyone I thought I loved is part of this conspiracy. All of them must die.

The street signs lead me to Queen's Gardens. I find my way back to where it all began. Pulling up to the Capello mansion, I park out of sight and open the glove box. After stuffing the gun, the knife, and the computer tablet into Miko's jacket, I place the garment over my shoulders and make my way to Pietro Fiore's house on foot.

———

Pietro's house is the perfect hideout. There's still food in the cupboards and a first-aid kit. The bullet I thought was lodged in my shoulder is actually just a flesh wound and after some pills and some thorough disinfecting, the pain is no longer all-consuming.

Two more men remain on my original list of people to kill: Edoardo Barone and Samson Capello. I still don't know what's real, but something tells me that If I don't kill Edoardo, he'll continue to haunt my nightmares. There's no question about what I want to do with Samson. He will die slowly.

I can't believe Mom is alive and working with Leroi. My mind skips back to the night I couldn't save her, and suddenly, everything makes sense.

She must have seen me through the gap in the door, watching her at the mercy of those men. Seen me standing there, not lifting a finger to help. I let her get beaten and violated, and that's why she teamed up with Anton and Leroi for revenge.

I clutch my temple, trying to quiet my racing thoughts. Time is running out. Samson is still out there with his assassins, and I can't fall back into his or anyone's clutches. Once he's dead, I'll work out how to deal with the others.

A quick search on Miko's tablet reveals three people in town called Edoardo Barone. One of them lives in a small house in Queen's Gardens within a one-minute walk from my new hideout.

This has to be my target.

I wait until after dark, using the rest of the day to gather weapons, fix an omelet, and dye my hair with a fresh batch of coffee. There's even time for a nap. When the streets are quiet and all the houses go dark, I change into a black shirt

I've stolen from Pietro's closet and sneak out of the house with a backpack.

The night is silent, with the only sounds coming from the distant traffic. I make my way down the street with my head bowed to avoid being seen under the streetlights.

Edoardo's house is in the corner, and there's a light on in the living room. My lips tighten. Infiltrating his house without Leroi's help will be difficult, but not impossible. After all, I killed dozens of targets before partnering up with a hitman. I walk around to the back of the house and find an unlocked window.

Hoisting myself up is painful with my flesh wound, but I clench my teeth, and climb into his kitchen. It's a dark space with every surface covered in trash. I land in a crouch, upsetting some plastic food wrappers.

The laugh track of a sitcom draws me out into the hallway and into the living room, where I find a man lounging on a leather couch in front of a wall-mounted television. He sits with his back to me, holding a can of beer, staring at the huge screen.

My lip curls.

How nice of him to unwind after a day's work.

Because of the likes of him, I will never know peace.

I don't really think what happened to Mom was staged. Even if it was, the nightmares I suffered were real, as were the five years I spent in that basement. Edoardo will tell me where I can find Samson or die horribly.

I extract the gun, creep up behind Edoardo, and press the barrel of the gun to the back of his head. "Don't move."

He stiffens, the beer can falling loose from his fat fingers.

"Who the fuck is this?" he snarls.

"The one who's going to blow your brains across your TV if you don't answer my questions."

He forces out a sharp exhale, his large frame trembling with restrained fury. Edoardo seems like the type of man who might grab my wrist and wrestle control of the gun, so I step back out of reach.

"What do you want?" he asks, his voice tight.

"Samson Capello is still alive. I want to know where he's hiding."

"Have you tried the big house?" he snaps.

I don't dignify that stupid question with an answer. Samson wouldn't return to the mansion until he was sure that all his enemies were dead. Instead, I flick off the gun's safety with a click, making Edoardo stiffen.

"Try again, asshole."

Edoardo raises his hands. "Alright, alright. Last thing I heard, he was staying with an associate out of town."

"Where?"

"He didn't say. Some house by Lake Alderney."

My nostrils flare.

He's with Anton.

"That's all I know," Edoardo says. "Now, could you please fuck off?"

I can't muster up the enthusiasm to give him an elaborate death. All my anger has been superseded by the overwhelming pain of everyone's betrayal.

Leroi's treachery cut the deepest. I'd come to terms with losing Mom. She was flawed, but hadn't deserved such a terrible death. Now, I don't know what to think.

My breathing becomes labored. Leroi crafted a persona of my perfect match. A man who knew the pain of being rejected by family and had spent his teens learning to kill, just like me. He gave me hope that there was someone out there who would see me as more than a pawn or prey, when all I was to him was both.

"Hello?" Edoardo snaps, his harsh voice snapping me out of my musings. "You got what you want, so—"

I cut off his rant with a bullet in the throat, and he falls off the sofa with a heavy thud. Killing is dull without an audience.

My journey out of his house is a blur of jumbled thoughts. Thoughts of Mom. thoughts of Gabriel, thoughts of Leroi and the hole I sliced into his gut. Thoughts of how on earth I'm going to find Anton's house. It's probably in Miko's address book. If not, maybe I'll find a clue in the photos.

Pain drags my heart down to my ankles, creating imaginary shackles. Even though I knew this thing I had with Leroi was too good to be true, I'd prepared my mind for a betrayal, but not of this magnitude. My worst-case scenario was Leroi being fickle, and one day casting me out. It never crossed my mind that he could be one of the masterminds conspiring to enslave my heart.

And Mom? I don't even know what to think.

The only way to clear my mind is to keep killing enemies until I get answers. With any luck, I'll find where Samson is hiding with Anton and pick them off one by one.

As I sneak back into Pietro's house, a sharp pain pierces my arm. I glance down what's sticking out of my skin: the red tailpiece of a tranquilizer dart.

I break into a run and yank it out, but it's already too late. It takes no time before my steps grow heavy and my muscles succumb to the sedative.

Darkness clouds my vision, and I stumble to my knees.

As I hit the floor, rough hands roll me onto my back and I stare into the furious eyes of my attacker.

Miko flashes his teeth. "You're going to pay for stabbing Leroi."

SEVENTY-ONE

LEROI

Pain lances through the stab wound, setting my insides aflame. My knees hit the ground, and I yell at Seraphine to stop. She thinks I'm attacking her mother, but she doesn't understand I was trying to stop her from running. Blood rushes from my abdomen at an alarming rate, and the edges of my vision fill with a dark mist.

Shit.

Of all the times to get stabbed, why is it when I'm still off balance from the explosion?

Seraphine slides in Miko's car and tears away in one direction, while Evangeline sprints down another. My vision fills with Miko's frantic features before everything goes black.

———

I don't know how much time passes, but the next time I awaken, it's on a cloud of opiates that fills my mind with fluff. The hard surface beneath my back rumbles, and my nostrils fill with the sharp scent of antiseptic.

The pain in my abdomen floats somewhere on the edge of my consciousness, almost like a memory. I struggle to open my eyes, but it feels like they're weighted down with sandbags. Where is Seraphine? Can she even drive a car?

A memory resurfaces of her telling me that she got lessons from her driver, when Miko's voice slices through the haze.

"Leroi?"

All I can think of is Seraphine. She's out there, frightened and alone and betrayed, maybe even adding me to the list of bastards who hurt her mother. I can't let her think our time together wasn't real.

"Doctor," Miko says. "He's awake."

"Let me take a look," replies a deeper voice.

Footsteps approach, and I peer into the eyes of a dark-skinned man with closely cropped hair. It's Sal, our resident doctor, who operates without a license.

My gaze darts around what looks like the interior of an ambulance, judging by the rumbling beneath me and how much medical equipment is stacked on the walls of this cramped space.

Thoughts of Seraphine race through my mind. What if seeing Evangeline triggered her to continue tracking Capello's guards alone? She has no tech, no weapons, and no backup. What if she crashes Miko's car on the highway and gets herself killed?

A fog closes in on my mind, trying to pull me under, but I clench my jaw and struggle.

I can't lie here while she's abandoned and suffering.

When I raise myself up on my elbows, Sal shoves me back down on the cot with a hand on my chest. "Relax," he says. "You're in a triage van with a minor laceration on your back and an abdominal wound that's lost you a fuckload of blood."

I turn to Miko, whose face is so pale that I wonder if he's the one who's nearly bleeding to death.

"You shot Seraphine." My voice comes out hoarse and gravelly.

He flinches, but before Miko can reply, Sal reappears at his side with a wide grin. "Heard you got taken down by a girl."

"This one is special," I mutter.

"You're lucky to be alive." The medic chuckles. "Good thing for you this girl of yours had a terrible aim, or you'd be dead."

My hackles rise. If she missed, it was on purpose. Seraphine's knife skills are impeccable. Anton would have trained her in advanced anatomy. I rear up, but Sal clenches my shoulder.

"I need to find her," I grind out.

Sal grips my other shoulder. "Take it easy, or you'll open up your wound."

Miko grabs my arm. "I'll find her. Just focus on getting better."

Sal injects something into my IV line, and my eyes droop under the weight of the fresh cocktail of drugs. I breathe harder, trying to fight the sedative's effects, but they keep pulling me under.

All I can see is Seraphine's pretty features, twisted with hurt and betrayal. I need to find her and explain that I wasn't hurting Evangeline.

Miko's voice filters through the growing haze. "The car tracker says she's heading toward Queen's Gardens. Don't worry, Leroi. I'll make everything right."

———

The next time I awaken, I'm staring at the white walls of a familiar-looking infirmary. It's our firm's out-of-town building beneath the abandoned warehouse. It's where I knew Seraphine was the one for me when she drilled through Paolo Rochas' urethra.

Seraphine.

Claws of worry reach through the wound in my gut and twist my heart until I'm gasping for air.

She's still out there, injured, confused, and probably thinking she doesn't have a single ally in the world. The last words Miko said to me as I fell unconscious sit in my gut like lead.

He shot at her. Now he's going to make things right?

Dread coils through my insides like a garotte.

I have to save her.

"Miko?"

I grip the hospital bed's metal frame and force myself up to sit.

The door at the end opens, and Sal walks in. "Did you know someone threw a grenade into your apartment?"

"Where is Miko?"

"He left about an hour ago."

"Shit."

I swing my legs out of bed. The infirmary tilts, and I reel back under a tidal wave of dizziness.

Sal grabs me by the midsection and holds me steady. "You're in no shape to go anywhere. Miko said he'd take care of the girl. Rest, and he'll be back soon."

"Out of my way." I shove past him and stumble to the closet door.

"At least pick up the phone and call Miko."

My stomach lurches at the thought of him getting caught by the bastards who blew up my apartment. I snatch my phone off the bedside table and dial Miko's number, but it goes straight to voicemail.

Damn it.

When I check my text messages, the last one from Miko reads:

I've agreed on a truce and will deliver her to Samson.

"What?"

My fingers grip the phone so tightly that my knuckles turn white. Rage burns through my veins at the thought that Miko has betrayed me and is delivering Seraphine to Samson.

The message is time stamped two hours earlier. I can't believe what I'm reading without context, so I scroll up to the text he sent five hours earlier:

I'll take care of it before you wake up.

I move on to the text before that one.

He must know you and S are working your way through the bodyguards.

Before that is the message:

Samson hired the Moirai Group to take you out. They're the ones who attacked your apartment.

The cold dread pooling in my gut evaporates under the force of my fury. I taught Miko better than to be an imbecile. How could he consider bartering Seraphine in exchange for Samson calling off the hit? He could have called Rita to mobilize the other operatives who work for the firm. Instead, he's chosen to stab me in the back.

Time is running out. I have to find Miko before Seraphine gets hurt. I fling open the closet door and throw on some sweats and a pair of shoes.

"Boss." Sal follows me out of the infirmary.

"Give me your keys." I hold out my hand.

"I'll drive." He darts back into the infirmary and reemerges, holding a set of car keys in one hand and a doctor's bag in the other. "Do you know where we're going?"

I scroll through my phone to the app that tracks all our vehicles and devices. Miko's phone has stopped at a location in Alderney Heights. I find the house number and bark out the address.

Sal hurries to keep up with my long strides as I march toward the garage. I make a frenzied call to Roman, barely able to hear him over my racing heart. His mansion is half a mile away, further up in Alderney Heights, and he still owes me for the Capello job.

When he agrees to storm the house, I can't even feel a flicker of relief. Not when Miko is handing Seraphine over to a rapist so vile that she had no choice but to bite through his penis.

If Seraphine gets so much as a scratch, I'm killing everyone.

SEVENTY-TWO

SERAPHINE

I can't move, not even to blink. Whatever was in that tranquilizer is that strong. Even breathing is an effort, and the only part of my body that works is my overactive heart. Cold sweat breaks out across my skin as he drags me down the street to the back of his car, each movement making my flesh wound burn like a brand.

Is he taking me back to Leroi? A shiver runs down my spine. It won't be Leroi. He's injured. Miko is taking me back to Anton.

He opens the back door of a car and hauls me onto the leather seat. My breath hitches and tears burn the backs of my eyes. If I don't find a way to overcome this drug, I'll relive my last five years in the basement, only it will be worse.

There will be no Dad telling the twins not to break me because Anton will be in charge. He'll finally have the access he always wanted to my body, but he won't make the same mistakes as Samson. I wasn't collared that time I bit him—only bound by rope. Anton will bury a new chip somewhere so deep inside me, no one will be able to set me free.

The car pulls out and speeds down the road, jostling me around on the back seat. It reminds me of the first time Miko transported me out of Queen's Gardens, when I was relieved to be leaving but a little wary.

Now, I'm terrified.

One sharp turn has me rolling off the seat and slamming onto the floor. Pain shoots up my spine, but it's nothing compared to the fear gripping my heart. I try to scream, but my vocal cords won't cooperate. I try to thrash, but my body won't move. Miko has rendered me completely helpless.

As the car races down the highway, regret surges through my veins like acid. After leaving the basement, I could have escaped Leroi or killed him in his sleep, but I fell for the lure of finally having a protector. Leroi had played the perfect gentleman and had even refused my advances until Anton gave him permission to cross the line.

I've been so bloody stupid.

All this time, I fantasized about finding companionship and I even fooled myself that it might be love. Now, I see the truth. My time in Leroi's apartment only brought me one step closer to falling into the clutches of Anton.

Bitter thoughts continue to wind through my mind as the car careens around the sharp bends of a hillside. Now, I can see the clues in the conspiracy that I should have spotted. Cold-blooded killers like Leroi don't lose control of their emotions or break their own rules unless it's part of an act. Leroi's slow surrender was just part of his and Anton's elaborate plan.

He probably isn't even allergic to chocolate. That was just a ploy to make the fountain seem like a huge sacrifice.

The overwhelming scent of juniper trees seeping

through the window tells me we're in Alderney Heights. Terror grips my heart and my veins surge with icy panic. What if I miscalculated and Miko is taking me back to the Montesano mansion, and the three brothers want to punish me for killing their father? That would make sense, since I confessed the murder to Leroi. I don't think I can survive another day of captivity.

The car comes to a sudden stop, jolting me back to the present. Miko winds down the window and has a hushed conversation with some men. Someone opens the back door and scoops me off the floor.

"Alright," Miko says. "I've delivered the girl. Tell your boss to call off the hit."

"He wants to see you, too."

As I try to make sense of what's happening, the man flings me over his shoulder and takes long strides toward a building. Each step over the gravel makes my gut churn. The drugs still have a tight grip on my muscles, but I can at least move my eyes.

With a muttered curse, Miko exits the car and has to jog to keep up with the man's brisk pace. All I can see of my surroundings is the man's back.

"Take her upstairs," says a voice that makes the fine hairs on the back of my neck stand on end.

Samson.

My breath catches. I don't know if that's better or worse. With no one to restrain Samson from his twisted urges, I'll be facing an unimaginably brutal fate.

By the time the man carrying me ascends the stairs, the drugs have worn off enough to allow my limbs to twitch. Rough hands thread through my hair and yank up my head, forcing me to meet Samson's eyes.

They're even more soulless than ever. Blown pupils

ringed with a thin strip of green and surrounded by dark circles. "Welcome back, Sera. You've caused me a lot of trouble."

I want to spit in his face, but the muscles around my mouth won't cooperate.

"Mr Capello?" Miko asks. "You said things would be even between us if I brought Seraphine?"

The tremor in Miko's voice tells me he's just realized he's walked into the stronghold of a psychopath and won't be allowed to leave. Samson will use Miko as a hostage to lure Anton and Leroi out of hiding. If the trio are truly a family, there will be a fight. If not, then Miko might not live to see tomorrow.

Nausea ripples through my insides. I'm so sickened at the thought of falling into Samson's clutches again that I can't even find any pleasure that Miko just walked into a trap.

The man carrying me stops mounting the stairs, and Samson directs him to a white room that smells of antiseptic. When he lays me on a hard surface, I finally get to see my surroundings.

We're in an infirmary, but I don't think Samson wants to provide me with medical attention. I scan the room for weapons or any means of escape, but it's windowless, with a single door that's blocked by two leering guards.

I'm lying on an operating table, and there's a small trolley beside me containing surgical tools. Alarm squeezes my chest at the horror of my situation, but I slide an arm toward the scalpel.

"Should I strip her, boss?" the man asks.

My skin crawls, and I try to roll off the table, but Samson holds my neck in a tight grip, his fingers digging into my flesh.

"No," he says with a wide grin. "Sera will strip for us after our guest installs the new chip."

I shudder, my flesh crawling at the thought of exposing myself to these monsters. It took me years to build a tolerance for Samson, yet that's now crumbled under the pretense of freedom I enjoyed with Leroi.

Miko's breath catches. "Wait. I don't know how to implant electronics into humans."

Samson releases my throat, spins on his heel, and grabs Miko by the scruff of the neck. "Then you'd better learn. You and that bastard tampered with my sister and I can't track her on the app. I want her back exactly as you found her."

My jaw tightens. I'm not his sister.

"What's with that face?" Samson grips my chin. "I went to all this trouble to bring you home, and you're not even grateful."

"It's probably the muscle relaxant," Miko says.

Samson leans so close that I can smell his acrid breath. It's a stomach-churning mix of alcohol and something metallic. He's probably back on the drugs.

"Did you fuck him?" he asks, his gaze trailing down the borrowed male clothes I'm still wearing. "Of course you did. I saw the way you were with him when you stepped out of that club. But what I want to know is why he isn't dead like all the others?"

My nostrils flare, and I jerk my head, but the drugs slow my attempt to escape his grasp.

Samson can go to hell. Leroi might have been a liar and a schemer, but he was the first man who didn't make me feel like an object. At least until I discovered he was warming me up for Anton.

The grip on my chin releases, only for Samson to return holding a collar.

"Put it on her and plug it to the mains socket," he says.

Miko takes the collar with trembling hands and fastens it around my neck. My eyes water as the cold metal digs into my skin. I can't let this happen.

"Boss," a deep voice says from the doorway. "There's a convoy of vehicles approaching from the top of the hill. Some of them are armored."

"What?" Samson roars. "We weren't supposed to be on their radar until next week."

He charges out of the room with his guards, and the tightness in my chest loosens long enough for me to grab the scalpel.

SEVENTY-THREE

LEROI

Sal crawls up the winding roads, gripping the steering wheel as though that's the only thing stopping the car from careening down the side of the hill. No matter how many times I call, Miko's phone still goes straight to voicemail. I can't shake off the image of Samson torturing Seraphine.

"Faster," I growl, my fingers curling around the device. "We have to reach her before it's too late."

"I'm trying," he says, his gaze fixed on the road ahead.

The car lurches forward, making the tires screech around the corner. I grab hold of the handle above my head and brace myself for another sharp turn.

The distant sound of gunshots offers zero reassurance. I knew Roman would pull through with his men, but if Seraphine gets hurt in the crossfire...

Bright light from an oncoming vehicle fills the windshield, and I have to squint against the glare. Sal slams on the brakes and swerves to the side, avoiding a head-on collision. Pain shoots through my abdomen as the seat belt digs into my wound, making me hiss.

"You okay?" Sal shoots me a worried glance.

"Fine," I grind out through gritted teeth. "Keep going."

We round another bend, and I catch sight of activity within the trees. Vehicles are parked haphazardly, with men advancing toward a mansion already alight with gunfire.

"Stop the car." I unbuckle my seatbelt, already opening the door before Sal can park.

"I'll wait for you here," he yells as I rush into the trees.

The canopy blocks out the moonlight, but I'm guided by the sight and sound of gunfire. I run toward the building, each step hitting like a sucker punch to my wound. Pushing past the excruciating pain, I pull out my gun and run through the twisted scraps of metal Romans trucks have made of the gate.

His men have already breached the mansion's front doors and have littered its grand foyer with corpses. Movement out of the corner of my eye has me swinging my pistol to the left. Roman steps out of a doorway with a semi-automatic.

He lowers his weapon and smirks. "You're late."

"What's the situation?" I rush toward the staircase with Roman following close behind.

"We've taken out most of his guys. Samson either fled at the first sign of trouble or he and some guards are holed up behind a fortified door on the third floor."

Shit.

If it's as well-guarded as the basement where I found Seraphine, the security will be impenetrable. "Any other ways in?"

He flicks his head toward the front door. "There's a balcony."

"Show me."

Roman runs outside, and I follow suit, having to clutch

my wound to absorb the impact of my steps. We race around to the back of the building, where one of his trucks has barreled through the rose garden, and men in bullet proof armor scale a woody vine covering the wall toward an iron balcony.

My gaze snaps up to the balcony and a pair of Samson's guards pointing automatic weapons downward, hindering their progress. I shake my head. They're going about this the wrong way.

"Cesare wants to end this siege with a bazooka," Roman mutters.

"Where is he?" I growl.

"I sent him home."

Good. I always preferred dealing with Benito and Roman. Cesare is a brat who never thinks further than satisfying his own temper. His plan would wipe out the last Capello, but it would also kill Miko and Seraphine.

"I'm beginning to think Cesare has a point," Roman says. "Those assholes have been shooting down on my men for ten minutes straight and still haven't run out of ammo."

My jaw tightens, and I squint up toward the balcony. Samson's men are well protected, but not completely. They've lifted their visors to get a better view of the climbers, and I catch glimpses of their necks between their helmets and the collars of their armor.

"Order your guys to retreat to the van," I mutter.

Roman passes on the commands to one of his men, who sprints toward the others trying to scale the walls. Then he turns to me and asks, "What's the plan?"

"I need those bastards' attention on a fixed spot."

"To make an easier target?"

"Exactly."

Minutes later, Roman's men position themselves

around the van, while the shooters on the balcony direct their fire at the vehicle. I can't even find satisfaction in them acting as I predicted because that Capello psychopath could be up there mutilating Seraphine.

I slink around the side of the building, close one eye, and peer up to the third floor. The man standing on the side closest to me leans over the balcony and shoots.

Taking aim at an exposed patch of skin on his neck, I fire off a single round.

He drops his weapon and topples over the side. I don't bother to follow the trajectory of his body because I'm already aiming at his companion. As the second man falls, the garden fills with a chorus of cheers.

Roman claps my back so hard that I feel the force of his blow in both of my knife wounds. "Nice shooting, man."

It's too early for congratulations. Seraphine is still in the house, and there's no sign of Samson Capello.

"Let's go," I say from clenched teeth.

Roman follows me to the wall, where the men from around the van gather. I turn to one who's about my size and demand his armor. My cousin does the same.

Moments later, we're scaling the walls, using the branches of the climbing plant to pull ourselves up. Sweat gathers on my brow and the wound in my gut pounds to the beat of my heart. There's no doubt that I'm breaking out in a fever. I don't need to feel the warm trickle of blood down my front to know that I've busted my stitches.

I can't stop now. Not until I save Seraphine. Not until I hold Samson Capello down while she carves out his heart.

We reach the balcony, and I'm the first one at its glass doors. Beyond them is an empty room, where two guards in black suits stand with their backs to me, their guns pointed at a reinforced metal door. I'm assuming Roman's men are standing on the other side, trying to shoot their way in.

There's no sign of Seraphine, but I spot a door to the left of the space.

Roman joins my side, and we both take aim at the men and fire through the glass. They drop to the ground, and Roman opens the door.

"After you."

"Don't shoot Samson," I say. "He belongs to Seraphine."

Roman scowls and is about to argue when there's a scream from the door on the left. My stomach lurches. It's her.

I push past Roman and rush through the door into an infirmary. Seraphine is lying strapped to a table, her chest rising and falling with rapid breaths. Two figures stand over her, one of them I recognize as Miko, and he's holding a scalpel. The larger one whirls around, revealing the twisted features of Samson Capello.

Samson's eyes widen. His gaze bounces from me to Roman before he bursts into a high-pitched giggle.

"Montesano? You've come to rescue the girl who—"

I shoot Samson in the gut.

Roman shoots me a glare.

"He and his twisted family kept her as their toy since she was sixteen," I snarl. "He doesn't get to disrespect her honor."

Roman's eyes soften, and he nods, seeming to understand.

It wasn't a complete lie. Seraphine might have killed Uncle Enzo, but she had no choice. Samson doesn't get to recast what she did as a cold-blooded assassination.

As I move toward Seraphine, Miko edges around the

table brandishing the scalpel. "Stay back," he says. "I haven't finished installing the chip."

"Put down the scalpel," I say through clenched teeth.

"You don't get it. The only way Samson will call off that hit on you is if we give back Seraphine. Then we can get on with our lives and no one else will blow up the apartment."

"Are you really that dense?" I growl. "Let. Her. Go."

Miko flinches, his features hardening. "You've been obsessed with her from the beginning. Can't you see she's crazy? Now, you've shot Samson because you don't want anyone to know—"

Seraphine stabs him in the groin with a metal object, just as I shoot him between the eyes. Whatever Miko was about to reveal about Seraphine dies with his last breath.

Time stills as he falls to the floor. A kaleidoscope of memories assault my mind at once, starting with the moment a skinny and broken kid walked in on me while I was killing his stepfather.

A fist of emotion punches through my ribcage and seizes my heart, squeezing so tightly that I can't breathe. Miko was supposed to be the one whose hands I kept clean. He was supposed to have a better life than the one he escaped when I took him from his addict mother.

And I killed him without hesitation.

My gaze drops to Seraphine, whose face looks even paler with her new dye job. Her figure appears even more frail when she's wearing men's clothes.

The fist around my heart releases, and I exhale. I would kill every motherfucker a hundred times if it meant keeping Seraphine safe. She is everything.

"Hey." Roman's voice cuts through the blood roaring between my ears. "Isn't that the boy you adopted?"

"He tried to make a truce with Capello." I rush forward to unbuckle Seraphine's restraints.

That's not the reason why I killed Miko. He was about to reveal to my cousin that Seraphine Uncle Enzo. Roman would shoot Seraphine without a moment's hesitation, and I would have to shoot Roman. Even if she survived Roman, Cesare, Benito, and every man loyal to the Montesano brothers wouldn't stop hunting us until we were dead.

Roman hesitates behind me for several heartbeats too long, making the fine hairs on the back of my head stand on end. Before I can work out how the hell I'm going to deal with my cousin's suspicions, he clears his throat.

"While I scout the rest of the house for survivors, make sure that Capello bastard dies," Roman says as he jogs out of the room and down a flight of stairs.

I'm about to answer when I'm distracted by the press of cold steel on my neck.

Seraphine is holding the scalpel to my throat.

SEVENTY-FOUR

SERAPHINE

My breath comes in shallow pants and I dart my gaze from side to side, trying to figure out what the hell just happened. Leroi shot Miko. Why?

I quiet my mind long enough to hear Leroi explain his reasons to Roman Montesano. Maybe Leroi wasn't working with Samson, but he must have taken me out of the basement on the orders of Anton.

My jaw clenches.

Dad only paid Anton for six months of training, after that, the twins became my handlers. After Dad dismissed Anton from training me, Anton must have worked out a way to break through the basement's security. He couldn't extract me himself because he knew I wouldn't leave with him.

That's why Anton chose a fresh face. A handsome face. A face I would find appealing.

Roman leaves, and Leroi begins to unfasten the straps of the operating table with urgent movements, his breathing harsh and labored. Now that he's trained me to accept sexual pleasure, he's anxious to deliver me to his father figure.

My heart pounds so hard that the bones of my ribcage tremble. I only have one chance of freedom, and I won't let it go to waste.

The moment he leans close enough to unbuckle the restraint around my neck, I grab hold of his lapel and press the scalpel to his throat.

"Seraphine." Leroi hisses through his teeth.

"Don't move," I say.

He raises both palms.

I ease myself up and slide the blade of the scalpel toward the thick vein running down the side of his neck. Leroi's breathing quickens, but he makes no move to escape.

"You're not taking me back to Anton," I say, my voice low.

"He's dead," Leroi says between panting breaths.

I press the scalpel deeper into his flesh and nick his skin. A bead of blood gathers on the dirty blade before it rolls down Leroi's neck.

"Don't lie to me," I say. "I overheard the doorman say your father was on his way up."

Leroi swallows, his Adam's apple bobbing up and down. He's calculating whether he can step away without his throat slit. I press the scalpel a little harder, and he shudders.

"Why do you think I rushed upstairs so quickly and left you behind in the room? It was to keep you hidden from Anton."

Clashing thoughts and emotions swirl through my mind, making a mess of confusion. I shake off the doubts and stay focused on Leroi and his half-truths.

"But you were working for him all this time."

"No," he snarls. "Anton retired over five years ago. He left his firm to me."

"That doesn't mean a thing. I saw the fishing photos."

He closes his eyes, every muscle in his face tightening. "It's been months since I took Miko to Anton's lake house, but that doesn't mean we were working together."

"Why did you lie about not knowing him?"

"I..." He sighs. "I should have said something, but I didn't want to overload you with the truth. Seraphine, you've got to believe me when I tell you that I wanted to keep you away from Anton."

"Why are you lying about him being dead?"

"I shot him upstairs and wanted to present you with his head." He swallows. "It's waiting for you in the refrigerator."

My eyes narrow. Would he really decapitate his father figure?

"Finding you in Capello's basement was a coincidence. The next day, Anton called to say that the girl he'd trained to be an assassin was missing, and I thought I could keep you hidden."

"So you could train me to work for you?"

He clenches his teeth. "Because you were innocent. Because you didn't deserve to be corrupted by those sick bastards. Because I wanted to keep you safe."

There's a harshness to his voice that betrays his emotions, and the way he stares down at me with glistening eyes says he means every word. I shake off that thought. Leroi has already proven himself to be a liar. At least by omission.

"You killed Miko," I say.

"He shot at you, brought you to your abuser." His gaze

darts toward the exit, where Roman just left. "You'd be dead if he'd finished what he was about to say."

Tears sting the backs of my eyes. The bitterness in his voice makes me pause, because Leroi hardly ever shows so much emotion.

Maybe he's telling the truth?

My throat thickens, and it's my turn to swallow. He's trying to throw me off. Make me think I'm confused. At any moment, he's going to find an opening, and I'll be the one with a blade to my throat.

Or a pistol to my head.

"Why haven't you reached for your gun?" I ask.

His jaw tightens. "I don't want to hurt you."

"Why not?"

"I've killed two of the most important people in my life for you. For your protection," he says through gritted teeth. "Isn't it obvious, Seraphine?"

I shake my head. "No."

"Because I love you," he adds.

The words hit like a punch to the throat, and I gasp for breath. Leroi can't mean it. He's just saying whatever is necessary to save me from cutting open his veins.

"And you love me, too," he says.

"You're wrong," I snap.

"Every man who has ever touched you is either dead or disfigured," he says. "Yet I'm still here with only a stab wound. You purposely missed my vital organs. That's your way of showing me love, angel."

"That's stupid."

He chuckles. "Is it? You're holding this scalpel to my throat and not cutting it. That's your way of saying you want us to be together."

I huff a laugh. "You're delusional."

"I love you, Seraphine, and you know it. I don't kill people for free, but I've murdered more than I can count just to keep you safe."

"Four kills is nothing. I've murdered over twice as many."

The corner of his lips lifts into a smirk. "Keep telling yourself that, sweetheart. I owed Anton my life, yet I killed him because he hurt you. I loved Miko like a little brother, but I was ready to put a bullet through his head for trying to reinsert that chip."

"What about the man in the nightclub?" I ask, my voice wavering.

"He touched what was mine," Leroi says with a snarl. "And the bum in the gas station deserved what he got for showing you disrespect."

My breath shallows and my heart beats so hard I can barely sift through my thoughts. His words are unsettling. He's using facts to prove his point and make me give into his charm.

"That doesn't explain what you were doing with Mom," I rasp.

He exhales a long breath. "Anton told me she was alive. There was even an address on his phone. After the assassins blew up the apartment, I decided to track her down and see for myself."

"Wait." My fingers tighten around the scalpel. "Someone tried to kill you?"

"Samson put a hit out on me. Rosalind must have shared the location of my apartment with her employer because two of them came to the door while I was cleaning up Anton's blood."

The way he says it is so convincing, and he has so much evidence to back up his lies. I saw Rosalind twice, heard her little sister come to the door to ask if she was in the apartment, and then there was that meeting in Alderney Hills to discuss the assassins.

Leroi's too skilled at lying because everything sounds like the truth.

"Why didn't you tell me about Mom?" I ask.

"By the time I found out, you and Miko had already left to find Gabriel. Besides, I didn't want to raise your hopes in case what Anton told me was bullshit."

"But you were hugging her."

"No," he rasps. "I was trying to stop her from running away. All this time, Gabriel has thought you were dead. He yelled at her to tell the truth."

I flinch, the word hitting like a slap. Leroi is trying to shift my anger to Mom by saying she knew Dad kept me in his basement.

"Don't change the subject," I snarl. "We're talking about you and your lies."

Leroi closes his eyes and inhales a deep, calming breath the way he does when he's meditating or trying not to be impatient. The only thing missing is him rubbing a finger on the bridge of his nose. "If you're so determined to see me as the villain, then kill me."

"What?" I whisper.

He opens his eyes again, his gaze boring so deeply into my soul that I draw back. "Don't think I haven't seen the pictures you drew of me in that little sketchbook. You used up so much red ink, I had to buy you replacement pens. If you're so desperate to spill my blood, then do it."

I try to pull my hand away, but he snatches my wrist.

"Say you don't love me, Seraphine."

He leans into the blade, letting it cut into his skin. Blood pours freely from the wound, trickles down the scalpel's handle, and onto my fingers.

"What are you doing?" I jerk my hand away, but Leroi's grip holds it in place.

"If you don't love me, then finish me."

Tears blur my vision. I blink them away, but they're only replaced by more. I don't want Leroi dead. Who would I cuddle up to if he dies? Who would supply me with chocolate fountains and mind-blowing orgasms? Who would make me breakfast and chase away my nightmares?

My fingers loosen around the scalpel, and it falls to the floor with a clang.

"Don't die." I fling my arms around his neck. "I couldn't stand it if you were gone."

Leroi pulls me into a hug. "I'm not going anywhere, angel. But you'll need to let go of me if you don't want Samson Capello to crawl out the door."

SEVENTY-FIVE

LEROI

Tearing myself away from Seraphine on the operating table, I cross the room to where the last Capello shuffles on his hands and knees toward his fallen lackey's pistol.

My footsteps are light, but I doubt he can hear me through his labored breaths. Gunshot wounds to the gut are excruciating, but not immediately fatal, and I intend to deliver him to Seraphine alive.

Overtaking him, I kick the pistol away, sending it skidding across the floor. Samson's eyes snap up to meet mine, his features twisted into a rictus of pain.

"Let me go, and I won't kill you," he says.

I pull him up by the lapels. Pain flares across my abdomen, and I clench my teeth. "You're in no position to make demands."

"What the fuck do you want?" he asks with a pained moan.

"Call your contact at the Moirai Group and cancel the hit."

He laughs, the sound grating my eardrums. "So you can kill me?"

"Your men are all dead, as is your family. That leaves you with two choices. I can kill you slowly until you beg for death, or you can die fast with a bullet through the skull."

Samson's features drop, and his face pales. "I'll call off the hit, but only on the condition that you don't kill me."

"Fine."

"Swear on your life."

My brow rises. "Are you serious?"

"Swear on your fucking life."

Sweat beads across my brow. and I clench my jaw. Of all the ridiculous bullshit. But I'll play along because the Moirai are like a hydra. Cut down one assassin, and two more will spring up to avenge their fallen comrade. They're relentless, focusing on quantity over quality, not caring about the collateral damage they inflict to guarantee results.

"Alright then," I rasp.

Spots dance in my vision. I suck in a deep breath and chase them away. "I, Leroi Montesano, swear on my life that I will not put a bullet through Samson Capello's head. Nor will I keep him alive and give him a lingering death."

Samson nods, and I release him. He hits the ground with a pained grunt. I reach into the back pocket of his pants and pull out his phone.

"Don't try anything stupid." I push the device into his trembling fingers.

"I won't."

He dials a number. As it rings, I lean down and put the phone on speaker.

"Moirai?" asks a deep voice.

"This is client number 732," Samson says, his breath

labored. "I'm calling to cancel the contract on the lone gunman."

The person on the other end of the line hesitates for a moment before asking, "Are you under duress?"

"No," he grinds out.

"Cancellations at this stage in the process are non-refundable," the man from Moirai says. "Are you sure you wish to proceed?

"Yes," Samson growls.

"Very well. Consider it done."

Snatching the phone off the floor sends a lash of agony through my insides that makes my breath catch. Ignoring it, I hang up and slip it into my pocket.

Samson slumps to the floor with a large exhale. "Now, call me a fucking ambulance."

Sweat soaks my front as I drag him back toward where I left Seraphine sitting on the operating table. She hops down and moves to a tray holding the surgical equipment and a brand new collar.

"What are you doing?" Samson asks, his voice rising several octaves. "You swore—"

"Not to kill you," I say and haul him onto the operating table with a grin. The wound in my stomach screams with protest, but the pain is worth the effort. "I made no promises about Seraphine."

"Let go of me," Samson yells.

Seraphine returns to my side. "Turn him over," she says, her voice cold. "We're going to stick this collar around his neck and then implant a chip."

Samson struggles, but I use the momentum of his movements to lay him on his front. Sharp pains punctuate each breath as I strap him in, and blood soaks the front of my black shirt and down my pants. At this rate, I won't stay conscious long enough to enjoy the show.

"Don't do this, Sera," Samson says, his voice breaking. "We can work something out. Whatever you want."

I back away, prop myself against the wall, and text Sal my location.

Seraphine turns around and gives me a dazzling smile, which fades to alarm. "Leroi?"

"I'm alright." I shake my head. "It's just a scratch."

Her gaze falls to the blood pooling at my feet. She drops the collar and rushes to my side. "You're hurt."

"It's nothing."

She rips open my shirt, revealing the soaked bandage. "I did this," she cries. "Oh, Leroi. I'm so sorry."

Of all the violent acts I've seen Seraphine commit, she has never once shown a scrap of remorse. Remorse for damaging furniture, making messes, or getting blood on food, but never for the carnage she's inflicted on another human being.

As the edges of my vision go black, I wonder if this is her way of showing love. If so, I'll take it.

———

Much later, I'm lounging on imaginary clouds. Fingertips running up and down my chest pull me out of slumber. I inhale a deep breath and inhale the faint scent of strawberries.

"Seraphine?" I croak.

"Go back to sleep," she murmurs. "Dr. Sal says you're not allowed out of bed for a week."

"Where am I?"

"Roman said we could stay in his cottage."

I crack open an eye to find Seraphine cuddled up to my side. There's a lightness in her expression I've never seen before. I'm not hopeful enough to believe that I've solved all her problems, but the darkness in her eyes has retreated to let in more light.

"Why not one of his spare rooms?"

She raises a shoulder. "He didn't want to house a Capello."

My brow furrows, and I wonder how much Seraphine told my cousin about her past.

"Not me," she says with a bright smile. "Samson."

I pinch the bridge of my nose. "He's still alive?"

She gives me an eager nod. "Roman let me bring him back with us. I was saving the best part for you."

"Seraphine," I say, my breaths going shallow. "What have you done?"

She lowers her gaze and walks her fingers up my chest, her lips curving with mischief. I let out an exasperated chuckle.

I knew what I was getting into when I allowed myself to kiss Seraphine. She isn't the kind of woman who would balk at my line of work because her hands are just as steeped in blood as mine. Besides, nothing she could ever do to Samson would compensate for the horrors of her five years in that basement.

"Don't huff and puff when I prove you wrong," she says.

"Wrong about what?" I ask.

"See, you're already getting huffy," she says, her voice light.

"Seraphine," I growl.

"Alright."

She sits up, letting the sheets slide down her body, revealing delicate curves that steal my breath. The wound in my gut throbs, but it's nothing compared to what she's doing to my aching cock.

I groan as she stretches, her body arching so beautifully that I lose track of my suspicions. Then she glances over her shoulder at me, her eyes gleaming, a smile playing on those pretty lips. It's not difficult to see why she's such a successful killer. Seraphine is a siren and I would let her lure me to a watery death.

"Want to see?" she asks.

"No." I lean back against the pillows. "Dr. Sal says I should stay in this bed for a week."

She hops off the mattress. "If you don't come now, he'll start to smell."

"What?"

She giggles, puts on a satin robe, and disappears behind another door. Throwing off the covers, I swing my legs off the edge of the bed. The pain in my gut isn't as acute as it was the night before, and there are no red patches seeping through the dressings.

"After Dr. Sal fixed your wounds, I made him heal Samson," she says from beyond the door, seeming to read my mind.

"Why?"

"To keep him alive for this," she replies.

Curiosity gives me an energy boost. I've never seen her so happy or light-hearted. I pad after her in my boxers, still not knowing what to expect.

Samson Capello lies in a bathtub of diluted blood. The handle of a scalpel protrudes from one closed eye, and the other is wide open in a rictus of horror. Deep gouges criss-cross his chest, some of them revealing glimpses of muscle and tendons.

"And before you complain, I didn't touch his junk directly," she says. "I used a knife and fork."

It takes a few moments for my brain to process the lumps of flesh floating in the red water are his testicles and what remained of his half-rotted penis. Gruesome wouldn't fully encompass the scene. It looks like one of Seraphine's pictures.

His rasping breaths fill the room, punctuated by the occasional moan. I'm impressed at how she's managed to keep him alive.

She has outdone herself.

The sound of a hairdryer breaks me out of my thoughts, and I tear my gaze away from Samson's disembodied genitals to find Seraphine standing over him holding a hairdryer attached to the mains.

My eyes widen. "What are you—"

She drops the appliance into the tub. Samson's body thrashes, splashing red-tinged water over her pretty robe, and then falls still.

She turns to me, her smile bright. "I told you!"

"Told me what?" I ask.

"You said my story about the man I electrocuted in the bathtub was bullshit," she says. "Now that you've seen the proof, it's time for you to apologize."

My gaze darts from the smartphone balancing on the sink, the metal scalpel embedded in his eye, and the empty bags of salt strewn on the floor. She must have searched to find a way to make the water more conductive just to prove her point.

My heart swells with pride at the thought of her researching ways to hone her craft.

"Come here," I say.

She walks over with her chin raised, looking triumphant.

I pull her into my chest. "You're perfect just the way you are. Don't ever change."

"And?"

"And I'm sorry."

Seraphine rocks forward on her tiptoes and places a kiss on my lips. "I love you, too."

SEVENTY-SIX

ONE WEEK LATER
SERAPHINE

I spend the next few days taking care of Leroi, making sure he takes his meds and sits still while I change his wounds. He pretends to be exasperated at all my fussing, but the twinkle in his eyes says he enjoys seeing me so caring.

In between meals and baths, we sleep. Right now, I'm snuggled against his side with an arm slung over his chest. The afternoon sun shines through the cottage's patio doors, bathing its whitewashed walls in warm light.

I trace the contours of his chest with my fingertips and enjoy the feel of the rise and fall of his breath. His skin is warm under my touch, and I marvel at the slow beat of his heart. The veins running under his skin are still beautiful, but all those fantasies I had about shedding Leroi's blood are gone. I can't imagine anything so horrific.

Leroi was right. Family isn't always built on blood. It's built on loyalty, love, sacrifice, and trust. He murdered his two closest friends to keep me safe, and that has erased all my doubts.

There aren't enough words to express my remorse for stabbing him in the stomach, and I plan to spend the rest of my life making sure he feels loved.

Leroi has forgiven me and says I was still reeling from the shock of several discoveries: Samson being alive, Mom's death being a lie as well as the constant video feed I saw of an emaciated Gabriel.

Before Samson died, he confessed that the man I saw in the darkened room wasn't even my brother, but an addict who bore a resemblance. Samson now rests in several pieces thanks to Don and his clean-up crew, but I have another dilemma.

Mom and Gabriel.

Leroi stirs beneath me, his eyes fluttering open. His fingers thread through my hair, sending tingles across my scalp. I bury my head in the crook of his neck and pretend to be asleep.

"You need to stop shutting down every time I try to bring up your family," he says.

When I make a snoring sound, he gives my ass a gentle swat.

"Hey." I poke him in the ribs, making him flinch.

"Fuck," he growls.

I raise my head off his neck and frown. "Did I hurt your wound?"

His even features say he doesn't want to make me feel bad, but I know he's in pain. I trail my fingers toward his bandages, which probably need changing.

He grabs my hand. "You sacrificed everything to see Gabriel again. Now you finally have the chance."

I swallow hard and squeeze my eyes shut. This isn't like

me. I'm not normally such a coward. Seeing Gabriel and Mom isn't the same as hunting down a man I need to kill. I've held their memories on pedestals for so long, thought tirelessly about saving or avenging them, only for everything I endured to have been in vain.

How do I confront the reality that they were both alive and well, living their lives without me? How on earth do I tell them everything I've done, everything I've become? How do I face them, knowing they'd left me in that basement to rot?

Every day, Leroi brings up the subject of my family and every day, I brush him off. He insists Gabriel thought I was dead and had mourned me all those years. He's becoming more and more persistent, which has to be a sign that he's healing.

He rubs my back. "I won't force you to face them if you're not ready."

I crack open an eye to meet his warm brown gaze and try to lose myself in the varying shades that make up his irises. Walnut in the center with cinnamon highlights and ebony striations that radiate from the pupil. There's an outer ring of deep umber made up of tiny specs that seem to shift and change in the light.

"Seraphine?"

His hand rises to cup the side of my face, his thumb brushing over my cheekbone. The warmth of his touch is a reminder that I never have to face my demons alone.

"Alright," I say.

"Alright... what?"

"Let's go."

———

Hours later, Leroi pulls up at Mom and Gabriel's pristine two-story house. The sun hangs low in the sky, casting long shadows over the perfectly manicured lawn and the white picket fences border each property. My insides churn and I swallow back a bellyful of resentment at the thought of them living somewhere so idyllic when I was confined to that basement.

Gabriel still had to donate his liver. Twice.

Those bastards might have installed a chip under my skin, but they left my body pretty much intact. I really can't say the same for Gabriel. While Leroi was sleeping, I read an article that explained why a person should never make a second donation. I shudder at the thought of Gabriel left with a liver that's functioning at half than its full capacity.

Leroi reaches across the front seat and takes my hand and brings it to his lips. "Remember, I'm here for you."

The anxiety roiling in my belly calms to a gentle flutter. I turn to give Leroi a shaky nod.

He exits first and walks around the car to open my door and help me out. My heart thuds soon as my feet touch the sidewalk. It's part panic, part pain, part pressure not to lash out. It's the reason I came unarmed. After what I did to Leroi, I no longer trust my reactions in the face of betrayal.

We walk up to the front door and Leroi rings the bell. Footsteps rush toward us, and the door swings open, revealing Gabriel.

He's a few inches taller than I remember and willowier. His green eyes are tinged with yellow and shadowed by dark circles.

A knot forms in my stomach, and I shrink into Leroi's side. The pleasant life I imagined for Gabriel is now marred by the reality of his health. That looks like jaundice.

"Sera." Gabriel reaches for me with both hands.

Leroi steps forward to form a barrier between us. "Seraphine has been through a lot. Don't touch her."

Gabriel's gaze bounces from Leroi's to mine, his shoulders sagging. "Where have you been?"

"Let's discuss this inside," Leroi says.

My brother's features tighten. "Who are you and why do you act like you own my little sister?"

Sister.

The word hits me in the gut. It was used as an insult, a weapon, a mark of ownership. I grab Leroi's forearm, afraid of how I will react.

"He's with me."

I leave so much unsaid. Leroi isn't just my companion, he's my lover, my savior, the man who rescued me from the darkness.

Gabriel's shoulders sag, and he steps back to let us inside.

Forcing myself to keep an open mind, I step through the doorway and into a hallway lined with family photos. Gabriel walks into a living room that looks as though it's been hit by a cyclone. Books, papers, and broken ornaments lie scattered on the wooden floor.

Gabriel walks to an armchair and gestures for us to sit on the sofa.

Leroi perches on its arms and scans the debris while I sit beside him with my hands clasped on my knees. I try to make eye contact with my brother, but his head is bowed and I can't see his expression through a mop of dark curls.

"What happened?" I ask.

"Mom cleared out," he says, his voice hollow. "She took everything. All the valuables, the cash, and even Dad's watches."

"Why?"

He raises his head. "She said you were coming for her."

My jaw drops. Without meaning to, I rise off the sofa, but Leroi grabs my shoulder.

"What?" I whisper.

"Mom says she couldn't stick around and wait for you to come back and punish her for what she did."

The knot in my stomach twists. "What did she..." I clear my throat. "What did she say she did?"

Gabriel squeezes his eyes shut and chokes on a sob. "She lied about everything."

SEVENTY-SEVEN

LEROI

I could have spent the rest of my life in bed with Seraphine. Everyone on her list of men to kill was dead, and she finally confronted the most vicious of her tormentors, Samson Capello.

But her journey would be incomplete.

I promised to help her get revenge and reunite her with her brother. We had both imagined breaking into a well-guarded stronghold to rescue an emaciated figure tied to a chair.

Seeing Gabriel bounding down the stairs holding a gun was a shock, but it was nothing compared to how Seraphine must have felt. Discovering that the Capellos never planned on killing Gabriel had been bad enough. Seeing Gabriel alive and well had sent Seraphine's mind into a tailspin.

I know she was reluctant to face her family, but it was a necessary step for her to have closure. I rub the pad of my thumb over her collarbone, needing her to feel my support.

Seraphine sits on the edge of the sofa, her eyes wide as Gabriel bows his head and sobs. She jerks forward as though wanting to reach out and touch him, but I hold her back.

I love Seraphine with every fiber of my heart, but I still can't predict what she might do at a moment like this.

"What did she lie about?" Seraphine asks.

He shakes his head. "Everything."

"Why don't you start with the night five years ago when Seraphine went missing?"

Gabriel wipes his eyes with the backs of his hands and nods. "Two of his guards came to where I was staying and brought me home. They said there was a family emergency."

I glance down to find Seraphine nodding. This part of Gabriel's story matches up with what we learned after interrogating those bastards.

"When I got there, Mom was strapped to a gurney, and they were loading her into an ambulance. She looked terrible. Dad was raging and crying and waving a gun."

My gaze darts down to Seraphine, her face is a blank mask. According to her story, this was when the driver took her to her grandmother's house, where she stayed the night. I lean down and place a kiss on her temple.

"I kept asking what happened and where you were, but Dad said Enzo Montesano and his sons came to the house and murdered Raphael. Then they attacked Mom and took you."

"That's not what happened," she says.

Gabriel looks up, his expression pained. "Yeah. Mom finally told the truth. She said that Dad and his guards were her attackers."

"What else did she say?"

"That Dad took you in payment for the money he spent

raising you as his daughter under false pretenses." He hiccups. "Mom said you were trafficked."

Seraphine and I exchange glances.

"And probably overseas?" she asks, her words clipped.

I lean down and whisper into her ear, "Are you alright?" She nods.

Today is about getting closure for Seraphine. If she isn't ready to share the details of what happened in that basement, then I won't push her, but she needs to know what happened to her family after she was taken.

"What happened after that night?" I ask Gabriel.

"Mom spent the night in the ER and Dad told me to pack a bag because the house was compromised."

"What does that mean?" she asks.

"He said Enzo Montesano would be looking for me."

"But why?"

"Enzo was Dad's boss, who liked to punish his underlings for their mistakes by attacking their families." Gabriel raises both shoulders. "Dad said his numbers were declining... Something like that, and Enzo took you and hurt Mom as an incentive for him to bring in more money."

My nostrils flare. He probably made up that lie to isolate and subdue his liver donor. If Gabriel thought he was hunted by Enzo, then he was more likely to leave behind his life to go into hiding.

"Dad moved me to an apartment and let Mom join a few days later, after she was released from the hospital. He said we'd be safe there from the Montesano family as long as we didn't leave."

Seraphine places a hand on my thigh, and I give it a gentle squeeze. The last time I saw her look so expressionless was after the poker massacre.

"Did your father explain what the Montesano family were supposed to have done with Seraphine?" I ask.

He nods. "A couple of weeks later, Dad came to visit us, looking devastated, and said Enzo Montesano had killed Seraphine along with the cook, the driver, and our grandma."

She inhales a sharp breath, her body tensing. I wrap an arm around her shoulders and pull her into my chest.

"How long did you stay in that apartment?" I ask.

"Until the first transplant." Gabriel rubs the spot beneath his right rib cage and grimaces.

"Were you still in hiding?" I ask. "Enzo Montesano had died by then and Roman was in prison."

"Dad told us he murdered Enzo for what he did to Sera, and his sons would be hunting me down for revenge. After the first transplant, he drove me to the burned ruins of our old apartment."

I glance down at Seraphine to gauge her reaction, but her eyes are closed and her lips are pursed. Gabriel pauses until she exhales an annoyed breath and meets his gaze.

"Dad said he was doing everything he could to keep his family together. He said he needed me to be strong and donate my liver so he could continue defending us from the Montesanos."

"Mom knew all along that it was bullshit," Seraphine says, her voice bitter.

Gabriel nods. "Before she left, she told me she had no choice. Dad held her hostage and forced her to keep up his lie."

"What do you think?" she asks.

"Mom and Dad got along just fine after he recovered from the first transplant." He shrugs. "When Dad needed my liver again, I kept asking her to leave with me, but she kept telling me it wasn't safe."

"Wow," she whispers.

Gabriel swallows. "You've got to believe me, Sera. If I'd known you weren't dead—" He breaks off, his voice choked with emotion. "If I'd known for one second that you were alive, I would have done everything in my power to find you."

"I know," she murmurs. "Dad told me Mom was dead, and he threatened to kill you if I didn't do what he said."

"What did he..."

She closes her eyes again and inhales several ragged breaths. I can't even begin to imagine her inner turmoil. One of the reasons she wanted to tame her killer instincts was to hide them from Gabriel.

"He turned me into an assassin," she says.

"What?" Gabriel whispers.

"He and his other sons made me kill Enzo Montesano."

My jaw tightens at the reminder of the circumstances of Uncle Enzo's death. "Everyone who knows this secret is dead," I snarl. "You must never repeat it, not even to Seraphine."

Gabriel shoots me a glance. "Who is this guy?"

"The one who saved me." She squeezes my hand. "Leroi has been my protector since he found me in Dad's basement."

His features drop, and he stares between Seraphine and me with wild eyes. I can already imagine him putting pieces together to create a picture of the truth.

"What are you saying?" he rasps.

"Dad kept me in a basement, and his sons only let me out to kill his enemies."

Gabriel turns his attention back to me. "And you're the

one who killed Dad?"

I nod.

"Thank you," he says, his words choked with sobs. "Thank you for saving my sister. Thank you for killing that bastard. You freed us both."

Seraphine releases my hand and rises off the sofa. I resist the urge to hold her back. Gabriel isn't in any trouble. This isn't the same as our other interrogations. He's just as much of a victim of Capello.

Gabriel stands, his thin chest rising and falling with each breath. He gazes down at Seraphine through tears. "I'm sorry, Sera. I'm sorry for everything that happened to you. I should have known you were alive. I should have looked."

She places a hand over his heart. "I'm sorry, too. I should have known Dad's threats were pointless. I could have tried to break free and rescued you."

My chest tightens. I don't like how they're both taking responsibility for not seeing through Capello's actions when they were both victims of his sick machinations.

"Neither of you are to blame," I say. "You were kids, trying to survive a psychopath."

Seraphine rests her head on Gabriel's chest, and he wraps his arms around her shoulders. They cling to each other, whispering words of comfort, reconnection, and love.

I stand back and turn away, both to afford them some privacy and in awe of their sibling bond. My former family was once the same: a mother, two children, and a violent maniac.

When I think back at their rejection, I feel nothing. No sense of betrayal, no loss, no regrets. If I could relive the time I spent with them, I wouldn't change a thing because their contempt led me to Seraphine.

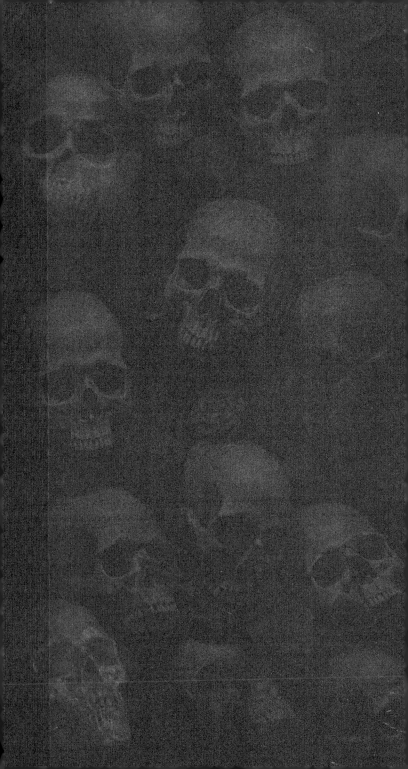

EPILOGUE

ONE YEAR LATER

SERAPHINE

Jobs like these need a full crew of trained professionals, including a medic like Dr. Sal, because you never know what state the girls will be in when they're rescued. That's what I tell Gabriel in the triage van as he readies himself for casualties.

My big brother pulls me into a tight hug. "Is this what you do with Leroi?"

I gaze into his worried green eyes and smile. "Tonight's going to be a breeze."

Gabriel gives my shoulders a squeeze, but his expression doesn't relax. I get why. It took a few weeks for me to share the horrors of my past with him, but talking about it with someone who knew me from before really helped.

Leroi only ever got to see the broken part of me, which he helped to put together, but Gabriel has known me from birth. When I'm with my big brother, I can connect with the person I used to be before my life turned dark.

Gabriel releases his grip on my shoulders and sweeps his gaze down my bulletproof vest.

"Be careful, Sera," he murmurs.

"I always am." I pick up my tactical helmet and head out into the parking lot.

That isn't an understatement. If I had been more observant, Miko would never have been able to get the jump on me and drag me over to Samson's hideout. If Leroi had kept his hookup away from his home, assassins wouldn't have set it on fire.

I'm nowhere near perfect, but I'm trying. I couldn't stand for my big brother to get hurt because I was reckless.

Leroi stands close by in the parking lot, a block away from our target location. Six members of the clean-up crew stand around him, listening to last-minute instructions.

He's dressed in black tactical gear, looking as intimidating as he did the day I saw him in the basement. Two huge pistols are strapped to a holster at his sides for backup in case something happens with the shotgun. I can't help but admire his commanding presence and my thoughts drift to taking it all off him tonight.

As though listening to my thoughts, he turns around and catches my gaze. A smirk lifts the corner of his lips, and he mouths the word, 'Behave.'

I give him an innocent shrug, silently telling him I was focused on the job and not what I planned on doing to him afterward. Besides, we're not expecting much trouble. Leroi's colleagues already took out the perimeter guards with long-range rifles, and Gabriel has redirected the security cameras to loop a feed from last week.

My brother moved out soon after we visited the cozy little house he shared with Mom. He now lives in the apartment next door, where he works in cybersecurity, and we see each other every day. Two liver donations left him with imperfect health, but Leroi sent him to a specialist to help improve his liver function.

Knowing that Mom didn't die that night closed one wound and opened up another. I no longer blame myself for what happened the night she was attacked, but it hurts that she traded my life to save hers.

Leroi says Mom is just a different type of monster, and I think he's right. She's living in New Jersey with some flunky who works for a distant cousin of Dad's. The man has a terrible reputation with women, but maybe she thinks he'll protect her from Leroi. As far as I'm concerned, she's still dead.

Months after Gabriel moved next door, I read something in the Alderney Times about a sex trafficker, and discovered that Dad and the twins weren't the only monsters keeping women in their basements.

That's when I knew exactly what I wanted to do with the rest of my life. Leroi thought it was a great idea, but Gabriel took a little more convincing because he worried that I might get hurt. After we showed him what I was capable of, he realized I was no longer his helpless little sister.

Gabriel now helps our vigilante group with tech support and intel. We're still a small team of people from Leroi's firm, but we've saved dozens of children and young women. With every raid, we get closer to finding the trafficker.

Leroi breaks away from the crew to cross the space and cups my face with both hands.

"Let's go over the ground rules," he says in a low voice.

"We go inside, we grab the girls, and we get out. No side quests, no heroics. Is that understood?"

"What if he's there?" I ask, resisting the urge to roll my eyes at his fussing. "We can't just shoot him in the head and give him a quick death."

Leroi's gaze flickers.

"What?" I ask.

"It was going to be a surprise."

My eyes widen. "What?"

"I got a call two nights ago from someone at the Phoenix, saying he had a table at the VIP section, so I drugged him while he was taking a piss and now he's waiting for you in the kill room."

"Why didn't you tell me?"

"It was supposed to be a surprise," he says, and I can tell he's holding back a smile. "After we got the girls settled at the lake house, I planned on taking you down there for a little celebration."

My breath catches. Some men give their lovers flowers, others give them chocolates or even jewelry, but Leroi gives me the satisfaction of revenge and vigilante justice. It's one of the many reasons I love him so much.

I rock forward on my tiptoes and place a kiss on his lips. "Thank you," I murmur against his mouth. "I can't wait to return the favor."

His gaze wanders over the armor he commissioned to fit my frame. "Ready, angel?"

I place both hands on my pistols. "Ready."

"Let's go save some lives."

We move toward the building with the rest of our small team, ready to rescue those who need us the most. It's the perfect ending to the fairytale that kept me sane during my darkest hours.

I didn't just get a happy ending with my knight in black armor. I get to create happy endings for those who need it most.

Preview Roman and Emberly's story at:
www.gigistyx.com/roman

ABOUT THE AUTHOR

Gigi lives with her husband and two cats in London. When she's not crafting twisted dark romances with fiesty heroines and the morally grey villains who love them, she's cuddled up on the sofa with a cup of tea and a book.

Sign up for Gigi's updates at:
www.gigistyx.com/newsletter

ALSO BY GIGI STYX

Snaring Emberly

Breaking Rosalind

Printed in Great Britain
by Amazon

36860882R00364